For Woman's Love

A Novel

by

Emma Dorothy Eliza Nevitte Southworth

For Woman's Love
A Novel
by Emma Dorothy Eliza Nevitte Southworth

ISBN: 978-93-61424-81-6

Published by

DOUBLE 9 BOOKS

2/13-B, Ansari Road
Daryaganj, New Delhi – 110002
info@double9books.com
www.double9books.com
Tel. 011-40042856

ABOUT THE AUTHOR

Emma Dorothy Eliza Nevitte Southworth (December 26, 1819 - June 30, 1899) was an American novelist who wrote over 60 books in the late nineteenth century. She was the most popular American novelist of her day. In her works, her heroines frequently challenge modern ideas of Victorian feminine domesticity by demonstrating that virtue is naturally coupled with wit, adventure, and rebellion to fix any terrible situation. Though The Hidden Hand (1859) was her most popular novel, Southworth preferred Ishmael (1876). Emma Nevitte was born on December 26, 1819, in Washington, D.C., to Susannah Wailes and Charles LeCompte Nevitte, a trader from Virginia. Her father died in 1824, and she was given the name Emma Dorothy Eliza Nevitte at his final wish. She attended a school run by her stepfather, Joshua L. Henshaw. She later described her youth as lonely, with her best times spent exploring Maryland's Tidewater region on horseback. During such rides, she developed a deep interest in the area's history and mythology. After attending her stepfather's school, she finished her secondary education at the age of 15 in 1835.

CONTENTS

CHAPTER I
A BRILLIANT MATCH

"I remember Regulas Rothsay—or Rule, as we used to call him—when he was a little bit of a fellow hardly up to my knee, running about barefooted and doing odd jobs round the foundry. Ah! and now he is elected governor of this State by the biggest majority ever heard of, and engaged to be married to the finest young lady in the country, with the full consent of all her proud relations. To be married to-day and to be inaugurated to-morrow, and he only thirty-two years old this blessed seventh of June!"

The speaker, a hale man of sixty years, with a bald head, a sharp face, a ruddy complexion, and a figure as twisted as a yew tree, and about as tough, was Silas Marwig, one of the foremen of the foundry.

"Well, I don't believe Regulas Rothsay would ever have risen to his present position if it had not been for his love of Corona Haught. No more do I believe that Old Rockharrt would ever have allowed his beautiful granddaughter to be engaged to Rothsay if the young man had not been elected governor," observed a stout, florid-faced matron of fifty-five. "How hard he worked for her! And how long she waited for him! Why, I remember them both so well! They were the very best of friends from their childhood— the wealthy little lady and the poor orphan boy."

"That is very true, Mrs. Bounce," said a young man, who was a newcomer in the neighborhood and one of the bookkeepers of the great firm. "But how did that orphan get his education?"

"By hook and by crook, as the saying is, Mr. Wall. I think the little lady taught him to read and write, and she loaned him books. He left here when he was about thirteen years old. He went to the city, and got into the printing office of *The National Watch*. And he learned the trade. And, oh, you know a bright, earnest boy like that was bound to get on. He worked hard, and he studied hard. After awhile he began to write short, telling paragraphs for the *Watch*, and these at length were noticed and copied, and he became assistant editor of the paper. By the time he was twenty-five years old he had bought the paper out."

"And, of course, he made it a power in politics. I see the rest. He was elected State representative; then State senator."

"Yes, indeed. You've hit it. And now he is going to marry his first love to-day, and to take his seat as governor to-morrow," continued the matron, with a little chuckle.

"Regulas Rothsay will never take his seat as governor," spoke a solemn voice from the thicket on the right of the road along which the party were walking to the scene of the grand wedding. All turned to see a strange form step out from the shelter of the trees—a tall, gaunt, swarthy woman, stern of feature and harsh of tone; her head covered with wild, straggling black hair; her body clothed in a long, clinging garment of dark red serge.

"Old Scythia," muttered the matron, shuddering and shrinking closer to the side of the bookkeeper, for the strange creature was reported and believed by the ignorant and superstitious of the neighborhood to be powerful and malignant.

"Regulas Rothsay will never take his seat as governor of this State!"

As the beldame repeated and emphasized these words, she raised her hand with a prophetic gesture and advanced upon the group of pedestrians.

"Now, then, you old crow! What are you up to with your croaking?" demanded Mr. Marwig. "Look here, Mistress Beelzebub! Do you know that you are a very lucky woman to live in a land where not only may a barefooted boy rise to the highest honors by talent and perseverance, but where a malignant old witch may torture and terrify her neighbors without fear of the ducking stool or the stake?" he demanded.

The beldame looked at him scornfully, and disdained to reply.

"Wait!" said a stout, dark, middle-aged, black-whiskered man, Timothy Ryland by name, and one of the managers of the "works" by state. "Wait, I want to question this miserable lunatic. She may have got wind of something. Tell me, old mother, why will not the governor-elect take his seat to-morrow?"

"Because Fate forbids it," solemnly replied the crone.

"Will the governor be—murdered?"

"No; Regulas Rothsay has not an enemy in the world!"

"Will he be killed on the railroad, or kidnapped?"

"No!"

"Will he be taken suddenly ill?"

"No!"

"What then in the fiend's name is to prevent his taking his seat to-morrow?" impatiently demanded the manager.

"An evil so dire, so awful, so mysterious, that its like never happened on this earth!"

"Arrest her, Mr. Ryland! She ought to be locked up until she could be sent to the asylum!" exclaimed old Marwig.

"I have no power to do so, my friend," replied the manager.

"Why, where is she?" inquired Mrs. Bounce, trembling. "Who saw her go?"

No one answered, but every one looked around. Not a trace of the witch could be seen. She had passed like a dark cloud from among them, and was gone.

It was a glorious day in June. A long, deep, green valley lay low between two lofty ridges of the Cumberland mountains, running north and south for ten miles, and near the boundary lines of three States. This lovely vale was watered by a merry, sparkling little river called the Whirligig, which furnished the power for the huge machinery of the great firm of Rockharrt & Sons, proprietors of the Plutus iron mines and the North End foundries, which supplied the mighty engines on the great lines of railroad from the East to the West, and whose massive buildings, forges, furnaces, store-houses and laborers' cottages occupied all the ground between the foot of the mountain and the banks of the river, on both sides of the Whirligig, at the upper or north end of the valley, where a substantial bridge connected the two shores.

This settlement, called, from its position, North End, was quite a thriving little village. North End was not only blessed with a mission church, having a schoolroom in its basement, but it was provided with a post-office, a telegraph, a drug store, kept by a regular physician, who dispensed his own physic (advice and medicine, one dollar), and a general store, where everything needed to eat, drink, wear or use (except drugs), was kept for sale.

On this bright June morning, however, the great works were all stopped. There was a general holiday, and as this was at the cost of the firm, it gave general satisfaction. All the people of North End, except the aged, infirm and infantile, were trooping down the valley, on the rough road between the foot of the West Ridge and the side of the river, to a fete to be given them at Rockhold on the occasion of the marriage of old Aaron Rockharrt's granddaughter, Corona Haught, to Regulas Rothsay, the governor-elect of the State.

It was a marriage of very rare interest to the workmen and their families. To the men, because the governor-elect had been one of their own class. The elders remembered him from the time when he was a friendless orphan child, glad to run the longest errand or do the hardest day's work for a dime, but also a very independent little fellow, who would take nothing in the shape of alms from anybody. To the women, because he was going to marry his first and only sweetheart, and on the very day before his inauguration, so that she might take part in the pageantry that was to be his first great success and triumph.

On one side of the river, at the foot of the East Ridge, stood Rockhold, the country seat of the Rockharrts, in its own park, which lay between the mountain and the river. The house itself was a large, heavy, oblong building of gray stone, two stories high, with cellar and garret. From the front of the house to the edge of the river extended a fair green lawn, shaded here and there by great forest trees. Under many of these trees, tables with refreshments were set, and seats were placed for the accommodation and refreshment of the out-door guests. In sunny spots, also, some white tents were raised and decorated with flags.

As a group of working men and women sat on the west bank of the river, waiting impatiently for the return of the ferryboat, they saw, from minute to minute, carriages drive up the lawn avenue, discharge the occupants at the main entrance of the house, and then roll off to the stable yard in the rear.

These seemed to come in a slow procession.

"Only the nearest relations and most intimate friends of the family are invited to the ceremony. There have only been five carriages passed since we have been sitting here, and I don't believe there was one come before we came, or that there'll be another come after that last one, which was certainly the groom's," said Old Marwig.

"Oh! was it, indeed? But how do you know?" demanded Mrs. Bounce.

"It is the new carriage from North End Hotel! And he and his groomsmen had engaged it. That's how I know! Here comes the ferryboat! Now for it!"

The boat touched the banks, and as many as could find room crowded into it, and were speedily rowed across the river and landed on the other side, where they found a few of the lawn party there before them.

"There is Mr. Clarence Rockharrt coming toward us!" said Mrs. Bounce, as the party walked up from the landing, and a medium-sized, plump, fair man of middle age, with a round, fresh face, a smiling countenance, blue eyes and light hair, and in "a wedding garment" of the day, came down to meet them, and shook hands with all, warmly welcoming them in the name of his father. Then he led them up to the lawn and gave them chairs among the unoccupied seats at the various tables.

"If you please, Mr. Clarence, is the groom in good health and sperrits?" meaningly inquired Mrs. Bounce.

"Mr. Rothsay is in excellent health and spirits, thank you," replied the gentleman, looking a little surprised at the question: an then moving off quickly to receive some new arrivals.

The guests for the lawn party were constantly arriving, and the ferryboat was kept busy plying from the shore to shore.

It is time now to introduce our readers to the house of Rockharrt.

Old Aaron Rockharrt, the head of that house, was at this time seventy-five years of age and a wonder of health and strength. He was called the "Iron King," no less from his great hardihood of body and mind than from his vast wealth in mines and foundries. In size he was almost a giant, with a large head covered by closely-curling, steel-gray hair. His character may be summed up in a very few words:

Aaron Rockharrt was an incarnation of monstrous selfishness.

His manners to all, but especially to his dependants, were arrogant, egotistical and overbearing. He was utterly destitute of sympathy or compassion. There was no room for either in a soul so full of self. In his opinion there was no one on earth, neither king nor Kaiser, saint nor hero, so important to the universe as Aaron Rockharrt, head of Rockharrt & Sons.

Yet Aaron Rockharrt had two redeeming points. He was strictly truthful in word and honest in deed.

His wife was near his own age, a quiet, gentle, little old lady, small and slim, with white hair half hidden by a lace cap. If she ever had any individuality, it had been quite crushed out by the hard heel of her husband's iron will. Their eldest son and second partner in the firm was Fabian Rockharrt, a fine animal of fifty years old, though scarcely looking forty. He had inherited all his father's great strength of body and of mind, with more than his father's business talent; but he had not inherited the truth and honesty of his father.

Yet there is no one wholly evil, and Fabian Rockharrt's one redeeming quality was a certain good nature or benevolence which is more the result of temperament than of principle. This quality rendered his manner so kind and considerate to all his employes that he was the most popular member of his family.

Clarence, the second son, was much younger than his elder brother, and so diametrically opposite to him and to their father, both in person and character, that he scarcely seemed to come of the same race.

He was really thirty-five years old, but looked ten years less, and was a fair blonde, medium-sized and plump, with a round head covered with light, curling yellow hair, a round, rosy face as bare as a baby's and almost as innocent. He had not the satanic intellect of his father or his brother, but he had a fine moral and spiritual nature that neither could understand or appreciate.

There were yet two other exceptions to the family character of worldliness and selfishness. There were Corona and Sylvanus Haught, a sister and brother, orphan grand-children of Aaron Rockharrt, left him by his deceased only daughter. Sylvanus, a fine, manly young fellow, resembled his Uncle Clarence in person and in character, having the same truthfulness, generosity and sincerity, but with a mocking spirit, which turned evil into ridicule rather than into a subject of serious rebuke. He was three years younger than his sister. Corona was a beautiful brunette, tall, like all the Rockharrts, with a superbly developed form, a fine head, adorned with a full suit of fine curly black hair, delicate classic features, straight, low forehead, aquiline nose, a "Cupid's bow" mouth, and finely curved chin. This was her wedding-day and she wore her bridal dress of pure white satin, with veil of thread lace and wreath of orange buds. Hers was the very triumph of a love match, for she was about to wed one whom she had loved from earliest childhood, and for whom she had waited long years.

Here was Corona Haught's great victory. She had seen his opponents, her own family, bow down and worship her idol. Yet, at the culmination of her triumph, on this her bridal day, why did she sit so pale and wan?

From her deep, sad reverie she was aroused by the entrance of her six gay bridesmaids.

"Corona, love, good morning! Many happy returns, and so on!" said Flora Fields, the first bridesmaid, coming up to the pale bride and kissing her.

All the others followed the example, and then Miss Fields said:

"Cora, dear, 'the scene is set'—otherwise, the company are all assembled in the drawing-room. Grandpapa and grandmamma are in their seats of honor. The bishop, in his canonicals, is waiting; the groom and his groomsmen are expectant. Are you ready?"

"I know getting married must be a serious, a solemn, even an awful thing when it comes to the point. And most brides do look pale! But you— you look ghastly! Come, take some composing spirits of lavender—do!"

"Yes; you may give me some. You will find the vial on the dressing-table."

The restorative was administered, and then the "bevy of fair maids" left the chamber and went down stairs.

There, in the great hall, they met the bridegroom and his six groomsmen; for it was the custom of that time and place to have a groomsman for each bridesmaid. The bridegroom and governor-elect was not a handsome man— that was conceded even by his best friends—but he was tall and muscular, with a look of strength, manliness and nobility that was impressive. A son of the people truly, but with the brain of the ruler. The whole rugged form and face assumed a gentleness and courtesy that almost conferred grace and beauty upon him, as he advanced to greet his bride.

Why did she shrink from him?

No one knew. It was only for a moment; and happily, he, in the simplicity of a single, honest heart, had not seen the momentary shudder.

He drew her hand within his arm, looked down on her with a beam of ineffable tenderness and adoration, and then waited, as he had been instructed to do, until the groomsmen and bridesmaids had formed the procession that was to usher them into the drawing-room and before the officiating bishop. They entered the crowded apartment. The bishop, in his white robes, stood on the rug, supported by the Rev. Mr. Wells, temporary minister of the mission church at North End, and the ceremony began. All went on well until he came to that part where the officiating minister must read—though a mere form this solemn adjuration to the contracting lovers:

"'I require and charge ye both, as ye shall answer at the dreadful day of judgment, when the secrets of all hearts shall be disclosed, that if either of you know just cause why ye may not be united in matrimony, ye do now declare it.'"

There was a pause, to give opportunity for reply, if any reply was to be made—a mere form, as the adjuration itself was. Yet the bride shuddered throughout her frame. Many noticed it, but not the bridegroom.

The ceremony went on.

"'Who giveth this woman to be married to this man?'"

Old Aaron Rockharrt, who stood on the right of the bridal party, stepped forth, took his granddaughter's hand, and placed it in that of the groom, saying, with visible pride:

"I do."

The rites went on to their conclusion, and the whole party were invited into the dining-room, where the marriage feast was spread, where the revelry lasted two full hours, and might have lingered longer had not the bride withdrawn from the table, and, attended by her bridesmaids, retired to her chamber to change her bridal robes for a plain traveling suit of silver gray silk, with hat and gloves to match.

There the gentle, timid, old grandmother came to bid her pet child a private good-by.

"Are you happy, my love—are you happy?" she inquired. "Why don't you answer?"

"My heart is full—too full, grandma," evasively answered Corona Rothsay.

"Ah, yes; that is natural—very natural. 'Even so it was with me when I was young,'" sighed the old lady, who detected no evasion in the words of her darling.

The bride went down stairs, where the bridegroom awaited her. There, in the hall, were collected the members of her family, friends, neighbors and wedding guests.

Some time was spent in bidding good-by to all these.

"But it is not good-by, really; for the majority of us will follow by a later train, and be on hand for the inauguration to-morrow," said old Aaron Rockharrt, who seemed to have recovered his youth on this proud day.

"And, grandpa, be sure to bring grandma. Don't say that she is too old, or too feeble, or too anything, to travel, because she is not; and she has set her heart on seeing the pageantry to-morrow. Promise me before I leave you," pleaded the bride.

"Very well; I will bring her," said Mr. Rockharrt, who would have promised anything to his granddaughter on this auspicious occasion.

"You will find your traps all right, Cora. They went off by the early train this morning," said Mr. Clarence.

"And I trust, Rothsay, that you will find my town house comfortably prepared for your reception," said Mr. Rockharrt.

The bridegroom handed his bride into the carriage that was to convey them to the railway station. The carriage crossed the ferry, and in a few minutes reached the other side, and rolled toward the railway station.

The road was at this hour very solitary, and the bridegroom and his bride found themselves for the first time that day tete-a-tete. He turned to her, and drew her head to his heart and whispered:

"Cora, speak to me! Call me your husband!"

"I—cannot. My heart is too full," the girl muttered evasively.

But his grand, simple, truthful spirit perceived no prevarication in her words. If her heart was full, it was with responsive love of him, he thought. He bent his face lower over her beautiful head, that lay upon his bosom, and kissed her.

Soon they reached North End, where all the aged, infirm and infantile who could not come to the wedding were seated at their cottage doors, to see the carriage with the bridegroom and bride go by.

Smiling and bowing in response, the pair passed through the village and went on their way toward the station which they reached at half-past one o'clock.

They had to wait about ten minutes for the train to come up. They remained in the carriage; for here, too, a small crowd of country people had collected to see the bride and the bridegroom, who was also the governor-elect.

The train from the East ran into the station. The bridal pair left the carriage and went on the cars, and the governor-elect and his bride set out for the State capital. It was a long afternoon ride, and the sun was low when the train drew in sight of the State capital, and slowed into the station.

An immense crowd had gathered to welcome the governor-elect, and as he stepped out upon the platform, and stood with his bride on his arm, the cheers were deafening. When these had in some measure subsided, the hero of the hour returned thanks in a simple little speech. Then the committee of reception came up and shook hands with the governor-to-be, who next presented them in turn to his wife.

At last the pair were allowed to enter the carriage that was in waiting to convey them to the town house of Aaron Rockharrt. Other carriages containing members of the committee attended them. They passed through the main street of the city.

The procession of carriages passed until it reached the Rockharrt residence, opposite the government mansion, where the committee took leave of the governor-elect and his bride, who entered their temporary home alone, to be received and attended by obsequious servants.

There we also will leave them.

Visitors to the inauguration were arriving by every train.

Among the arrivals from the East came Aaron Rockharrt, with his wife, his two sons, Fabian and Clarence, and his grandson, Sylvan, the younger brother of Cora.

The main door of the mansion was open, and several gentlemen, wearing official badges, stood without or just within it.

"By Jove! we are just in time, and it has been a close shave! That is the committee come to take him to the State house!" exclaimed old Aaron Rockharrt as he stepped out of the carriage, and helped his feeble little wife to alight. He led her up the steps, followed by the other three men of his party.

"Good morning, Judge Abbot. We are just in time, I find. We came up by the night train, and a close shave it has been. Well, a miss is as good as a mile, and we are safe to see the whole of the pageant," said the old man, speaking to a tall, thin, gray-haired gentleman, who wore a rosette on the lapel of his coat.

"Yes, sir; but here is a very strange difficulty—very strange, indeed," replied the official, with a deeply troubled and perplexed air, which was shared by all the gentlemen who stood with him.

"What's the trouble, gentlemen? Is the chief justice ill, that his honor cannot administer the oath, or what?"

"It is much worse than that—if anything could be worse," gravely replied one of the committee.

"What is it then? A contested election at this late hour?"

"The governor-elect cannot be found. No one has seen him since eleven o'clock last night. He is missing."

CHAPTER II
A LOST GOVERNOR AND BRIDEGROOM

"Missing!" echoed old Aaron Rockharrt, drawing up his huge frame to its fullest height, and staring with strong black eyes in a defiant and aggressive manner. "Missing! did you say, sir?" he repeated sternly.

"Yes, Mr. Rockharrt; ever since last night," replied Judge Abbot, chairman of the committee, in much distress and anxiety.

"Impossible! Never heard of such a thing in the whole course of my life! A bridegroom lost on the evening of his marriage! A governor lost on the morning of his inauguration! I tell you, sir, it is impossible—utterly and entirely impossible! How do you know, sir, that he has not been seen by some one or other since last night? How do you know that he cannot be found, somewhere, this morning?"

"All his household have failed to find him. Our messengers have been sent in every direction without discovering the slightest clew to his—fate," gloomily replied the judge.

Mr. Rockharrt turned to the porter, who was still in attendance at the door, and demanded:

"Where is your mistress?"

The man, a negro and an old family servant of the Rockharrts, replied:

"The young madam is in the back drawing room, sir; and if you please, sir, I think she would be all the better for seeing the old madam."

"Who is with her now?" shortly demanded Mr. Rockharrt, ignoring his servant's suggestion, although Mrs. Rockharrt looked nervously anxious to follow it "There is no one with her, sir."

"Alone! Alone! My granddaughter left alone on the morning after her marriage? What do you mean by that? Where is your master?

"Show me in to your mistress at once. I will get at the bottom of this mystery, or this villainy, as it is more likely to prove, before I am through with the matter. And if my granddaughter's husband is not to be found before the day is out, I will have all concerned in the plot arrested for conspiracy!"

exclaimed Mr. Rockharrt, with that utter recklessness of assertion to which he was addicted in moments of excitement.

The dismayed negro lowered his eyes and led the way. Aaron Rockharrt strode on, followed by his timid and terrified old wife, his stalwart sons, his mocking grandson, and the members of the committee. But the old man, not liking such an escort, turned upon them, and said, with sarcastic politeness and dignity:

"Gentlemen, permit me. It is expedient, under existing circumstances, that I should first see my granddaughter alone."

The members of the committee bowed with offended dignity and withdrew to the front of the hall.

Meanwhile Aaron Rockharrt sent back the members of his own family, and strode solemnly into the drawing room, which was half darkened by the closed window shutters.

"Now leave the room, sir; shut the door after you and stand on the outside to keep off all intruders," commanded Mr. Rockharrt to the servant who had admitted him.

When the door was closed upon him, Aaron Rockharrt discerned his granddaughter, who sat in an easy chair in a dark corner of the back drawing room, which was divided from the front by blue satin and white lace portieres. Her deadly pallid face gleamed out from the shadows in startling contrast to her jet black hair and the black dress which, against all precedent, she wore on this the morning after her marriage.

The old man of iron went up and stood before her, looking at her in silence for a few moments.

"Corona Rothsay," he began, sternly, "what is the meaning of this unparalleled situation?"

"I—I—do not know."

"You do not know where your husband is on the morning after his marriage and on the day of his expected inauguration?"

"No; I do not know."

"You seem to take this desertion or this death very quietly."

"What would be gained by taking it any other way?" she murmured, though indeed she was not taking the situation quietly, but controlling herself.

"How dare you say so to me?" severely demanded the old man, scarcely able to control his wrath, though at a loss to know against whom to direct it.

"You ask me a direct question. I give you a truthful answer."

"Answer me, truly!" rudely exclaimed Aaron Rockharrt, giving way, in his blind egotism, to utter recklessness of assertion, to gross injustice and exaggeration. "What have you done to him, Corona? Tell me that!"

She started violently and looked up quickly; her face was whiter, her eyes wilder than before.

"What—have—you—done to him?" he sternly repeated, looking her full in the deathly face.

"I? Nothing!" she answered, but her voice faltered and her frame shook.

"I believe that you have! You look as if you had! I have seen the devil in you since we brought you home from Europe against your will; especially within the last few days!"

Having hurled upon her this avalanche of abuse, he turned and strode wrathfully up and down the room until he had got off some of his excitement. Then, he came and stood before his granddaughter.

"How long has your husband been missing?" he abruptly inquired.

"Since last night," in a very low tone.

"When did you see him last? Tell me that!"

"I have already told you—last evening."

"Tell me all that has occurred from the time you both left Rockhold to the time you entered this house which I placed at your disposal and to which I sent you, to save you from the noise and bustle and excitement of a crowded hotel, and to give you rest and quiet and seclusion. Yes! and this the result! But go on and tell me. From the time you left Rockhold to this time, mind you!"

"Very well, sir, I will tell you. Our journey, a series of ovations. Our reception in this city was a triumph. We were met at the depot by a great crowd, and by the committee with carriages, and we were escorted to this house by a military and civil procession with a band of music. They left us at the gate.

"We entered, and were received by the servants. As soon as I had changed my dress we went down to dinner. After dinner we went into the drawing room. A gentleman was announced on official business connected with the ceremonies of to-day. He was shown into the library, and my husband went to him. Many callers came. They talked with Mr. Rothsay in the library. I remained in this room. At last the crowd began to thin off, and soon all were gone. Mr. Rothsay came into this room—and sat down by my side. We talked together for an hour or more. Then a card was brought in. Mr. Rothsay took it, looked at it, and said:

"'I will see the gentleman. Show him into the front room.'

"Mr. Rothsay arose and went into the front room to receive his visitor. It was late, and I was very tired, so I went up stairs to my chamber and retired to bed. I have never seen my husband since."

And Corona dropped her face upon her hands and sobbed as if her heart would break. She had utterly broken down for the first time.

"Good heavens! I don't understand it all! Had you had a lover's quarrel now in that hour when you talked together in this parlor?" inquired the old gentleman, his insane anger being now merged in wonder. "Had you reproached him for spending so much time with his political friends while you were waiting here alone?"

"Oh, no, no," replied Corona, between her convulsive sobs.

"Good heavens!" again exclaimed the old man. "When did you first miss him?"

"When I came down in the morning. I thought then that he had been kept up all night by his friends, and that I should meet him at breakfast. He did not appear at breakfast. The servants searched for him all over the house, but could not find him. I waited breakfast until I was faint with fasting and suspense. Then I took a cup of coffee. On inquiry it was found that Jasper had been the last to see him, and that he had not seen him since he showed the visitor in. He did not show the visitor out. He waited some time to do so, and fell asleep. When he awoke the visitor had gone, and the drawing rooms were empty. The man supposed that Mr. Rothsay had seen his friend to the door, and had then retired to bed. And so he shut up the house and went to his room. No one discovered that Mr. Rothsay was missing until this morning. When the inaugural committee came two hours ago, the servants told them all that I have just told you."

"Who was the last visitor? He might throw some light upon this dark, evil subject. Who was he?" abruptly demanded Aaron Rockharrt.

"I do not know. No one seems to know. Jasper says he never saw him before, nor ever heard his name."

"Couldn't he see it on his card?"

"Jasper cannot read, you must remember."

"Where is that card? Let me see it!"

"It cannot be found."

"Conspiracy! Treason! Murder!" interrupted Aaron Rockharrt. "The governor-elect has been decoyed away from the house by that last caller, and has been murdered! And the people in the house may not be as innocent or ignorant as they pretend to be. I will go out and take counsel with the committee," he said, and he turned and strode out of the drawing room.

When he reached the hall, however, he found that the officials had gone to pursue their search for the missing man elsewhere. The men of his own party were nowhere to be seen. The porter, Jasper, was the only occupant of the hall, and Aaron Rockharrt opened the hall door and walked out. The military and civil escort were still on parade before the house, waiting for the governor-elect.

Mr. Rockharrt's carriage was standing before the door. He entered it and ordered the coachman to drive to police headquarters.

The hour for the inauguration of the new governor was approaching. The procession to the State house should have been in motion by this time. The people on the sidewalks, at the doors and windows, on the balconies, and on the roofs, all along the line of march, were beginning to be weary of waiting.

The officials who had the ceremonies of the occasion in hand waited until three o'clock in the afternoon, and then, as the governor-elect was nowhere to be found, as the necessity was imminent, the inaugural procession was ordered to begin its march.

"Where is he? Where is Rothsay?" demanded the spectators one of the other.

No one knew. No one had seen him. No one could, therefore, answer.

When the procession reached the State house, the lieutenant-governor, Kennelm Kennedy, was sworn in, and the military companies and the civic societies and the spectators all dispersed.

But where was the governor? That was the question of the hour. Why had he not been inaugurated? was asked by everybody of everybody else. The secret of his total and unexplained disappearance had not, indeed, been closely kept. His intimate friends, his household servants and the public officials knew it, but the general public did not.

The next morning the news came out, and the papers had sensational head-lines and long accounts of the sudden and mysterious disappearance of the governor-elect on the eve of his inauguration and of a bridegroom on the evening of his wedding day.

Also there were rewards offered for any intelligence of Regulas Rothsay, living or dead, and for the identification of the unknown visitor who was supposed to have been the last to have seen him on the night of his disappearance.

Days passed, and nothing came in answer to the advertisements. The public at length reached in theory this conclusion: that the governor-elect had been decoyed from the house by his latest visitor, and had been secretly murdered in some remote quarter.

The Rockharrts did not return to Rockhold, but remained in town through all the heat of that hot summer, because Aaron Rockhartt thought he could best pursue his investigations on the scene of the mystery. But he sent his sons to North End to look after the works.

Corona would see no one save the members of her own family. She kept her room, and grieved without ceasing. On the ninth day after the disappearance of her lover-husband she made an effort and came down into the drawing room, to please the gentle old grandmother.

She sat there with the old lady, reading to her, until Mrs. Rockharrt was called out by her tyrant to get something, it might be a book or a paper, a cigar or a pipe, that he himself or a servant might have got just as well, except that Aaron Rockharrt liked to have the ladies of his family wait upon him.

What happened during the hour of the old lady's absence from the drawing room no one knew, but when she returned she found her granddaughter in a swoon on the carpet. In great alarm she called the servants to her assistance. The unconscious girl was laid upon a sofa, and all means were taken to restore her to her senses. Corona recovered her faculties only to fall into the most violent paroxysms of anguish and despair.

From her ravings and self-reproaches Mrs. Rockharrt gathered that the unfortunate girl had heard, or in some way learned, some fatal news.

She sent all the servants out of the room, locked the door, administered a sedative to her child, and then, when the latter was somewhat calmer, questioned her as to the cause of her distress.

"I have nothing to tell—nothing, nothing to tell! But take me away from this place! Take me home to Rockhold, where I may be alone!"

"I will do all I can to comfort you, my dear," said Mrs. Rockharrt. "I will speak to Mr. Rockharrt when he comes in."

No one but the snubbed, brow-beaten and humiliated wife knew all that she engaged to suffer when she promised to speak to her lord and master.

Corona, soothed by the sedative that had been given her, and consoled by the love and sympathy that had been lavished upon her, grew more composed, and finally fell into a deep sleep from which she awoke refreshed. But a rumor went through the house that the young lady had got news which she did not choose to communicate.

Later in the day Mrs. Rockharrt deferentially proposed to the domestic despot that they should return to Rockhold, as the weather was so oppressive and the town house was so obnoxious to dear Corona, which was quite natural under the trying circumstances.

Aaron Rockharrt glared at her until she cowered, and then he told her that he should direct the movements of his family as he thought proper, and that any suggestions from her or from his granddaughter were both unnecessary and impertinent.

So they both had to bend under the iron will of Aaron Rockharrt.

At length, however, something happened to relieve them.

Mr. Rockharrt had not been neglecting his own business, while looking after the missing governor-elect, nor had he been leaving it to his sons and partners, whom he refused to trust. He had been corresponding with his chief manager, Ryland. This correspondence had not been entirely satisfactory, so at length he wrote to Ryland to come to the city for a business talk. It was about the middle of August that the manager arrived and was closeted with his chief. After two hours' discussion of business matters, which ended satisfactorily, the manager, rising to leave the study, observed:

"This is a bad job about the governor, sir!"

"I do not wish to talk of this matter," said Mr. Rockharrt.

"Very well, sir, I am dumb," replied the manager, taking up his hat to leave the house.

"Do you go back to North End by the night train?" inquired Mr. Rockharrt.

"Yes, sir! I must be at my post to-morrow morning, in order to carry out your instructions."

"Quite right," said the head of the great firm. Then with strange inconsistency, since he had declared that he wished to talk no more on the subject of the lost governor, he suddenly inquired:

"What do the people of North End say about the disappearance of Governor Rothsay?"

"Some say he was beguiled away by that man who called on him late at night, and that he was murdered and his body made away with. But I beg your pardon, sir, for repeating such dreadful things."

"Go on! What else do they say?"

"Well, sir, one says one thing, and one another; but they all agree that Old Scythia could tell something if she chose."

"Old Scythia? And what has she to do with the loss of the governor?"

"Nothing that I know of, sir. But the people at North End say that she has."

"Why do they say it?"

"Because, sir, on the day of the wedding, and the eve of the inauguration, she did foretell, in the hearing of a score, that Mr. Rothsay would never take his seat as governor."

"What! Absurd! Preposterous!"

"Of course it was, sir! Yet she did say that, sir, in the hearing of twenty or more of us, and it was a strange coincidence, to say the least, that her words came true. She said it in the presence of many witnesses on the day before the intended inauguration, and when there seemed no possibility of her words coming true. And strange to say, they have come true."

Old Aaron Rockharrt mused for a few minutes and then replied:

"There is no such thing as divination, or soothsaying, or prophesy, or fortune telling in this world. It is all coarse imposture, that can deceive only the weakest mortals. You know that, of course, Ryland. It follows, then, that this old woman could have had no knowledge of what was going to happen unless she was in league with conspirators who had planned to kidnap or murder the governor-elect."

"But, sir, if Old Scythia had been in league with any conspirators, would she have betrayed them—beforehand?"

"No; unless she was too crazy to keep their secret. But—she may have got wind of their plots in some way without their knowledge."

"Yes, sir," said Manager Ryland, who agreed to every opinion advanced by his chief.

"Well, then, I shall go down to Rockhold to-morrow, and investigate this matter for myself. In my capacity of justice of the peace I shall issue a warrant to have that woman brought before me on a charge of vagrancy, and then I shall examine her on this point. But, Ryland, you are to be careful not to drop even a hint of my intention."

"Of course I will not, sir," replied the manager, and then, as there seemed no more to do or say, he took his leave.

Old Aaron Rockharrt strode into the drawing room where his wife and granddaughter sat, and astonished them by saying:

"Pack up your things this afternoon. We leave for Rockland by the first train to-morrow morning."

He deigned no explanation, but turned and stalked off.

The three reached North End at noon. As their arrival was to be a surprise, no carriage had been ordered to meet them. But the large, comfortable hack from the North End Hotel was engaged, and in it they rode on to Rockhold, where they pulled up two hours later, to the astonishment and consternation of the household, who, be it whispered, had almost as lief been confronted with his satanic majesty as to be surprised by their despotic master.

Leaving his womenkind to get domestic affairs into order, the Iron King went to the little den at the end of the hall, which he called his study, and there made out a warrant for the arrest of Hyacinth Woods on the charge of vagrancy. This he directed to William Hook, county constable, and sent it off to the county seat by one of his servants. He waited all the rest of the day for the return of the warrant with the prisoner, but in vain.

The next day, in the afternoon, Constable Hook made his appearance before the magistrate without the prisoner, and reported:

"She cannot be found. I went first to her hut on the mountain, but it was in ruins. It had fallen in. I searched for the woman everywhere, and only found out that she had not been seen by anybody since the day of the grand wedding here," replied the officer.

"The old crone is lost on the same day that the young governor was missing, eh? Very significant. I want you to take a paper for me to the *Peakeville Gazette*. I will advertise a thousand dollars reward for the discovery of that woman. She knows the fate of Rothsay."

CHAPTER III
A MOUNTAIN IDYL—THE GIRL AND THE BOY

On a fine day near the end of October, several years before the opening of this story, the express train from the southwest was speeding on toward North End. In one of the middle cars, which was not crowded, nor, indeed, quite full, sat a girl and a boy—both dressed in deep mourning, and both in charge of a tall, stout gentleman, also in deep mourning. These children were Corona, aged seven, and Sylvanus, aged four, orphans and co-heirs of John Haught, a millionaire merchant of San Francisco, and of his wife, Felicia, only daughter of Aaron and Deborah Rockharrt, of Rockhold. They had lost their parents during the prevalence of an epidemic fever, and had been left to the guardianship of Aaron Rockharrt. They were now coming, in charge of their Uncle Fabian—who had been sent to fetch them—to their grandparents' house, which was to be their home during their minority.

In front of these children sat a man of middle age and a boy of about twelve years. They seemed to belong to the honorable order of working men. Their clothing was old, worn and travel-stained. They had been picked up only at the last past station, and looked as if they had tramped a long way—weary and dejected. Each wore on his battered hat a little wisp of a dusty black crape band. This was a circumstance which much interested the little girl, Corona, who had a longer memory than her baby brother, and had not yet done grieving after her father and her mother, and she wanted to speak to the poor boy, and to tell him how very sorry she was for him, but was much too timid for such a venture. Neither the boy nor the man looked behind them, and so the children never saw their faces during the ride to North End. Both parties got out at the station. The Rockhold carriage was waiting for Fabian and his charges. Nothing was waiting for the tramp and his son. Mr. Fabian looked at them, and took in the whole situation. He put his nephew and niece into the carriage, told the coachman to wait for him, and then went up to the tramps.

"Looking for work?" he said, addressing the elder.

"Yes, sir," replied the latter, touching his old hat. "I have come a long way to look for it, and I am bound now for Rockharrt & Sons' Locomotive Works. Could you be so kind as to direct me where to find them?"

"About three miles down this side of the river. You cannot miss them if you follow this road. Stay—I am one of the firm. We have rather more men than we want just now, but I will give you a line to our manager, and he will find a place for you, and the boy, also," said plausible, good-natured, lying, dishonest Fabian Rockharrt, as he drew a card from his pocket and just wrote above his name:

"Take the bearer and his boy on."

Then on the opposite side of the card he wrote the superscription: "Timothy Ryland, Manager North End Foundries."

He gave this to the tramp, who touched his hat again, and led off his boy for their long walk to the works.

Fabian Rockharrt, with his nephew and niece, reached Rockland two hours later.

Aaron Rockharrt and his younger son, Clarence, were absent, at the works; but little Mrs. Rockharrt was at home.

Little Cora became the constant companion of the grandmother, who found her well advanced in learning for a child of seven years. She could read, write a little, and do easy sums in the first four simple rules of arithmetic.

A school room was fitted up on the first floor back of the Rockhold mansion. A nursery governess was found by advertisement.

She was a young and beautiful girl of the wax doll order of beauty, and of not more than sixteen years of age. In person she was tall, slim and fair, with red cheeks, blue eyes and yellow hair. Her very name, as well as her presence, was full of the aromas of Araby the Blest. It was Rose Flowers.

Rose smiled and bloomed and beamed on all, but most of all on Mr. Fabian, who was at that time a very handsome and fascinating man of no more than thirty, and to do her justice, she brought her young pupils well on in elementary education.

No more was seen or heard of the tramp and his boy, who had come to seek work at the foundries. They seemed to have been forgotten even by the little girl whose sympathies had been touched by their appearance on the train with their own party.

But early in February a catastrophe occurred which brought them back most painfully to, her memory. There was an explosion in the foundry, by which the man was instantly killed.

"Uncle Clarence," asked Cora of that person, "where is the boy belonging to the poor man that was killed? You know they came in the cars with us to North End Station. Oh! and they were so poor! Oh, and the boy had a bit of old crape on his old hat! Oh, and I know he had no mother! But I don't know whether the man was his father or his uncle. But, oh, Uncle Clarence, dear, where is the boy?"

"I don't know anything about the boy, little one, but I will inquire and tell you. I think the little chap has two more friends left, dear. You are one. I am the other."

"Oh, Uncle Clarence, you are a dear ducky-ducky-darling! And when I am a grown-up woman, I will marry you."

"Oh! well, all right, if you remain in the same mind, and—"

"I will never, never change my mind. I love you better than I do anybody in the world, except Sylvan and grandma, and Miss Flowers and Tip!"

Clarence kept his word with the child about making inquiries as to the fate of the boy in whom she was interested.

The boy was motherless, and, by the death of his father, had been left utterly destitute. He had found a home with Scythia Woods, an eccentric woman, who lived in a hut on the mountain side, half way between North End and Rockhold, and he supported himself in a poor way by running errands and doing little jobs about the works.

Little Cora Haught listened to this account of the poor, friendless, self-reliant lad with the deepest sympathy.

"Uncle Clarence," she pleaded, "you are so rich. Why don't you give that poor boy clothes, and shoes, and hats, and all he ought to have?"

"My good little girl, nothing would give me more delight, but that fellow would see Rockharrt & Sons swallowed up by an earthquake before he would take a cent from them that he had not earned."

"Oh, I like that—that is grand! But why don't you take him on and give him good pay?"

"But, my dear, he is a boy, and cannot do regular heavy work. He is quite uneducated, and cannot do any other except what he does."

Two months later, one lovely spring day, she saw him again for the first time since their meeting on the train six months previous. He came to Rockhold one Saturday afternoon to bring a letter from the manager to the head of the firm. He came to the back door which opened from the porch. He sent in his letter by the servant who came at his knock, and he said he was to wait for an answer. Cora, in the back parlor, saw him, recognized him, and ran out to speak to him.

Perhaps the tiny lady had some faint idea of the duties and responsibilities of wealth and station. So she spoke to the boy.

"Are you Regulas Rothsay?" she inquired, in a soft tone.

"Yes, miss," replied the boy.

There was an awkward pause, and then the little girl said slowly:

"You won't let anybody give you anything, although you have no father nor mother. Now, why won't you?"

"Because, I can work for all I want, all—but—" the boy began, and then stopped.

"You have all but what?"

"A little schooling."

"Here's the answer, Rule! You are to run right away as fast as you can and take it to Mr. Ryland," said a servant, coming out upon the porch and handing a letter to the boy.

It was a week after this interview with the lad before Cora saw him again.

He was on the lawn in front of the house. She was at the window of the front drawing room. As soon as she espied him she ran out to speak to him, and eagerly begged that she might teach him to read.

The boy, surprised at the suddenness and the character of such an offer, blushed, thanked the little lady, and declined, then hesitated, reflected, and then, half reluctantly, half gratefully, consented.

Cora was delighted, and frankly expressed her joy.

"Oh, Regulas, I am so glad! Now every afternoon when I have done my lessons—I am in Comly's first speller, Peter Parley's first book of history, and first book of geography, and I am as far as short division in arithmetic, and round hand in the copy book—so as soon as I get through with my lessons, and you get through with your work, you come to this back porch, where I play, and I will bring my old primer and white slate, and I will teach you. If you get here before I do, you wait for me. I will never be long away. If I get here before you, I will wait for you," she concluded.

The Iron King, Mr. Fabian, or Mr. Clarence, passing out of the back door for an afternoon stroll in the grounds, would see the little lady seated in one of the large Quaker chairs, her feet dangling over its edge, busy with her doll's dresses, and furtively watching her pupil, who, seated before her on one of the long piazza benches, would be poring over his primer or his slate.

As time went on every one began to wonder at the earnestness and constancy of this childish friendship.

So the lessons went on through all the spring and summer and early autumn of that year.

Before the leaves had fallen Regulas had learned all she could teach him.

Then their parting came about naturally, inevitably. When the weather grew cold, the lessons could no longer be given out on the exposed piazza, and the little teacher could not be permitted to bring her rough and ragged pupil into the house.

Cora begged of her kind Uncle Clarence some of his old school books, which she knew to be among the rubbish of the garret, which was her own rainy-day play room in summer, and offered the books to the boy as a loan from herself, because she dared not offer the lad a gift.

Later, she loaned him a "Boy's Life of Benjamin Franklin." It was that book, perhaps, that decided the boy's destiny. He read it with avidity, with enthusiasm. The impression made upon his mind was so deep and intense that his heart became fired with a fine ambition. He longed to tread in the steps of Benjamin Franklin—to become a printer, to rise to position and power, to do great and good things for his country and for humanity. He brooded over all this.

To begin, he resolved to become a printer.

So, when the spring opened, he came to Rockhold and bade good-by to his little friend, and went, at the age of fourteen, to the city to seek his fortune, walking all the way, and taking with him testimonials as to his character for truth, honesty, and industry.

There were at that time three printing offices in that city. Rule applied to the first and to the second without success, but when he applied to the third—the office of the *Watch*—and showed his credentials, the proprietor took him on.

He and his little friend corresponded regularly from month to month.

No one objected to this letter writing, any more than to the lesson giving. It was but the charity of the little lady given for the encouragement of the poor, struggling orphan boy.

It was nearly four years after the departure of Rule from the works at North End to seek his fortune in a printing office of the neighboring city. He had never yet returned to see his friends, though his correspondence with Cora had been kept up.

In the four years that Rose Flowers had lived at Rockhold she had won the hearts of all the household, from the master down to the meanest drudge. She was, indeed, the fragrance of the house. All admired her much and loved her more, and yet—

And yet in every mind there was a latent distrust of her, which seemed unjust, and for which all who felt it reproached themselves—in every mind but one.

The Iron King felt no distrust of the submissive, beautiful creature, whom he continually held up to other members of his family as the very model of perfect womanhood.

He did not see, he said, why she should now, when it was finally decided that Cora should be sent to the young ladies' institute, at the city, why Rose should leave the house. She might remain as companion for Mrs. Rockharrt. But when this was proposed to Miss Flowers, the young governess explained, with much regret, that, not anticipating this generous offer, she had already secured another situation.

With tears in her beautiful eyes, Rose Flowers took the old man's hand and pressed it to her heart and then to her lips as she bent her head and cooed:

"I will remember all you have told me—all the wise and good counsel you have ever given me, all the precious acts of kindness you have ever shown me. And when I cease to remember them, sir, may heaven forget me!"

"There, there, my child. You are a baby—a mere baby!" said the Iron King, as he patted her on the head and left her.

This interview occurred a few days before Christmas.

It was now Christmas morning, nearly four years after the departure of Rule Rothsay. It was a fine clear, cold day. Bright with color was the village of North End, where all the houses were decorated with holly, and the people, in their Sunday clothes, were out in the streets on their way to the church, which had been beautifully decorated for the occasion.

The Rockharrt family—with the exception of old Aaron Rockharrt, who did not choose to turn out that day, and Miss Rose Flowers, who stayed home to keep him company and to wait on him—came early in their capacious and comfortable family carriage. They had a large, square, handsomely upholstered pew in the right-hand upper corner of the church.

When they were all quietly settled in their seats and the voluntary was going on, the elders of the party bowed their heads to offer up their preliminary prayers. But Cora, girl-like, looked about her, letting her glances wander over the well-filled pews, and then up toward the galleries. A moment later she suddenly gave a little start and half-suppressed exclamation of delight.

Mrs. Rockharrt, who had finished her prayer, looked around in surprise at the girl, who had committed this unusual indecorum.

"Oh, grandma, it is Rule! Rule, up there in the boys' gallery—look!" Cora whispered, in eager delight.

The old lady raised her eyes and recognized Regulas Rothsay—but so well grown, so well dressed, and well looking as to be hardly recognizable, except from his strong, characteristic head and face. He wore a neatly fitting suit of dark-blue cloth; neat woolen gloves covered his large hands; his hair was trimmed and as nicely dressed as such rough, tawny locks could be.

At length the beautiful service was finished, and the congregation filed out of the church into the yard, where all immediately began shaking hands with each other.

Presently Cora saw the youth come out of the church, look earnestly about him until he descried her party, and then walk directly toward her.

"Oh, Rule, I am so glad to see you! When did you get here? Why didn't you come straight to Rockhold? Why didn't you write and tell me you were coming?" Cora eagerly demanded, as she met him, and hurrying question upon question before giving him time to answer the first one.

The youth raised his cap and bowed to the elder members of the party before answering the girl. Then he said:

"I did not know that I could come until an hour before I started. I came by the midnight express, and reached here just in time for church. I have not seen, or I should say, I have not spoken to, any one here yet except yourself.

"Last evening, being Friday evening, we were at work very late on our Saturday's supplement, and a Christmas story in it. Very often we have to work on Christmas night, if the next day is a week day; and every Sunday night—that is, from twelve midnight, when the Sabbath ends—we have to work to get out Monday morning's paper."

"Oh, yes; of course," said Fabian.

"Well, I never have had a whole holiday since I have been in the *Watch* office; but last night, about half-past ten, after the paper had gone to press, the foreman came to me, paid my wages up to the first of January, and told me that I need not return to the office at midnight after Sunday, but might have leave of absence until Monday morning, so as to have time to go and spend Christmas with my friends if I wished to do so."

Just then Clarence Rockharrt joined them and said, anxiously:

"Mother, dear, I think you had better get into the carriage. It is very bleak out here, and you might take cold."

Mrs. Rockharrt at once took the arm of her youngest and best-beloved son and let him lead her away to the spot where the comfortable family coach awaited them.

Mr. Fabian started to follow with Cora.

"Come with us to the carriage door, Rule," said the girl, looking back and stretching her hand out toward the youth.

"Yes! Come!" added pleasant Mr. Fabian.

Regulas touched his hat and followed. Fabian put his niece in the seat beside her grandmother, and then turned to the youth and inquired:

"What are you going to do with yourself to-day?"

"I shall go down to my old home, sir, Mother Scythia's hut."

"Oh! Ah! Yes; I remember. You are going to stop there?"

"Yes, sir; but I shall try to see all old friends to-day or to-morrow, and I should like to go to Rockhold to thank all the friends there who have been kind to me, and to tell Mrs. Rockharrt and Miss Cora, who were kindest of all, how I have got on in the city."

"Certainly! Certainly, Rule! Come whenever you like! And see here! It is a long, rough road from here to old Scythia's Roost, which is right on our way to Rockhold. Sorry we cannot offer you a seat in the carriage but you see there are but four seats and there are already five people to fill them."

"Oh, sir, I should not expect such a thing," said the youth.

"But I was about to say if you will mount to a seat beside the coachman, you will be heartily welcome to what used to be my own 'most favoryte' perch in my younger days. And we can set you down at the foot of the path leading up to old Scythia's hut," concluded Mr. Fabian.

"Oh, do, Rule! Please do!" pleaded Cora.

Regulas, with his sturdy independence of spirit, would most likely have declined this favor had not the girl's beseeching face and voice persuaded him to accept it.

"I thank you very much, sir," he said, and promptly climbed to the seat.

Three miles down the road the carriage was pulled up at the foot of the highest point of the mountain range, and Rule came down from his perch beside the coachman, stepped up to the carriage window, took off his hat, thanked the occupants for his ride, and then drew a neat, white inch-square parcel from his vest pocket, and holding it modestly, said:

"I hope you will accept this, Miss Cora."

The girl took it with a smile, but before she could open her lips to express her thanks, the youth had bowed, turned from the carriage, and was speeding his way up the rough mountain path, springing from crag to crag up to the ledge on which old Scythia's hut stood.

Cora opened the parcel and found an inch-square little casket of red morocco. She opened this with a spring, and found a small gold heart reposing in a bed of white satin.

"How pretty it is!" she said softly to herself, as she took the trinket from its case. "Look, grandma, what Rule has brought me for a Christmas gift! A little gold heart! A pure gold heart! His is a pure gold heart, is it not?" she added, earnestly, as she placed the trinket in the lady's hand.

Mrs. Rockharrt looked at it with interest, and then passed it on to her eldest son.

The ride was continued, and presently the carriage was driven off the boat and up the avenue leading to the house. As the vehicle drew up before the front doors, a pretty picture might have been seen through the drawing-room windows.

A bright fireside, an old man reclining in his luxurious arm-chair; a beautiful girl seated on a hassock at his feet, reading to him, and at intervals lifting her lovely blue eyes in childish adoration to his face. They might have been grandfather and granddaughter, but they were, in fact, old Aaron Rockharrt and Miss Rose Flowers—Merlin and Vivien again, except that the Iron King was rather a rugged and unmanageable Merlin.

Meanwhile, Regulas Rothsay had climbed the rugged mountain path that led to Scythia's hut. On the back of the broad shelf of rock on which the hut stood was a hollow in the side of the precipice. Scythia had cleared out this hollow of all its natural litter. Before this apartment she had built another room, with no better material than fragments of rock found on the spot, and filled in with earth, moss and twigs. She had roofed this over with branches of evergreens piled thick and high, to keep off rain and sun. A heavy buffalo robe, fastened with large wooden pins at its top to the roof of the hut, served for a door. There was no window. In the inner or cavernous apartment she had built a rude fire-place and chimney going up through a hole in the rock. A pallet of rough furs and coarse blankets lay in one corner of this room, and a few rude cooking utensils occupied another. In the outer room there was a rough oak table and two chairs.

Up before the edge of this natural shelf on which the hut stood appeared the tops of a thicket of pine trees that grew on the mountain side fifty feet below. Up behind this shelf arose other pines, height above height, until their highest tops seemed to pierce the clouds.

When Rule reached this shelf, he found the tops of the pine trees, the ground, and the hut all covered with snow.

"Good morning, mother! A merry Christmas to you!" said Rule, gayly.

"I hope you have made yourself as comfortable as possible in this place," said the youth, anxiously.

"Yes, Rule! always as happy and as much at ease as my past will permit."

"Oh! what is—what was this terrible past?" inquired the youth—not for the first time.

"It was, it is, and it ever will be! This past will be present and future so long as I live on this earth. And some day, when time and strife and woe have made you strong and hard and stern, I will lift the veil and show you its horrible face! But not now, my boy! not now! Come in."

As the weird woman said this she led the way into the hut, where the rude table stood covered with a coarse white cloth and adorned with two white plates and two pairs of steel knives and forks. Here the Christmas dinner was eaten, and afterward the two began a close conversation.

"Mother," said the youth, "I shall have to leave here to-morrow night. I should go away so much more contented if I could see you living down in the village among people. Here you are dwelling alone, far from human help if you should require it. The winter coming on!"

"Rule! I hate the village! I hate the haunts of human beings! I love the wilderness and the wild creatures that are around me!"

"But, mother, if you should be taken ill up here alone!"

"I should get well or die; and it would not in the least matter which."

"But you might linger, you might suffer."

"I am used to suffering, and however long I might linger, the end would come at last. Recovery or death, it would not matter which."

"Oh, Mother Scythia!" said the youth, in a voice full of distress.

"Rule! I am as happy here as my past will permit me to be. I abhor the haunts of the human! I love the solitude of the wilderness. The time may come when you too, lad, shall hate the haunts of the human and long for the lair of the lion! You will rise, Rule! As sure as flame leaps to the air, you will rise! The fire within you will kindle into flame! You will rise! But—beware the love of woman and the pride of place! See! Listen!"

The face of the weird woman changed—became ashen gray, her form became rigid, her eyes were fixed, her gaze was afar off in distant space.

"What is it, mother?" anxiously demanded the youth.

"I see your future and the emblem of your future—a splendid meteor, soaring up from the earth to the sky, filling space with light and glory! Dazzling a million of eyes, then dropping down, down, down into darkness and nothingness! That is you!"

"Mother Scythia!" exclaimed the youth, in troubled tones.

The weird woman never turned her head, nor withdrew her fearful, far-off stare into futurity.

"That is you. You are but a poor apprentice. But from this year you will soar, and soar, and soar to the zenith of place and power among your fellows! You will be the blazing meteor of the day! You will dazzle all eyes by the splendor of your success, and then, 'in an instant, in the twinkling of an eye,' you will drop into night, and nothingness, and be heard of no more!"

"Mother! Mother Scythia! Wake up! You are dreaming!" said Rule, laying his hand on the woman's shoulder and gently shaking her.

"Oh, what is this? Rule! What is it?"

"You have been dreaming, Mother Scythia."

"Have I?" said the woman, putting her hands to her forehead and stroking away the raven locks that over-shadowed it.

And gradually she recovered from her trance and returned to her normal condition. When Rule was quite sure that she was all right again, he said:

"Mother Scythia, I am going to Rockhold to see the friends there who have been kind to me. But I will come back to spend the night with you."

"Well, lad, go. Why should I try to hinder you? You must work out your destiny and bear your doom," she said, wearily, with her forehead bowed upon her hands, as if she felt the heavy prophetic cloud still over-shadowing and oppressing her.

"Mother Scythia, why do you speak so solemnly of me, and I only in my nineteenth year?" gravely inquired the youth, who, though he had been accustomed to the weird woman's strange moods and stranger words and deemed them little less than the betrayals of insanity, yet now felt unaccountably troubled by them.

"Yes; you are young, but the years fly fast; and I—I see the future in the present. But go, my boy! enjoy the good of the present—your best days, lad!—and come back this evening and you shall find your pallet of sweet boughs and soft blankets ready for you," she said.

Rule stooped and kissed her corrugated forehead and then left the hut.

The sun was setting behind the mountain, which threw a dark shadow over Scythia's Ledge and Rule's path, as he ran springing from rock to rock down the precipice to the river's side. It was dark when he reached the spot. But the lights from the windows of Rockhold on the opposite shore gleamed out upon the snow with splendid effect.

Every window in the front of the building was shining with light that streamed out upon the snow; for the shutters had been left unclosed on purpose, this Christmas night.

Rule crossed the ferry and went, as he had been used to go, to the back door, opening on the back porch, where, four years before, Cora used to keep school for her one pupil. He rapped at the door, and Sylvan sprang up and opened it. He was warmly welcomed, and spent a pleasant evening. The rest of his vacation was spent in a way equally pleasant, and at seven a.m., Monday, Rule was at work, type-setting in the *Watch* office.

On the third of January following that Christmas there were three departures from Rockhold. Miss Rose Flowers went East to enter upon her new engagement. Corona Haught, in charge of her grandmother and her Uncle Clarence, went West to enter the Young Ladies' Institute, in the capital, and Master Sylvanus Haught went North, in the care of his Uncle Fabian, to enter a boy's school.

CHAPTER IV
A RETROSPECT

It was near the close of a cold, bright day early in January, that Mrs. Rockharrt and Corona Haught, escorted by Mr. Clarence, stepped from the train at the depot of the capital city of their State—which must, for obvious reason, be nameless—and were driven to the Young Ladies' Institute, where the girl was left, and as the adieus were being said it was explained to Cora that discretion and social conventionality dictated that her correspondence with young Rothsay should cease. Clarence stated that he would write to the youth and explain that the rules of the school, also, forbade such a correspondence.

"I will also tell him that he can continue to send the *Watch* to you, with his own paragraphs marked as before," said Corona's uncle. "There can be no law against that. I will correspond with Rule occasionally, and keep you posted up as to how he is getting on. There can be no school law against your uncle writing to you."

Cora Haught graduated when she was eighteen. In all these years she had not seen Rule Rothsay. She only heard from him through his letters to her Uncle Clarence, reported second hand to herself. She knew that in these five years Rule had risen, step by step, in the office where he had begun his apprenticeship; that he had risen to be foreman, then sub-editor, and now he was part proprietor and one of the most powerful political writers on the paper.

The workingmen's party wished to put him up as a candidate for the State legislature. What a power he would have been for their cause in that place! but when the subject was proposed to him, he admonished the spokesman that he was, as yet, a little less than of legal age for an office that required its holder to be at least twenty-five years old.

After Cora's graduation the Rockharrt family spent a week in their town house, preparatory to a summer tour through the Northern States and Canada.

One morning, while the whole family were sitting around the breakfast table, old Aaron Rockharrt suddenly spoke:

"Fabian! Now that my granddaughter has left school, she will want a companion near her own age. Miss Rose Flowers would suit very well. Have you any idea where she is?"

"Miss Rose Flowers, my dear sir, is now Mrs. Slydell Stillwater, the—"

"Married!" interrupted all voices except that of the Iron King, who bent his heavy gray brows as he gazed upon his son.

"Stuff and nonsense! How did you know anything about her marriage?" demanded old Aaron Rockharrt.

"In the simplest and most natural way, sir. I saw it in the newspapers, about three years ago. And, in point of fact, I forgot it and should never have thought of it again but for your inquiries about the young woman this morning. Her husband is Captain Slydell Stillwater, captain and half owner of the East Indiaman Queen of Sheba," replied Mr. Fabian.

"Poor child! To be parted from her husband more than half her time. Is Captain Stillwater now at sea?"

"I think he must be, sir, as there has hardly been time for his return since he sailed soon after his marriage."

"Do you know where Mrs. Stillwater lives?"

"I do not, sir; but I might find out by inquiring of some mutual acquaintance."

"Do so. And, Mrs. Rockharrt," the King added, turning to his little old wife, "you will write a note to Mrs. Stillwater, inviting her to join our party for a summer tour, and as our guest, remember. Fabian, you will see that the note reaches the lady in time."

"I will do my best, sir," said Mr. Fabian.

"Very well," said the wife.

The note of invitation to Mrs. Stillwater was written. Mr. Fabian used such dispatch in his search for the lady that his efforts were soon rewarded with success. A letter came from Mrs. Stillwater, postmarked Baltimore, in which she cordially thanked Mrs. Rockharrt for her invitation, gratefully accepted it, and offered to join the Rockharrt party at any point most convenient to the latter. This answer was communicated to the family autocrat, who thereupon issued his commands:

"Write and say to Mrs. Stillwater that we will stop at Baltimore on our way, and call for her at her hotel on Friday; but say that if she should not be ready, we will wait her convenience."

This letter was also written and sent off.

Three days later the whole family left the capital for Baltimore, which they reached at night. They went directly to the hotel where Mrs. Stillwater was staying, and engaged rooms for their whole party.

They scarcely took time enough to wash the travel dust from their faces and brush it from their hair, and change their traveling suits for fresher dresses, before they hurried down stairs to their private parlor, whence Mrs. Rockharrt sent her own and her granddaughter's cards to Mrs. Stillwater's room.

A few minutes after, the young siren appeared.

"Heavens! how beautiful she is! More beautiful than before! Look, Cora! Was there ever such a perfect creature?" said Mr. Clarence, under his breath.

Cora looked at her former governess with a start of involuntary wonder and admiration. Rose Stillwater was more beautiful than ever. Her exquisite oval face was a little more rounded. Her fair complexion had a richer bloom on the cheeks and lips. Her hair was darker in the shade and brighter in the light; her blue eyes were softer and sweeter; her graceful form fuller. She was dressed in some floating material that enveloped her figure like a cloud.

She came, blooming, beaming, smiling, into the room, where all arose to meet her. She went first to Mr. Rockharrt, and bent and almost knelt before him, and raised his hand to her lips as if he had been her sovereign; and then, before he could respond—for she saw that he was slightly embarrassed as well as greatly pleased by this adoration—she turned and sank into the arms of old Mrs. Rockharrt, and cooed forth:

"How sweet of you to remember your poor, lonely child and call her to your side!"

"Why didn't you tell me you were going to be married, my dear?" was the practical question of the old lady.

"It was shyness on my part. I dared not obtrude my poor affairs on your attention until you should notice me in some way," she meekly replied, and then she gracefully slipped out of Mrs. Rockharrt's embrace and went and folded Cora to her bosom, murmuring:

"My own darling, how happy I am to meet you again! How lovely you are, my sweet angel!"

"Oh, why did you not write to me that you were going to be married? I should have so liked to have been your bridesmaid!" complained Cora.

"Sweetest sweet, if I had dreamed such honor and happiness were possible for me, I should have written and claimed them with pride and delight. But I dared not, my darling! I dared not. I was but a poor governess, without any claims to your remembrance, and should not now be with you had not the dear lady, your grandmamma, kindly recalled her poor dependant to mind and brought me into her circle."

"Oh, Rose, do not speak so! I should hate to hear even the poorest maid in our house speak so. You were never grandma's dependant, or anybody's dependant. You were one of the noble army whom I honor more than I do all the monarchs on earth," said Cora earnestly.

With remembrances and delightful chat the evening was wearing away, and it was time for the party to retire to rest.

Two days after this the Rockharrts, with Cora Haught and Mrs. Stillwater, left Baltimore for the North, *en route* for Canada and New Brunswick.

The party went first directly to Boston, where they stayed for a few days, to attend the commencement of the collegiate school at which Master Sylvanus Haught was preparing himself to become a candidate for admission to the military academy at West Point; but where, as yet, he had not distinguished himself by application to his studies.

On promising to do better, Sylvan was permitted to accompany his friends on their summer tour.

The party spent the season in traveling, and it was not until the 15th of September that they set out on their return South. They reached Baltimore late in September, yet found the weather in that latitude still oppressively warm, and roomed at a hotel.

Here it had been tacitly understood from the first that Mrs. Stillwater was to remain, while the rest of the party should proceed on their journey West.

But the family despot had become so habituated to the incense hourly offered up to his egotism by Circe, that he felt her society to be essential to his contentment. So he issued his commands to his wife to invite Mrs. Stillwater to accompany the family party to Rockhold for a long visit.

The old lady very willingly obeyed these orders, for she also desired the visit from the fascinator, whose presence kept the tyrant in a good humor and on his good behavior. So she pressed Rose Stillwater to accompany them to their mountain home.

Rose Stillwater raised her beautiful soft blue eyes, brimming with tears that ever came at will, gazed sorrowfully, penitently, deprecatingly, into the lady's face and cooed:

"I feel as if it were a sin to refuse you! You who have been a mother to me. And, oh! how dearly I should love to stay with you and wait on you forever and forever! I could not conceive a happier life! But duty constrains me to deny myself this delight, and to wrench myself away from all I love."

"Duty? What duty, my dear girl? I do not understand that. You have no children to take care of, no house to look after, no husband to please, for Captain Stillwater is at sea. What duty, then, can you have which is so pressing as to keep you away from your friends?"

"The Queen of Sheba was spoken and passed by the Liverpool and New York ocean steamer Arctic on Saturday, within three days' sail of land. And he may arrive here any hour. I must wait to receive him."

"Indeed! I did not know that. My dear, I congratulate you on your coming happiness. I can urge you no more, of course. It is a sacred duty as well as a sweet delight for you to remain here and meet your husband. So, of course, we must resign ourselves to our loss; but I hope, my dear, that you and your husband will come together at an early date and make us a long visit."

"I hope so, too, dearest lady!"

When, a little later in the evening, the Iron King heard the result of this interview, he was—as his wife had feared—dreadfully disappointed, and consequently in one of his morose and diabolical tempers, and sullenly set his despotic will against the reasonable wishes of everybody else. He announced that they should all set forward the next day. It was high time they should all be at home looking after house and business. So it was settled.

As the party needed rest, they retired very early.

That night Cora Haught had a rather strange adventure, to relate which intelligibly I must describe the situation of their rooms.

The suite occupied by the Rockharrt party was on the third floor of the house, and consisted of five rooms in a row, on the left hand side of the corridor, from the head of the stairs. The front room, overlooking an avenue, was tenanted by Mr. and Mrs. Rockharrt, the next one was occupied by Cora Haught, the third room was the private parlor of the suite, the fourth room was that of Mrs. Stillwater, and the fifth, and largest, was a double-bedded room, tenanted jointly by Mr. Fabian and Mr. Clarence. All these rooms had doors communicating with each other, and also with the corridor, all or any of which could be left open or made fast at discretion.

Cora's room, between her grandparents' bed-chamber and their private parlor, was the smallest, the closest and the warmest of the suite. That

September night was sultry and stifling. Scarcely a breath of air came from without.

The girl could not sleep for the heat. Anathematizing her room as a "black hole" of Calcutta, she lay tossing from side to side, and listening for the hourly strokes of a neighboring clock, and praying for the night to be over. She heard that clock strike eleven, twelve, one.

At length Cora thought that she would go into the private parlor next her own room to get a breath of fresh air. She felt sure that there she should be perfectly safe from intrusion, as she knew that the door leading from the parlor into the corridor was secured from within by a strong bolt, and the other two doors led, the one into her own little room, and the other, on the opposite side, into Mrs. Stillwater's. So that she would be as secluded as in her own chamber.

She slipped on a thin, dark blue silk dressing gown, thrust her feet in slippers, opened the door and passed into the parlor.

The room was very dark, still and cool. The two side windows overlooking the alley were open, and a rising breeze from the harbor blew in. Cora went and sat down in an easy chair in the angle of the corner between an open side window and her own room door.

The room was pitch dark. The darkness, the coolness, and the stillness were all so soothing and refreshing to the girl's heated and excited nerves that she sank back in her high, cushioned chair and dozed off into sleep—into such a deep and dreamless sleep that she knew nothing until she was awakened, or rather only half awakened, by the sound of a key turning in a lock and a door creaking upon its hinges. The sound seemed to come from the direction of Mrs. Stillwater's room; but Cora was still half asleep, and almost unconscious of her whereabouts. As in a dream, she heard some one tiptoe slowly across and jar a chair in the deep darkness. She heard the bolt of the door leading into the corridor grate as it was slipped back. This awakened her thoroughly. She was about to call out:

"Who is there?"

Then a voice that she recognized even in its low, whispering tones spoke and arrested the words on her lips. It said:

"Fabe! Fabe! is that you?"

"Yes. Is all quiet?"

"Yes; and has been so for hours. Come in. Pass around, feeling by the wall until you reach the sofa. If you attempt to cross the room, you may strike a chair or table and make a noise, as I did."

The unseen man cautiously crept around by the wall, feeling his way, but occasionally striking and jarring a picture frame or looking glass as he passed, and muttering good-humored little growls of deprecation, and finally making the sofa creak as he struck and sat heavily down upon it.

Cora was wide awake now, and quite cognizant of the identity of the invisible persons in the room as that of Mr. Fabian Rockharrt and Mrs. Rose Stillwater.

It did not once occur to the girl that she was doing any wrong in remaining there, in the parlor common to the whole party. Surprise and wonder held her spellbound in her obscure seat.

The sofa on which they sat was between the two windows. She reclined in the easy chair in the corner between the right-hand window and the door of her room. She was so near them that she might have touched the sofa by stretching out her hand.

Without dreaming of harm, she overheard their conversation.

Mr. Fabian was the first to speak.

"I say, Rose," he began, "I have a deuce of a hard time to get a tete-a-tete with you. This is the first we have had for two months."

"And we could not have had this but for the accidental arrangement of these convenient rooms," she whispered.

"Exactly. We must arrange for future plans to-night. I understand that the old folks have been trying to persuade you to return home with us?"

"Yes; but, of course, I shall not go."

"Of course not; but how did you get out of it?"

"Oh, by raising the old gentleman."

"Do you mean the—the—the—de—"

"Certainly not. I mean my husband, the gallant Captain Stillwater, of the East Indiaman Queen of Sheba, who has been spoken within three days' sail of port, and is expected here every hour. So that, you see, I must remain here to welcome my husband. It is my sacred duty," said the woman demurely.

"Ha-ha-ha!" laughed Mr. Fabian, in a low, half-suppressed chuckle.

"Hush! Oh, be careful! You will be heard!" murmured Rose Stillwater, in a frightened whisper.

"What! at this hour? Why, everybody in this suite is in his or her deepest sleep. I say, Rosebud."

"What?"

"His Majesty the King of the Cumberland Mines has been in a demoniac humor ever since he learned that you were not coming home with us."

"I know it, and I am very sorry for it, especially on his family's account, but I could not help it."

"Certainly not. It would have been inconvenient and embarrassing. Look here, Rosalie."

"Well?"

"If the aged monarch was not such a perfect dragon of truth, honesty and fidelity, and all the cast-iron virtues, I should think that he was over head and ears in love with you."

"Nonsense, Fabian! Mr. Rockharrt is old enough to be my grandfather, and his hair is quite gray."

"If he were old enough to be your great-grandfather, and his hair was quite white, it need make no difference in that respect, my dear. The fires of Mt. Hecla burn beneath eternal snows."

"What rubbish you are talking, Fabian! But—to change the subject— when will my house be ready? I warn you that I will not go back to that brick block on Main Street in your State capital."

"You should not, Rosebella. Your home is finished and furnished; and a lovelier bower of roses cannot be found out of paradise! It is simply perfection, or it will be when you take possession of it."

"Yes; tell me all about it," whispered the lady, eagerly.

"It is a small, elegant villa, situated in the midst of beautiful grounds in a small, sequestered dell, inclosed with wooded hills rising backward into forest-crowned mountains, and watered by many little springs rising among the rocks and running down to empty into a miniature lake that lies shining before the house. It seems to be in the heart of the Cumberlands, in the depth of solitude, yet it is not fifteen minutes' walk by a forest footpath to the railway station at North End."

"What shall we name this little Eden?"

"Rose Bower, and the locality Rose Valley."

"And when may I take possession?"

"Whenever you please. All is prepared and waiting the arrival of Mrs. Stillwater, who has taken the house and engaged the servants through her agent, and who is expected to reside there during the absence of her husband, Captain Stillwater, on long voyages."

"How long are these false appearances to be kept up, and when are our true relations to be announced?"

"Before very long, my sweet!"

"I hate this concealment! I know that I am a favorite with your father and mother, so I cannot see why you have not told them and will not tell them."

"Now, Rosamunda, don't be a little idiot! Be a little angel, as you always have been! Am I not doing everything I can for your comfort and happiness, only asking you in turn to be faithful and patient until I can make you my wife before the whole world? My father does not like the idea of my marrying—anybody! If he knew we were engaged to each other, he would never forgive me, and that means he would cut me off from all share in the patrimony. And we could not afford to lose that! Let me tell you a secret, Rose. Though our firm does business under the name 'Rockharrt & Sons,' yet 'Sons' have a merely nominal interest in the works while Rockharrt lives. So you see, I have very little of my own, and if the autocrat should learn, even by our own confession, that we had been—been—been—concealing our engagement from him, he would never forgive either of us."

At this moment a step was heard passing along the corridor outside.

It caused the two unseen inmates of the parlor to shrink into silence, and even when it had passed out of hearing it caused them, in renewing their conversation, to speak only in the lowest tones, so that Cora could no longer catch a word of their speech.

She would before this have risen and retired to her own room; but she was afraid of making a noise, and consequently causing a scene.

Were those two, her Uncle Fabian and Mrs. Stillwater, only secretly engaged? Secretly engaged? But whoever heard of a betrothed lover providing a home for his betrothed bride to live in before marriage! And then, again, was her Uncle Fabian really so dependent on his father as he had represented to Rose? Cora had always understood that he had a quarter share in the great business, and that Clarence had an eighth. And, worse than all, had they been so deceived as to the condition of Rose that, if she was Mrs. Stillwater at all, she was the widow and not the wife of Captain Stillwater, since she was engaged to be married, if not already married, to Mr. Fabian Rockharrt?

Altogether the affair seemed a blinding and confusing tissue of falsehood and deception that amazed and repulsed the mind of the girl.

Bewildered by the mystery, lulled by the hum of voices whose words she could not distinguish, fanned by the breeze from the harbor, and calmed by the darkness, the wearied girl sank back into her resting chair, closed her eyes, and lost the sequence of her thoughts in dreams—from which she presently sank into dreamless sleep, which lasted until she was awakened by the noise of the hotel servants moving about on their morning duties, opening windows, rapping at doors to call up travelers for early trains, dragging along trunks, and so on.

At breakfast Cora watched Mr. Fabian and Rose, because she could not help doing so, and she certainly discovered signs of a secret understanding between them—signs so slight that they would have been unnoticed by any one who had not the key to the mystery. But how sickening and depressing was all this! Rose Flowers, or Stillwater, or Rockharrt—whichever name she could legally claim—was a fraud. Mr. Fabian Rockharrt was another fraud. Those two were secretly engaged or secretly married.

After breakfast the party were ready for their journey Then came the leave-taking.

Every one, except Cora Haught, shook hands warmly with Rose Stillwater. Mrs. Rockharrt embraced and kissed her fondly, and renewed and pressed her invitation to the beauty to come and make a long visit.

Rose put her arms around the old lady's neck and clung to her, and, with tearful eyes and trembling tones and loving words, assured her that she would fly to Rockhold on the first possible opportunity, and, after many caresses, she reluctantly turned away and went toward Cora.

The girl had lowered her blue veil, and tied it mask-like over her face, in a way that women often do, but which Cora never did, except on this occasion, when she wished to evade the sure to be offered kiss of Rose Stillwater.

But Rose embraced her strongly and kissed her through the veil, endearments which the young girl could not repel without attracting attention, but which she only endured and did not return.

The party reached Rockhold on the evening of the second day's travel.

Old Aaron Rockharrt found himself so weary of traveling that he announced his intention of remaining in Rockhold for the entire winter, nor leaving it even to go to his town house for a few weeks during the session of the legislature.

Cora was disappointed. She longed to go to Washington for the season—to go into company, to go to balls and parties, concerts and operas, to see new people and make new friends, perhaps to attract new admirers; and as she was now nineteen years of age, she need not be too severely criticised for so natural an aspiration.

Mr. Fabian was the most zealous and active member of the firm. He would go to North End and stay two days at a time to be near his scene of duty.

Time passed, but Rose Stillwater did not make her promised visit.

Old Aaron often referred to it, and worried his wife to write to her and remind her of her promise. The old lady always complied with her husband's requirements, and wrote pressing letters; but the beauty always wrote back excusing herself on the ground of "the captain's" many engagements, which confined him to the ship and her to his side.

So time passed, and nearly another year went by. The Rockharrts were still at Rockhold.

A political crisis was at hand—the election for the State legislature.

The candidate for representative of the liberal party in that election district was Regulas Rothsay.

The election day came at length, as anxious a day for Cora Haught as for any one.

It was a grand success, a glorious triumph for the printer boy and for the workingmen's cause as well. Rule Rothsay was elected representative for his district in the State legislature by an overwhelming majority.

Cora was destined to a joyful surprise the next morning, when the domestic autocrat suddenly announced:

"I shall take the family to my town house on the first of next week. My last bill, which was defeated last year, may be passed this session."

Cora now, on the Irishman's principle of pulling the pig backward if you want him to go forward, ventured on the assurance of counseling her grandfather by saying:

"I would not approach Mr. Rothsay on the subject of this bill, if I were you, sir."

"But you are not I, miss!" exclaimed the old man, opening his eyes wide to stare her down. "And the new man is the very one to whom I shall first speak. He is the most proper person to present the bill. He represents my own district. His election is largely due to the men in my own employ. I am surprised that you should presume to advise upon matters of which you can know nothing whatever."

Cora bowed to the rebuke, but did not mind it in the least, since now she felt sure of meeting Rule Rothsay in town.

On the following Monday the Rockharrts went to town.

Mr. Rockharrt met and compared notes with some of the lobbyists.

One veteran lobbyist gave him what he called the key to the riddle of success.

"You appealed to reason and conscience!" said he. "My dear sir, you should have appealed to their stomachs and pockets. You should have given them epicurean feasts, and put money in your 'purse' to be transferred to theirs!"

"Bribery and corruption! I would lose my bill forever! And I would see the legislature—*exterminated*, before I would pay one cent to get a vote," said the Iron King. And he used a much stronger as well as much shorter word than the one underscored; but let it pass.

As soon as the morning papers announced—among other arrivals—that of the new assemblyman, the Hon. Regulas Rothsay, Aaron Rockharrt sought out the young legislator, and explained that he wished to get a charter for a railroad that he wished to build. The company—all responsible men—had been incorporated some time, but he had never succeeded in getting a charter from the legislature.

Rule saw that the enterprise would be a benefit to the community at large, and especially to the workingmen, the farmers, shop keepers and mechanics; so when he had heard all the old Iron King had to say on the subject, he promptly gave a promise which neither favor, affection nor self-interest could ever have won from him, but which reason, conscience and the public good constrained him to give—namely, to present the petition for the charter to the assembly, and to support it with all his might.

After this Regulas Rothsay came often and more often, until at length he passed every evening with the Rockharrts when they were at home. Old Aaron Rockharrt esteemed him as he esteemed very, very few of his fellow creatures. Mrs. Rockharrt really loved him. Mr. Fabian and Mr. Clarence liked him. Cora admired and honored him. He was made so welcome in the family circle that he felt himself quite at home among them.

On the second of January the first business taken up was that of the bill to charter the projected railroad. It was presented by Mr. Rothsay, and referred to the proper committee.

The charter bill was reported with certain amendments, sent back again and reported again, with modified amendments, laid on the table, taken up and generally tormented for ten days, and then passed by a small majority.

Rule had conscientiously done his best, and this was the result: Old Aaron Rockharrt thanked him stiffly.

"You have worked it through, sir! No one but yourself could have done it! And it is a wonder that even you could do so with such a set of pig-headed rascals as our assemblymen. And now, will it pass the senate?"

"I believe it will, Mr. Rockharrt. I have been speaking to many of the senators, and find them well disposed toward it," said Rule.

To be brief, the bill was soon taken up by the senate; and after much the same treatment it had received in the assembly, it came safely through the ordeal, and was passed—again by a small majority.

Old Aaron Rockharrt was triumphant, in his sullen, dogged and undemonstrative way.

But having gained his ends, for which alone he had come to the city, he ordered his family to pack up and be ready to leave town for Rockhold the next day but one.

But the worst was to come.

When all the household were assembled at luncheon, he shot his last bolt.

"Now look you here, all of you! We are going to Rockhold to-morrow. I do not wish to have any company there. I am tired of company! I hate company! I am going to the country to get rid of company. So see that you do not, any of you, invite any one to visit us."

The next morning the Rockharrt family left town for North End, where they arrived early in the afternoon.

A monotonous season followed, at least for the two ladies, who led a very secluded life at the dreary old stone house on the mountain side.

Winter, spring, summer and autumn crept slowly away in, the lonely dwelling. In the last days of November he announced to his family, with the usual suddenness of his peremptory will, that he should go to Washington City for the winter, taking with him his wife and granddaughter, and leaving his two sons in charge of the works, and that they would be joined in Washington at Christmas by his grandson, for whom he was about to apply for admission into the military academy at West Point.

Regulas called frequently, and his attentions to Cora were marked.

The Rockharrt party went to Washington on the first of December, and took possession of the suite of rooms previously engaged for them at one of the large West End hotels.

One morning, when Rule was out of the way, being on a canvassing round with Mr. Rockharrt among such members of Congress as had remained in the city, Sylvan suddenly asked his sister:

"Cora, what's to make the pot boil?"

"What do you mean?" inquired the young lady, looking up from "Bleak House," which she was reading.

"Who's to get the grub?"

"I—don't understand you."

"Oh, yes, you do. What are you and Rothsay to live on after you are married? He is poor as a church mouse, and you are not much richer. You are reported to be an heiress and all that, but you know very well that you cannot touch a cent of your money until you are twenty-five years old, and not even then if you have married in the interim without our great Mogul's consent. Such are the wise provisions of our father's will. Now then, when you and Rule are married, what is to make the pot boil?"

"There is no question of marriage between Mr. Rothsay and myself," replied Cora, with a fine assumption of dignity, which was, however, quite, lost on Sylvan, who favored her with a broad stare and then exclaimed:

"No question of marriage between you? My stars and garters! then there ought to be, for you are both carrying on at a—at a—at a most tremendous rate!"

Cora took up her book and walked out of the room in stately displeasure.

No; there had been no question of marriage between them; no spoken question, at least, up to this day.

This was true to-day, but it was not true on the following day, when Cora and Rule, being alone in the parlor, fell into thoughtful silence, neither knowing exactly why.

This was broken at last by Rule.

"Cora, will you look at me, dear?"

She raised her eyes and meet his fixed full and tenderly on hers.

"Cora, I think that you and I have understood each other a long time, too long a time for the reserve we have practiced. My dear, will you now share the poverty of a poor man who loves you with all his heart, or will you wait for that man until he shall have made a home and position more worthy of you? Speak, my love, or if you prefer, take some time to think of this. My fate is in your hands."

These were calm words, uttered with much, very much, self-restraint; yet eyes and voice could not be so perfectly controlled as language was, and these spoke eloquently of the man's adoration of the woman.

She put her hand in his large, rough palm—the palm inherited from many generations of hard workers—where it lay like a white kernel in a brown shell, and she answered quietly, with controlled emotion:

"Rule, I would rather come to you now forever, and share your life, however hard, and help your work, however difficult, than part from you again; or, if this happiness is not for us now, I would wait for years—I would wait for you forever."

"God bless you! God bless you, my dear! my dear! But is not this in your own choice, Cora?"

"No; it is in my grandfather's."

"You are of age, dear."

"Yes. But not because I am of age would I disobey his will. He has always done his duty by me faithfully. I must do mine by him. He is old now. I must not oppose him. He may consent to our union at once, for you are a very great favorite with him. But his will must be consulted."

"Of course, dear. I meant to speak to Mr. Rockharrt after speaking to you."

"And to abide by his wishes, Rule?"

"If I must. But I would rather abide by yours only, since you are of age," said the young man.

And what more was spoken need not be repeated here. The next day Rule Rothsay called early, and asked to see Mr. Rockharrt.

"Ah! Ah! You come to tell me that you have seen Hunter, I suppose? How does he stand affected toward my bill?" exclaimed the Iron King, pointing to one chair for his guest and dropping into another himself.

"The truth is, Mr. Rockharrt, I came to see you on quite another matter—"

The young man paused. The old man looked attentive and curious.

"It is a matter of the deepest interest to me—"

Again Rule paused, for Mr. Rockharrt was looking at him with bent brows, staring eyes, and bristling iron gray hair and beard, or hair and beard that seemed to bristle.

"Your granddaughter—" began Rule. "Your granddaughter has made me very happy by consenting to become my wife, with your approbation," calmly replied Rule.

"Oh!" exclaimed the old man, in a peculiar tone, between surprise and derision. "And so you have come to ask my consent to your marriage with my granddaughter?"

"If you please, Mr. Rockharrt."

"And so that is the reason why you worked so hard to get my railroad bill through the legislature. Well, I always believed that every man had his price; but I thought you were the exception to the general rule. I thought you were not for sale. But it seems that I was mistaken, and that you were for sale, and set a pretty high price upon yourself, too—the hand of my granddaughter!"

The young man was not ill-tempered or irritable. Perfectly conscious of his own sound integrity, he was unmoved by this taunt; and he answered with quiet dignity:

"If you will reflect for a moment, Mr. Rockharrt, you will know that your charge is untrue and impossible, and you will recall it. I took up your railroad bill because I saw that its provisions would be beneficial to the small towns, tradesmen and farmers all along the proposed line—interests that many railroads neglect, to the ruin of parties most concerned. And I took up this cause before I had ever met your granddaughter since her childhood or as a woman."

"That is true. Well, well, the selfish and mercenary character of the men, and women, too, that I meet in this world has made me, perhaps, too suspicious of all men's motives," said the champion egotist of the world, speaking with the air of the great king condescending to an apology—if his answer could be called an apology.

Rule accepted it as such. He knew it was as near to a concession as the despot could come. He bowed in silence.

"And so you want my granddaughter, do you?" demanded the old man.

"Yes, sir; as the greatest good that you, or the world, or heaven, could bestow on me," earnestly replied the suitor.

"Rubbish! Don't talk like an idiot! How do you propose to support her?"

"By the labor of my brain and hands," gravely and confidently replied Rule.

"Worse rubbish than the other! How much a year does the labor of your brain and hands bring you in?—not enough to keep yourself in comfort! And you would bring my granddaughter down to divide that insufficient income with you"

"My income would provide us both with modest comforts," replied Rule.

"I think your ideas and our ideas of comfort may differ importantly. Now see here, Mr. Rothsay, I do believe you to be a true, honest, straightforward man; I believe you are attracted to Cora by a sincere preference for herself, irrespective of her prospects; and you are a rising man. Wait a year or two, or three. Take a few steps higher on the ladder of rank and fame, and then come and ask me for my granddaughter's hand, and if you are both of the same mind, I will give it to you. There!"

"Mr. Rockharrt—" began Rule.

"There, there, there! I will not even hear of an engagement until that time shall arrive. How do I know how you will pass through the ordeal of a political career, or into what bad company, evil habits, riotous living, dissipation, drunkenness, bribery and corruption, embezzlements, ruin and disgrace you may not be tempted?"

"Heaven forbid!" exclaimed Rule.

"Amen! I believe you will stand the test, but I have seen too many brilliant and aspiring young politicians go up like a rocket and come down a burnt stick, to be very sure of any man in the same circumstances."

"But, Mr. Rockharrt, such men were most probably brought up in wealth and luxury. They were not trained, perhaps, as I have been, in the hard but wholesome school of labor and self-denial."

"There may be something in that; but if you advance it as an argument for me to change my mind in this matter of a prudent delay, it is thrown away upon me. You should know me well enough to know that I never change my mind."

Rule did know it. But he answered earnestly:

"I accept your conditions, Mr. Rockharrt. I will wait and work as long for Cora as Jacob did for Rachel, if necessary. Cora has been the inspiration of all that I have wrought, endured and achieved—and she was all that to me long before I dreamed of aspiring to her hand in marriage, and she will be as long as we both shall live in this world or the world to come."

Rule bowed and left. He at once recounted to Cora the interview and the condition imposed on him.

When the short season ended, and the city was tilted upside down and emptied like a bucket of half its contents, the Rockharrts went with the rest.

Old Aaron was in his very worst fit of sullen ferocity. He had not been able to get a charter for clearing out the channel of the Cumberland River (another pet project of his), or even to form a company strong enough to undertake the enterprise.

After a while, out of restlessness, he started with his wife, granddaughter and grandson for a tour to the Northern Pacific Coast. He spent some time in traveling through that region of country, and returned East.

He stopped at West Point to leave Sylvan Haught, who had successfully passed his examination and received his appointment at the military academy.

Then he took his womenkind home to Rockhold.

A few days later young Rothsay was elected senator.

Some weeks later Rothsay again pressed his suit on the attention of Mr. Rockharrt.

But the old man was adamant.

"No, sir, no! You must have a firmer foundation to build upon than the fickle favor of the public. Wait a year or two longer. Let us see whether your success is to be permanent."

"But," urged Rule, "my chosen bride is twenty-three years of age, and I am twenty-seven. Time is flying."

"What has that got to do with the question? If you were to marry this morning, would that stop the flight of time? Would not time fly just as fast as ever? Suppose you should not marry for two years? My granddaughter would then be twenty-five and you thirty, and many wise philosophers think that such are the relative ages at which man and woman should marry. Then the Iron King cast a thunderbolt. He said:

"I am going to take my girl on a trip to Europe this summer. When we return, it will be time enough to talk about marriage."

Rule bowed a reluctant admission to this mandate. He knew well that argument would be thrown away upon the Iron King, and he knew that, even if he himself were tempted to try to persuade Cora to marry him at present, she would not do so in opposition to her grandfather's will.

Mr. Rockharrt had not as yet said one word to his family concerning his intended trip to Europe, although he had been thinking of it, and laying his plans, and making his arrangements, preparatory to the voyage, all the winter.

So it was with amazement that Cora first heard of the matter from Rule Rothsay, who came to her to report the result of his last attempt to gain the consent of the old gentleman to his marriage with the granddaughter.

A few days later the family despot announced to his subjects that he should start for Europe in two weeks, taking his wife and granddaughter with him, and leaving his two sons in charge of the works.

Active preparations went on for the voyage. Mr. Rockharrt went every day to the works to lay out plans for the summer to be completed during his absence.

Mrs. Rockharrt and Cora had few arrangements to make, for the autocrat had warned them that they were to take only sufficient for the voyage, as they could buy whatever they needed on the other side.

A few days before they left Rockhold, Rule Rothsay came uninvited to visit his beloved Cora.

Mr. Rockharrt happened to be the first to see him, and received him well.

When they were seated, Rule said:

"You refused to allow me to marry your granddaughter at present, and—"

"Now begin all that over again, Rothsay. I said that in two years you can marry her and take her fortune, if you both choose, whether I like it or not. That is all."

"Do you, however, sanction our engagement, Mr. Rockharrt? Shall your granddaughter and myself be betrothed, openly betrothed, so that all may know our mutual relations, before the ocean divides us? That is what I would know now. That is what I have come down here to ask."

The old man ruminated for a few moments, and then answered:

"Well, yes; you may be, with the understanding that you will wait to marry for two years longer. These two years will be a probation to both. If you fulfill the promise of your youth, and rise to the position that you can, if you will, attain, and if you remain faithful to her, and if she remains true to you, you may then marry. With all my heart I shall wish you well. But if either of you fail in truth and fidelity, the defaulting one, whether it be you or she, shall never look me in the face again," concluded the Iron King.

Rule's eyes lighted up with the fire of love and faith. He seized the hand of the old man and shook it warmly, saying:

"You have made me very happy by your words, Mr. Rockharrt, and I assure you, by all my hopes on earth or in heaven, that whatever may change in time or eternity, my heart will never vary a hair's breadth from its fidelity to its queen."

"I believe you, or rather I believe you think so."

A kind impulse, a rare one, moved the old man. Perhaps he reflected that these two young people might, have defied him and married without his consent had they pleased to do so; but they had submitted themselves to his will, and as his favorite motto told him that "Government is maintained by reward and punishment," he may have reasoned that this was an occasion for reward. So he said to the young man, who had risen, and was standing before him:

"Rothsay, we shall leave here for New York on Tuesday, to sail by the Saturday's steamer for Liverpool. If your engagements admit of it, and if you would like to spend the intervening time near Cora, we should be pleased to have you stay here."

Rule spent three happy days at Rockhold, and in the evening of the third day, the evening before they were to leave for Europe, he asked Mr. Rockharrt if he might have the privilege of attending the travelers to the seaport, and seeing them off by the steamer.

The Iron King found no objection to this plan. Mrs. Rockharrt was pleased, and Cora was delighted with it.

Accordingly, on the next morning, they left Rockhold for New York, where they arrived on the evening of the next day.

And on Saturday morning they went on board the steamer Persia, bound for Liverpool.

They bade good-by to Regulas Rothsay, on the deck, at the last moment.

The signal gun was fired, and our party sailed away to a new life, in which the faith of a woman was to be tempted and lost, and the career of a man was to be wrecked.

It was in the third year of their absence that they returned from the Continent to England. They reached London in February, in time to see the grand pageant of the queen opening parliament. After which they attended the first royal drawing room of the season, on which occasion Mrs. Rockharrt and Miss Haught were presented to her Majesty by the wife of the American minister.

Cora Haught was a new beauty and a new social sensation. She was, indeed, more beautiful than she had been when she left America. A richly colored Southern brunette was unique among British blondes. It was for this, perhaps, she was so much admired.

Moreover, she was reported to be the only descendant of her grandfather and the sole heiress of his fabulous wealth.

There was at this time another *debutant* in society, a young man, the Duke of Cumbervale, who had lately reached his majority and come into his estates, or what was left of them—an ancient castle and a few barren acres in Northumberland, an old hall and a few acres in Sussex, and a town house in London; but his title was an historical one. His person was handsome, his manners attractive, and his mind highly cultivated.

Cora met him first at the queen's drawing room, and afterward at every ball and party to which she went.

It was, perhaps, natural—very natural—that the handsome blonde man should be attracted by the beautiful brunette woman, without thought of the supposed fortune that might have redeemed his mortgaged estates and supported his distinguished title. But why should the betrothed of Regulas Rothsay have been fascinated by this elegant English aristocrat?

Surely no two men were ever more diametrically opposite than the American printer and the English duke.

Regulas Rothsay was tall, muscular, and robust, with large feet and hands, inherited from many generations of hard-working forefathers. His movements were clumsy; his manners were awkward, except when he was inspired by some grand thought or tender sympathy, when his whole person and appearance became transfigured. His sole enduring charms were his beautiful eyes and melodious voice.

The Duke of Cumbervale was slight and elegant in form, with small, perfectly shaped hands and feet—derived from a long line of idle and useless ancestors—finely cut Grecian profile, pure, clear, white skin, fine, silken, pale yellow hair and mustache, calm blue eyes, graceful movements, and refined manners.

Regulas Rothsay was a man of the people, who did not know any ancestry behind his laboring father, who could not have told the names of his grandparents.

The Duke of Cumbervale was descended from eight generations of noblemen.

Cora Haught saw and felt this contrast between the two men, so opposite in birth, rank, person, manner, character, and cultivation.

Not all at once could she become an apostate to her faith, pledged to Rule. But, in truth, she had always loved him more as a sister loves a dear brother than as a maiden loves her betrothed husband. She had not seen him for three years. And she had seen so much since they had parted! In truth, his image had grown dim in her imagination.

She wrote to him briefly from London that her engagements were so numerous as to preclude the possibility of her writing much, but that at the end of the London season they expected to return home. This was before she had—

"Foregathered with the de'il,"

in the shape of the handsome, eloquent, and fascinating Duke of Cumbervale.

Afterward a strange madness had seized her; a sudden revulsion of feeling, amounting almost to repugnance, against the rugged man of the people who had hewn out his own fortune, and who looked, she thought, more like a backwoodsman than a gentleman. Yes; it was madness—such madness as is sometimes the wreck of families.

The duke grew daily more impressive in his attentions, and Cora more delighted to receive them. So the season went on. People began to connect the names of the Duke of Cumbervale and the beautiful American heiress.

Just about this time old Aaron Rockharrt walked into the breakfast room of their apartments at Langham's with an American newspaper, which had just come by the morning's mail, in his hands.

"Here is news!" he said. "Rothsay has been nominated as governor of ----! But perhaps this is no news to you, Cora. You may have received a letter?" he added, turning to his granddaughter.

"I had a letter from Mr. Rothsay yesterday, but he said nothing on the subject," replied the girl somewhat coldly.

"Well, if he should be elected—and I really believe he will be, for he is the most popular man in the State—I shall throw no obstacles in the way of your immediate marriage with him. You have been engaged long enough—long enough! We shall set out for home on the first of next month, and so be in full time for the election."

Cora did not reply. She grew pale and cold.

The Iron King looked at his granddaughter, bending his gray brows over keenly penetrating eyes.

"See here, mistress!" he said. "You don't seem to rejoice in this news. What is the matter with you? Have any of these English foplings and lordlings, with more peers in their pedigrees than pennies in their pockets, turned your head? If so, it is time for me to take you home."

Cora did not reply. Only the night before, at the ball given by the Marchioness of Netherby, the Duke of Cumbervale had proposed to her, and had been referred to her grandfather. He was coming that very morning to ask the hand of the supposed heiress of the Iron King. Cora was that very day intending to write to Rule and tell him the whole truth, and ask him to release her from her engagement; and she knew full well that he would have no alternative but to grant her request.

"Why do you not answer me, Corona? What is the matter with you?" again demanded old Aaron Rockharrt.

But at that moment a waiter entered, and laid a card on the table before the old gentleman. He took it up and read:

The Duke of Cumbervale.

"What in the deuce does the young fellow want of me? Show him into the parlor, William, and say that I will be with him in a few minutes."

The waiter left the room to do his errand, and was soon followed by Mr. Rockharrt, who found the young duke pacing rather restlessly up and down the room.

"Good morning, sir," said old Aaron, with stiff politeness.

The visitor turned and saluted his host.

"Will you not be seated?" said Mr. Rockharrt, waving his hand toward sofa and chairs.

The visitor bowed and sat down. The host took another chair and waited. There was silence for a short time. The old man seemed expectant, the young man embarrassed. At length, when the latter opened his mouth and spoke, no pearls and diamonds of wisdom and goodness dropped from his lips; he said:

"It is a fine day."

"Yes, yes," admitted the Iron King, taking his hands from his knees, and drawing himself up with the sigh of a man badly bored—"for London. We wouldn't call this a fine day in America. But I have heard it said that it is always a fine day in England when it don't pour."

"Yes," admitted the visitor; and then he driveled into the most inane talk about climates, for you see this was the first time the poor young fellow had ever ventured to

"Beard the lion in his den,"

so to speak, by asking: a stern old gentleman for a daughter's hand, and this Iron King was a very formidable-looking beast indeed.

At length, Mr. Rockharrt, feeling sure that his visitor had come upon business—though he did not know of what sort—said:

"I think, sir, that you are here upon some affairs. If it is about railway shares—"

The old man was stopped short by the surprised and insolent stare of the young duke.

"I know nothing of railway shares, sir," he answered.

"Oh, you don't! Well, I did not think you did. In what other way can I oblige you?"

Indignation generally deprives a man of self-possession, but on this occasion it restored that of the embarrassed lover. Feeling that he—the descendant of a dozen dukes, whose ancestors had "come over with William the Conqueror," had served in Palestine under King Richard, had compelled King John to sign the Magna Charta, had gained glory in every generation—was about to do this rude, purse-proud old tradesman the greatest honor in asking of him his granddaughter in marriage, he said, somewhat coldly:

"Miss Haught has made me happy in the hope of her acceptance of my hand, pending your approval, and has referred me to you."

The Iron King stared at the speaker for a moment, and then said, quite calmly:

"Please to repeat that all over again, slowly and distinctly."

The duke flushed to the edges of his hair, but he repeated his proposal in plain words.

"You have asked Cora Haught to marry you?" demanded the Iron King.

"Yes, sir."

"What did she say?"

"She did me the honor to give me some hope, and she referred me to you, as I have already explained."

"I don't believe it!" blurted the old man.

"Sir!" said the duke, in a low voice.

"I don't believe it! What! My granddaughter—mine—break her faith and wish to marry some one else?"

"Mr. Rockharrt," began the duke, in a smooth tone—though his blood was hot with anger—"I am sorry you should so forget the—"

"I forget nothing. I remember that you charge my granddaughter—mine—with unfaithfulness! It is an insult, sir!"

"Really, Mr. Rockharrt, I do not understand you."

"I don't suppose you do! I never gave your order much credit for intelligence."

Is this old ruffian mad or drunk? was the secret question of the duke, whose tone and manner, always calm and polite, grew even calmer and more polite as the Iron King grew more sarcastic and insulting.

"I would suggest that you speak to Miss Haught on this subject, that she may confirm my statement," he said.

"I shall do nothing of the kind! I shall not entertain for an instant the thought of the possibility of my granddaughter breaking her plighted faith."

"I never knew that she was engaged. May I ask the name of the happy man?"

"Regulas Rothsay; he is not a duke; he is a printer; also a senator, and nominated for governor of his native State; sure to be elected, and then he is to marry my granddaughter, who has been engaged to him many years."

"But Miss Haught certainly authorized me to ask her hand of you."

When did this extraordinary acceptance take place?"

"Yesterday evening, at Lady Netherby's ball."

"After supper?"

"After supper."

"That accounts for it! You took too much wine, and misunderstood my granddaughter's reply She must have referred you to me for an explanation of her engagement, and consequent inability to entertain any other man's proposal. That was it!"

"May I refer you to Miss Haught for confirmation of my words?"

"I say, as I said before, no."

"May I see the young lady herself?"

"No; but I will tell you something that may console you under your disappointment. I have seen in several of your papers, in the society columns, my granddaughter referred to as my sole heiress. I do not know who is responsible for these reports, but you may have believed them, though there is not a word of truth in them. My granddaughter is not my sole heiress; not my heiress in the slightest degree. I have two stalwart sons, partners in my business, both now in charge of the works at North End, Cumberland mountains, and managing them extremely well, else I could not be taking a long holiday here. These sons are heirs to all my property. Nor is my granddaughter the heiress of her late father. She has a brother, now a cadet at our military academy at West Point. He inherits the bulk of his father's estate. My granddaughter's fortune is, therefore, very moderate— quite beneath the consideration of an English nobleman," concluded the old man, very grimly.

The young duke heard him out, and then answered;

"I trust, sir, that you will credit me with better motives in seeking the hand of the young lady. It was her charm of person and of mind that attracted me to her."

"Of course, of course; but, my dear duke, there is a plenty of sole heiresses among the wealthy trades-people of London who would be proud to buy a title with a fortune. Let me advise you to strike a bargain with one of them. Now, as I have pressing business on hand, you will excuse me."

The young duke arose, with a bow, and left the room, muttering to himself: "What an unmitigated beast that old man is! I do like the girl; she is a beautiful creature, but—I am well out of it after all."

Old Aaron Rockharrt made no false pretense of business to get rid of his unwelcome visitor; he never made false pretense of any sort for any purpose. He had pressing business on hand, though it was business which had suddenly arisen during his interview with the duke, and had in fact come out of it. No sooner had the young man left the house than the Iron King went to the agency of the Cunard line, and secured staterooms for himself and party in the Asia, that was to sail on the following Saturday from Liverpool for New York.

When he re-entered his parlor at the Langham, he found his wife and Cora seated there, the girl reading the *Court Journal* to her grandmother.

"Put that tomfoolery down, Cora, and listen to me, both of you! This is Wednesday. We leave London for Liverpool on Friday morning, and sail from Liverpool for New York on Saturday. So you sent that man to me, mistress?"

"Yes, sir," without looking up.

"For my consent to a marriage with him!"

"Yes, sir!"

"Then the fellow did not mistake your meaning! Cora Haught! I could not have believed that any girl who had any of my blood in her veins could be guilty of such black treachery as to break faith with her betrothed husband, and wish to marry another, just for the snobbish ambition to be a duchess and be called 'her grace'!" said the Iron King, with all the sardonic scorn and hatred of any form of falsehood that was the one redeeming trait in his hard and cruel nature.

"Grandpa, it was not so! Indeed, it was not! Oh, consider! I had known Rule Rothsay from my childhood, and loved him with the affection a sister gives a brother; I knew of no other love, and so I mistook it for the love surpassing all others that a betrothed maiden should give her betrothed. But when I met Cumbervale and he wooed me, I loved truly for the first time! loved, as he loves me!" she concluded, with trembling lips and downcast eyes and flushed cheeks.

"Stuff and nonsense! Don't talk to me about love or any such sentimental trash! I am talking of good faith between man and woman—words of which you don't seem to know the meaning!"

"Oh, grandpa! yes, I do! But would it be good faith in me to marry Rule Rothsay, when I love Cumbervale?"

"It would be good faith to keep your word, irrespective of your feelings, and bad faith to break it in consideration of your feelings! But you are too false to know this!"

"Oh, sir! pray do not set your face against my marriage with Cumbervale, or insist on my marrying Rule! It would not be for Rule's good," pleaded Cora.

"No; Heaven knows it would not be for his good! It had been better for Rothsay that he had been blown up in the explosion that killed his father, than that he had ever set eyes on your false face! But you have given him your word, and you must keep it, or never look me in the face again! You shall be married as soon as we reach Rockhold."

Cora raised her tearful face from her hands, and looked astonished and wretched.

"Oh, you may gaze, but it is true. The fortune hunter has discovered that he is on a false scent. There is no fortune on the trail. I told him everything about you. I told him that you were not my heiress at all, because I had two sons who would inherit all my property; that you were not even your father's heiress, because you had a brother who would inherit the larger portion of his; that, in point of fact, you were only moderately provided for. He was startled, I assure you. I also told him that for years you had been engaged to a young printer in your native country, who would probably be the next governor of his native State. He bowed himself out. I engaged our passage to New York by the Saturday's steamer. You will never see the little dandy again. He was after a fortune, and finding that you have none, he has forsaken you—and served you right, for a base, treacherous, and contemptible woman, unworthy even of his regard; for you are much lower in every way than he is, for while he was seeking a fortune and you were seeking a title, you were concealing from him the fact of your engagement to Rule Rothsay. You were doubly false to Rule and to Cumbervale. Oh, Cora Haught! Cora Haught! Are you not ashamed of yourself! Ashamed to look any honest man or woman in the face! Ah! you do well to hide yours!"

he concluded, for Cora had lost all self-control, dropped her head upon her hands, and burst into hysterical sobs and tears.

Did you ever see a small bantam hen ruffle up all her feathers in angry defense of her chick? So did poor little, timid Mrs. Rockharrt in protection of her pet. She ventured to expostulate with her tyrant for, perhaps, the first time in their married life.

"Oh, Aaron, do not scold the child so severely. She is but human. She has only been dazzled and fascinated by the young duke's rank, and beauty, and elegance. She could not help it, being thrown in his company so much. And you know they say that half the girls in London society are in love with the handsome duke. We will take her home, and she will come all right, and be our own, dear, faithful Cora again, and—"

Old Aaron Rockharrt, who had gazed at his wife in speechless astonishment at her audacity in reasoning with him, now burst forth with:

"Hold your jaw, madam," and strode out of the room.

A minute later a waiter came in and laid a note on the table before Cora and immediately withdrew.

Cora took the missive, recognized the handwriting and seal, tore it open and eagerly ran her eyes along the lines. This was the note:

Cumbervale Lodge, London,May,
1, 18—

Miss Haught: For my indiscretion of last evening I owe you an humble apology, which I beg you to accept with this explanation, that, had I known, or even suspected, that your hand was already promised in another quarter, I should never have presumed to propose for it. I beg now to withdraw such a false step.

Accept my best wishes for your happiness in a union with the more fortunate man of your choice, and believe me to be now and ever,

Your obedient servant,

Cumbervale.

Scarcely had Cora's eyes fallen from the paper when Lady Pendragon's carriage drove up to the door.

Glad of the interruption that enabled her to escape from the parlor, and give way to the passion and grief and despair that were swelling her heart to breaking, Cora hastened to her bed chamber and threw herself down upon the couch in a paroxysm of sobs and tears.

Mrs. Rockharrt waited in the parlor to receive the visitor, but no visitor came up. Only two cards were left for the two ladies, and then the Countess of Pendragon rolled away in her carriage.

On Friday morning the Rockharrts left London. And on Saturday morning they sailed from Liverpool. After a prosperous voyage of ten days they landed at New York.

"My soul! there is Rothsay on the pier, waving his hand to us!" exclaimed the Iron King, as he led his little wife down the gang plank, while Cora came on behind them.

Yes; there was Rule, his tall figure towering above the crowd on the pier, his rugged face beaming with delight, his hand waving welcome to the returning voyagers. He received his friends as they stepped upon the pier. He shook hands warmly with Mrs. Rockharrt, heartily with the Iron King, and then, behind them, with Cora, and before Cora knew what was coming she was folded in the arms and to the faithful breast of her life-long lover— only for a moment; and then he drew her arm within his own and led her on after the elder couple, whispering:

"Dear, this is the happiest day I have ever seen as yet, but a happier one is coming—soon, I hope. Dear, how soon shall it be?"

"You must ask my grandparents, Rule. Their judgment and their convenience must be consulted," she answered in a low, steady tone.

She had no thought now of breaking her engagement with Rule, though her heart seemed breaking. She still loved that rugged man with the sisterly affection she had always felt for him, and which, in her ignorance of life and self, she had mistaken for a warmer sentiment, and resolved, in wedding him, to do her whole duty by him for so long as she should live, and she hoped and believed that that would not be very long.

Rothsay led the way to a carriage. When all were seated in this, the old man leant toward the young one, and said:

"Well, I haven't had a chance to ask you yet. The election is over. How did it go? Who is their man?"

"They chose me," answered Rothsay, simply.

Cora Haught's bosom was wrung by hopeless passion and piercing remorse.

Yet she tried to do her whole duty.

"If it craze or kill me I will wed Rule, and he shall never know what it costs me to keep my word," she said to herself, as she lay sleepless and restless in her bed on the night before her wedding morn. "Yes; I will do my duty and keep my secret even unto death."

"'Even unto death!' but unto whose death?" whispered a voice close to her ear—a voice clear, distinct, penetrating.

Cora started and opened her eyes. No one was near her. She sat up in bed, and looked around the apartment. The night taper, standing on the hearth, burned low. The dimly lighted room was vacant of any human being except herself.

"I have been dreaming," she said, and she laid down and tried to compose herself to sleep again. In vain! Memories of the near past, dread of the nearer future, contended in her soul, filling her with discord. When Cora arose on her wedding morning, she said to herself:

"Yes, this day I am going to marry Rule, dear, loving, faithful, hardworking, self-denying Rule! A monarch among men, if greatness of soul could make a monarch. In that sense no woman, peeress or princess, ever made a prouder match. May Heaven make me worthier of him! May Heaven help me to be a true, good wife to him!"

She said these words to herself, but oh! oh! how she shuddered as she breathed them, and how she reproached herself for such shuddering! The girl's whole nature was at war with itself. Yet through all the terrible interior strife she kept her firm determination to be faithful to Rule; to go through the ordeal before her, even though it should cost her life or reason.

The external circumstances of this wedding were given in the first chapter, and need not be repeated here.

My readers may remember the marble-like stillness of the bride as she sat in her bridal robes, looking out from the front window of her chamber on the bright and festive scene below, where all the work people from the mines and foundries were assembled; they will remember how she shivered when she was summoned with her bridesmaids to meet her bridegroom and his attendants in the hall below; how when she met him at the foot of the stairs she shrank from his greeting—emotion in which he in his simple, loyal soul saw no repugnance, but only maiden reserve to be reverenced, as he drew her arm within his own to lead her before the bishop; how she faltered during the whole of the marriage ceremony; how like a woman in a trance she passed through the scenes of the wedding breakfast and those that immediately followed it; how in her own room, where she went to change her wedding dress for a traveling suit, and whither her gentle old grandmother had followed her for a private parting, she had answered the old lady's anxious question as to whether she was "happy," first by silence and then by muttering that her heart was too full for speech; how when the bridegroom and the bride had taken leave of all their friends at Rockhold, and were seated *tete-a-tete* in their traveling carriage, bowling along the river road, at the base of the East Ridge toward the North End railway station, when he passed his arm around her and drew her to his heart and murmured of his love and his joy in her ear, and pleaded for some response from her, she had only said that her heart was too full for speech, and he in his confiding spirit had perceived no evasion in her reply, but thought, if her heart was full, it was with responsive love for him.

My readers will recollect the railway journey to the State capital; the procession through the decorated streets between the crowded sidewalks from the railway station to the town house of Mr. Rockharrt, which had been placed at the disposal of the governor-elect for the interval between his arrival in the State capital and his inauguration.

The committee of reception escorted them to the gates of the Rockharrt mansion and left them at the door. There we also left them, in the second chapter of this story—and there we return to them in this place.

CHAPTER V
THE GREAT RENUNCIATION

When the governor-elect and his bride entered the Rockharrt town house, they were received by a group of obsequious servants, headed by Jason, the butler, and Jane, the housekeeper, and among whom stood Martha, lady's maid to the new Mrs. Rothsay.

"Will you come into the drawing room and rest, dear, before going upstairs?" inquired Mr. Rothsay of his bride, as they stood together in the front hall.

"No, thank you. I will go to my room. Come, Martha!" said the bride, and she went up stairs, followed by her maid.

Rule stood where she had so hastily left him, in the hall, looking so much at a loss that presently Jason volunteered to say:

"Shall I show you to your apartment, sir?"

"Yes," answered Mr. Rothsay. And he followed the servant up stairs to a large and handsomely furnished bed chamber, having a dressing room attached.

Jason lighted the wax candles on the dressing table and on the mantel piece, and then inquired:

"Is there anything else I can do for you, sir?"

"No," replied Mr. Rothsay. And the servant retired.

Rothsay was alone in the room. He had never set up a valet; he had always waited on himself. Now, however, he was again at a loss. He was covered with railway dust and smoke, yet he saw no conveniences for ablution.

While he stood there, a shout arose in the street outside. A single voice raised the cheer:

"Hoo—rah—ah—ah for Rothsay!"

He went to the front window of the room. The sashes were hoisted, for the night was warm; but the shutters were closed. He turned the slats a little and looked down on the square below. It was filled with pedestrians, and every window of every house in sight was illuminated. When the shouts had died away, he heard voices in the room. He was himself accidentally concealed by the window curtains. He looked around and saw his bride emerge from the dressing room, attired in an elegant dinner costume of rich maize-colored satin and black lace, with crocuses in her superb black hair. She passed through the room without having seen him, and went down stairs followed by her maid.

He saw the door of the dressing room standing open and went into it. It was no mere closet, but a large, well lighted and convenient apartment, furnished with every possible appurtenance for the toilet. Here he found his trunk, his valise, his dressing case, all unpacked—his brushes and combs laid out in order, his dinner suit hung over a rack—every requirement of his toilet in complete readiness as if prepared by an experienced valet. All this he had been accustomed to do, and expected to do, for himself. Who had served him? Had Corona and her maid? Impossible!

He quickly made a refreshing evening toilet and went down stairs, for he was eager to rejoin his bride. He found her in the drawing room; but scarcely had he seated himself at her side when the door was opened and dinner announced by Jason.

They both arose; he gave her his arm, and they followed the solemn butler to the dining room, which was on the opposite side of the front hall and in the rear of the library.

An elegant tete-a-tete dinner but for the presence of the old butler and one young footman who waited on them.

They did not linger long at table, but soon left it and returned together to the drawing room.

They had scarcely seated themselves when the door bell rang, and in a few moments afterward a card was brought in and handed to Mr. Rothsay, who took it and read:

A.B. Crawford.

"Show the judge into the library and say that I will be with him in a few moments," he said to the servant.

"He is one of the judges of the supreme court of the State, dear, and I must go to him. I hope he will not keep me long," said Mr. Rothsay, as he raised the hand of his bride to his lips and then left the room.

With a sigh of intense relief Cora leaned back in her chair and closed her eyes.

People have been known to die suddenly in their chairs. Why could not she die as she sat there, with her whole head heavy and her whole heart faint, she thought.

She listened—fearfully—for the return of her husband, but he did not come as soon as he had hoped to do; for while she listened the door bell rang again, and another visitor made his appearance, and after a short delay was shown into the library.

Then came another, and still another, and afterward others, until the library must have been half full of callers on the governor-elect.

And presently a large band of musicians halted before the house and began a serenade. They played and sang "Hail to the Chief," "Yankee Doodle," "Hail Columbia," and other popular or national airs.

Mr. Rothsay and his friends went out to see them and thank them, and then their shouts rent the air as they retired from the scene.

The gentlemen re-entered the house and retired to the library, where they resumed their discussion of official business, until another multitude had gathered before the house and shouts of—

"Hoo-rah-ah ah for Rothsay!" rose to the empyrean.

Neither the governor-elect nor his companions responded in any way to this compliment until loud, disorderly cries for—

"Rothsay!"

"Rothsay!"

"Rothsay!"

constrained them to appear.

The governor-elect was again greeted with thundering cheers. When silence was restored he made a short, pithy address, which was received with rounds of applause at the close of every paragraph.

When the speech was finished, he bowed and withdrew, and the crowd, with a final cheer, dispersed.

Mr. Rothsay retired once more to the library, accompanied by his friends, to renew their discussion.

Cora, in her restlessness of spirit, arose from her seat and walked several times up and down the floor.

Presently, weary of walking, and attracted by the coolness and darkness of the back drawing room, in which the chandeliers had not been lighted, she passed between the draped blue satin portieres that divided it from the front room and entered the apartment.

The French windows stood open upon a richly stored flower garden, from which the refreshing fragrance of dewy roses, lilies, violets, cape jasmines, and other aromatic plants was wafted by the westerly breeze.

Cora seated herself upon the sofa between the two low French windows, and waited.

Presently she heard the visitors taking leave.

"The committee will wait on you between ten and eleven to-morrow morning," she heard one gentleman say, as they passed out.

Then several "good nights" were uttered, and the guests all departed, and the door was closed.

Cora heard her husband's quick, eager step as he hurried into the front drawing room, seeking his wife.

She felt her heart sinking, the high nervous tension of her whole frame relaxing. She heard the hall clock strike ten. When the last stroke died away, she heard her husband's voice calling, softly:

"Cora, love, wife, where are you?"

She could bear no more. The overtasked heart gave way.

When, the next instant, the eager bridegroom pushed aside the satin portieres and entered the apartment, with a flood of light from the room in front, he found his bride had thrown herself down on the Persian rug before the sofa in the wildest anguish and despair and in a paroxysm of passionate sobs and tears.

What a sight to meet a newly-made, adoring husband's eyes on his marriage evening and on the eve of the day of his highest triumph, in love as in ambition!

For one petrified moment he gazed on her, too much amazed to utter a word.

Then suddenly he stooped, raised her as lightly as if she had been a baby, and laid her on the sofa.

"Cora—love—wife! Oh! what is this?" he cried, bending over her.

She did not answer; she could not, for choking sobs and drowning tears.

He knelt beside her, and took her hand, and bent his face to hers, and murmured:

"Oh, my love! my wife! what troubles you?"

She wrenched her hand from his, turned her face from him, buried her head in the cushions of the sofa, and gave way to a fresh storm of anguish.

When she repulsed him in this spasmodic manner, he recoiled as a man might do who had received a sudden blow; but he did not rise from his position, but watched beside her sofa, in great distress of mind, patiently waiting for her to speak and explain.

Gradually her tempest of emotion seemed to be raging itself into the rest of exhaustion. Her sobs and tears grew fainter and fewer; and presently after that she drew out her handkerchief, and raised herself to a sitting position, and began to wipe her wet and tear-stained face and eyes. Though her tears and sobs had ceased, still her bosom heaved convulsively.

He arose and seated himself beside her, put his arm around her, and drew her beautiful black, curled head upon his faithful breast, and bending his face to hers, entreated her to tell him the cause of her grief.

"What is it, dear one? Have you had bad news? A telegram from Rockhold? Either of the old people had a stroke? Tell me, dear?"

"Nothing—has—happened," she answered, giving each word with a gasp.

"Then what troubles you, dear? Tell me, wife! tell me! I am your husband!" he whispered, smoothing her black hair, and gazing with infinite tenderness on her troubled face.

"Oh, Rule! Rule! Rule!" she moaned, closing her eyes, that could not bear his gaze.

"Tell me, dear," he murmured, gently, continuing to stroke her hair.

"I am—nervous—Rule," she breathed. "I shall get over it—presently. Give me—a little time," she gasped.

"Nervous?" He gazed down on her woe-writhen face, with its closed eyes that would not meet his own. Yes, doubtless she was nervous—very nervous—but she was more than that. Mere nervousness never blanched a woman's face, wrung her features or convulsed her form like this.

"Cora, look at me, dear. There is something I have to say to you."

She forced herself to lift her eyelids and meet the honest, truthful eyes that looked down into hers.

"Cora," he said, with a certain grave yet sweet tone of authority, "there is some great burden on your mind, dear—a burden too heavy for you to bear alone."

"Oh, it is! it is! it is!" she wailed, as if the words had broken from her without her knowledge.

"Then let me share it," he pleaded.

"Oh, Rule! Rule! Rule!" she wailed, dropping her head upon his breast.

"Is your trouble so bitter, dear? What is it, Cora? It can be nothing that I may not share and relieve. Tell me, dear."

"Oh, Rule, bear with me! I did not wish to distress you with my folly, my madness. Do not mind it, Rule. It will pass away. Indeed, it will. I will do my duty by you. I will be a true wife to you, after all. Only do not disturb your own righteous spirit about me, do not notice my moods; and give me time. I shall come all right. I shall be to you—all that you wish me to be. But, for the Lord's love, Rule, give me time!" she pleaded, with voice and eyes so full of woe that the man's heart sank in his bosom.

He grew pale and withdrew his arm from her neck. She lifted her head from his breast then and leaned back in the corner of the sofa. She trembled with fear now, lest she had betrayed her secret, which she had resolved to keep for his own sake. She looked and waited for his words. He was very still, pale and grave. Presently he spoke very gently to the grieving woman.

"Dear, you have said too much and too little. Tell me all now, Cora. It is best that you should, dear."

"Rule! oh, Rule! must I? must I?" she pleaded, wringing her hands.

"Yes, Cora; it is best, dear."

"Oh, I would have borne anything to have spared you this. But—I betrayed myself. Oh, Rule, please try to forget what you have seen and heard. Bear with me for a little while. Give me some little time to get over this, and you shall see how truly I will do my duty—how earnestly I will try to make you happy," she prayed.

"I know, dear—I know you will be a good, dear wife, and a dearly loved and fondly cherished wife. But begin, dear, by giving me your confidence. There can be no real union without confidence between husband and wife, my Cora. Surely, you may trust me, dear," he said, with serious tenderness.

"Yes; I can trust you. I will trust you with all, through all, Rule. You are wise and good. You will forgive me and help me to do right." She spoke so wildly and so excitedly that he laid his hand tenderly, soothingly, on her head, and begged her to be calm and to confide in him without hesitation.

Then she told him all.

What a story for a newly-married husband to hear from his wife on the evening of their wedding day!

He listened in silence, and without moving a muscle of his face or form. When he had heard all he arose from the sofa, stood up, then reeled to an arm chair near at hand and dropped heavily into it, his huge, stalwart frame as weak from sudden faintness as that of an infant.

"Oh, Rule! Rule! your anger is just! It is just!" cried Cora, wringing her hands in despair.

He looked at her in great trouble, but his beautiful eyes expressed only the most painful compassion. He could not answer her. He could not trust himself to speak yet. His breast was heaving, working tumultuously. His tawny-bearded chin was quivering. He shut his lips firmly together, and tried to still the convulsion of his frame.

"Oh, Rule, be angry with me, blame me, reproach me, for I am to blame—bitterly, bitterly to blame. But do not hate me, for I love you, Rule, with a sister's love. And forgive me, Rule—not just now, for that would be impossible, perhaps. But, oh! do forgive me after a while, Rule, for I do repent—oh, I do repent that treason of the heart—that treason against one so worthy of the truest love and honor which woman gives to man. You will forgive me—after a while—after a—probation?"

She paused and looked wistfully at his grave, pained, patient face.

He could not yet answer her.

"Oh, if you will give me time, Rule, I will—I will banish every thought, every memory of my—my—my season in London, and will devote myself to you with all my heart and soul. No man ever had, or ever could have, a more devoted wife than I will be to you, if you will only trust me and be happy, Rule. Oh!" she suddenly burst forth, seeing that he did not reply to her, "you are bitterly angry with me. You hate me. You cannot forgive me. You blame me without mercy. And you are right. You are right."

Now he forced himself to speak, though in a low and broken voice.

"Angry? With you, Cora? No, dear, no."

"You blame me, though. You must blame me," she sobbed.

"Blame you? No, dear. You have not been to blame," he faltered, faintly, for he was an almost mortally wounded man.

"Ah! what do you mean? Why do you speak to me so kindly, so gently? I could bear your anger, your reproaches, Rule, better than this tenderness, that breaks my heart with shame and remorse!" cried Cora, bursting into a passion of sobs and tears.

He did not come near her to take her in his arms and comfort her as before. A gulf had opened between them which he felt that he could not pass, but he spoke to her very gently and compassionately.

"Do not grieve so bitterly, dear," he said. "Do not accuse yourself so unjustly. You have done no wrong to me, or to any human being. You have done nothing but good to me, and to every human being in your reach. To me you have been more than tongue can tell—my first friend, my muse, my angel, my inspiration to all that is best, greatest, highest in human life—the goal of all my earthly, all my heavenly aspirations. That I should love you with a pure, single, ardent passion of enthusiasm was natural, was inevitable. But that you, dear, should mistake your feelings toward me, mistake sisterly affection, womanly sympathy, intellectual appreciation, for that living fire of eternal love which only should unite man and woman, was natural, too, though most unfortunate. I am not fair to look upon, Cora. I have no form, no comeliness, that any one should—"

He was suddenly interrupted by the girl, who sprang from her seat and sank at his feet, clasped his knees, and dropped her head upon his hands in a tempest of sobs and tears, crying:

"Oh, Rule! I never did deserve your love! I never was worthy of you! And I long have known it. But I do love you! I do love you! Oh, give me time and opportunity to prove it!" she pleaded, with many tears, saying the same words over and over again, or words with the same meaning.

He laid both his large hands softly on her bowed head and held them there with a soothing, quieting, mesmeric touch, until she had sobbed, and cried, and talked herself into silence, and then he said:

"No, Cora! No, dear! You are good and true to the depths of your soul; but you deceive yourself. You do not love me. It is not your fault. You cannot do so! You pity, you esteem, you appreciate; and you mistake these sentiments as you mistook sisterly affection for such love as only should sanctify the union of man and woman."

"But I will, Rule. I will love you even so! Give me time! A little time! I am your own," she pleaded.

"No, dear, no. I am sure that you would do your best, at any cost to yourself. You would consecrate your life to one whom yet you do not love, because you cannot love. But the sacrifice is too great, dear—a sacrifice which no woman should ever make for any cause, which no man should ever accept under any circumstances. You must not immolate yourself on my unworthy shrine, Cora."

"Oh, Rule! What do you mean? You frighten me! What do you intend to do?" exclaimed Cora, with a new fear in her heart.

"I will tell you later, dear, when we are both quieter. And, Cora, promise me one thing—for your own sake, dear."

"I will promise you anything you wish, Rule. And be glad to do so. Glad to do anything that will please you," she earnestly assured him.

"Then promise that whatever may happen, you will never tell any human being what you have told me to-night."

"I promise this on my honor, Rule."

"Promise that you will never repeat one word of this interview between us to any living being."

"I promise this, also, on my honor, Rule."

"That is all I ask, and it is exacted for your own sake, dear. The fair name of a woman is so white and pure that the smallest speck can be seen upon it. And now, dear, it is nearly eleven o'clock. Will you ring for your maid and go to your room? I have letters to write—in the library—which, I think, will occupy me the whole night," he said, as he took her hand and gently raised her to her feet.

At that moment a servant entered, bringing a card.

Mr. Rothsay took it toward the portiere and read it by the light of the chandelier in the front room.

"Show the gentleman to the library, and say that I will be with him in a few minutes," said Rothsay.

"If you please, sir, the lights are out and the library locked. I did not know that it would be wanted again to-night. But I will light up, sir."

"Wax candles? It would take too long. Show the gentleman into this front room," said the governor-elect.

The servant went to do his bidding.

Then Rothsay turned to Cora, saying:

"I must see this man, dear, late as it is! I will bid you good night now. God bless you, dear."

And without even a farewell kiss, Rothsay passed out.

And Cora did not know that he had gone for good.

She rang for her maid and retired to her room, there to pass a sleepless, anxious, remorseful night.

What would be the result of her confession to her husband? She dared not to conjecture.

He had been gentle, tender, most considerate, and most charitable to her weakness, never speaking of his own wrongs, never reproaching her for inconstancy.

He had said, in effect, that he would come to an understanding with her later, when they both should be stronger.

When would that be? To-morrow?

Scarcely, for the ceremonies of the coming day must occupy every moment of his time.

And what, eventually, would he do?

His words, divinely compassionate as they had been, had shadowed forth a separation between them. Had he not told her that to be the wife of a husband she could not love would be a sacrifice that no woman should ever make and no man should ever accept? That she should not so offer up her life for him?

What could this mean but a contemplated separation?

So Cora lay sleepless and tortured by these harrassing questions.

When Rule Rothsay entered the front drawing room he found there a young merchant marine captain whom he had known for many years, though not intimately.

"Ah, how do you do, Ross?" he said.

"How do you do, Governor? I must ask pardon for calling so late, but—"

"Not at all. How can I be of use to you?"

"Why, in no way whatever. Don't suppose that every one who calls to see you has an office to seek or an ax to grind. Though, I suppose, most of them have," said the visitor, as he seated himself.

Rothsay dropped into a chair, and forced himself to talk to the young sailor.

"Just in from a voyage, Ross?"

"No; just going out, Governor."

Rothsay smiled at this premature bestowal of the high official title, but did not set the matter right. It was of too little importance.

"I was going to explain, Governor, that I was just passing through the city on my way to Norfolk, from which my ship is to sail to-morrow. So I had to take the midnight train. But I could not go without trying for a chance to see and shake hands with you and congratulate you."

"You are very kind, Ross. I thank you," said Rothsay, somewhat wearily.

"You're not looking well, Governor. I suppose all this 'fuss and feathers' is about as harrassing as a stormy sea voyage. Well, I will not keep you up long. I should have been here earlier, only I went first to the hotel to inquire for you, and there I learned that you were here in old Rockharrt's house, and had married his granddaughter. Congratulate you again, Governor. Not many men have had such a double triumph as you. She is a splendidly beautiful woman. I saw her once in Washington City, at the President's reception. She was the greatest belle in the place. That reminds me that I must not keep you away from her ladyship. This is only hail and farewell. Good night. I declare, Rothsay, you look quite worn out. Don't see any other visitor to-night, in case there should be another fool besides myself come to worry you at this hour. Now good-by," said the visitor, rising and offering his hand.

"Good-by, Ross. I wish you a pleasant and prosperous voyage," said Rothsay, rising to shake hands with his visitor.

He followed the young sailor to the hall, and seeing nothing of the porter, he let the visitor out and locked the door after him.

Then he returned to the drawing room. Holding his head between his hands he walked slowly up and down the floor—up and down the floor—up and down—many times.

"This is weakness," he muttered, "to be thinking of myself when I should think only of her and the long life before her, which might be so joyous but for me—but for me! Dear one who, in her tender childhood, pitied the orphan boy, and with patient, painstaking earnestness taught him to read and write, and gave him the first impulse and inspiration to a higher life. And now she would give her life to me. And for all the good she has done me all her days, for all the blessings she has brought me, shall I blight her happiness? Shall I make her this black return? No, no. Better that I should pass forever out of her life—pass forever out of sight—forever out of this world—than live to make her suffer. Make her suffer? I? Oh, no! Let fame, life, honors, all go down, so that she is saved—so that she is made happy."

He paused in his walk and listened. All the house was profoundly still—all the household evidently asleep—except her! He felt sure that she was sleepless. Oh, that he could go and comfort her! even as a mother comforts her child; but he could not.

"I suppose many would say," he murmured to himself, "that I owe my first earthly duty to the people who have called me to this high office; that private sorrows and private conscience should yield to the public, and they would be right. Yet with me it is as if death had stepped in and relieved me of official duty to be taken up by my successor just the same—"

He stopped and put his hand to his head, murmuring:

"Is this special pleading? I wonder if I am quite sane?"

Then dropping into a chair he covered his face with his hands and wept aloud.

Does any one charge him with weakness? Think of the tragedy of a whole life compressed in that one crucial hour!

After a little while he grew more composed. The tears had relieved the overladen heart. He arose and recommenced his walk, reflecting with more calmness on the cruel situation.

"I shall right her wrongs in the only possible way in which it can be done, and I shall do no harm to the State. Kennedy will be a better governor than I could have been. He is an older, wiser, more experienced statesman. I am conscious that I have been over-rated by the people who love me. I was elected for my popularity, not for my merit. And now—I am not even the man that I was—my life seems torn out of my bosom. Oh, Cora, Cora! life of my life! But you shall be happy, dear one! free and happy after a little while. Ah! I know your gentle heart. You will weep for the fate of him whom you loved—as a brother. Oh! Heaven! but your tears will come from a passing cloud that will leave your future life all clear and bright—not darkened forever by the slavery of a union with one whom you do not—only because you cannot—love."

He walked slowly up and down the floor a few more turns, then glanced at the clock on the mantel piece, and said:

"Time passes. I must write my letters."

There was an elegant little writing desk standing in the corner of the room and filled with stationery, mostly for the convenience of the ladies of the family when the Rockharrts occupied their town house.

He went to this, sat down and opened it, laid paper out, and then with his elbow on the desk and his head leaning on the palm of his hand, he fell into deep thought.

At length he began to write rapidly. He soon finished and sealed this letter. Then he wrote a second and a longer one, sealed that also. One—the first written—he put in the secret drawer of the desk; the other he dropped into his pocket.

Then he took "a long, last, lingering look" around the room. This was the room in which he had first met Cora after long years of separation; where he had passed so many happy evenings with her, when his official duties as an assemblyman permitted him to do so; this was the room in which they had plighted their troth to each other, and to which, only six hours before, they had returned—to all appearance—a most happy bride and groom. Ah, Heaven!

His wandering gaze fell on the open writing desk, which in his misery he had forgotten to close. He went to it and shut down the lid.

Then he passed out of the room, took his hat from the rack in the hall, opened the front door, passed out, closed it behind him, and left the house forever.

Outside was pandemonium. The illuminations in the windows had died down, but the streets were full of revelers, too much exhilarated as yet to retire, even if they had any place to retire to; for on that summer night many visitors to the inauguration chose to stay out in the open air until morning rather than to leave the city and lose the show.

Once again the hum and buzz of many voices was broken by a shrill cry of:

"Hooray for Rothsay!" which was taken up by the chorus and echoed and re-echoed from one end to the other of the city, and from earth to sky.

Poor Rothsay himself passed out upon the sidewalk, unrecognized in the obscurity.

An empty hack was standing at the corner of the square, a few hundred feet from the house.

To this he went, and spoke to the man on the box:

"Is this hack engaged?"

"Yes, sah, it is—took by four gents as can't get no lodgings at none of the hotels, nor yet boarding houses—no, sah. Dere dey is ober yonder in dat dere s'loon cross de street—yes, sah. But it don't keep open, dat s'loon don't, longer'n twelve o'clock—no, sah. It's mos' dat now, so dey'll soon call for dis hack—yes, sah!"

Rothsay left the talkative hackman and passed on.

A hand touched him on the arm.

He turned and saw old Scythia, clothed in a long, black cloak of some thin stuff, with its hood drawn over her head.

Rothsay stared.

"Come, Rule! You have tested woman's love to-day, and found it fail you; even as I tested man's faith in the long ago, and found it wrong me! Come, Rule! You and I have had enough of falsehood and treachery! Let us shake the dust of civilization off our shoes! Come, Rule!"

CHAPTER VI
THE WIDOWED BRIDE

The amazement and confusion that followed the discovery of the mysterious disappearance of Governor-elect Regulas Rothsay, on the morning of the day of his intended inauguration, has been already described in an earlier chapter of this story.

The most searching inquiries were made in all directions without any satisfactory result.

Then advertisements were put in all the principal newspapers in all the chief towns and cities throughout the country, offering large rewards for any information that should lead to the discovery of the missing man or of his fate.

These in time drew forth letters from all points of the compass from people anxious to take a chance in this lottery of a reward, and who fabricated reports of the lost governor having been seen in this, that, or the other place, or of his body having been found here, there or elsewhere.

Prompt investigation proved the falsehood of these fraudulent letters in every instance.

No one really knew the fate of the missing man. No one but Cora Rothsay had even the clew to the cause of his disappearance; and she—from her sensitive pride, no less than from her sacred promise not to reveal the subject of her communicaton to her husband on that fatal evening of his flight or of his death—kept her lips sealed on that subject.

Days, weeks and months passed away without bringing any authentic news of the lost ruler.

At length hope was given up. The advertisements were withdrawn from the papers.

Still occasionally, at long intervals of time, vague rumors reached his friends—a sailor had seen him in the streets of Rio de Janeiro; a fur trader had found him in Washington Territory; a miner had met him in California—but nothing came of all these reports.

One morning, late in December, there came some news, not of the actual fate of the governor, but of the long-lost man who had seen the last of him alive.

Despite the bitter pleading of the poor, bereaved bride, who dreaded the crowded city and desired to remain in seclusion in the country, old Aaron had removed his whole family to their town house for the winter.

They had been settled there only a few days, and were gathered around the breakfast table, when a card was brought in to Mr. Rockharrt.

"'Captain Ross!' Who, in the fiend's name, is Captain Ross? And what does he want at this early hour of the morning?" demanded the Iron King, after he had read the name on the card. Then, as he scrutinized it, he saw faintly penciled lines below the name and read:

"The late visitor who called on Governor-elect Rothsay on the evening of his disappearance."

"Show the man in the library, Jason," exclaimed old Aaron Rockharrt, rising, leaving his untasted breakfast, and striding out of the room.

In the library he found a young skipper, tall, robust, black bearded and sun burned.

"Captain Ross?" said the old man, interrogatively.

"The same, at your service, sir—Mr. Rockharrt, I presume?" said the visitor with a bow.

"That's my name. Sit down," said the Iron King, pointing to one chair for his visitor and taking another for himself.

"So you were the last visitor to Mr. Rothsay, eh?"

"Yes, sir."

"Well, can you give any information regarding the disappearance of my grandson-in-law?"

"No, sir; but learning that I had been advertised for, I have come forward."

"At rather a late date, upon my soul and honor! Where have you been all this time?"

"At sea. When I called upon Mr. Rothsay, it was to congratulate him on his position and to bid him good-by. I was on the eve of sailing for India, and, in fact, left the city by the night's express and sailed the next morning. I think we must have been out of sight of land before the news of the governor's disappearance was spread abroad."

"What explanation can you give of his sudden disappearance?"

"None whatever, sir."

"Then, in the demon's name, why have you come forward at all at this time?"

"Because I was advertised for."

"That was months ago."

"But months ago I was at sea and knew nothing of the matter. I have but just returned from a long voyage, and hearing among other matters that Governor Rothsay had been missing since the day of his inauguration, that Governor Kennedy reigned in his stead, and that the latest visitor of the missing man had long been wanting, I have come."

"Do you appreciate the gravity of your own position, sir, under the circumstances?" sternly demanded the Iron King.

"I—don't—understand you," said the skipper, in evident perplexity.

"You don't? That is strange. You are the last man—the last person—who saw Governor-elect Rothsay alive, at eleven o'clock on the night of his disappearance. After that hour he was missing, and you had run away."

The young sailor smiled.

"Steamed away, and sailed away, you should say, sir. I see the suspicion to which your words point, and will answer them at once: On that night in question I was a guest of the Crockett House. I was absent from that house only half an hour—from a quarter to eleven to a quarter after eleven—during which time I walked to this house, saw the governor-elect, and walked back to the hotel, only to pay my bill, take a hack and drive to the railway station. Do you think that in half an hour I could have done all that and murdered the governor, and made away with his body besides, Mr. Rockharrt?"

"You would have to prove the truth of your words, sir," replied the Iron King.

"That is easily done by the people at the hotel. I did not tell them where I was going. I never even thought of telling them. But they know I was only gone half an hour; for before going out, or just as I was going out, I ordered the carriage to be ready to take me to the depot at a quarter past eleven."

"They may have forgotten all about you."

"Not at all. I am an old customer, though a young man. They know me very well."

"Then it is very strange that when every anxious inquiry was made for this latest visitor of the governor-elect, these hotel people did not come forward and name you."

"But I repeat, sir, that they did not know that I was that latest visitor. I did not think of telling any one that I was going to see Rothsay before I went, or of telling them that I had been to see him after I went. They had no more reason to identify me with that late caller than any other guest at the hotel, or, in fact, any other man in the world. Come, Mr. Rockharrt, you have complimented me with one of the blackest suspicions that could wrong an honest man, but I will not quarrel with you. I know very well that the last person seen with a missing man is often suspected of his taking off. As for me, I invite the most searching investigation."

"Why did you come here, after so long an interval?" demanded the Iron King, in no way mollified by the moderation of his visitor.

"As I explained to you, I come now because I have just heard that I had been advertised for; and after this long interval because I have been for months at sea. I had, however, another motive for coming—to tell you of the strange manner of Regulas Rothsay during my interview with him—a manner that does not seem to have been observed by any one else, for all speak and write of his health and extraordinarily good spirits on the evening of his arrival in the city only a few hours before I saw him, when he seemed very far from being in good health or good spirits. In fact, a more utterly broken man I never saw in my life."

"Ah! ah! What is this you tell me? Give me particulars! Give me particulars!" said the Iron King, rising and standing over his visitor.

"Indeed, I do not think I can give you particulars. The effect he seemed to produce was that of a general prostration of body and mind. On coming into the room where I waited for him, he looked pale and haggard; he tottered rather than walked; he dropped into his chair rather than sat down in it; his hands fell upon the arms rather than grasped them; he was gloomy, absent-minded, and when he spoke at all, seemed to speak with great effort."

"Ah! ah! ah!" exclaimed the Iron King.

"I thought the fatigue and excitement of the day had been too much for him. I made my visit very short, and soon bade him good-night. He wished me a prosperous voyage, but did not invite me to visit him on my return—a kindness that he had never before omitted."

"Ah, ah ah!" again exclaimed old Aaron Rockharrt.

"Then I thought his manner and appearance only the effect of excessive fatigue and excitement. Now, seen in the light of future events, I attach a more serious meaning to them."

"What! what! what!" demanded the Iron King.

"I think that some fatal news, from some quarter or other, had reached him; or that some heavy sorrow had fallen upon him; or, worse than all, sudden insanity had overtaken him! That, under the lash of one or another, or all of these, he fled the house and the city, and—made away with himself."

"Now, Heaven forbid!" exclaimed old Aaron Rockharrt, dropping into his chair.

"One favor I have to ask you, Mr. Rockharrt, and that is, that the most searching investigation be made of my movements on that fatal evening of the governor's disappearance."

"It shall be done," said the Iron King.

"I shall remain at the David Crockett until all the friends of the late governor are satisfied so far as I am concerned. And now, having said all I have to say, I will bid you good morning," concluded the visitor as he arose, took up his hat, bowed, and left the room.

Old Aaron Rockharrt returned to the breakfast table, where his subservient family waited.

The coffee, that had been sent to the kitchen to be kept hot, was brought up again, with hot rolls and hot broiled partridges.

The old man resumed his breakfast in silence. He did not think proper to speak of his visitor, nor did any member of the family party venture to question him.

And this was well, so far as Cora was concerned.

Any allusion to the agonizing subject of her husband's mysterious disappearance was more than she could well bear; and to have hinted in her presence that some hidden sorrow had driven him to self-destruction might almost have wrecked her reason.

Cora now never mentioned his name; yet, as after events proved, he was never for a moment absent from her mind.

The old grandmother, who could not speak to Cora on the subject, and who dared not speak to her lord and master on any subject that he did not first broach, and yet who felt that she must talk to some one of that which oppressed her bosom so heavily, at length confided to her youngest son.

"I do think Cora's heart is breaking in this suspense, Clarence! If Rule had died there would have been an end of it, and she would have known the worst and submitted to the inevitable! But this awful suspense, anxiety, uncertainty as to his fate, is just killing her! I wish we could do something to save her, Clarence!"

"I wish so, too, mother! I see how she is failing and sinking, and I own that this surprises me! I really thought that Cora was fascinated by that fellow in London." (This was the irreverent manner in which Mr. Clarence spoke of his grace the Duke of Cumbervale.) "And I thought that she only married Rothsay from a sense of duty, keeping her word, and all that sort of thing! I can't understand her grieving herself to death for him now!"

"Oh, Clarence! she was fascinated by the rank and splendor and personal attractions of the young duke! Her fancy, vanity, ambition and imagination were fired; but her heart was never touched! She had not seen Rothsay for so long a time that his image had somewhat faded in her memory when this splendid young fellow crossed her path and dazzled her for a time! It was a brief madness—nothing more! But you can see for yourself how really she loved Rothsay when you see that anxiety for his fate is breaking her heart."

"I see, mother dear; but I don't understand! And I don't know what on earth we can do for her! If my father does not think proper to suggest something, we must not, for if we should do so it would make matters much worse."

"Yes," sighed the old lady; and the subject was dropped.

Clarence had said that he did not understand Cora's state of mind. No; nor did old Mrs. Rockharrt. How could they, when Cora had not understood herself, until suffering brought self-knowledge?

From her childhood up she had loved Rule Rothsay as a sister loves a favorite brother. In her girlhood, knowing no stronger love, on the strength of this she accepted the offered hand of Rothsay, and was engaged to be married to him. She meant to have been faithful to him; but it was a long engagement, during which she traveled with her grandparents for three years, while the memory of her calmly loved betrothed husband grew rather dim. Then came her meeting with the handsome and accomplished young Duke of Cumbervale, and the infatuation, the hallucination that enslaved her imagination for a period. Then began the mental conflict between inclination and duty, ending in her resolution to forget her English lover and to be true to Rule.

Up to the very wedding day she had suppressed and controlled her feelings with heroic firmness, but on the evening of that day, while waiting for her husband, the long, severe tension of her nerves utterly gave way, and when found in a paroxysm of tears and questioned by him, in her wretchedness and misery she had confessed the infidelity of her heart and pleaded for time to conquer it.

She had expected bitter reproaches, but there were none. She had dreaded fierce anger, but there was none. She had anticipated obduracy, but there was none. There was nothing but intense suffering, divine compassion, and infinite renunciation. He pitied her. He soothed her. He defended her from the reproaches of her own conscience. He protected her by an imposed provision that for her own sake she should not tell others what she had told him. And then—

He laid down all the honors that his life-long toil and self-denial had won for her sake, and he went out from his triumphs, went out from her life—out, out into the outer darkness of oblivion, to be seen no more of men, to be heard of no more by men. All for her sake. And before the majesty of such infinite love, such infinite renunciation, her whole soul bowed down in adoration. Yes, at last, in the hour of losing him she loved him as he longed to be loved by her. She had but one desire on earth—to be at his side. But one prayer, and that was her "vital breath"—for his return.

She felt herself to be unworthy of the measureless love that he had given her—that he still gave her, if he still lived, for his love had known no shadow of turning, nor ever would suffer change.

But, oh! where in space was he? How could she reach him? How could she make him hear the cry of her heart?

One message, like a voice from the grave, had, indeed, come to her from him since his disappearance, but it had been sent before he left the house; it was in the letter he had written and placed in the secret drawer of her writing desk before he went forth that fatal night, a "wanderer through the world's wilderness."

She had found it on that day, about three weeks after his loss, when she had come into the parlor for the first time since her illness, and when, left alone for a few minutes by her grandmother, she had gone to her writing desk, and in the idleness of misery had begun carelessly, aimlessly, to turn over her papers. In the same mood she pressed the spring of the secret drawer, and it sprang open and projected the letter before her. She recognized his handwriting, seized the paper and opened it. It contained only a few words of farewell, with a prayer for her happiness and a parting blessing.

There was no allusion made to the cause of their separation. Probably Rule had thought of the letter falling into other hands than hers; so he had refrained from referring to her secret, lest she should suffer reproach from her family.

Cora read this letter with deep emotion over and over again, until she found herself staring at the lines without gathering their meaning, and then she felt herself growing giddy and faint, for she was still very weak from recent illness, and she hastily dropped the letter into the desk and shut down the lid, only just before a film came over her eyes, a muffled sound in her ears, and oblivion over her senses. This is the swoon in which she was found by Mrs. Rockharrt, and for which she could give no satisfactory reason.

When Cora recovered from that swoon her first care, on the first opportunity, was to go to her writing desk to look for her precious letter— Rothsay's last letter to her. No one had opened her desk or disturbed its contents.

She found her letter; pressed it to her heart and lips many times; then made a little silken bag, into which she put it; then tied it around her neck with a narrow ribbon.

And from that day it rested on her heart. It was her priceless treasure to be cherished above all others, "the first to be saved in fire or flood." It was the only relic of her lost love with his last good-by, and prayers and blessings. It was her magic talisman, still connecting her in some occult way with the vanished one. It was her anchor of hope, still promising in some mysterious manner the final return of her lost husband.

While Cora mourned and dreamed away these first days of the family's return to their town house, old Aaron Rockharrt was sifting the evidence of the story told by Captain Ross; he proved the truth of the skipper's account; and he failed to connect the young man's late visit on that fatal night with the almost simultaneous disappearance of Rothsay.

The season passed on. Mr. and Mrs. Rockharrt gave dinner parties and supper parties; and received and accepted invitations to similar entertainments in return; but no persuasions nor arguments could prevail on Cora to go into any society. Not even the iron will of the Iron King could conquer in this matter. His granddaughter was his own personal property, and one of the attractions of his house; it was in her place to wear her best clothes and costliest jewels, and to show herself to his guests; and her persistent refusal to do this put him in a gloomy, teeth-grinding, impotent rage.

"Cora is of age! She has a very sufficient provision. And now if she does not return to her duty and render herself amenable to my authority and obedient to my commands, I shall order her to find another home; for I mean to be master of my own house and of everybody in it!" he said, savagely, to his timid wife, one evening when she was doing valet's duty by dressing his hair for a dinner party.

"Oh, Aaron! Aaron! have pity on the poor, heartbroken girl!" pleaded the old lady, falling into a fit of trembling that interfered with her task.

"Hold your tongue and heed my words, for I shall do as I say. And mind what you are about now! You have scratched my ear with the bristles of the brush."

"I beg your pardon, Aaron, but my hand shakes so."

"If that young woman don't submit herself to my will, and obey my orders, I will pack her out of this house. And then, perhaps, your nerves will be quieter! I'll do it, for I am not particularly fond of having grass widows about me," he growled.

She made no reply. She could not trust herself to speak. It required all her self-control to steady her hands so as to complete her master's toilet.

Then she had to dress herself in haste and agitation to be ready in time to accompany her husband to the dinner party at the executive mansion, which was now occupied by Lieutenant-Governor Kenelm Kennedy—and from which the Iron King would not allow his wife to absent herself.

Old Aaron Rockharrt was the lion of the evening, as he was the lion of every party in the State capital, probably because he owned the lion's share of the State's wealth, and had more money, perhaps, than the State's treasury. He enjoyed this beast worship, and came to his town house every season and went into general society to receive it.

Mrs. Rockharrt was very anxious to have a talk with her granddaughter, to warn her of impending danger and to implore her to obey the wishes of her grandfather, but the poor old lady had no opportunity.

Cora sat up for her grandparents, in case they should need any of her services on their return.

They came in very late, and then the exactions of the domestic tyrant kept his wife in attendance on him until they were all in bed.

CHAPTER VII
NEWS OF THE MISSING MAN

The next morning, while Aaron Rockharrt slept the sleep of the dead-in-selfishness, his wife arose and crept into the bedroom of her granddaughter.

Cora was awake, but not yet up.

"Oh, grandma, you will get your death of cold! walking about the house in your night gown. What is it? What do you want? Can I do anything for you?" cried the girl, springing out of bed to turn on the heat of the register, and then wrapping a large shawl around the old lady, and putting her into the cushioned easy chair.

"Now what is it, dear grandma? What can I do for you?" she inquired, as she drew on her own wadded dressing gown and sat on the side of the bed near the old lady.

"You can do something to set my mind at ease, my dear; but it will be painful for you, and I do not know whether you will do it," said the old lady with timid hesitation.

"I can do this, dear? Then, of course, I will do it," replied the girl.

"It is almost too much to ask of you, my child."

"There is nothing, nothing that I would not do to give you peace—you, poor dear, who have so little peace," said Cora, tenderly, smoothing the silver hair away from the wrinkled brow of the old lady, who began to drop a few weak tears of self-pity, excited by Cora's sympathy.

"Well, my child," she said, "your grandfather is going to have a little talk with you soon—on the subject of your self-seclusion. Oh! my poor child, do not resist him, do not provoke, do not disobey him. Oh! for my sake, Cora, for my sake, do not!"

"Dearest dear, I will leave undone anything in the world you wish me not to do. I will no longer rebel against my grandfather's authority, even when he exercises it in such a despotic manner," said Cora, raising the clasped hands of the old lady and pressing them to her lips.

Mrs. Rockharrt gathered the girl in her arms and kissed her, with a few more weak tears, but with no more words.

She did not tell Cora of the cruel threat made by the tyrant to turn her out of doors if she failed to obey him, and she hoped that the girl might never hear of it, lest in her wounded pride she might forestall the threat and leave the house of her own accord.

"Now be at ease, dear," said Cora, soothingly. "No more trouble—"

A bell rang sharply and cut off the girl's speech.

"Oh, there he is awake! I must go to him," exclaimed the timid old creature.

Cora made her toilet, and then went down to the breakfast parlor, where she found the two old people about to sit down to the table. She bade her grandfather good morning and then took her place.

During breakfast Aaron Rockharrt said:

"Mrs. Rothsay, you will come to me in the library as soon as we leave the table. I have something to say to you that must be said at once and for the last time."

"Very well, sir," replied the girl.

Half an hour later she was closeted with her grandfather.

"Madam, I do not intend to waste much time over you this morning. I merely mean to put a test question, whose answer shall decide my future course in regard to you."

"Very well."

"I must preface my question by reminding you that you have constantly disregarded my wishes and disobeyed my orders by refusing to see my guests or to go out in company with me."

"Yes."

"When honored with an invitation to the state dinner at the executive mansion you declined to go, even though I expressed my will that you should accompany me."

"Yes."

"But for the future I intend to be master of my own house and of every living soul within it. Now, then, for my test question. You have received cards to the ball to be given at the house of the chief justice to-morrow evening. I wish you to attend it, and my wish should be a command."

"Of course."

"What is your answer? Think before you speak, for on your answer must depend your future position in my house."

Cora was silent for a few moments.

"Sir," she began at length, "you are a just man, at least, and you will not refuse to hear and consider my reasons for seclusion."

"I will consider nothing! I know them as well as you do. Morbid sensitiveness about your peculiar position; morbid dread of facing the world; morbid love of indulging in melancholy. And I will have none of it! None of it! I will be obeyed, and you shall go out into society, or else—"

"'Or else' what will be the alternative, sir?"

"You leave my house! I will have no rebel in my family!"

Had Cora followed the impulse of her proud and outraged spirit, she would have walked out of the library, gone to her room, put on her bonnet and cloak, and left the house, leaving all her goods to be sent after her; but the girl thought of her poor, gentle, suffering grandmother, and bore the insult.

"Sir," she said, with patient dignity, "do you think that it would have been decorous, under the peculiar circumstances, for me to appear in public, and especially at a state dinner at the executive mansion?"

"Madam, I instructed you to accept that invitation and to attend that dinner! Do you dare to hint that I would counsel you to any indecorous act?"

"No, sir; certainly not, if you had stopped to think of it; but weightier matters occupied your mind, no doubt."

"Let that go. But in the question of this ball? Do you mean to obey me?"

"Grandfather, please consider! How can I mix with gay scenes while the fate of my husband is still an awful mystery?"

"You must conquer your feelings, and go, or—take the consequences!"

"Even if I could forget the tragedy of my wedding day, and mix with the gay world again, what would people say?"

"What would people say, indeed? What would they dare to say of my granddaughter?"

"But, sir, it would be contrary to all the laws of etiquette and conventionality."

"My granddaughter, madam, should give the law to fashion and society, not receive it from them!" said the Iron King, throwing himself back in his arm chair as if it had been his throne.

Cora smiled faintly at this egotism, but made no reply in words.

"To come to the point!" he suddenly exclaimed—"Will you obey me and attend this ball, or will you take the other alternative?"

Cora's heart swelled; her eyes flashed; she longed to defy the despot, but she thought of her meek, patient, long-suffering grandmother, and answered coldly:

"I will go to the ball, sir, since you wish it."

"Very well. That will do. Now leave the room. I wish to read the morning papers."

Cora went out to find her grandmother and to relieve the lady's anxiety; old Aaron Rockharrt threw himself back in his arm chair with grim satisfaction at having conquered Cora and set his iron heel upon her neck. Yes; he had conquered Cora through her love for her poor, timid, abused grandmother. But now Fate was to conquer him.

But Fate had decided that Cora should not attend that ball, or any other place of amusement, for a long time. And he was just on the brink of discovering the impertinent interference of Fate in human affairs, and especially those of the Iron King.

He took up a Washington paper—a government organ—and read, opening his eyes to their widest extent as he read the following head-lines:

A MYSTERY CLEARED UP.

THE FATE OF GOVERNOR REGULAS ROTHSAY .

Killed by the Comanches on November 1st.

A dispatch from Fort Security to the Indian Bureau, received this morning, announces another inroad of the Comanches upon the new settlement of Terrepeur, in which the inhabitants were massacred and their dwellings burned. Among the victims who perished in the flames in their own huts was Regulas Rothsay, late Governor-elect of — —, and at the time of his death a volunteer missionary to this treacherous and bloodthirsty tribe.

Another man, under the circumstances, might have been unnerved by such sudden and awful news, and let fall the paper, but not the Iron King. He grasped it only with a firmer hand, and read it again with keener eyes.

"What under the heavens took that man out there? Had he gone suddenly mad? That seems to be the only possible explanation of his conduct. To abandon his bride on the day of his marriage—to abandon his high official position as governor of this State on the day of his inauguration, and without giving any living creature a hint of his intention, to fly off at a tangent and go to the Indian country and become a missionary to those red devils, and be massacred for his pains—it was the work of a raving maniac. But what drove him mad? Surely it was not his high elevation that turned his head, for if it had been, his madness would never have taken this particular direction of flying from his honors. No! it is as I have always suspected. He heard, in some way, of the girl's English lover, and he, with his besotted devotion to her, was just the man to be morbidly, madly jealous, and to do some such idiotic thing as he has done, and get himself murdered and burned to ashes for his pains! Yes; and it serves him right!—it serves him—right!"

He sat glowering at the paragraph, and growling over his news for some time longer, but at length he took it up and walked over to the back parlor, where he felt sure he should find his two women.

Mrs. Rockharrt and Cora, who sat at a table before the gloomy coal fire, and were engaged in some fancy needlework, looked up uneasily as he entered; not that they expected bad news, but that they feared bad temper.

"Cora," he began, "I shall not insist on your going to the ball to-morrow."

She looked up in surprise, and a grateful exclamation was on her lips, but he forestalled it by saying:

"I suppose the news is all over the city by this time. I am going out to hear what the people are saying about it, and to see if the government house and the public offices are to be hung in mourning. There—there it is told in the first column of this paper."

And with cruel abruptness he laid the newspaper on the table between the two women, and pointed out the fatal paragraph.

Then he stalked out of the room, and called his man-servant to help him on with his heavy overcoat.

That house, on the previous night, had been one blaze of light in honor of the State dinner. Now, as well as he could see dimly through the falling snow, it was all closed up, and men on ladders were festooning every row of windows with black goods.

"Yes, of course. It is as I expected. The news has gone all over the town already," said old Aaron Rockharrt, as he strode through the snowstorm to the business center of the city.

Every acquaintance whom he met stopped him with the same question in slightly different words.

"Have you heard?" and so forth.

Every intimate friend he encountered asked:

"How does Mrs. Rothsay bear it?" or—

"What on earth ever took the governor out there?"

To all questions the Iron King gave curt answers that discouraged discussion of the subject. He walked on, noticing that the stores and offices of the city were being festooned with mourning, and that notwithstanding the severity of the storm the street corners were occupied by groups talking excitedly of the fatal news.

He went into the editorial rooms of all the city newspapers and wished and attempted to dictate to the proprietors the manner in which they should write of the tragic event which was then in the minds and on the tongues of all persons.

As he spent an hour on the average at each office, it was late in the winter afternoon when he got home. It was not yet dark, however, and he was surprised to see a man servant engaged in closing the shutters.

He entered and demanded severely why the servant shut the windows before night.

The old man looked nervous and distressed, and answered vaguely:

"It is the missus, sah."

The idea that his wife should take the liberty of ordering the house to be closed for the night at this unusual hour of the afternoon, without his authority, enraged him:

"Help me off with my ulster," he said.

When the servant had performed this office the master said:

"Serve dinner at once."

And then he strode into the back parlor, which was the usual sitting room of his wife and granddaughter. The room was empty and darkened. More than ever infuriated by fatigue, hunger, and the supposed disregard of his authority, he came out and walked up stairs to look for his wife in her own room. He pushed open the door and entered. That room was also dark, only for the faint red light that came from the coal fire in the grate. By this he dimly perceived a female form sitting near the bed, and whom he supposed to be his wife.

"Why, in the fiend's name, is the whole house as dark as pitch?" he roughly demanded, as he went to a front window and threw open the shutters, letting in the white light of the snow storm.

"Grandfather!"

It was the voice of Cora that spoke, and there was a something in its tone that struck and almost awed even the Iron King.

He turned abruptly.

Cora had risen from her chair and was now standing by the bed. But on the bed lay a little, still, fair form, with hands folded over its breast, with the eyes shut down forever, and all over the fair, wan, placid face was "the peace of God which passeth all understanding."

"What is this?" demanded Old Aaron Rockharrt, as he came up to the bed.

"Look at her. She rests at last. I have been with her twenty years, and this is the first time I have ever seen her rest in peace."

Old Aaron Rockharrt stood like a stone beside the bed, gazing down on the dead.

"She is safe now, never more to be startled, or frightened, or tortured by any one. 'Safe, where the wicked cease from troubling, and the weary are at rest,'" continued Cora.

Still Old Aaron stood like a stone beside the bed and gazed down on the dead.

Suddenly, without moving or withdrawing his gaze from where it rested, he asked in a low, gruff tone:

"How did this happen?"

"She fainted in her chair, and died in that faint."

"When? where? from what?"

"Within an hour after you had left us together in the back parlor, with the paper containing the news of my husband's death," answered Cora, speaking in a tone of most unnatural calmness.

"Had that excitement anything to do with her swoon?"

"I do not know."

"Give me the particulars."

"We—or, rather, she—first took up the paper, and without knowing what the news was that you told us to look at, gave it to me, and asked me to read it. I, as soon as I saw what it was—I lost all control over myself. I do not know how I behaved. But she took the paper, to see what it was that had so disturbed me, and then, she, too, became very much agitated; but she tried to console me, tried for a long while to comfort me, standing over my chair, and caressing and talking. At last she left me, and sat down and leaned back in her own chair. I was trying to be quiet, and at last succeeded, and then I arose and went to her, meaning to tell her that I would be calm and not distress her any more. When I looked at her, I found that she had fainted. I rang and sent off for a doctor instantly, and while waiting for him did all that was possible to revive her, but without effect. When the doctor came and examined her condition he pronounced her quite dead."

"This must have occurred four or five hours ago. Why was I not sent for?"

"You were sent for immediately. Messengers were dispatched in every direction. But you could nowhere be found. They did not, indeed, know where to look for you."

"Now close the window again, and then go and leave me alone; and do not let any one disturb me on any account," said the old man, who had not once moved from the bedside, or even lifted his gaze from the face of the dead.

"I have telegraphed to North End for Uncle Fabian and Clarence, also to West Point for Sylvanus. Sylvan cannot reach here before to-morrow, but my uncles will be here this evening. Shall I send you word when they arrive?"

"No. Let no one come to me to-night."

"Shall I send you up anything, grandfather?"

"No, no. If I require anything I will ring for it. Go now, Cora, and leave me to myself."

The girl went away, closing the door behind her. As she descended the stairs she heard the key turned, and knew that her grandfather had so shut out all intruders.

He who had come home hungry and furious as a famished wolf never appeared at the dinner that he had so peremptorily ordered to be served at once, but shut himself up fasting with his dead. If his eyes were now opened to see how much he had made her suffer through his selfishness, cruelty, and despotism all her married life—if his late remorse awoke—if he grieved for her—no one ever knew it. He never gave expression to it.

CHAPTER VIII
"THE PEACE OF GOD WHICH PASSETH ALL UNDERSTANDING"

In the late dawn of that dark winter day Mr. Clarence came down into the parlor, and found Cora still there, with one gas jet burning low.

"Up so early, my dear child?" he said, as he took her hand and gave her the good morning kiss.

"I have not been in bed," she replied.

"Not in bed all night! That was wrong. How cold your hands are? Go to bed now, dear."

"I cannot. I do not wish to."

"My poor, doubly bereaved child, how much I feel for you!" he said, in a tender tone, and still holding her hand.

"Do not mind me, Uncle Clarence. I do not feel for myself. I am numb. I feel nothing—nothing," she replied.

Mr. Clarence, still holding her hand, led her to a large easy chair, and put her in it.

Then he went and rang the bell.

"Tell the cook to make a strong cup of coffee as quickly as she can, and bring it up here to Mrs. Rothsay," he said to the man who answered the call.

The latter touched his forehead and left the room.

Mr. Clarence had tact enough not to worry his niece with any more words. He went and opened one of the front windows to look out upon the wintry morning. The ground was covered very deeply with the snow, which was now falling so thickly as to obscure every object.

When the servant entered with the coffee, Mr. Clarence himself took it from the man's hand, and carried it to his niece and persuaded her to drink it.

The servant meanwhile, mindful of the proprieties, when he saw the front window open, went and closed it, and then passed down the room and opened both the back windows, which gave sufficient light to the whole area of the apartment.

Finally he turned off the gas, and taking up the empty coffee service, left the room.

Presently after Mr. Fabian came in, and greeted his niece and his brother in a grave, muffled voice.

A little later breakfast was served.

"Some one should go up to see if grandpa will have anything sent to him. Will you, Uncle Fabian?" inquired Cora, as they seated themselves at the table.

Mr. Fabian left his chair for the purpose, but before he had crossed the room they heard the heavy footsteps of the Iron King coming down the stairs.

He entered the dining room, and all arose to receive him. He came up and shook hands with each of his sons in turn and in silence. Then he took his place at the table. The three younger members of the family looked at him furtively, whenever they could do so without attracting his attention, and, perhaps, awakening his wrath.

Some change had come over him, but not of a softening nature. His hard, stern, set face was, if possible, more stony than ever.

Neither Mr. Clarence nor Cora dared to speak to him; but Mr. Fabian, feeling the silence awkward and oppressive, at length ventured to say:

"My dear father, in this our severe bereavement—"

But he got no further in his speech. Old Aaron Rockharrt raised his hand and stopped him right there, and then said:

"Not one word from any one of you to me or in my presence on this event, either now or ever. It happened in the course of nature. Drop the subject. Fabian, how are matters going on at the works?"

"I do not know, sir," replied Mr. Fabian, speaking for the first and last and only time, abruptly and indiscreetly to his despotic father.

But the Iron King took no notice of the words, nor did he repeat the question. He drank one cup of coffee, ate half a roll, and then arose and left the table, without a word. He did not return to his dead wife's chamber, which he probably knew would now have to be given up to dressers of the dead and to the undertakers.

He went and locked himself in the library, and was seen no more that day.

Cora, with her woman's intuition, understood the accession of hardness that was worn as a mask to conceal grief and remorse.

"Be patient with him, Uncle Fabian. He is your father, after all. And he suffers! Oh, he suffers! Yes; much more than any of us do," she said.

"Do you think so, Cora?" inquired Mr. Fabian, looking at her in surprise.

"I know he does," she answered.

"Well, he has good reason to!" concluded Mr. Fabian. Then, after a pause, he added: "But I am sorry I spoke roughly to my father! I will make it up to him, or try to do so, by extra deference."

Then they all arose from the table.

Mr. Fabian and Mr. Clarence to attend to the business of the mournful occasion, which Old Aaron Rockharrt, in his proud, reserved, absorbed sorrow, seemed to have ignored or forgotten.

Cora stepped away to her grandmother's room, to have a quiet hour beside the beloved dead before the undertaker should come in and take possession.

"It is only her body that is dead, I know. But the hands had caressed me and the lips kissed me; and, right or wrong, I love that body as well as the heavenly soul that lived within it! The flesh cleaves to the flesh. And so long as we are in the flesh we will, we must, haunt the shrines that contain the bodies of those we love," she thought, as reverently she entered the chamber of death, closed the door, and went up to the bed whereon lay the tenantless temple in which so lately lived the most loving, the most patient spirit she had ever known!

But what is this! Into what strange sphere of ineffable peace has Cora entered? She could not understand the change that came over her. She had a gentle impulse to close her eyes to all visible matters and yield herself up to the sweetness of this sphere. Her dear one was living, was young again, was happy, was sleeping, watched by angels, who would presently awaken her to the eternal life.

Cora knelt down by the bed and lifted up her heart to the Lord of life in silent, wordless, thoughtless, profoundly quiet aspiration. She did not wish to move or speak, or form a sentence even in her mind. She found her state a strange one, but she did not even wonder at it, so deep was the calm that enveloped her spirit.

Not long had she knelt there in this rapt serenity, when she was conscious that some one was rapping softly at the door. This did not disturb her. She arose from her knees, still in deep peace, went to the door, and said:

"Presently. I will open presently. Wait a moment."

Then she went back to the bed, turned down the sheet, and gazed upon the beloved face. How placid it was, and how beautiful. Death had smoothed every trace of age and care from that little fair old face. She lay as if sleeping, and almost smiling in her sleep—

"As though by fitness she had won
The secret of some happy dream."

Cora stooped and kissed the placid brow, then covered the face, and went to open the door.

The gray-haired old Jason was waiting outside.

"If you please, ma'am, it is the—"

"I know, I know," said Cora, quietly. "Show them in."

And she passed out and went to her own room.

Her front windows were closed; but through the slats of the shutters she saw that it was still snowing fast.

"What a winding sheet this will make for her grave," she thought, as she looked out upon the wintry scene.

There was no wind, the fine white snow fell softly and steadily, giving only the dimmest view of the government house on the opposite side of the square draped in mourning.

The funeral of Mrs. Rockharrt took place on the third day after her death. The snow had ceased, and the winter sun was shining brightly from a clear blue sky on a white world, whose trees wore pendent diamonds instead of green leaves, and as every house in the city was hung in black for the dead governor, the effect of all this glare and glitter and gloom was very weird and strange, as the funeral cortege passed from the Rockharrt home to the Church of the Lord's Peace.

After the rites were over, the family returned to their city home, but only for the night; for preparation had been already completed for their removal to Rockhold, there to pass the year of mourning.

Old Aaron Rockharrt never changed from his look of stony immobility. If he mourned for his patient wife of more than half a century, no outward sign betrayed his feelings. If his spirit suffered with suppressed grief, his strong frame bore up under it without the slightest weakening.

On the afternoon of his return from his wife's funeral he shut himself up in his library and remained there all the evening, refusing to come to dinner, calling for a bottle of wine and a sandwich and desiring afterward to be left alone.

Later in the evening he sent for Mr. Fabian to come to him, and there opened to his eldest son and partner, in whose business talents he had great confidence, a scheme of speculation so venturous, so gigantic that the younger man was shocked and staggered, and began to lose faith in the sound intellect of the Iron King.

"This will make us twice told the wealthiest men in the United States, if not in the whole world," concluded Old Aaron Rockharrt.

"If it should succeed," said Mr. Fabian, dubiously.

"It shall succeed; I say it. We shall go down to Rockhold to-morrow morning and the next day to the works, and there I shall give my whole mind to this matter and make it succeed, do you hear? Make it succeed! And place my name at the head of the list of wealthy men of this age."

Mr. Fabian did not dare to raise any objection.

"I am pleased, sir," he said, "that you find in this new enterprise an object of so much interest to engage your mind. Employ me in any way you think fit. I am quite at your service, as it is my bounden duty to be."

"Very well; that is as it should be. Now I am going to bed. Good night," said the Iron King, abruptly dismissing his son, then rising and ringing for his valet, whose office, since the patient old lady's death, was now no longer a sinecure.

It seems passing strange that a man of seventy-six years, who had just lost his life-long and beloved companion—for in his own selfish way he loved her after a sort, and perhaps more than he loved any human being in the world—and who must expect before many years to follow her, should be so full of this world's avarice and ambition; so eager to make more, and more, and more money, and to stand at the head of the list of all the wealthiest men in the land. Strange, yet the name of such a one is legion. But in the case of Old Aaron Rockharrt there might have been this additional motive—the necessity to seek refuge from the pains of grief and remorse in the anxieties and activities of speculation. So he was very eager to get back as soon as possible to business and to enter at once upon the enterprise he had planned.

Cora was also anxious to leave the city, which she knew was in a fresh ferment of gossip and conjecture on the subject of her lost husband, the deceased governor-elect. The news from the Indian Territory had renewed all the public interest in the mystery of his disappearance.

For some months before this news arrived, the community had settled down to the conviction that the missing governor had been murdered and his body made away with, although, as there was no proof to establish the fact of their theory, there was no thought of inaugurating the lieutenant-governor as chief magistrate of the State.

Yet, now, when the startling news came that the missing statesman had been killed by the Comanches in the wilds of the Indian Reservation, far from any agency, and that he had been living and preaching there as a volunteer missionary for many months before the massacre, the mystery of his sudden and unexplained disappearance from the State capital on the day of his inauguration was not cleared up and made intelligible, but darkened and rendered more inscrutable.

It was easy enough to understand why a missing man might have been lured away from his dwelling by some false letter or plausible message, and murdered in some secret place where his body lay buried in earth or water, for such crimes were not unfrequent.

But that a bridegroom should secretly depart on the evening of his wedding day, that a governor should take flight on the evening before his inauguration, was a course of action only to be explained on the ground of insanity; and yet Regulas Rothsay was always considered one of the most level-headed and mentally well balanced among the rising young statesmen of the country.

Conjecture had once been wild as to the cause of his disappearance— had he been murdered, or kidnapped, or both? Those were the questions then.

Conjecture was now rampant as to the cause of his sudden flight and self expatriation to the Indian Territory. Had he suddenly gone mad? Or committed a capital crime which was on the eve of discovery? These were the questions now.

Every newspaper was full of the problem, which none but one could solve, and she was bound to secrecy.

But it gave her inexpressible pain to know that his motives and his character were being discussed and censured for that course of conduct for which only herself was to be blamed, and which only she could explain. A word from her would show him in a very different light before his critics. But she must not speak that word to save his reputation.

So Cora was anxious to leave the city.

The next morning the whole family set out on their return journey to Rockhold, where they arrived early in the afternoon. They found everything in good order, for Cora had taken the precaution to write to the housekeeper, and warn her of the return of the family.

The grief of the servants for the loss of their kind and gentle old mistress broke out afresh at the sight of the young lady. And it was long before the latter could soothe and quiet them.

Fortunately Mr. Rockharrt had gone at once to his room, and so he escaped annoyance from their loud lamentations, and they escaped stern rebuke for their want of self-control.

The two young Rockharrts had left the family party at North End, to inspect the condition of the works, and were to remain there overnight. Old Aaron Rockharrt, Sylvanus Haught, and Cora Rothsay were, therefore, the only ones who sat down at the once full dinner table.

The meal passed in almost utter silence, for neither Sylvan nor Cora ventured to address one word to the hard old man who, whenever they had spoken to him since his loss of his wife, had replied in short, harsh words, or not replied at all. The brother and sister, therefore, only spoke in suppressed tones, at intervals, to each other.

After dinner the old man bade them an abrupt good night, and left the room to retire to his own chamber. Cora felt sorry for him, despite all his harshness. She stepped after him and asked:

"Grandfather, can I be of any service to you at all? Help you at your—"

He stopped her by turning and bending his gray brows over the fierce black eyes which fixed her motionless. He stared at her for an instant and then said:

"No. Certainly not," and turned and went up stairs.

Cora walked slowly back into the drawing room, at the open door of which stood Sylvan, who had heard all that passed.

"You had better let the old man alone, Cora. Or you'll have your head bitten off. I don't want to break the fifth commandment by saying anything irreverent of our grandfather, but indeed, indeed, indeed it is as much as one's life, or at least as one's temper, is worth to speak to him," said the young man.

"I never reverenced my grandfather as much as I do now, Sylvan," gravely replied the young lady.

"That is all right! Reverence him as much as you please; but don't go too near the old lion in his present mood. Come and sit down on the sofa by me, sister, and let us have a pleasant talk—"

"Pleasant talk! Oh, Sylvan!"

"Well, then, Cora, dear sister, a cozy, confidential talk. Do you know we have not had one for years and years and years?"

They sat down side by side holding each other's hands in silence for a little while, when Cora said:

"Do you think you will graduate next year, Sylvan?"

"Yes, Cora, certainly."

"And then you will come home for a long visit."

"For a short one, on leave."

"And afterward, Sylvan?"

"Well, afterward I shall be ordered out to 'The Devil's Icy Peak.'"

"What!"

"That was Aunt Cassy's name for all remote parts, you know. 'Devil's Icy Peak,' which in my destination means some remote frontier fort, among hostile Indians, border ruffians, grizzly bears, buffaloes, rattlesnakes, mosquitoes, malaria, and other wild beasts. There is where they send all the new-fledged military officers from West Point, and there they may spend the best part of their lives," said Sylvan.

"Unless they have influence with the higher authorities. If they have such influence, they may be sent to choice posts near the great cities, in reach of all the best society, best libraries, and all the luxuries and advantages of the highest civilization."

"Yes, I know; but—" said the young cadet, hesitatingly.

"You, or rather our grandfather, has influence enough to have you ordered to Washington, New York, Portsmouth—any place."

"Yes, I know; but—"

"But what, Sylvan?"

"Cora, our grandfather's influence is that of wealth—great wealth—and it is a mighty power in this world at this age; but, you see, Aaron Rockharrt would not use it in such a way. He would not consider it honest to do so. Nor would I have it either. No; since the government has given me a free military education, I think it my duty to go exactly wherever they may order me, without attempting to evade orders through the influence of friends or money."

"You are entirely right, dear brother. And I tell you this: Though I must and will remain with my grandfather so long as he shall need me—so long as he shall live—yet, when he departs, if you should be stationed at one of those border posts, I will go out and join you, Sylvan," said Cora Rothsay, taking both his hands and pressing them warmly.

"No, dear sister; you shall not make such a sacrifice for me," he answered.

"But after my aged grandfather, whose days on earth cannot be long, whom have I in this world to live for but you, Sylvan?"

"Other interests in life, I hope, will arise, sister, to give you happiness," he replied.

Cora shook her head, and as the waiter now entered the parlor with the bedroom candles, she lighted one, bade her brother good night, and retired.

The next morning, as but one day of his leave of absence remained, the young cadet bade good-by to his friends, and left Rockhold for West Point, where he arrived the next morning just in time to report for duty, and save his honor.

Old Aaron Rockharrt went up to North End, where his sons awaited him; there to inspect the works, and commence proceedings toward that vast enterprise which the Iron King had planned out while in the city.

And from this day forth. "Rockharrt & Sons" devoted all their energies to this mammoth speculation, while, as the months passed, it grew into huge and huger proportions, and great and greater success.

Old Aaron Rockharrt's spirits rose with the splendor of his fortune.

He was nearly seventy-seven years of age, yet he said to himself, in effect: "Soul, thou hast much goods laid up for many years."

Cora, meanwhile, living a secluded and almost solitary life at Rockhold, occupied herself with a labor of love, in writing the life of her late husband, with extracts from his letters, speeches, and newspaper articles. In doing this her soul seemed once more joined to his.

In this manner the year of mourning passed, and the month of January was at hand.

CHAPTER IX
TURMOIL OF THE WORLD

The Rockharrts were again in the State capital. It was but thirteen months since the death of his wife and since the news of the murder of his grandson-in law had been received—calamities which had doubly bereaved the family, and thrown them in the deepest mourning—yet the Iron King, elated by his marvelous financial success, had thrown open his house to society, and insisted that his granddaughter should do its honors.

Cora, who, since the death of the grandmother, had deeply pitied the grandfather, yielded to his wishes in this respect, though much against her secret inclination. She did not leave off her widow's mourning, but she modified it when she presided at the head of the Rockharrt table on those frequent occasions of the sumptuous and unrivaled dinners given by the Iron King to those whose fortunes he was making, with his own, by his mammoth enterprise.

The old man was certainly the lion of the season. He had steadily gone on from step to step on the ladder of fame (for enormous wealth), until now he was quoted as not only the richest man of his State, but as one of the ten richest men in the world.

It was at this time that Mr. Fabian bethought himself of taking a wife. It was indeed quite time that he should marry, if he ever intended to do so. He was nearly fifty-two years of age, though looking no more than forty; his erect and active figure, his fresh and smooth complexion, his curling brown hair and beard, his smiling countenance and cheerful demeanor, rendered him quite an attractive man to young ladies, who credited him with fully twenty years less than his due.

There was, at this time, among the lovely "rosebuds" opening in the fashionable drawing rooms of the city, a sweet "wood violet," otherwise Violet Wood; a perfect blonde, with perfect features and a petite figure. Her beauty was peculiar; she was very small, very dainty; her hair the palest yellow, her face so white that almost the only color on her features were her deep blue eyes and crimson lips.

She was an orphan heiress, without any near relation in the world. Though but eighteen years of age, and just from school, she had already entered on the possession of her fortune by the terms of her father's will. She lived with her former guardians, the Chief Justice Pendletime and his wife.

They had given a grand ball to introduce their ward into society. The Rockharrts had been invited, of course. And they had all been present. The Wood Violet, as admirers transposed her name, was equally, of course, the belle of the evening.

The tall, towering sunflower, Mr. Fabian, fell instantly and irrecoverably in love with this tiny white wood violet. Many others fell in love with her, but none to the depth of Mr. Fabian. He resolved to "take time by the forelock," "not to let the grass grow under his feet" in this love chase.

The very next morning he said to his father:

"You have lately expressed a wish to see me married, sir. I have been, in obedience to your commands, looking out for a wife. I think I have found a woman to suit me, and, what is more to the purpose, to suit you, sir. However, if I should be mistaken in your taste, I shall, of course, give up the thought of proposing to her," added artful Mr. Fabian, who felt perfectly sure that his father would approve his choice.

"Who is she?" demanded the Iron King.

"Miss Violet Wood, the ward of Chief Justice Pendletime."

"You could not have made a wiser choice. You have my full approval. And the sooner you are married, the better I shall like it."

Mr. Fabian bowed in silence.

"And you remember that we were planning to send a confidential agent to Europe to establish syndicates for our shares in the principal cities. Now you can utilize your wedding tour by taking your bride to Europe and looking after this business in person."

"Yes, of course," assented Mr. Fabian.

"Other details may be thought of afterward. You had better begin to call on the lady. It is well to be the first in the market."

"Of course, sir."

This ended the conference.

Mr. Fabian groomed himself into as charming a toilet as a gentleman's morning suit would admit. He then set forth in his carriage and made the round of the three conservatories of which the town could boast before he could find a cluster of white wood violets to pin on the lapel of his coat. He also got a splendid and fragrant bouquet, and armed with these fascinators he drove to the house of the chief justice and sent in his card.

The ladies were at home. He was shown into the drawing room, where, oh! beneficence of fortune, he found his inamorata alone.

In a pale blue cashmere home dress trimmed with swan's down and lace, she looked fairer, sweeter, daintier, more suggestive of a wood violet than ever.

She left her seat at the piano and came to meet him, saying simply:

"Good morning, Mr. Rockharrt. Mrs. Pendletime will be down presently. She is not in good health, and so she slept late this morning after the ball. Oh! what lovely, lovely flowers! For me? Oh! thank you so much, Mr. Rockharrt," she added, as Mr. Fabian, with a deep bow and a sweet smile, presented his offering.

Mr. Fabian made good use of his time, and had advanced considerably in the good graces of his fair little love before the lady of the house entered.

Mrs. Chief Justice Pendletime greeted Mr. Fabian most graciously, inquiring after the health of his father.

A little small talk, a few compliments, and the delightful chat was broken into by the arrival of other callers, fine youths, admirers of Violet Wood and secret aspirants to her favor. Even most amiable Mr. Fabian felt a strong desire to kick them all out of the drawing room, through the front door and into the street.

He made himself doubly agreeable to the beauty and her chaperon, and finally offered them a box at the opera for the next evening, and when it was accepted he at last took leave.

"I have got the inside track and mean to keep it!" he said to himself, as he drove homeward. And he did keep it. He was really a very fascinating man when he chose to be so, and he generally did choose to be so. And he could "make love like an angel." Now, whether he really won the affections of Violet Wood by his charms of person and address, or whether he only dazzled the girl's imagination by the splendor of his wealth and position, or whether her guardians advocated his cause with the beauty, or whether there was something of all these influences at work upon her will, I do not quite know. But certain it is that when Mr. Fabian, after two weeks' courtship, offered his heart, hand, and fortune to the little beauty, she accepted them, and not only accepted, but seemed very happy in doing so.

The betrothed lover pleaded for an early wedding day. Violet Wood answered that she would consult her chaperon and abide by her decision. Mr. Fabian then took the precaution to see Mrs. Pendletime, and pray that the marriage might take place early in February. The lady answered that she would consult her young protegee and be governed by her wishes.

Mr. Fabian bowed, thanked her warmly, shook hands with her cordially and left the house. He went straight home, took from his safe a casket of diamonds he had bought for his bride, and saying to himself:

"I can get Violet another and twice as costly a set; and what I need now is to save time." He called Jason and dispatched him with this casket and his card done up in a neat parcel, and directed to Mrs. Chief Justice Pendletime. So prompt had been his action that the chaperon received this silent bribe before she had spoken to her protegee on the subject of fixing a day for her marriage.

Now the fire of these diamonds threw such a radiant light on the matter that Mrs. Pendletime saw at once, and quite clearly, that February, early in February, was the very best time for the wedding.

She sent for her protegee, and had a talk with her. Now Violet Wood was by nature a simple-hearted, good-humored girl, who loved to be well dressed, well housed, well served, and, above all, to be much petted, especially by such a charming master of the art as was Mr. Fabian. She also loved to oblige her friends.

So she yielded to the arguments of Mrs. Pendletime and consented to be married in February—only not during the first week in February, but about the middle of the month—the fourteenth, say. Saint Valentine's day, the birds' bridal day, would be a very appropriate time for a wood violet to wed.

When Mr. Fabian came to pay his usual visit the next morning, Mrs. Pendletime received him, thanked him profusely for his munificent gift, telling him at the same time that she should certainly never have accepted such a costly present from any one who was not connected or about to be connected with her family. Mr. Fabian bowed deprecatingly and asked if he might be permitted to see Miss Wood. Surely he might, she had only intercepted him to thank him for his gift. Then she told him that he would find Violet alone in the drawing room. He went in, and found the little creature perched upon the music stool, before the open piano, trying a new piece of music. She lighted down like a little bird from a twig and came to meet him. He greeted his betrothed with more warmth of love than a younger man might have ventured upon—but, then, Mr. Fabian was no freshman in the college of love. And Violet, though she did not like to be squeezed so tight and kissed so much, thought it was all right, since he was her first lover and her betrothed husband. She was not sufficiently in love with him to be afraid of him. This was as if one of her school girl friends had hugged and kissed her so much. When they were seated side by side on the sofa, Mr. Fabian told her that immediately after their wedding breakfast they should take the train for New York and thence sail for Liverpool. They should reach London near the beginning of the fashionable season, which is not winter, as with us, but spring.

Violet listened in the rapture of anticipation.

"And at the end of the London season we will make a leisurely tour through England—see the monuments of its great old history; palaces and castles of kings and chieftains who have been dust for ages. Then the homes and haunts of the great poets and painters."

The door opened, and the servant announced a visitor. Mr. Fabian, secure now of his prize, arose and said good morning, leaving Violet to entertain one of her young adorers. Mr. Fabian went home and sought his father in the library, where the old man now passed much of his time.

"Well, my dear sir, it is all settled. With your approbation, we—Miss Violet Wood and myself—will be married on the fourteenth proximo, and leave for Europe immediately afterward," said Mr. Fabian, seating himself.

"That is right. I am glad that you will sail in February. You will thereby escape the winds of March and the tempests of the spring equinox," said the Iron King, sententiously.

"I am very glad you approve," said Mr. Fabian.

Old Aaron Rockharrt nodded in silence.

Fabian looked at him; saw that the old man looked grave, depressed, yet stern and strong as adamant. He felt very sorry for his father. His own present happiness rendered good-natured Mr. Fabian very compassionate toward the lonely old widower. He had something, inspired by this compassion, to suggest to the old man, yet he feared to do so straightforwardly.

"Father," he said at length, for he didn't mind lying the least in the world—"Father, I heard a strange report about you this morning."

"Indeed! What was it? That I had failed in business, or quadrupled my fortune?" inquired the egotist, who was always interested when the question concerned himself.

"Neither, sir. I heard you were going to be married."

"Fabian!" sternly exclaimed the Iron King, darkly gathering his brows.

"Yes, sir," said the benevolent Mr. Fabian, who, now that the ice was broken, could go on lying glibly with the best intentions and without the slightest scruple; "yes, sir; you know such rumors must necessarily get afloat about such a fine-looking, marriageable man as yourself."

"Ah! and since the community have made so free, pray what lady's name have they honored me by associating with mine?" inquired the Iron King somewhat sarcastically, yet not ill-pleased to learn that he was still to be considered a great prize in the matrimonial market.

"Why, of course there could be but one lady in the question; and equally, of course, you will be able to place her," said Mr. Fabian, smiling.

"Upon my soul, I am not."

"Well, then, the lady to whom you are reported to be engaged is the beautiful Mrs. Bloomingfield."

"Who?"

"The beautiful and accomplished Mrs. Bloomingfield, with whom you sat and talked during the whole evening of the governor's State dinner party."

"Oh, the widow of General Bloomingfield, who died three years ago. Yes, I remember her—a very fine creature, most certainly—but I never dreamed of her in the light of a wife. In fact, I never dreamed of marrying again," said the Iron King, speaking with unusual gentleness.

Mr. Fabian laughed in his sleeve. He thought of the soft place in the hard head of the Iron King, a weak part in the strong character of old Aaron Rockharrt—personal vanity.

"With all possible respect and submission, my dear father, I would suggest that if you never thought of marrying again, you should do so now."

"Fabian, I am seventy-seven years old."

"In years, yes; but that is nothing to you. You are not half that age in health, strength, vigor, and activity of mind and body. What man of forty do you know who has anything approaching your energy?"

"None that I know of, indeed, Fabian," said the Iron King, softening into complacency.

"No, none," assented Mr. Fabian. "Men die of old age at almost any time in their lives—at forty, fifty, sixty, seventy—but you in your strength of manhood are likely to reach your hundredth year and to be a hale old man then. Now, and for many years to come, you will not be old at all."

"Yes; I think I have twenty-five or thirty years longer to live."

"And will you live those years in loneliness? Cora will be sure to marry. A young woman like Cora will not wear the willow long, believe me. And when Cora leaves you, what then will you do? You have no other daughter or granddaughter. As for my promised wife, you yourself made it a condition of our marriage that we should have an establishment of our own."

"For the dignity of the house of Rockharrt. Yes, Fabian."

"And when Cora shall have left you, you will be alone—you who require the gentle ministrations of woman more than any man I ever knew."

"Fabian!" exclaimed old Aaron Rockharrt, suddenly and suspiciously, bringing his strong black eyes to bear pointedly upon the face of his son. "What is your motive in wishing me to marry?"

"Heaven bear me witness, sir, that my motive, my only motive, is your own comfort and happiness," said Fabian, and this time he spoke the truth.

"I believe you, Fabian. But this lady with whom the world associates my name is too young for me. She cannot be more than twenty-five," said Old Aaron Rockharrt reflectively.

"Well, sir! What did the sages and prophets recommend to David? A young woman to comfort the king. I am not very well posted in Bible history, but I think that is the story," said Mr. Fabian.

CHAPTER X
ANOTHER FINE WEDDING

The marriage of Mr. Fabian Rockharrt and Miss Violet Wood was to be the great event of the winter.

When the approaching wedding was announced in the newspapers of the day, it caused a sensation, I assure you. Mr. Fabian Rockharrt, the eldest son of the renowned millionaire, the confirmed bachelor, for whom "caps" had been "set" for the last twenty-five years; who had flirted with maidens who were now wives of elderly men and mothers of grown-up daughters, and in some cases even grandmothers of growing boys and girls—Mr. Fabian Rockharrt to be won at last by a little wood violet! Preposterous!

The fourteenth of February, Saint Valentine's Day, the Birds' Wedding Day, dawned in that Southern climate like a May day. The snow had vanished weeks before; the ground was warm and moist; the grass was springing; the trees were budding; the wood violets were opening their sweet eyes in sheltered nooks of the forest.

I do not know in what mood Violet Wood arose on that momentous morning of her life—probably in a very pleasant one. Her chaperon confided to an intimate friend that the child was not in love; that she had never been in love in her life, and did not even know what being in love meant; but that she was rather fond of the fine fellow who adored her, flattered her, petted her, promised her everything she wanted, and whose enormous wealth constituted him a sort of magician who could command the riches, the splendors, the luxuries, and all the delights of life! She was full of rapturous anticipations of extravagant enjoyments.

Mr. Fabian Rockharrt, utterly unprincipled as he was, yet had the grace to recognize the purity of the young being whom he was about to make his wife. He was very kind hearted and good humored with every one; he really loved this girl, as he had never loved any one in all his life; and it was his pleasure to indulge her in every wish and whim—even to suggest and create in her mind more wishes and more whims, such as she never could have imagined, so that he might have the joy of gratifying them.

Before starting to church that morning his father called him into the library for a private interview, and lectured him as if he had been a lad of twenty-one, who was about to contract marriage—lectured him on the duties of a husband, of the master of a household and the head of a family.

The arrival of Mr. Clarence from North End, and of Mr. Sylvan from West Point by the same train, to be present at the wedding, interrupted the bridegroom's reflections.

"It is now nine o'clock, boys. You have just time to get your breakfast comfortably and dress yourselves properly before we leave for the church. So look sharp," was the greeting of Mr. Fabian, as he shook hands with his brother and his nephew.

At ten o'clock the carriage containing Mr. Rockharrt, Mrs. Rothsay and Cadet Haught left the house for the church, which they entered by the central front door, from which they were marshaled up the center aisle to their seats in the right hand front pew.

At a quarter past ten the bridegroom, with his best man, Clarence Rockharrt, followed in another very handsome carriage.

They drove around to the side of the church, and passed in through the rector's door to the vestry on the left of the chancel, where they awaited the arrival of the bride's party, and through the open door of which they looked in upon the splendidly decorated and crowded church. An affluence of rare exotic flowers everywhere. The green-houses of the State capital and of three neighboring cities had been laid under contribution by Mr. Fabian, and had yielded up their sweetest treasures for this occasion. Floral arches spanned the center aisle from side to side, all the way up from the door to the chancel; festoons of flowers were looped from the galleries on three sides of the church; wreaths of flowers were wound around the pillars from floor to ceiling; the railing around the chancel was covered with flowers; the pulpit and reading desk were hidden under flowers. The pews were filled with the beauty, fashion, and aristocracy of the capital, and a splendid crowd they formed. Every lady held a rich bouquet; every gentleman wore a rare boutonniere.

Mr. Fabian looked at his watch from moment to moment. We have scarcely ever seen a more impatient bridegroom than Mr. Fabian Rockharrt. But, then, childish disorders go hard with elderly folks. Just as the clock struck eleven, with dramatic punctuality, the gentlemanly white-satin-badged ushers threw open the double doors, and the bride's procession entered. She wore a trained dress of rich white satin, with an overskirt, berthe and veil, all of duchess lace, looped, fastened and festooned here and there and everywhere with orange buds; and a magnificent set of diamonds, consisting of a coronet, necklace, ear-drops, brooch, and bracelets—too much for the little creature—lighting her up like fireworks as she passed under the blaze of the sunlit windows. She carried in her white-gloved hand a bouquet of white wood violets, with her monogram in purple violets in the center. She was leaning on the arm of her guardian, the chief justice, followed by eight bridesmaids.

The bishop, with two other clergymen, in their white vestments, entered and took their places at the altar. The choir struck up Mendelssohn's wedding march. The bride's procession came slowly up under all the floral arches of the center aisle to the floral hedge around the chancel.

The bridegroom came gayly out of the vestry room to meet her, smiling, radiant, tripping as if he had been a slim young lover of twenty, instead of a tall and heavy giant of fifty odd. He took her hand, lifted it to his lips, and led her to the altar, where both knelt. The bridesmaids grouped behind them. The best man stood on the groom's right. Old Aaron Rockharrt, Mrs. Rothsay and Cadet Haught came out of their pew and formed a group behind the bridegroom.

Mrs. Chief Justice Pendletime, and a few intimate friends, came out of her pew and grouped behind the bride and her maids.

The rest of the congregation remained in their pews, but stood up, and those in the rear raised on tiptoes and craned their necks to witness the proceedings. As soon as the bridegroom and the bride had knelt under the floral arch, from the high center of which hung a wedding bell of white wood violets, the bishop and his assistants stepped down from the high altar steps, and opened their books.

The rites commenced, and went on without any unusual disturbance of their course until they came to the question:

"Who giveth this woman to be married to this man?"

Her guardian, the chief justice, a portly, ponderous person, was moving solemnly forward to perform this duty, when—

Old Aaron Rockharrt—not from officiousness, but out of pure simple egotism—took the bride's hand and placed it in that of the groom, saying:

"I do."

You may judge the effect of this. The bride was mildly amazed; the bridegroom was deeply annoyed; the chief justice, the rightful owner of the thunder, was highly offended, and withdrew back in solemn dignity. Meanwhile the ceremony went on to its end. The benediction was pronounced, and congratulations were in order.

The marriage feast was a great success, like most other affairs of the kind. The chief justice had not got over the affront given him at the church, but he could not show resentment in his own house, and on the occasion of his young ward's wedding breakfast. As for Old Aaron Rockharrt, he had not the faintest idea that he had committed any breach of propriety. The deuce, you say! Was it not his own eldest son's wedding? Had he not a right to give away the bride? He never even asked himself the question. He took it for granted as a matter of course. Besides, was not he the greatest man present? And should not he do just as he thought fit? So in utter ignorance of any offense given to any one, the Iron King unbent his stiffness for once, and was very genial to every one, especially to the chief justice, who, secretly offended as he was, could not but respond to this friendliness.

Among the wedding guests around the board was the beautiful widow, Mrs. Bloomingfield. Mrs. Pendletime had requested Mr. Rockharrt to take her to the table, and he had offered her his arm, placing her at the board, and seated himself beside her. The Iron King looked at the lady with more interest than he would have felt had not Mr. Fabian invented a rumor to the effect that he, Aaron Rockharrt, was addressing her.

He looked at the lady on his left critically. Yes; she was very beautiful—very beautiful indeed! And, of course, she would accept him at once if he should offer her his hand! Very beautiful! A tall, finely rounded, radiant blonde, with a suit of warm auburn hair, which she wore in a mass of puffs and coils high on her head; a brilliant, blooming complexion, damask rose cheeks, redder lips, blue eyes, and a pure, fine Roman profile—that means, among the rest, a hooked nose—a very elegant and aristocratic nose indeed, but still a hooked nose. She carried her head high, and her well turned chin a little forward, her lip a little curled. All that meant a high spirit, intolerance of authority, and danger, much danger, to a would-be despot. Oh! very handsome, and very willing to marry the old millionaire. But—no! the Iron King thought not! She would give him too much trouble in the process of subjugation. He would none of her.

Cadet Haught, watching this pair from the opposite side of the table, whispered to his sister, who sat on his right:

"As I live by bread, Cora, there is the aged monarch flirting with the handsome widow! A thing unparalleled in human history. Or is it dreaming I am?"

Cora lifted her languid dark eyes, looked across the table and answered:

"She is trying to flirt with him, I rather fancy."

"Wasted ammunition, eh, Cora?"

"I do not know," replied the young lady.

And then the increasing talk and laughter all around the table rendered any tete-a-tete difficult or impossible. And now began the toast drinking and the speech making. It need not be told how Mr. Rockharrt toasted the bride, how the chief justice responded in behalf of his late ward, how Mr. Fabian toasted the bridesmaids, how Mr. Clarence responded on the part of the young ladies, how with this and that and the other observance of forms, the breakfast came to an end and the bishop gave thanks.

The bride retired to change her dress for a traveling suit of navy blue poplin, with hat and feather to match, and a cashmere wrap. Then came the leave-taking, and the jubilant bridegroom handed his bride into the elegant carriage, while his best man, Clarence, gave the last order.

"To the railway station."

This was the final farewell, for Mr. Fabian had asked as a particular favor that no one of the wedding party should attend them to the depot. Their luggage had been sent on hours before, in charge of the maid and the valet. Half an hour's drive brought them to the station in time to catch the 3:30 train East.

"At last, at last I have you away from all those people and all to myself!" exulted Fabian, as he seated his wife in the corner of the car, and turned the opposite seat that they might have no near fellow passenger. For as yet palace cars were not.

The maid and valet were seated on the opposite side of the car.

The train started.

The speed was swift, yet seemed slow. It was the way train they were on, and it stopped at every little station. They could not have got an express before midnight, and that would have been perilous to their chance of catching the steamer on which their passage to Europe was engaged.

The journey was made without events until about sunset, when the train reached the little mountain station of Edenheights, where it stopped twenty minutes for refreshments.

"What a lovely scene!" said the bride, looking down from the window on her left, into the depths of a small valley lighted up by the last rays of the setting sun streaming through the opening between two wooded hills.

"Yes, dear, lovely, if I can think anything lovely besides yourself," he replied.

"Look, what a sweet cottage that is almost hidden among the trees. An elegant cottage of white freestone built after the Grecian order. How strange, Fabian, to find such a bijou here in this wild, remote section."

"Probably the residence of some well-to-do official connected with our works," said Mr. Fabian, carelessly; then—"Will you come out to the refreshment rooms and have some tea? See, they are on the opposite side of the train."

Violet turned and looked on a very different scene. No wooded and secluded valley with its one lovely cottage, but a row of open saloons and restaurants, crowded and noisy.

"No; I think I will not go in there. It is not pretty. You may send me a cup of tea. I will sit here and enjoy this beautiful valley scene. And oh, Fabian! Look there, coming up the hillside, what a beautiful woman!"

Mr. Fabian looked out and saw and recognized Rose Stillwater and saw that she had recognized him. She was coming directly toward the train.

"Sit here, my love; I will go and bring you some refreshments. Don't attempt to get out, dearest; to do so might be dangerous. I will not be long," he said, hastily, and rising, he hurried after the other passengers out of the car.

But instead of going into the railway restaurant he went back to the rear of the train, placed himself where he stood out of sight of his wife and of all his fellow passengers, yet in full view of the approaching woman.

"What devil brings that serpent here?" he muttered to himself. "I must intercept her. She must not go on board the train. She must not approach my little wood violet. Good heavens, no!"

But the woman turned aside voluntarily from her course to the stationary train and walked directly toward himself.

"Well, Rose," he said, in as pleasant a voice as his perturbation of mind would permit him to use.

"Well, Fabian," she answered.

She was as white and hard as marble; her lips when she ceased to speak were closed tightly, her blue eyes blazed from her hard, white face.

"What brings you here?" he inquired.

"What brings me here, indeed! To see you. Only this morning I heard of your intended business. Only this morning, after the morning train had left. If there had been another train within an hour or two, I should have taken it and gone to the city and should have been in time to stop the wicked wedding."

"What a blessing that there was not! You could not have stopped the marriage. You would only have exposed yourself and made a row."

"Then I should have done that."

"I don't think so. It would not have been like you. You are too cool, too politic to ruin yourself. Come, Rose," looking at his watch, "there are but just sixteen minutes before the train starts. I have just fifteen to give you, because it will take me one minute to reach my seat. Therefore, whatever you have to say, my dear, had better be said at once."

"I have not come here to reproach you, Fabian Rockharrt," she said, fixing him with her eyes.

"That is kind of you at all events."

"No; we reproach a man for carelessness, for thoughtlessness, for forgetfulness; but for baseness, villainy, treachery like yours it is not reproach, it is—"

"Magnanimity or murder! I suppose so. Let it be magnanimity, Rose. I have never done you anything but good since I first met your face, now twenty years ago. You were but sixteen then. You are thirty-six now, and, by Jove! handsomer than ever."

"Thank you; I quite well know that I am. My looking glass, that never flatters, tells me so."

"Then why, in the name of common sense, can you not be happy? Look you, Rose, you have no cause to complain of me. When even in your childhood, you—"

"How dare you throw that up to me!" she exclaimed.

He went on as if he had not heard her.

"Were utterly lost and ruined through the villainy of your first lover— what did I do? I took you up, got a place for you in my father's house as the governess of my niece."

"Well, I worked for my living there, did I not? I gave a fair day's work for a fair day's wages, as your stony old father would say."

"Certainly, you did. But you would not have had an opportunity of doing so in any honest way if it had not been for me."

"How dare you hit me in the teeth with that!"

"Only in self-defense, my Rose."

"It was with an ulterior, a selfish, a wicked end in view. You know it."

"I know, and Heaven knows that I served you from pure benevolence and from no other motive. Gracious goodness! why, I was over head and ears in love with another woman at that time. But you, Rose, you made a dead set at me. You did not care for me the least in life, but you cared for wealth and position, and you were bound to have them if you could."

"Coward!" she hissed, "to talk to me in this way."

"I am not finding fault with you the least in the world. You acted naturally on the principles of self-interest and self-preservation. You wanted me to marry you, but I could not do that under the circumstances. By Jove! though, I did more for you than I ever did for any other living woman and with less reward—with no reward at all, in fact. When your time was up at Rockhold I settled an income on you, and afterward, in addition to that, I gave you that beautiful cottage, elegantly furnished from basement to roof. And what did I ever get in return for all that? Flatteries and fair words— nothing more. You were as cold as a stone, Rose."

"I would not give my love upon any promise of marriage, but only for marriage itself."

"And that you know I could not offer you, and you also knew why I could not."

"Poltroon! to reproach me with the great calamity of my childhood."

"I repeat that I do not reproach you at all. I am only stating the facts, for which I do not blame you in the least, though they prevented the possibility of my ever thinking of marriage with you. I gave you a house furnished, land, and an income to insure you the comforts, luxuries, and elegances of life. I did not bargain with you beforehand. I thought surely you would, as you led me to believe that you would, give me love in return for all these. But no. As soon as you were secure in your possessions you turned upon me and said that I should not even visit you at your house without marriage. Now, what have you to complain of?"

"This! that you have broken faith with me!"

"In what way, pray you?"

"You swore that, if you did not marry me, no more would you ever marry any woman."

"If you would love me. Not if you would not. Besides, I had not seen my sweet wood violet then," he added, aggravatingly.

She turned upon him, her eyes flashing blue fire.

"I will be revenged!" she said.

"Be anything you like, my dear, only do not be melodramatic. It's bad form. Come, now, Rose, you have your house and your income. You are still young, and much handsomer than ever. Be happy, my dear. And now I really must leave you and run to the train."

"Go. I will not detain you. I came here only to tell you that I will be revenged. I have told you that and have no more to say."

She turned and went down the hill toward the cottage in the dell.

Mr. Fabian hurried to the train and sprang on board just as it began to move.

"Fabian! Oh, Fabian!" cried the alarmed bride, "you were almost knocked under the wheels!"

"All right, my dear little love. I am safe now," he laughed.

"Where is my tea?"

"Oh, my dear child," exclaimed the conscience-stricken man. "I am so very sorry! But the tea was detestable—perfectly detestable! I could not bring you such stuff. I am so very sorry, Violet, my precious."

"Well, never mind. Bring me a glass of ice water from the cooler."

He obeyed her, and when she had drank, took back the tumbler.

A porter came along and lighted the lamps in the cars, for it was now fast growing dark.

The train sped on.

Our travelers reached Baltimore late at night, changed cars at midnight for New York, and reached that city the next morning in time to secure the passage they had engaged.

At noon they sailed in the Arctic for Liverpool.

CHAPTER XI
THE WILES OF THE SIREN

When the bridal pair had started on their journey the wedding guests dispersed.

Old Aaron Rockharrt and his family returned to their town house.

The next morning Mr. Clarence went back to North End to look after the works. Cadet Haught left for West Point.

Mr. Rockharrt and Mrs. Rothsay were alone in their city home.

Old Aaron Rockharrt continued to give dinners and suppers to noted politicians until the end of the session and the adjournment of the legislature.

The family returned to Rockhold in May. Here they lived a very monotonous life, whose dullness and gloom pressed very heavily upon the young widow.

Mr. Rockharrt and Mr. Clarence rode out every day to the works and returned late in the afternoon.

Cora occupied herself in completing the biography of her late husband, which had been interrupted by the season in the city.

Mr. Clarence often spent twenty-four hours at North End looking after the interests of the firm, and eating and sleeping at the hotel.

Mr. Rockharrt came home every evening to dinner, but after dinner invariably shut himself up in his office and remained there until bedtime.

Cora's evenings were as solitary as her mornings. But a change was at hand.

One evening, on his return home, Mr. Rockharrt brought his own mail from the post office at North End.

After dinner, instead of retiring to his office as usual, he came into the drawing room and found Cora.

Dropping himself down in a large arm chair beside the round table, and drawing the moderator lamp nearer to him, he drew a letter from his breast pocket and said:

"My dear, I have a very interesting communication here from Mrs. Stillwater—Miss Rose Flowers that was, you know."

"I know," said Cora, coldly, and wondering what was coming next.

"Poor child! She is a widow, thrown destitute upon the cold charities of the world again," he continued.

Cora said nothing. She was marveling to hear this harsh, cruel, relentless man speaking with so much pity, tenderness, and consideration for this adventuress.

"But I will read the letter to you," he said, "and then I will tell you what I mean to do."

"Very well, sir," she replied, with much misgiving.

He opened the letter and began to read as follows:

Wirt House, Baltimore, MD.,
May 15, 18—

My Most Honored Benefactor: I should not presume to recall myself to your recollection had you not, in the large bounty of your heart, once taken pity on the forlorn creature that I am, and made me promise that if ever I should find myself homeless, friendless, destitute, and desolate, I should write and inform you.

My most revered friend, such is my sad, hopeless, pitiable condition now.

My poor husband died of yellow fever in the West Indies about a year ago, and his income and my support died with him.

For the last twelve months I have lived on the sale of my few jewels, plate, and other personal property, which has gradually melted away in the furnace of my misfortunes, while I have been trying with all my might to obtain employment at my sometime trade as teacher. But, oh, sir! the requirements of modern education are far above my poor capabilities.

Now, at length, when my resources are well nigh exhausted — now, when I can pay my board here only for a few weeks longer, and at the end of that time must go forth—Heaven only knows where!—I venture, in accordance with your own gracious permission, to make this appeal to you! Not for pecuniary aid, which you will pardon me if I say I could not receive from any one, but for such advice and assistance as your wisdom and benevolence could afford me, in finding me some honest way of earning my bread. Feeling assured that your great goodness will not cast this poor note aside unnoticed, I shall wait and hope to hear from you, and, in the meanwhile, remain,

Your humble and obedient servant,
Rose Stillwater.

"That is what I call a very pathetic appeal, Cora. She is a widow, poor child! Not such a widow as you are, Cora Rothsay, with wealth, friends, and position! She is a widow, indeed! Homeless, friendless, penniless—about to be cast forth into the streets! My dear, I got this letter this morning. I answered it within an hour after its reception! I invited her to come here as our guest, immediately, and to remain as long as she should feel inclined to stay—certainly until we could settle upon some plan of life for her future. I sent a check to pay her traveling expenses to North End, where I shall send the carriage to meet her. You will, therefore, Cora, have a comfortable room prepared for Mrs. Stillwater. I think she may be with us as early as to-morrow evening," said the Iron King.

And he arose and strode out of the parlor, leaving his granddaughter confounded.

Rose Stillwater the widow of a year's standing! Rose Stillwater coming to Rockhold as the guest of her aged and widowed grandfather! What a condition of things! What would be the outcome of this event? Cora shrank from conjecturing.

She felt that there had been two factors in bringing about the situation: first, the death of her grandmother; second, the marriage of her Uncle Fabian. The field was thus left open for the operations of this scheming adventuress and siren.

Cora had been so dismayed at the communication of her grandfather that she had scarcely answered him with a word. But he had been too deeply absorbed in his own thoughts and plans to notice her silence and reserve.

He had expressed his wishes, given his orders, and gone out. That was all.

What could Cora do?

Nothing at all. Too well she knew the unbending nature of the Iron King to delude herself for a moment with the idea that any opposition, argument, or expostulation from her would have so much as a feather's weight with the despotic old man.

If he had asked Mrs. Stillwater to Rockhold under present circumstances, Mrs. Stillwater would come, and he would have her there just as long as he pleased.

Cora was at her wits' end. She resolved to write at once to her Uncle Fabian. Surely he must know the true character of this woman, and he must have broken off his very questionable acquaintance with her before marrying Violet Wood. Surely he would not allow his father to be so dangerously deceived in the person he had invited to his house—to the society of his granddaughter. He would unmask her, even though in doing so he should expose himself.

She would also write to Sylvan, who from the very first had disliked and distrusted "the rose that all admire." And she thanked Heaven that Cadet Haught would graduate at the next exhibition at West Point and come home on leave for the midsummer holidays.

While waiting answers from the two absent men she would consult her Uncle Clarence. Truth to tell, she had but little hope of help in this affair from her younger uncle. Mr. Clarence was so far from thinking evil of any one. He was so loath to give pain or have any disturbance in the domestic circle. He would be sure to feel compassion for Rose Stillwater. He would be sure to recall her pretty, helpful, pleasant ways, and the comfort both his father and his mother used to take in her playful manners and affectionate ministration. Mr. Clarence was much too benevolent to wish to interfere with any arrangement that was likely to make the house pleasant and cheerful to his aged father, and give a comfortable home and support to a desolate young widow. And that the Iron King should ever be seriously taken in by the beautiful and bewitching creature he would never believe. Yet Cora knew from all past experience that Rose Stillwater was more esteemed by old Aaron Rockharrt and had more influence over him than any living creature. Strange that a man so hard headed as the Iron King, and so clear brained on all occasions when not blinded by his egotism, should allow himself to be so deceived in any one as he was in Rose Stillwater.

But, then, she knew how to flatter this egotism. She was beautiful and attractive in person, meek and submissive in manner, complimentary and caressing in words and tones.

Cora asked herself whether it would be right, proper, or expedient for her to give information of that secret interview between Mr. Fabian and Mrs.

Stillwater, to which she herself had been an accidental and most unwilling witness, on that warm night in September, in the hotel parlor at Baltimore.

She could not refer to it in her intended letter to her Uncle Fabian. To do so would be useless and humiliating, if not very offensive. Her Uncle Fabian knew much more about that interview than she could tell him, and would be very much mortified and very indignant to learn that she knew anything of it. He might accuse her of being a spy and an eavesdropper, or he might deny and discredit her story altogether.

No. No good could come of referring to that interview in her letter to her Uncle Fabian. She would merely mention to him the fact that Mrs. Stillwater had written to Mr. Rockharrt an appealing letter declaring herself to be widowed and destitute, and asking for advice and assistance in procuring employment; and that he had replied by inviting her to Rockhold for an indefinite period, and sent her a check to pay her traveling expenses. She would tell Mr. Fabian this as a mere item of news, expressing no opinion and taking no responsibility, but leaving her uncle to act as he might think proper.

She could not tell her brother Sylvan of that secret interview, for she was sure that he would act with haste and indiscretion. Nor could she tell her Uncle Clarence, who would only find himself distressed and incapable under the emergency. Least of all could she tell her grandfather, and make an everlasting breach between himself and his son Fabian.

No. She could tell no one of that secret interview to which she had been a chance witness—a shocked witness—but which she only half understood, and which, perhaps, did not mean all that she had feared and suspected. On that subject she must hold her peace, and only let the absent members of the family know of Mrs. Stillwater's intended visit as an item of domestic news, and leave any or all of them to act upon their own responsibility unbiased by any word from her.

Cora's position was a very delicate and embarrassing one. She did not believe that this former nursery governess of hers was or ever had been a proper companion for her. She herself—Cora Rothsay—was now a widow with an independent income, and was at liberty to choose her own companions and make her home wherever she might choose.

But how could she leave her aged and widowed grandfather, who had no other daughter or granddaughter, or any other woman relative to keep house for him? And yet how could she associate daily with a woman whose presence she felt to be a degradation?

As we have seen, she knew and felt that it would be vain to oppose her grandfather's wish to have Mrs. Stillwater in the house, especially as he had already invited her and sent her the money to come—unless she should tell him of that secret interview she had witnessed between Mr. Fabian and Mrs. Stillwater. That, indeed, might banish Rose from Rockhold, but it would also bring down a domestic cataclysm that must break up the household and separate its members.

No, she could say nothing, do nothing that would not make matters worse. She must let events take their course, bide her time and hope for the best, she said to herself, as she arose and rang the bell.

John, the footman, answered the call.

"It is Martha whom I want. Send her here," said the lady.

The man went out and the upper housemaid came in.

"You wanted me, ma'am?"

"Yes. Do you remember the room occupied by my nursery governess years ago?"

"Yes, ma'am; the front room on the left side of the hall on the third story."

"Yes; that is the room. Have it prepared for the same person. She will be here to-morrow evening."

"Good—Lord!" involuntarily exclaimed old Martha; "why, we haven't heard of her for a dozen years. What a sweet creeter she was, though, Miss Cora. I thought as she'd a married a fortin' long ago."

"She has been married and widowed. At least she says so."

"A widow, poor thing! And is she comin' to be a companion or anything?"

"She is coming as a guest."

"Oh! very well, Miss Cora; I will have the room ready in time."

When the old woman had left the room Cora sat down to her writing desk and wrote two letters—one to Mr. Fabian Rockharrt, Hotel Trois Freres, Paris; the other to Cadet Sylvanus Haught, West Point, N.Y.

When she had finished and sealed these she put them in the mail bag that was left in the hall to be taken at daybreak by the groom to North End post office. Then she retired to rest.

The next morning she breakfasted tete-a-tete with her grandfather, Mr. Clarence having remained over night at North End. While they were still at the table the man John entered with a telegram, which he laid on the table before his master.

"Who brought this?" inquired the Iron King, as he opened it.

"Joseph brought it when he came back from the post office. It had just come, and Mr. Clarence gave it to Joseph to fetch to you, sir. Yes, sir!" replied John.

"It is from Mrs. Stillwater. That lady is a perfect model of promptitude and punctuality. She says—but I had better read it to you. John, you need not wait," said Mr. Rockharrt.

The negro, who had lingered from curiosity to hear what was in the telegram, immediately retired.

Old Aaron Rockharrt took up the long slip, adjusted his spectacles and read:

Wirt House, Baltimore, Md., May 16th, 18—

A thousand heartfelt thanks for your princely munificence and hospitality. I avail myself of both gladly and at once. I shall leave Baltimore by the 8:30 a.m., and arrive at the North End Station at 6:30 p.m.

"That is her message. Now I wish you to have everything in readiness for her. I shall go in person to the depot and bring her home with me when I return in the evening. Of course it will be two hours later than usual when I get back here. You will, therefore, have the dinner put back until nine o'clock on this occasion."

Cora bowed. She could scarcely trust her voice to answer in words.

Mr. Rockharrt, absorbed in his own thoughts and plans, never noticed her coldness and silence. He soon finished breakfast, left the table, and a few minutes later entered his carriage to drive to North End.

"'Pears to me old marse is jes' wonderful, Miss Cora. To go to his business every day like clock work, and he 'bout seventy-seven years old. And jes' as straight and strong as a pine tree! Yes, and as hard as a pine knot! He's wonderful, that he is!" said old Jason, the gray haired negro butler, when he came in from seeing his master off and began to clear away the breakfast service.

"Yes; your master is a fine, strong man, Jason—physically," replied Cora, who was beginning to doubt the mental soundness of her grandfather!

"Physicking! No, indeed! 'Tain't that as makes the old g'eman so strong. He nebber would take no physic in all his life. It's consternation, that's w'at it is—his good, healthy consternation!"

"Very likely!" replied Cora, who was too much disturbed to set the old man right.

She left the breakfast parlor, and went up stairs to superintend in person the preparation for the comfort of the expected guest.

CHAPTER XII
THE SIREN AND THE DESPOT

That May night was clear and cool. The sky was brilliant with stars, sparkling and flashing from the pure, dark blue empyrean.

In the house it was chilly, so Cora had caused fires to be built in all the grates.

The drawing room at Rockhold presented a very attractive appearance, with its three chandeliers of lighted wax candles, its cheerful fire of sea coal, its warm crimson and gold coloring of carpets and curtains, and its luxurious easy chairs, sofas and ottomans, its choice pictures, books, bronzes and so forth. In the small dining room the table was set for dinner, in the best spare room all was prepared for its expected occupant.

Cora, in her widow's cap and dress, sat in an arm chair before the drawing room fire, awaiting the arrival. Half past eight had been the hour named by her grandfather for their coming. But a few minutes after the clock had struck, the sound of carriage wheels was heard on the avenue approaching the house.

Old Jason opened the hall door just as the vehicle drew up and stopped.

Mr. Rockharrt alighted and then gave his hand to his companion, who tripped lightly to the pavement, and let him lead her up stairs and into the house. Cora stood at the door of the drawing room. Mr. Rockharrt led his visitor up to his granddaughter, and said:

"Mrs. Stillwater is very much fatigued, Cora. Take her at once to her room and make her comfortable; and have dinner on the table by the time she is ready to come down."

He uttered these words in a peremptory manner, without waiting for the usual greeting that should have passed between the hostess and the visitor.

Cora touched a bell.

"Oh! let me embrace my sweet Cora first of all! Ah! my sweet child! You and I both widowed since the last time we met!" cooed Rose, in her most dulcet tones, as she drew Cora to her bosom and kissed her before the latter could draw back.

"How do you do?" was the formal greeting that fell from the lady's lips.

"As you see, dearest—'Not happy, but resigned,'" plaintively replied the widow.

"You quote from a king's minion, I think," said Cora, coldly.

Rose took no notice of the criticism, but tenderly inquired.

"And you, dearest one? How is it with you?"

"I am very well, thank you," replied the lady.

"After such a terrible trial! But you always possessed a heroic spirit."

"We will not speak of that, Mrs. Stillwater, if you please," was the grave reply.

Mr. Rockharrt looked around, as well as he could while old Jason was drawing off his spring overcoat, and said:

"Take Mrs. Stillwater to her room, Cora. Don't keep her standing here."

"I have rung for a servant, who will attend to Mrs. Stillwater's needs," replied the lady, quietly.

The Iron King turned and stared at his granddaughter angrily, but said nothing.

The housemaid came up at this moment.

"Martha, show Mrs. Stillwater to the chamber prepared for her, and wait her orders there."

The negro woman wiped her clean hand on her clean apron—as a mere useless form—and then held it out to the visitor, saying, with the scorn of conventionality and the freedom of an old family servant:

"How do Miss Rose! 'Deed I's mighty proud to see you ag'in—'deed I is! How much you has growed! I mean, how han'some you has growed! You allers was han'some, but now you's han'somer'n ever! 'Deed, honey, you's mons'ous han'some!"

This hearty welcome and warm admiration, though only from the negro servant, helped to relieve the embarrassment of the visitor, who felt the chill of Cora's cold reception.

"Thank you, Aunt Martha," she said, and followed the woman up stairs.

"Why did you not attend Mrs. Stillwater to her room?" sternly demanded the Iron King, fixing his eyes severely on his granddaughter, as soon as the visitor was out of hearing.

"It is not usual to do anything of the sort, sir, except in the case of the guest being a very distinguished person or a very dear friend. My ex-governess is neither. She shall, however, be treated with all due respect by me so long as she remains under your roof," quietly replied Cora.

"You had best see to it that she is," retorted the Iron King, as he stalked up stairs to his own room, followed by his valet.

Cora returned to the drawing room, and seated herself in her arm chair, and put her feet upon her foot-stool, and leaned back, to appearance quite composed, but in reality very much perturbed. Had she acted well in her manner to her grandfather's guest? She did not know. She could not, therefore, feel at ease. She certainly did not treat Mrs. Stillwater with rudeness or hauteur; she was quite incapable of doing so; yet, on the other hand, neither had she treated her ex-governess with kindness or courtesy. She had been calm and cold in her reception of the visitor; that was all. But was she right? After all, she knew no positive evil of the woman. She had only strong circumstantial evidence of her unworthiness. She recalled an old saying of her father's:

"Better trust a hundred rogues than distrust one honest man."

Yet all Cora's instincts warned her not to trust Rose Stillwater.

After all, she could do nothing—at least at present. She would wait the developments of time, and then, perhaps, be able to see her duty more clearly. Meanwhile, for family peace and good feeling, she would be civil to Rose Stillwater. Half an hour passed, and her meditations were interrupted by the entrance of the guest. Mrs. Stillwater seemed determined not to understand coldness or to take offense. She came in, drew her chair to the fire, and spread out her pretty hands over its glow, cooing her delight to be with dear friends again.

"Oh, darling Cora," she purred, "you do not know—you cannot even fancy—the ineffable sense of repose I feel in being here, after all the turbulence of the past year. You read my letter to your dearest grandfather?"

"Yes," answered Mrs. Rothsay.

"From that you must have seen to what straits I was reduced. Think! After having sold everything I possessed in the world—even all my clothing, except two changes for necessary cleanliness—to pay my board; after trying in every direction to get honest work to do; I was in daily fear of being told to leave the hotel because I could not pay my board."

"That was very sad! but was it not very expensive—for you—living at the Wirt House? Would it not have been better, under your circumstances, to have taken cheaper board?"

"Perhaps so, dear; but Captain Stillwater had always made his home at the Wirt House when his ship was in port, and had always left me there when his ship sailed, so that I felt at home in the house, you see."

"Yes, I see," said Mrs. Rothsay.

"Oh, my fondly cherished darling—you, loved, sheltered, caressed—you, rich, admired, and flattered—cannot understand or appreciate the trials and sufferings of a poor woman in my position and circumstances. Think, darling, of my condition in that city, where I was homeless, friendless, penniless, in daily fear of being sent from the house for inability to pay my board!"

"I am sorry to hear all this," said Cora. And then she was prompted to add: "But where was Mr. Fabian Rockharrt? He was your earliest friend. He first introduced you to my grandfather. He never lost sight of you after you left us, but corresponded with you frequently, and gave us news of you from time to time. Surely, Mrs. Stillwater, had he known your straits, he would have found some way of setting you up in some business. He never would have allowed you to suffer privation and anxiety for a whole year."

While Cora spoke she fixed her eyes on the face of her listener. But Rose Stillwater was always perfect mistress of herself. Without the slightest change in countenance or voice, she answered sweetly:

"Why, dear love, of course I did write to Mr. Fabian first of all, and told him of the death of my dear husband, and asked him if he could help me to get another situation as primary teacher in a school or as a nursery governess."

"And he did not respond?"

"Oh, yes; indeed he did. He replied very promptly, writing that he had a situation in view for me which would be better suited to my needs than any I had ever filled, and that he should come to Baltimore to explain and consult with me."

"Well?"

"The next day, dear, he came, and—I hate to betray his confidence and tell you."

"Then do not, I beg you."

"But—I hate more to keep a secret from you. In short, he asked me to marry him."

"What!" exclaimed Cora, in surprise and incredulity.

"Yes, my love; that was what he had to explain. The position of his wife was the situation he had to offer me, and which he thought would suit me better than any other I had ever filled."

"When was this proposal made?"

"About five months ago, and about seven months after the death of my dear husband. He said that he would be willing to wait until the year of mourning should be over."

"Oh, that was considerate of him."

"But I was still heart-broken for the loss of my dear husband. I could not think of another marriage at any time, however distant. I told him so. I told him how much I esteemed and respected him and even loved him as a dear friend, but that I could not be faithless to the memory of my adored husband. I was very sorry; for he was very angry. He called me cold, silly and even ungrateful, so to reject his hand. I began to think that it was selfish and thankless in me to disappoint so good a friend, but I could not help it, loving the memory of my sainted husband as I did. I was grieved to hurt Mr. Fabian, though."

"I do not think he was seriously injured. At least I am sure that his wounds healed rapidly; for in a very few weeks afterward he proposed to Miss Violet Wood, and was accepted by her. They were married on the fourteenth day of February, and sailed for Europe the next day," said Mrs. Rothsay.

"Yes; I know. Disappointed men do such desperate deeds; commit suicide or marry for revenge. Poor, dear girl!" murmured Rose Stillwater, with a deep sigh.

"Why poor, dear girl?" inquired Cora.

"Oh, you know, she caught his heart in the rebound, and she will not keep it. But let us talk of something else, dear. Oh, I am so happy here. So free from fear and trouble and anxiety. Oh, what ineffable peace, rest, safety I enjoy here. No one will pain me by presenting a bill that I cannot pay, or frighten me by telling me that my room will be wanted for some one else. Oh, how I thank you, Cora. And how I thank your honored grandfather for this city of refuge, even for a few days."

"You owe no thanks to me," replied Cora.

"A thousand thanks, my darling!" said Rose, and hearing the heavy footsteps of the Iron King in the hail, she added—as if she heard them not: "And as for Mr. Rockharrt, that noble, large brained, great hearted man, I have no words to express the gratitude, the reverence, the adoration with which his magnanimous character and munificent benevolence inspires me. He is of all men the most—"

But here she seemed first to have caught sight of the Iron King, who was standing in the door, and who had heard every word of adulation that she had spoken.

"Cora, is not dinner ready?" he inquired, coming forward.

"Yes, sir; only waiting for you," answered the lady, touching a bell.

The gray haired butler came to the call.

"Put dinner on the table," ordered Mr. Rockharrt.

The old butler bowed and disappeared; and after awhile reappeared and announced:

"Dinner served, sir."

Mr. Rockharrt gave his arm to Mrs. Stillwater, to take her to the table.

"Will not my Uncle Clarence be home this evening?" inquired Cora, as the three took their seats.

"No; he will not be home before Saturday night. Since Fabian went away there has been twice as much supervision over the foremen and bookkeepers needed there, and Clarence is very busy over the accounts, working night and day," replied the Iron King, as he took a plate of soup from the hands of the butler and passed it to Mrs. Stillwater, who received it with the beaming smile that she always bestowed on the Iron King.

She was the life of the little party. If she was a broken hearted widow, she did not show it there. She smiled, gleamed, glowed, sparkled in countenance and words. The moody Iron King was cheered and exhilarated, and said, as he filled her glass for the first time with Tokay, "Though you do not need wine to stimulate you, my child. You are full of joyous life and spirits."

"Oh, sir, pardon me. Perhaps I ought to control myself; but I am so happy to be here through your great goodness; so free from care and fear; so full of peace and joy; so safe, so sheltered! I feel like a storm beaten bird who has found a nest, or a lost child who has found a home, and I forget all my losses and all my sorrows and give myself up to delight. Pardon me, sir; I know I ought to be calmer."

"Not at all, not at all, my child! I am glad to see you so gay. I approve of you. You have suffered more than either of us, for you have not only lost your life's companion, but home, fortune, and all your living. My granddaughter here, as you may see, is a monument of morbid, selfish sorrow, which she will not try to throw off even for my sake. But you will brighten us all."

"I wish I might; oh, how I wish I might! It seems to me it is easy to be happy if one has only a safe home and a good friend," said Rose.

"And those you shall always have in me and in my house, my child," said the Iron King.

Cora listened in pure amazement. Her grandfather sympathetic! Her grandfather giving praise and quoting poetry! What was the matter with him? Not softening of the heart; he had never possessed such a commodity. Was it softening of the brain, then? As soon as they had finished dinner and returned to the drawing room, the Iron King said to his guest:

"Now, my child, I shall send you off to bed. You have had a very long and fatiguing journey and must have a good, long night's sleep."

And with his own hands he lighted a wax taper and gave it to her. Rose received it with a grateful smile, bade a sweet toned good night to Mr. Rockharrt and Mrs. Rothsay, and went tripping out of the room.

"I shall say good night, too, Cora; I am tired. But let me say this before I go: Do you try to take pattern by that admirable child. See how she tries to make the best of everything and to be pleasant under all her sorrows. You have not had half her troubles, and yet you will not try to get over your own. Imitate that poor child, Cora."

"'Child,' my dear grandfather! Do you forget that Mrs. Stillwater is a widow thirty-six years old?" inquired Cora.

"'Thirty-six.' I had not thought of it, and yet of course I knew it. Well, so much the better. Yet child she is compared to me, and child she is in her perfect trust, her innocent faith, her meekness, candor and simplicity, and the delightful abandon with which she gives herself to the enjoyment of the passing hour. This will be a brighter house for the presence of Rose Stillwater in it," said the Iron King, as he took up his taper and rang for his valet and left the room.

Cora sat a long time in meditation before she arose and followed his example. When she entered her chamber, she was surprised and annoyed to find Rose Stillwater there, seated in the arm chair before the fire. Old Martha was turning down the bed for the night.

"Cora, love, it is not yet eleven o'clock, though the dear master did send us off to bed. But I wanted to speak to you, darling Cora, just a few words, dear, before we part for the night; so when I met my old friend, Aunt Martha, in the hall, I asked her to show me which was your room, so I could come to you when you should come up; but Aunt Martha told me she was on the way to your room to prepare your bed for the night, and she would bring me here to sit down and wait for you. So here I am, dear Cora."

"You wished to speak to me, you say?" inquired Mrs. Rothsay, drawing another chair and seating herself before the fire.

"Yes, darling; only to say this, love, that I have not come here to sponge upon your kindness. I will be no drone. I wish to be useful to you, Cora. Now you are far away from all milliners and dress makers and seamstresses, and I am very skillful with my needle and can do everything you might wish to have done in that line—I mean in the way of trimming and altering bonnets or dresses. I do not think I could cut and fit."

"Mrs. Stillwater," interrupted Cora, "you are our guest, and you must not think of such a plan as you suggest."

"Oh, my dear Cora, do not speak to me as if I were only company. I, your old governess! Do not make a stranger of me. Let me be as one of the family. Let me be useful to you and to your dear grandfather. Then I shall feel at home; then I shall be happy," pleaded Rose.

"But, Mrs. Stillwater, we have not been accustomed to set our guests to work. The idea is preposterous," said the inexorable Cora.

"Oh, my dear, do not treat me as a guest. Treat me as you did when I was your governess. Make me useful; will you not, dear Cora?"

"You are very kind, but I would rather not trouble you."

"Ah, I see; you are tired and sleepy. I will not keep you up, but I must make myself useful to you in some way. Well, good night, dear," said the widow, as she stooped and kissed her hostess. Then she left the room.

CHAPTER XIII
THE SPELL WORKS

Rose Stillwater was very near overdoing her part. She rose early the next morning and came down in the drawing room before any of the family had put in an appearance. She had scarcely seated herself before the bright little sea coal fire that the chilly spring morning rendered very acceptable, if not really necessary, when she heard the heavy, measured footsteps of the master of the house coming down the stairs. Then she rose impulsively as if in a flutter of delight to go and meet him; but checked herself and sat down and waited for him to come in.

"How heavily the old ogre walks! His step would shake the house, if it could be shaken. He comes like the statue of the commander in the opera."

She listened, but his footsteps died away on the soft, deep carpet of the library into which he passed.

"Ah! he does not know that I am down!" she said to herself, complacently, as she settled back in her chair. Cora came in and greeted Rose with ceremonious politeness, having resolved, at length, to treat Mrs. Stillwater as an honored guest, not as a cherished friend or member of the household.

"Good morning, Mrs. Stillwater. I hope you have had a good night's rest and feel refreshed after your journey," she said.

Rose responded effusively:

"Ah, good morning, dear love! Yes; thank you, darling, a lovely night's rest, undisturbed by the thoughts of debts and duns and a doubtful future. I slept so deeply and sweetly through the night that I woke quite early this morning. The birds were in full song. You must have millions of birds here! And the subtile, penetrating fragrance of the hyacinths came into the window as soon as I opened it. How I love the early spring flowers that come to us almost through the winter snows and before we have done with fires."

Cora did not reply to this rhapsody. Then Rose inquired:

"Does your grandfather go regularly to look after the works as he used to do?"

"Mr. Rockharrt drives to North End every day," replied Cora.

"It is amazing, at his age," said Rose.

"Some acute observer has said that 'age is a movable feast.' Age, no more than death, is a respecter of persons or of periods. Men grow old, as they die, at any age. Some grow old at fifty, others not before they are a hundred. I think Mr. Rockharrt belongs to the latter class."

"I am sure he does."

Cora did not confirm this statement.

Rose made another venture in conversation:

"So both the gentlemen go every day to the works?"

"Mr. Rockharrt goes every day. Mr. Clarence usually remains there from Monday morning until Saturday evening."

"At the works?"

"Yes; or at the hotel, where he has a suite of rooms which he occupies occasionally."

"Dear me! So you have been alone here all day long, every day but Sunday! And now I have come to keep you company, darling! You shall not feel lonely any longer. And—what was that Mary Queen of Scots said to her lady hostess on the night she passed at the castle in her sad progress from one prison to another:

"'We two widows, having no husbands to trouble us, may agree very well,' or words to that effect. So, darling, you and I, having no husbands to trouble us, may also agree very well. Shall we not?"

"I cannot speak so lightly on so grave a subject, Mrs. Stillwater," said Cora.

Old Mr. Rockharrt came in.

"Good morning, Cora! Good morning, Mrs. Stillwater! I hope you feel quite rested from your journey."

"Oh, quite, thank you! And when I woke up this morning, I was so surprised and delighted to find myself safe at home! Ah! I beg pardon! But I spent so many years in this dear old house, the happiest years of my life, that I always think of it as home, the only home I ever had in all my life," said Rose, pathetically, while tears glistened in her soft blue eyes.

"You poor child! Well, there is no reason why you should ever leave this haven again. My granddaughter needs just such a bright companion as you are sure to be. And who so fitting a one as her first young governess?"

"Oh, sir, you are so good to me! May heaven reward you! But Mrs. Rothsay?" she said, with an appealing glance toward Cora.

"I do not need a companion; if I did, I should advertise for one. The position of companion is also a half menial one, which I should never associate with the name of Mrs. Stillwater, who is our guest," replied Cora, with cold politeness.

"You see, my dear ex-pupil will not let me serve her in any capacity," said Rose, with a piteous glance toward the Iron King.

"You have both misunderstood me," he answered, with a severe glance toward his granddaughter, "I never thought of you as a companion to Mrs. Rothsay, in the professional sense of that word, but in the sense in which daughters of the same house are companions to each other."

"I should not shrink from any service to my dear Cora," said Rose Stillwater, and she was about to add—"nor to you, sir," but she thought it best not to say it, and refrained.

When breakfast was over, and the Rockhold carriage was at the door to convey the Iron King to North End, the old autocrat arose from the table and strode into the hall, calling for his valet to come and help him on with his light overcoat.

"Let me! let me! Oh, do please let me?" exclaimed Rose, jumping up and following him. "Do you remember the last time I put on your overcoat? It was on that morning in Baltimore, years ago, when we parted at the Monument House; you to go to the depot to take the cars for this place, I to remain in the city to await the arrival of my husband's ship? Nine years ago! There, now! Have I not done it as well as your valet could?" she prattled, as she deftly assisted him.

"Better, my child, much better! You are not rough; your hands are dainty as well as strong. Thank you, child," said Mr. Rockharrt, settling himself with a jerk or two into his spring overcoat.

"Oh, do let me perform these little services for you always! It will make me feel so happy!"

"But it will give you trouble."

"Oh, indeed, no! not the least! It will give me only pleasure."

"You are a very good child, but I will not tax you. Good morning! I must be off," said Mr. Rockharrt, shaking hands with Rose, and then hurrying out to get into his carriage.

Rose stood in the door looking after him, until the brougham rolled away out of sight.

At luncheon Rose Stillwater seemed so determined to be pleasant that it was next to impossible for Cora Rothsay to keep up the formal demeanor she had laid out for herself.

"It is very lonely for you here, my dear. How soon does your grandfather usually return? I know he must have been later than usual last night, because he had to go to the depot to meet me," Rose said.

"Mr. Rockharrt usually returns at six o'clock. We have dinner at half-past," replied Cora.

"And this is two! Four hours and a half yet!"

"The afternoon is very fine. Will you take a walk with me in the garden?" inquired Cora, as they left the dining room, feeling some compunction for the persistent coldness with which she had treated her most gentle and obliging guest.

"Oh, thank you very much, dear. With the greatest pleasure! It will be just like old times, when we used to walk in the garden together, you a little child holding on to my hand. And now—But we won't talk of that," said Rose.

And she fled up stairs to get her hat and shawl.

And the two women sauntered for half an hour among the early roses and spring flowers in the beautiful Rockhold garden.

Then they came in and went to the library together and looked over the new magazines. Presently Cora said:

"We all use the library in common to write our letters in. If you have letters to write, you will find every convenience in either of those side tables at the windows."

"Yes. Just as it used to be in the old times when I was so happy here! When the dear old lady was here! Ah, me! But I will not think of that. She is in heaven, as sure as there is a heaven for angels such as she, and we must not grieve for the sainted ones. But I have no letters to write, dear. I have no correspondents in all the world. Indeed, dear Cora, I have no friend in the world outside of this house," said Rose, with a little sigh that touched Cora's heart, compelling her to sympathize with this lonely creature, even against her better judgment.

"Is not Mr. Fabian friendly toward you?" inquired Cora, from mixed motives—of half pity, half irony.

"Fabian?" sweetly replied Rose. "No, dear. I lost the friendship of Mr. Fabian Rockharrt when I declined his offer of marriage. You refuse a man, and so wound his vanity; and though you may never have given him the least encouragement to propose to you, and though he has not the shadow of a reason to believe that you will accept yet will he take great offense, and perhaps become your mortal enemy," sighed Rose.

"But I think Uncle Fabian is too good natured for that sort of malice."

"I don't know, dear. I have never seen him since he left me in anger on the day I begged off from marrying him. Really, darling, it was more like begging off than refusing."

But little more was said on the subject, and presently afterward the two went up stairs to dress for dinner.

Punctually at six o'clock Mr. Rockharrt returned. And the evening passed as on the preceding day, with this addition to its attractions: Mrs. Stillwater went to the piano and played and sang many of Mr. Rockharrt's favorite songs—the old fashioned songs of his youth—Tom Moore's Irish melodies, Robert Burns' Scotch ballads, and a miscellaneous assortment of English ditties—all of which were before Rose's time, but which she had learned from old Mrs. Rockharrt's ancient music books during her first residence at Rockhold, that she might please the Iron King by singing them.

Surely the siren left nothing untried to please her patron and benefactor.

When he complained of fatigue and bade the two women good night, she started and lighted his wax candle and gave it to him. The next day she was on hand to help him on with his great coat, and to hand him his gloves and hat, and he thanked her with a smile.

So went on life at Rockhold all the week.

On Saturday evening Mr. Clarence came home with his father and greeted Rose Stillwater with the kindly courtesy that was habitual with him.

There were four at the dinner table. And Rose, having so excellent a coadjutor in the younger Rockharrt, was even gayer and more chatty than ever, making the meal a lively and cheerful one even for moody Aaron Rockharrt and sorrowful Cora Rothsay.

After dinner, when the party had gone into the drawing room, Mrs. Stillwater said:

"Here are just four of us. Just enough for a game at whist. Shall we have a rubber, Mr. Rockharrt?"

"Yes, my child! Certainly, with all my heart! I thank you for the suggestion! I have not had a game of whist since we left the city. Ah, my child, we have had very stupid evenings here at home until you came and brought some life into the house. Clarence, draw out the card table. Cora, go and find the cards."

"Let me! Let me! Please let me!" exclaimed Rose, starting up with childish eagerness. "Where are the cards, Cora, dear?"

"They are in the drawer of the card table. You need not stir to find them, thank you, Mrs. Stillwater."

"No; here they are all ready," said Mr. Clarence, who had drawn the table up before the fire and taken the pack of cards from the drawer.

The party of four sat down for the game.

"We must cut for partners," said Mr. Rockharrt, shuffling the cards and then handing them to Mrs. Stillwater for the first cut.

"The highest and the two lowest to be partners?" inquired Rose, as she lifted half the pack.

"Of course, that is the rule."

Each person cut in turn, and fortune favored Mrs. Stillwater to Mr. Clarence, and Cora to Mr. Rockharrt. Then they cut for deal, and fortune favored Mr. Rockharrt.

The cards were dealt around.

Rose Stillwater had an excellent hand, and she knew by the pleased looks of her partner, Mr. Clarence, that he also had a good one; and by the annoyed expression of Mr. Rockharrt's face that he had a bad one. Cora's countenance was as the sphinx's; she was too sadly preoccupied to care for this game.

However, Rose determined that she would play into the hand of her antagonist and not into that of her partner.

Pursuing this policy, she watched Mr. Rockharrt's play, always returned his lead, and when her attention was called to the error, she would flush, exhibit a lovely childlike embarrassment, declare that she was no whist player at all, and beg to be forgiven; and the very next moment she would trump her partner's trick, or purposely commit some other blunder that would be sure to give the trick to Mr. Rockharrt.

Mr. Clarence was the soul of good humor, but it was provoking to have his own "splendid" hand so ruined by the bad play of his partner that their antagonists, with such very poor hands, actually won the odd trick.

In the next deal Rose got a "miserable" hand; so did her partner, as she discovered by his looks, while Mr. Rockharrt must have had a magnificent hand, to judge from his triumphant expression of countenance.

Rose could, therefore, now afford to redeem her place in the esteem of her partner by playing her very best, without the slightest danger of taking a single trick.

To be brief, through Rose's management Mr. Rockharrt and Cora won the rubber, and the Iron King rose from the card table exultant, for what old whist player is not pleased with winning the rubber?

"My child," he said to Rose Stillwater, "this is altogether the pleasantest evening that we have passed since we left the city, and all through you bringing life and activity among us! I do not think we can ever afford to let you go."

"Oh, sir! you are too good. Would to heaven that I might find some place in your household akin to that which I once filled during the happiest years of my life, when I lived here as your dear granddaughter's governess," said Rose Stillwater, with a sigh and a smile.

"You shall never leave us again with my consent. Ah, we have had a very pleasant evening. What do you think, Clarence?"

"Very pleasant for the winners, sir," replied the young man, with a good humored laugh, as he lighted his bed room candle and bade them all good night.

Soon after the little party separated and retired for the night.

As time passed, Rose Stillwater continued to make herself more and more useful to her host and benefactor. She enlivened his table and his evenings at home by her cheerful conversation, her music and her games. She waited on him hand and foot, helped him on and off with his wraps when he went out or came in; warmed his slippers, filled his pipe, dried his newspapers, served him in innumerable little ways with a childlike eagerness and delight that was as the incense of frankincense and myrrh to the nostrils of the egotist.

And he praised her and held her up as a model to his granddaughter.

Rose Stillwater was a proper young woman, a model young woman, all indeed that a woman should be. He had never seen one to approach her status in all his long life. She was certainly the most excellent of her sex. He did not know what in this gloomy house they could ever do without her.

Such was the burden of his talk to Cora.

Mrs. Rothsay gave but cold assent to all this. She had too much reverence for the fifth commandment to tell her grandfather what she thought of the situation—that Rose Stillwater was making a notable fool of him, either for the sake of keeping a comfortable home, or gaining a place in his will, or of something greater still which would include all the rest.

She tried to treat the woman with cold civility. But how could she persevere in such a course of conduct toward a beautiful blue eyed angel who was always eager to please, anxious to serve?

Cora felt that this woman was a fraud, yet when she met her lovely, candid, heaven blue eyes she could not believe in her own intuitions. Cora, like some few unenvious women, was often affected by other women's beauty. The childlike loveliness of her quondam teacher really touched her heart. So she could not at all times maintain the dignified reserve that she wished toward Rose Stillwater.

Meantime the day approached when it was decided that they should all go to West Point to the commencement, at which Cadet Sylvan Haught was expected to graduate.

Mr. Rockharrt had invited Mrs. Stillwater to be of their party, and insisted upon her accompanying them.

Rose demurred. She even ventured to hint that Mrs. Rothsay might not like her to go with them; whereupon the Iron King gathered his brow so darkly and fearfully, and said so sternly:

"She had better not dislike it," that Rose hastened to say that it was only her own secret misgiving, and that no part of Mrs. Rothsay's demeanor had led her to such a supposition.

And she resolved never again to drop a hint of her hostess' too evident suspicion of herself to the family autocrat, for it was the last mistake that Mrs. Stillwater could possibly wish to make—to kindle anger between grandfather and granddaughter. Her policy was to forbear, to be patient, to conciliate, and to bide her time.

"Cora," said the Iron King, abruptly, to his granddaughter, at the breakfast table, on the morning after this conversation, and in the presence of their guest, "do you object to Mrs. Stillwater joining our traveling party to West Point?"

"Certainly not, sir. What right have I to object to any one whom you might please to invite?"

"No right whatever. And I am glad that you understand that," replied Mr. Rockharrt.

Rose was trembling for fear that her benefactor would betray her as the suggester of the question, but he did not.

Cora had received no letter from her Uncle Fabian in answer to hers announcing the fact of Mrs. Stillwater's presence at Rockhold.

Mr. Fabian wrote no letters, except business ones to the firm, and these were opened at the office of the works, and never brought to Rockhold.

If Cora should ever inquire of her grandfather whether he had heard from Mr. and Mrs. Fabian Rockharrt, his answer would be brief—

"Yes; they are both well. They are at Paris. They are at Berne. They are at Aix," or wherever the tourists might then chance to be.

Sylvan was a better correspondent. He answered her letters promptly. His comments on the visit of Rose Stillwater were characteristic of the boy.

"So you have got the Rose 'that all admire' transplanted to the conservatories of Rockhold. Wish you joy of her. She is a rose without a single thorn, and with a deadly sweet aroma. Mind what I told you long ago. It contains the wisdom of ages. 'Stillwater runs deep.' Mind it does not draw in and submerge the peace and honor of Rockhold. I shall see you at the exhibition, when we can talk more freely over this complication. If Mrs. Stillwater is to remain as a permanent guest at Rockhold, I shall ask my sister to join me wherever I may be ordered, after my leave of absence has expired. You see I fully calculate on receiving my commission."

Cora looked forward anxiously to this meeting with her brother. Only the thought of seeing him a little sooner than she should otherwise have done could reconcile her to the proposed trip to West Point, where she must be surrounded by all the gayeties of the Military Academy at its annual exercises.

Cora had yielded to her grandfather's despotic will in going a little into society while they occupied their town house in the State capital. But she took no pleasure—not the least pleasure—in this.

To her wounded heart and broken spirit the world's wealth was dross and its honors—vapor!

The only life worth living she had lost, or had recklessly thrown away. Her soul turned, sickened, from all on earth, to seek her lost love through the unknown, invisible spheres.

She still wore around her neck the thin gold chain, and suspended from it, resting on her bosom, the precious little black silk bag that contained the last tender, loving, forgiving, encouraging letter that he had written to her on the night of his great renunciation for her sake, when he had left all his hard won honors and dignities, and gone forth in loneliness and poverty to the wilderness and to martyrdom.

Oh, she felt she was never worthy of such a love as that; the love that had toiled for her through long years; the love that had died for her at last; the love that she had never recognized, never appreciated; the love of a great hearted man, whom she had never truly seen until he was lost to her forever.

So long as he had lived on earth Cora had cherished a hope to meet him, "sometime, somehow, somewhere."

But now he had left this planet. Oh! where in the Lord's universe was he? In what immeasurably distant sphere? Oh! that her spirit could reach him where he lived! Oh, that she could cause him to hear her cry—her deep cry of repentance and anguish!

But no; he never heard her; he never came near her in spirit, even in her dreams, as the departed are sometimes said to come and comfort the loved ones left on earth.

During these moods of dark despair Cora was so gloomy and reserved that she seemed to treat her unwelcome guest worse than ever, when, in truth, she was not even seeing or thinking of the intruder.

The Iron King, however, noticed his granddaughter's coldness and reserve, and he deeply resented it.

One very rainy, dismal Sunday they were all at home and in the drawing room. Cora had sat for hours in silence, or replying to Mrs. Stillwater's frequent attempts to draw her into conversation in brief monosyllables, until at last the visitor arose and left the room, not hurt or offended, as Mr. Rockharrt supposed, but simply tired of staying so long in one place.

But the Iron King turned on his granddaughter and demanded:

"Corona Rothsay! why do you treat our visitor with such unladylike rudeness?"

Cora, brought roughly out of her sad reverie, gazed at the old man vaguely. She scarcely heard his question, and certainly did not understand it.

"Father," ventured Mr. Clarence, "I do not believe Cora could treat any one with rudeness, and surely she could never be unladylike. But you see she is absent-minded."

"Hold your tongue, sir! How dare you interfere?" sternly exclaimed the despot. "But I see how it is," he added, with the savage satisfaction of a man who has power to crush and means to do it—"I see how it is! That oppressed woman will never be treated by either of you with proper respect until I give her my name and make her my wife and the mistress of my house."

CHAPTER XIV
IN THE WEB

"Yes, sir and madam, you may stare; but I mean to place my guest in a position from which she can command due honor. I mean to give her my name and make her the mistress of my house," said old Aaron Rockharrt; and he leaned back in his chair and drew himself up.

Had a thunderbolt fallen among them, it could hardly have caused greater consternation.

The shock was more effective because both his hearers knew full well that old Aaron Rockharrt never used vain threats, and that he would do exactly what he said he would do. Having said that he meant to marry the unwelcome guest, he would marry her.

But what unutterable amazement fell upon the two people! Both had felt a vague dread of evil from the presence of this siren in the house; but their darkest, wildest fears had never shadowed forth this unspeakable folly. The Iron King, a man of seventy-seven, strong, firm, upright, honored, to fall into the idiocy of marrying a beautiful adventuress merely because she waited on him, ran his errands, warmed his slippers, put on his dressing gown or his overcoat, as he would come in or go out, and generally made him comfortable; but above all perhaps, because she flattered his egotism without measure. And yet the Iron King was considered sane, and was sane on all other subjects.

So thought Clarence and Cora as they gasped, glanced at the old man, gazed at each other, and then dropped their eyes in a sort of shame.

Neither spoke or could speak.

The dreadful silence was broken at last by Rose Stillwater, who burst into the room like a sunbeam into a cloud, and said with her childish eagerness:

"I have got such a lovely piece of music. I ran out just now to look for it. I was not sure I could find it; but here it is. It may be called sacred music and suitable to the day, I hope. Here is the title.

"'Glad life lives on forever.'

"Shall I play and sing for you, Mr. Rockharrt? Would you like me to do so, dear Cora? And you, Mr. Clarence?"

"Certainly, my dear," promptly responded the Iron King.

"As you please," coldly replied Cora.

"I—yes—thank you; I think it would be very nice," foolishly observed Mr. Clarence, who was just now reduced to a state of imbecility by the stunning announcement of his father's intended marriage.

But all three had spoken at the same time, so that Rose Stillwater heard but one voice clearly, and that was the Iron King's.

Mr. Clarence, however, went and opened the piano for her. Then old Mr. Rockharrt arose, went to the instrument slowly and deliberately, put his youngest son aside, wheeled up the music stool, seated her and then—

> "The monarch o'er the siren hung
> And beat the measure as she sung,
> And pressing closer and more near,
> He whispered praises in her ear."

"It is 'The Lion in Love,' of Æsop's fable. He will let her draw his teeth yet," said Mr. Clarence, in a low tone, quite drowned in the joyous swell of the music.

"No, it is not. A man of his age does not fall in love, I feel sure. And she will never gain one advantage over him. He likes her society and her servitude and her flatteries. He will take them all, and more than all, if he can; but he will give nothing, nothing in return," murmured Cora.

"But why does he give her this attention to-day? It is unusual."

"To show us that he will do her honor; place her above us, as he said; but that will not outlast their wedding day, if indeed they marry."

"They will marry unless something should happen to prevent them. I do wish Fabian was at home."

"So do I, with all my heart."

The glad bursts of music which had drowned their voices, slowly sank into soft and dreamy tones.

Then Clarence and Corona ceased their whispered conversation.

Soon the dinner bell rang and the family party went into the dining room.

On Monday morning active preparations were commenced for their journey to New York. Not one more word was spoken about the marriage of

June and January, nor could either Clarence or Corona judge by the manner of the ill sorted pair whether the subject had been mentioned between them.

On Wednesday of that week Mr. Rockharrt, accompanied by Mrs. Stillwater and Mrs. Rothsay, left Rockhold for New York, leaving Mr. Clarence in charge of the works at North End.

They went straight through without, as before, stopping overnight at Baltimore. Consequently they reached New York on Thursday noon.

Mr. Rockharrt telegraphed to the Cozzens Hotel at West Point to secure a suite of rooms, and then he took his own party to the Blank House.

When they were comfortably installed in their apartments and had had dinner, he said to his companions:

"I have business which may detain me in the city for several days. We need not, however, put in an appearance at the Military Academy before Monday morning. Meanwhile you two may amuse yourselves as you please, but must not look to me to escort you anywhere. Here are fine stores, art galleries, parks, matinees and what not, where women may be trusted alone;" and having laid down the law, his majesty marched off to bed, leaving the two young widows to themselves, in the private parlor of their suite.

They also retired to the double-bedded chamber, which, to Cora's annoyance, had been engaged for their joint occupancy. She detested to be brought into such close intimacy with Rose Stillwater, and longed for the hour of her brother's release from the academy, and his appointment to some post of duty, however distant, where she might join him, and so escape the humiliation of her present position. However, she tried to bear the mortification as best she might, thankful that she and her unwelcome chum, while occupying the same chamber, were not obliged to sleep in the same bed.

Truly, Rose Stillwater felt how unpleasant her companionship was to her former pupil, but she showed no consciousness of this. She comported herself with great discretion—not forcing conversation on her unwilling room mate, lest she should give offense; and it was the policy of this woman to "avoid offenses," nor yet did she keep total silence, lest she should seem to be sulky; for it was also her policy always to seem amiable and happy. So, though Cora never voluntarily addressed one word to her, yet Rose occasionally spoke sweetly some commonplace about the weather, their room, the bill of fare at dinner, and so on; to all of which observations she received brief replies.

Both were relieved when they were in their separate beds and the gas was turned off—Rose that she need act a difficult part no more that night, but could lie down, and, under the cover of the darkness, gather her features in a cloud of wrath, and silently curse Corona Rothsay; Cora, that she was freed from the sight of the deceitful face and the sound of the lying tongue.

Fatigued by their long journey, both soon fell asleep, and slept well, until the horrible sound of the gong awakened them—the gong in those days used to summon guests to the public breakfast table.

Cora sprang out of bed with one fear—that her grandfather was up and waiting for his breakfast, though that gong had really nothing to do with any of their meals, which were always to be served in their private parlor.

Cora and her room mate quickly dressed and went to the parlor, where they were relieved to find no Mr. Rockharrt and no table set.

Presently, however, the Iron King strode into the room, a morning paper in his hand.

"Breakfast not ready yet?" he sharply demanded, looking at Corona.

Then she suddenly remembered that whenever they had traveled before this time, her grandmother had ordered the meals, as she had done everything else that she could do to save her tyrant trouble.

"I—suppose so, sir. Shall I ring for it?" she inquired.

"Let me! Let me! Oh, please let me wait on you!" exclaimed Rose, as she sprang up, ran across the room, and rang a peal on the bell.

The waiter came.

"Will you also order the breakfast, Mrs. Stillwater, if such is your pleasure?" inquired Cora, who could not help this little bit of ill humor.

"Certainly I will, my dear, if you like!" said the imperturbable Rose, who was resolved never to understand sarcasm, and never to take offense—"Waiter, bring me a bill of fare."

The waiter went out to do his errand.

Old Aaron Rockharrt glared sternly at his granddaughter; but his fire did not strike his intended victim, for Cora had her back turned and was looking out of the window.

The waiter came in with the breakfast bill of fare.

"Will you listen, Mr. Rockharrt, and you, dear Cora, and tell me what to mark, as I read out the items," said Rose, sweetly, as she took the card from the hands of the man.

"Thank you, I want nothing especially," answered Cora.

"Read on, my dear. I will tell you what to mark, and you must be sure also to mark any dish that you yourself may fancy," said Mr. Rockharrt, speaking very kindly to Rose, but glaring ferociously toward Cora.

Rose read slowly, pausing at each item. Mr. Rockharrt named his favorite dishes, Rose marked them, and the order was given to the waiter, who took it away.

Breakfast was soon served, and a most disagreeable meal it must have been but for Rose Stillwater's invincible good humor. She chatted gayly through the whole meal, perfectly resolved to ignore the cloud that was between the grandfather and the granddaughter.

As soon as they arose from the table old Aaron Rockharrt ordered a carriage to take him down to Wall Street, on some business connected with his last great speculation, which was all that his granddaughter knew.

Before leaving the hotel, he launched this bitter insult at Cora, through their guest:

"My dear," he said to Mrs. Stillwater, as he drew on his gloves, "I must leave my granddaughter under your charge. I beg that you will look after her. She really seeds the supervision of a governess quite as much now as she did years ago when you had the training of her."

Corona's wrath flamed up. A scathing sarcasm was on her lips. She turned.

But no. She could not resent the insult of so aged a man; even if he had not been her grandfather.

Rose Stillwater said never a word. It was not—it would not have been prudent to speak. To treat the matter as a jest would have offended the Iron King; to have taken it seriously would most justly and unpardonably have offended Corona Rothsay. Truly, Rose found that "Jordan am a hard road to trabbel!" And here at least was an apt application of the old proverb:

"Speech is silver, silence is golden." So Rose said never a word, but looked from one to the other, smiling divinely on each in turn.

Old Aaron Rockharrt having discharged his shot, went down stairs, entered his carriage and drove to Wall Street.

Corona went to her room, or to the room she jointly occupied with Mrs. Stillwater, wishing from the depths of her heart that she could get entirely away from the sight and hearing of the woman who grew more repugnant to her feelings every day. At one time Cora thought that she would call a carriage, drive to the Hudson River railway station, and take the train for West Point, there to remain during the exercises of the academy. She was very strongly tempted to do this; but she resisted the impulse. She would not bring matters to a crisis by making a scene. So the idea of escaping to West Point was abandoned. Next she thought of taking a carriage and driving out to Harlem alone; but then she remembered that the woman Stillwater was, after all, her guest, so long as she herself was mistress, if only in name, of her grandfather's house; she could not leave her alone for the whole day; and so the idea of evading the creature's company by driving out alone was also given up.

Truly, Cora was bound to the rack with cords of conventionality as fine as cobwebs, yet as strong as ropes.

She did nothing but sit still in her chamber and brood; dreading the entrance of her abhorrent room-mate every moment.

But Rose Stillwater—who read Cora Rothsay's thoughts as easily as she could read a familiar book—acted with her usual discretion. As long as Cora chose to remain in their joint chamber, Rose forbore to exercise her own right of entering it.

Not until the afternoon did Corona come out into the parlor. Then she found Rose seated at the window, watching the busy scene on the Broadway pavement below, the hurried promenaders jostling as they passed each other on going up and coming down; the street peddlers, the walking advertisements, and all other sights never noticed by a citizen of the town, but looked at with curiosity by a stranger from the country.

Rose turned as Corona entered, and ignoring all reserve, said sweetly:

"I hope you have been resting, dear, and that you feel refreshed. Shall I ring and order luncheon? I wish to do all I can, dear, to prove my appreciation of all the kindness shown me; yet not to be officious."

Now, how could Cora repulse the advances of so very good humored a woman? She believed her to be false and designing. She longed with all her heart and soul to be rid of the woman and her insidious influence. Yet she could not hear that sweet voice, those meek words, or meet those soft blue eyes, and maintain her manner of freezing politeness.

"If you please," she answered, gently, and then said to herself: "Heavens! what a hypocrite this unwillingness to hurt the woman's feelings does make me!"

Rose rang the bell and ordered the luncheon.

They sat down in apparent amity to partake of it.

The afternoon waned and evening came, but brought no Iron King back to the hotel.

"Have you any idea at what hour Mr. Rockharrt will return, dear?" inquired Mrs. Stillwater, in her most dulcet tones.

"Not the slightest."

"I think he said something about going down to Wall Street to see after the forming of a syndicate in connection with his grand speculation. What is a syndicate, dear?"

"I don't know—it may be an agency or a company—"

"Or it may be something connected with the building of the new synagogue, which it is said is to be constructed of iron."

Cora was surprised into the first laugh she had had in two years. But the mirth was very short-lived. It came and passed in an instant, and then a pang of remorse seized her heart that she could have laughed at all. She was thinking of her lost Rule, and of her own guilty share in his tragic fate. If she had not let her fancy and imagination become so dazzled by the rank and splendor of the British suitor as to blind her heart and mind for a season, as to make her think and believe that she really loved this new man, and that she had never loved, and could never love, Ruth Rothsay, though she must keep her engagement with him and marry him—had she not broken down and given way to her emotions on that fatal evening of their wedding day— then Rule would never have made his great renunciation for her sake— would never have wandered away into the wilderness to meet his death from murderous hands. How could she ever laugh again? she asked herself.

"What is the matter with you, dear?" inquired Rose, surprised at the sudden change in Cora.

But before she could be answered the door opened and old Aaron Rockharrt came in, looking weary and careworn.

"How have you amused yourselves to-day?" he inquired of the two young women.

Cora was slow to speak, but Rose answered discreetly:

"I do not think we either of us did much but loll around and rest from our journey."

"Not been out?"

"No; I did not care to do so; nor did Cora, I believe."

Dinner was served. Afterward the evening passed stupidly.

Aaron Rockharrt sat in the large arm chair and slept. Cora, looking at him, thought he was aging fast.

As soon as he waked up he bade his companions good night and went to his apartment. The two others soon followed his example.

As this day passed, so passed the succeeding days of their sojourn in the city.

Mr. Rockharrt went out every morning on business connected with that great scheme which was going to quadruple his already enormous wealth. He came home every evening quite worn out, and after dinner sat and dozed in his chair until bedtime.

Cora watched him anxiously and wondered at him. He was aging fast. She could see that in his whole appearance. But what a strange infatuation for a man of seventy-seven, possessed already of almost fabulous wealth, to be as hotly in pursuit of money as if he were some poor youth with his fortune still to make! And what, after all, could he do with so much more money? Why could he not retire on his vast riches, and rest from his labors, leaving his two stalwart sons to carry on his business, and so live longer? Cora mournfully asked herself.

On Sunday a strange thing happened. Old Aaron Rockharrt announced at the breakfast table his intention of going to a certain church to hear a celebrated preacher, whose piety, eloquence and enthusiasm was the subject of general discussion; and he invited the two ladies to go with him. Both consented—Cora because she never willingly absented herself from public worship on the Sabbath; Rose because it was her cue to be amiable and to agree to everything that was proposed.

"We need not take a carriage. The church is only two blocks off," said Mr. Rockharrt, as he arose from the table.

The party was soon ready, and while the bell was still ringing, they set out to walk. As they reached the sacred edifice the bell ceased ringing and the organ pealed forth in a grand voluntary.

"You see we are but just in time," said Mr. Rockharrt, as he led his party into the building.

The polite sexton conducted the strangers up the center aisle and put them into a good pew. The church was not full, but was filling rapidly. Our party bowed their heads for the preliminary private prayer, and so did not see the great preacher as he entered and stood at the reading desk. He was an English dean of great celebrity as a pulpit orator, now on a visit to the United States, and preaching in turn in every pulpit of his denomination as he passed. He was a man of about sixty-five, tall, thin, with a bald head, a narrow face, an aquiline nose, blue eyes and a gray beard. He began to read the opening texts of the service.

"'If we say that we have no sin, we deceive ourselves, and the truth is not in us.'"

At the sound of his voice Rose Stillwater started violently, looked up and grew ghastly white. She dropped her face in her hands on the cushioned edge of the pew before her, and so sat trembling through the reading of the texts and the exhortations. Afterward followed the ritualistic general confession and prayer, during which all knelt.

When at the close all arose Mrs. Stillwater was gone from her seat. Mr. Rockharrt looked around him and then stared at Cora, who very slightly shook her head, as if to say:

"No; I know no more about it than you."

How swiftly and silently Rose Stillwater had left the pew and slipped out of the church while all the congregation were bowed in prayer!

Old Aaron Rockharrt looked puzzled and troubled, but the minister was pronouncing the general absolution that followed the general confession, and such a severe martinet and disciplinarian as old Aaron Rockharrt would on no account fail in attention to the speaker.

Nor did he change countenance again during the long morning service.

At its close he drew Cora's arm within his own and led her out of the church.

As they walked down Broadway he inquired:

"Why did Mrs. Stillwater leave the church?"

"I do not know," answered his granddaughter.

"Was she ill?"

"I really do not know."

"When did she go?"

"I do not know that either, except that she must have slipped out while we were at prayers."

"You seem to be a perfect know-nothing, Cora."

"On this subject I certainly am. I did not perceive Mrs. Stillwater's absence until we rose from our knees."

"Well, we shall find her at the hotel, I suppose, and then we shall know all about it."

By this time they had reached the Blank House.

They entered and went up into their parlor.

Rose was not there.

"Bless my soul, I hope the poor child is not ill. Go, Cora, and see if she is in her room, and find out what is the matter with her," said old Aaron Rockharrt, as he dropped wearily into the big arm chair.

Cora had just come from church, from hearing an eloquent sermon on Christian charity, so she was in one of her very best moods.

She went at once into the bedroom occupied jointly by herself and her traveling companion. She found Rose in a wrapper, with her hair down, lying on the outside of her bed.

"Are you not well?" she inquired in a gentle tone.

"No, dear; I have a very severe neuralgic headache. It takes all my strength of mind and nerve to keep me from screaming under the pain," answered Rose, in a faint and faltering voice.

"I am very sorry."

"It struck me—in the church—with the suddenness of a bullet—shot through my brain."

"Indeed, I am very, very sorry. You should have told me. I would have come out with you."

"No, dear. I did not—wish to disturb—anybody. I slipped out noiselessly—while all were kneeling. No one heard me—no one saw me except the sexton—who opened—the swing doors—silently to let me pass."

"You should not have attempted to walk home alone in such a condition. It was not safe. But I am talking to you, when I should be aiding you," said Cora; and she went to her dressing case and took from it a certain family specific for neuralgic headaches which had been in great favor with her grandmother. This she poured into a glass, added a little water, and brought to the sufferer.

"Put it on the stand by the bed, dear. I will take it presently. Thank you very much, dear Cora. Now will you please close all the shutters and make the room as dark as a vault—and shut me up in it—I shall go to sleep—and wake up relieved. The pain goes as suddenly as it comes, dear," said Rose, still in a faint, faltering and hesitating voice.

Cora did all her bidding, put the tassel of the bell cord in her reach, and softly left the room.

The chamber was not as dark as a vault, however. Enough of light came through the slats of the shutters and the white lace curtains to enable Rose to rise, take the medicine from the stand, cross the floor and pour it in the wash basin, under a spigot. Then she turned on the water to wash it down the drain. Then she turned off the water and went back to bed—not to sleep—for she had too much need to think.

Had the minister in that pulpit recognized her, as she had certainly recognized him? She hoped not. She believed not. As soon as she had heard the voice—the voice that had been silent for her so many years—she had impulsively looked up. And she had seen him! A specter from the past—a specter from the grave! But his eyes were fixed upon the book from which he was reading, and she quickly dropped her head before he could raise them. No; he had not seen her. But oh! if she had heard his name before she had gone to hear him preach, nothing on earth would ever have induced her to go into the church. But she had not heard his name at all. She had heard of him only as the Dean of Olivet. He was not a dean in those far-off days when she saw him last; only a poor curate of whose stinted household she had grown sick and tired. But he was now Dean of Olivet! He had come to make a tour of the United States. Should she have the mischance to meet him again? Would he go up to West Point for the exercises at the military academy? But of course he would! It was so convenient to do so. West Point was so near and easy to see. The trip up the Hudson was so delightful at this season of the year. And the dean was bound to see everything worth seeing. And what was better worth seeing by a foreigner than the exercises at our celebrated military academy? What should she do to avoid meeting, face to face, this terrible phantom from the grave of her dead past?

She could make no excuse for remaining in New York while her party went up to West Point—make no excuse, that is, which would not also make trouble. And it was her policy never to do that. She thought and thought until she had nearly given herself the headache which before she had only feigned. At length she decided on this course: To go to West Point with her party, and as soon as they should arrive to get up a return of her neuralgic headache, as her excuse for keeping her room at the hotel and absenting herself from the exercises at the academy.

As soon as she had formed this resolution she got up, opened one of the windows, washed and dressed herself and went out into the parlor.

She entered softly.

Old Aaron Rockharrt was sound asleep in his big arm chair.

Cora was seated at the table engaged in reading. She arose to receive the invalid.

"Are you better? Are you sure you are able to be up?" she kindly inquired.

"Oh, yes, dear! Very much better! Well, indeed! When it goes, it goes, you know! But had we better not talk and disturb Mr. Rockharrt?" inquired Rose.

"We cannot disturb him. He sleeps very soundly—too soundly, I think, and too much."

"Do you know by what train we go to West Point to-morrow?"

"By the 7:30 a.m. So that we may arrive in good time for the commencement. We must retire very early to-night, for we must be up betimes in the morning. But sit down; you really look very languid," said Cora, and taking the hand of her companion, she led her to the sofa and made her recline upon it. Then Cora resumed her own seat.

"Thank you, darling," cooed Rose.

There was silence in the room for a few moments. Mr. Rockharrt slept on. Cora took up her book. Rose was the first to speak.

"I wonder if the new lion, the Dean of Olivet, will go to West Point to-morrow," she said in a tone of seeming indifference.

"Oh, yes! It is in all the papers. He is to be the guest of the chaplain," replied Cora.

"I wonder what train he will go by."

"Oh, I don't know that. He may go by the night boat."

"The Dean of Olivet would never travel on Sunday night."

"But he might hold service and preach on the boat."

"Oh, yes; so he might."

"What on earth are you talking about? When will dinner be ready?" demanded old Aaron Rockharrt, waking up from his nap. Straightening himself up and looking around, he saw Rose Stillwater.

"Oh, my dear, are you better of your headache?"

"Yes, thank you, Mr. Rockharrt."

"You look pale, as if you had gone through a sharp siege, if a short one. You should have told me in the pew, and allowed me to take you here, not ventured out alone, when you were in such pain."

"But I did not wish to attract the least attention, so I slipped out unperceived while everybody's heads were bent in prayer."

"All very well, my dear; but pray don't venture on such a step again. I am always at your service to attend you. Now, Cora, ring for dinner to be served. It was ordered for five o'clock, I think, and it is five minutes past," said Mr. Rockharrt, consulting his watch.

Cora arose, but before she could reach the bell, the door was opened, and the waiter appeared to lay the cloth.

After dinner the Iron King went into a little room attached to the suite, which he used as a smoking den.

The two young women settled themselves to read.

They all retired at nine o'clock that night so as to rise very early next day.

CHAPTER XV
AT THE ACADEMY

It was a splendid May morning. Our travelers were out of bed at half-past four o'clock. The sun was just rising when they sat down to their early breakfast.

Mr. Rockharrt seemed stronger and brighter than he had been since his arrival in New York.

The Sabbath day's complete rest had certainly refreshed him.

Immediately after breakfast they left the hotel, entered the carriage which had been engaged for them and drove to the Hudson River depot.

"There's the dean!" exclaimed Mr. Rockharrt, as they entered the waiting room. "He must be going on the same train with us."

Rose Stillwater did not start or change color this time. She had prepared herself for contingencies by taking a dose of morphine just before she left the hotel. But she drew her veil closely over her face, murmuring that the brightness of the sun hurt her eyes.

Cora looked up and saw the tall, thin form of the church dignitary standing with a group of gentlemen near the gate leading to the train.

The waiting room was crowded; a multitude was moving toward West Point.

"It is well I engaged our rooms a week ago, or we might not have found accommodations," said Mr. Rockharrt, as he pressed with his party behind the crowd.

Among the group of gentlemen surrounding the dean, was a Wall Street broker with whom old Aaron Rockharrt had been doing business for the last few days.

This man was standing beside the dean, and both stood immediately in front of Mr. Rockharrt and his party.

Presently the broker turned and saw the Iron King.

"Oh, Mr. Rockharrt. Happy to meet you here. Going to the Point, as everybody else is? Fine day."

"Yes; a fine day," responded the Iron King.

At this moment the dean happened to turn his head.

"You know the Dean of Olivet, of course, Mr. Rockharrt?"

"No; I have not that pleasure."

"Let me present you. Dean of Olivet, Mr. Rockharrt."

Both gentlemen bowed.

The Iron King held out his hand.

"Happy to welcome you to America, Dean. Went to hear you preach yesterday morning. One of the finest sermons I ever heard in my life, I do assure you."

The dean bowed very gravely.

"Let me present you to my granddaughter, Mrs. Rothsay," said the old man.

The dean bowed gravely to the young lady, who bent her head.

"And to our friend, Mrs. Stillwater," continued the old gentleman, waving his hand again. "Why, where is she? Why, Cora, where is Mrs. Stillwater?" demanded the Iron King in amazement.

"I do not know. I have just missed her," said the young lady.

"Well, upon my soul! For the power of vanishing she excels all living creatures. Pray, Cora, does she carry a fairy cap in her pocket, and put it on when she wishes to make herself invisible?"

"I think, sir, that she has been pressed away from us in the crowd. We shall find her when we get through the gate into more space."

"Well, I hope so."

"She is quite able to take care of herself, sir. Pray do not be alarmed. She will be sure to find us."

"Well, I hope so. Yes; of course she will."

At this moment the gates were opened.

"Take my arm. Don't let me lose you in the crowd. I suppose Mrs. Stillwater cannot fail to join us. Oh! of course not! She knows the train, and there is but one."

He drew Cora's hand close under his arm, and holding it tightly, followed the multitude through the gate, looking all around in search of Rose Stillwater.

But she was nowhere to be seen.

"She may have gotten ahead of us, and be on the train. Come on!" said Mr. Rockharrt, as he hurried his granddaughter along and pushed her upon the platform.

The cars were rapidly filling.

Mr. Rockharrt seized upon four seats, in order to secure three. He put Cora in one and told her to put her traveling bag on the other, to hold it for Mrs. Stillwater. Then he took possession of the seat in front of her.

"As soon as this crowd settles itself down and leaves something like a free passageway, I will go through the train and find Mrs. Stillwater. She is bound to be on board. She is no baby to lose herself," said Mr. Rockharrt, and though his words were confident, his tone seemed anxious.

The people all got seated at last and the long train moved.

Mr. Rockharrt left his seat, and stooping over his granddaughter, he whispered:

"I am going now to look for Mrs. Stillwater and fetch her here."

He passed slowly down the car, looking from side to side, and then out through the back door to the rear cars, and so out of Cora's sight.

He was gone about fifteen minutes. At the end of that time he reappeared, and came up the car and stopped to speak to Cora: "She is not in any of the rear cars. I am going forward to look for her. This comes of traveling in a crowd."

He went on as before, looking carefully from side to side, passed out of the front door and again out of Cora's sight. This time he was gone twenty minutes. When he come back his face wore an expression of the greatest anxiety.

"She is not on the train. She has been left behind! Foolish woman, to let herself be separated from us in this stupid way!" testily exclaimed the Iron King, as he dropped himself heavily into his seat.

"What can be done?" exclaimed Cora, now seriously uneasy about her unwelcome companion, because she feared that Rose might have been seized with one of her sharp and sudden headaches and had stepped away from them as she had done in the church.

"I hope she has had the presence of mind, on finding herself left, to return to the hotel and wait for the next train. This is the express, and does not stop until we reach Garrison's. But when we get there I will telegraph to her and tell her what train to take. It is all an infernal nuisance—this being jostled about by a crowd."

Cora was consulting a time table. She looked up from it and said:

"It will all come right, sir. There is another train at half-past eight. If she should take that, she will reach West Point in full time for the opening of the exercises. We started unnecessarily early."

"I always take time by the forelock, Cora. That habit is one of the factors of my success in life."

The express train flew on, and in due time reached Garrison's, opposite West Point. The ferry boat was waiting for the train. As soon as it stopped, Mr. Rockharrt handed his granddaughter out. The other passengers followed, and made a rush for the boat.

"Let it go, Cora. We must take time to telegraph to Mrs. Stillwater, and we can wait for the next trip," said Mr. Rockharrt, still keeping a firm grip on his granddaughter's arm, lest through woman's inherent stupidity she should also lose herself, as he marched her off to the telegraph window of the station.

The telegram, a very long-winded one, was sent. Then they sat down to wait for the coming boat, which crossed the going one about midstream, and approached rapidly.

In a few minutes they were on board and steaming across the river.

They reached the opposite bank, and Mr. Rockharrt led his granddaughter out, and placed her in the carriage he had engaged by telegraph to meet them, for carriages would be in very great demand, he knew.

They drove up to the hotel in which he had taken rooms. Here they went into their parlor to rest and to wait for an answer to the telegram.

"It is no use going over to the academy now. We could not get sight of Sylvan. The rules and regulations of the military school are as strict and immutable as the laws of the Medes and Persians," said old Aaron Rockharrt, as he dropped heavily into a great armchair, leaned back and presently fell asleep.

Cora never liked to see him fall into these sudden deep slumbers. She feared that they were signs of physical decay.

She sat at a front window, which, from the elevated point upon which the hotel stood, looked down upon the brilliant scene below, where crowds of handsomely dressed ladies were walking about the beautiful grounds. She sat watching them some time, and until she saw the tide of strollers turning from all points, and setting in one direction—toward the academy.

Then she glanced at her grandfather. Oh! how old and worn he looked when he lost control of himself in sleep. She touched him lightly. He opened his eyes.

"What is it? Has the telegram come from Mrs. Stillwater?" he inquired.

"No, sir; but the visitors are pouring into the academy, and I am afraid, if we do not go over at once, we shall not be able to find a seat," said Cora.

"Oh, yes, we shall. Strange we do not get an answer from Mrs. Stillwater," said the old man anxiously, as he slowly arose and began to draw on his gloves and looked for his hat.

Cora went and found it and gave it to him.

Then she put on her bonnet.

Then they went down together, crossed the grounds, and entered the great hall, which was densely crowded. Good seats had been reserved for them, and they found themselves seated next the Dean of Olivet on Cora's right and the Wall street broker on Mr. Rockharrt's left.

I do not mean to trouble my readers with any description of this by-gone exhibition. They can read a full account of such every season in every morning paper. Merely to say that it was late in the afternoon when the exercises were over for the day.

Mr. Rockharrt and Cora Rothsay returned to the hotel to a very late dinner.

The first question that the Iron King asked was whether any telegram had come for him. He was told that there was none.

"It is very strange. She could not have received mine," he said, and he went directly to the telegraph office of the hotel and dispatched a long message to the clerk of the Blank House, telling him of how Mrs. Stillwater had been separated from her party by the pressure of the crowd, and how she had thereby missed their train, and inquiring whether she had returned to the hotel, whether she had got his message, and if she were well. Any news of her, or from her, was anxiously expected by her friends.

Having sent off this dispatch, Mr. Rockharrt went in to dinner. The dinner was long. The courses were many. Mr. Rockharrt and his granddaughter were still at table when the following telegram was placed in his hands:

Blank House, New York, May, 18—

Mrs. Stillwater is not here, and has not been seen by any of our people since she left the house with your party for the Hudson River Railway depot. We have made inquiries, but have no news.

M. Martin.

CHAPTER XVI
THE SEARCH

"This is intolerable," muttered old Aaron Rockharrt, in a tone as who should say: "How dare Fate set herself to baffle me?"

He then took tablets and pencil from his pocket and wrote the following telegram:

> Cozzens Hotel, West Point,
> May — —, 18—
>
> To M. Martin, Esq., Blank House, New York City:
>
> Just received your dispatch. There has been foul play. Report the case at police headquarters. Set private detective on the track of the missing lady. Last seen at the gate of the Hudson River Railway depot, waiting for 7:30 a.m. train for West Point yesterday morning, but not seen on train. Give me prompt notice of any news.
>
> Aaron Rockharrt.

He beckoned a waiter and sent the message to be dispatched from the office of the hotel.

Then he set himself to finish his dinner.

After dinner he went out on the piazza.

Cora followed him. There was quite a number of people out there, seeing whom, he walked out upon the open grounds.

"May I come with you, grandfather?" inquired Cora.

"If you like," was the short answer.

As they walked on he said:

"I think it possible that Mrs. Stillwater, after missing our train, left for North End."

"Yes, it is possible," assented Cora.

No more was said. They walked on for half an hour and then returned to the hotel and bade each other good night.

The next morning they met in the parlor.

Old Aaron Rockharrt was reading a New York morning paper. Cora went up and bade him good morning.

He merely nodded and went on reading. Presently he burst out with:

"By — —! This must be Mrs. Stillwater!"

"Who? What?" eagerly inquired Cora, going to his side.

"Here! Read!" exclaimed the Iron King, handing her the sheet and pointing out the paragraph.

Cora took the paper with trembling hands and read as follows:

> "A Mystery.—Yesterday morning at six o'clock an unknown young woman of about twenty-five or thirty years of age, of medium height, plump form, fair complexion and yellow hair, clothed in a rich suit of widow's mourning, was found in a state of coma in the ladies' dressing room of the Hudson River Railway station. She was taken to St. L——'s Hospital. There was nothing on her person to reveal her name or address."

"That must have been Mrs. Stillwater," said old Aaron Rockharrt.

"I think there is no question of it," replied Cora.

"No doubt the poor child was suddenly seized with one of her terrible neuralgic headaches, caused by the pressure of that infernal crowd at the gate, and she stole away, as before, lest she should disturb us and prevent our journey; the most self-sacrificing creature I ever met. No doubt she meant to telegraph to us, but was prevented by the sudden reaction from agony to stupor. Ah! I hope it is not a fatal stupor."

"I hope not, sir."

"Cora!"

"Yes, sir."

"We must leave for New York by the next train. If Sylvanus is not free to go with us, he can follow us. Come, let us go down and get some breakfast."

Cora arose and went with her grandfather down to the breakfast room.

When they had taken their places at one of the tables and given their orders to one of the waiters, old Aaron Rockharrt drew a time table from his pocket and consulted it.

"There is a down train stops at Garrison's at 10:50. We will take that."

As soon as they had breakfasted, and as they were leaving the table, another telegram was handed to Mr. Rockharrt. He opened it and read as follows:

Blank House, New York, May — —, 18—

The missing lady is in St. L— —'s Hospital.

M. Martin.

"It is true, then! true as we surmised. Mrs. Stillwater was the unknown lady found unconscious in the dressing room of the Hudson River Railroad and taken to St. L— —'s. Cora!"

"Yes, sir."

"Go and pack our effects immediately. I will go down and settle the bill and leave a letter of explanation for Sylvanus. Get your bonnet on and be ready. The carriage will be at the door in twenty minutes."

Cora hurried off to her room and to her grandfather's room, which adjoined hers, to prepare for the sudden journey. She quickly packed and labeled their traveling bags, and rang for a porter to take them down stairs.

Then she put on her bonnet and duster and went down and joined her grandfather in the parlor.

"Come," he said, "the carriage is at the door and our traps on the box. I have written to Sylvanus, telling him to join us at the Blank House, where we will wait for him."

He turned abruptly and went out, followed by Cora.

They entered the waiting carriage and were rapidly driven down to the ferry.

The boat was at the wharf. They alighted from the carriage and went on board.

Old Aaron Rockharrt's hot haste did not avail them much. The boat remained at the wharf for ten minutes, during which the Iron King secretly fumed and fretted.

"Does this boat connect with the 10:50 train for New York?" he inquired.

"Yes, sir," was the answer.

"Then you will miss it."

"Oh, no, sir."

The five remaining minutes seemed hours, but they passed at length and the boat left the shore, and old Aaron Rockharrt walked up and down the deck impatiently.

As they neared the other side the whistle of a down train was heard approaching.

"There! I said you would miss it!" exclaimed the Iron King.

"That train does not stop here, sir," was the good humored answer.

The boat touched the wharf at Garrison's, and the passengers got off.

Old Aaron Rockharrt led his granddaughter up to the platform to wait for the train; but no train was in sight or hearing.

Mr. Rockharrt looked at his watch.

"After all, we have seven minutes to wait," he growled, as if time and tide were much in fault at not being at his beck and call.

"Had we not better go into the waiting room?" suggested Cora.

"No, we will stand here," replied the Iron King, who on general principles never acted upon a suggestion.

So there they stood—the old man growling at intervals as he looked up the road; Cora gazing out upon the fine scenery of river and mountain.

Presently the whirr of the coming train was heard. In a minute more it rushed into the station and stopped. There were no other down passengers except Mr. Rockharrt and Mrs. Rothsay.

He handed her up, and took her to a seat. The car was not half full. The tide of travel was northward, not southward at this season.

They were scarcely seated when the train started again. They reached New York just before noon.

"Carriage, sir? Carriage, ma'am? Carriage? Carriage? Carriage?" screamed a score of hackmen's voices, as the passengers came out on the sidewalk.

Mr. Rockharrt beckoned the best-looking turnout and handed his granddaughter into it.

"Drive to St. L——'s Hospital," he said.

The hackman touched his hat and drove off. In less than fifteen minutes he drew up before the front of St. L——'s.

The hackman jumped down, went up and rang the bell. Then he came back to the carriage and opened the door.

Mr. Rockharrt got out, followed by his granddaughter.

"Wait here!" he said to the hackman, as he went to the door, which was promptly opened by an attendant.

"I wish to see the physician in charge here, or the head of the hospital, or whatever may be his official title," said the Iron King.

"You mean the Rev. Dr. — —"

"Yes, yes; take him my card."

"Walk in the parlor, sir."

The attendant conducted the party into a spacious, plainly furnished reception or waiting room, saw them seated, and then took away Mr. Rockharrt's card.

A few minutes passed, and a tall, white haired, venerable form, clothed in a long black coat and a round skull cap, entered the room, looking from side to side for his visitor.

Mr. Rockharrt got up and went to meet him.

"Mr. Rockharrt, of North End?" courteously inquired the venerable man.

"The same. Dr. — —, I presume."

"Yes, sir. Pray be seated. And this lady?" inquired the venerable doctor, courteously turning toward Cora.

"Oh—my granddaughter, Mrs. Rothsay."

The aged man shook hands kindly with Cora, and then turned to Mr. Rockharrt, as if silently questioning his will.

"I came to inquire about the lady who was found in an unconscious state at the Hudson River Railway depot. How is she?" The old man's anxiety betrayed itself even through his deliberate words.

"She is better. You know the lady?"

"More than know her—have been intimate with her for many years. She is our guest and traveling companion. She got separated from us in the crowd which was pressing through the railway gate to take the train yesterday morning. I surely thought when I missed her that she had found her way to some car. But it appears that she was seized with vertigo, or something, and so missed the train."

"Yes; a lady, one of our regular visitors, found her there, by Providence, in a state of deep stupor, and being unable to discover her friends, or name, or address, put her in a carriage and brought her directly here."

"She is better, you say? I wish to see her and take her back to our apartments," said Mr. Rockharrt.

"I will send for one of the nurses to take you to her room. You will excuse me. I am momentarily expecting the Dean of Olivet, who is on a visit to our city, and comes to-day to go through the hospital," said the doctor, and he rang a bell.

"The dean here? Why, I thought we left him at West Point," said Mr. Rockharrt.

"He came down by a late train last night, I understand. He makes but a flying tour through the country, and cannot stay at any one place," the venerable doctor explained. And then he touched the bell again.

The same man who had let our party in came to the door to answer the call.

"Say to Sister Susannah that I would like to see her here," said the doctor.

The man went out and was presently succeeded by a sweet faced, middle aged woman in a black dress and a neat white cap.

"Here are the friends of the young lady who was brought in yesterday morning. Will you please to take them to the bedside of your patient?"

The Protestant sister nodded pleasantly and led off the visitors.

As they went up the main staircase they heard the front door bell ring, the door opened, and the Dean of Olivet, with some gentlemen in his company, entered the hall.

Our party, after one glance, passed up the stairs, through an upper hall and a corridor, and paused before a door which Sister Susannah opened.

They entered a small, clean, neat room, where, clothed in a white wrapper, reclining in a white easy chair, beside a white curtained window, and near a white bed, sat Rose Stillwater. She was looking, not only pale, but sallow—as she had never looked before.

Rose Stillwater held out one hand to Mr. Rockharrt and one to Cora Rothsay, in silence and with a faint smile.

The sister, seeing this recognition, set two cane bottomed chairs for the visitors and then went out, leaving them alone with the patient.

"Good Lord, my dear, how did all this come about?" inquired old Aaron Rockharrt, as he sank heavily upon one of the chairs, making it creak under him.

"It was while we stood in the crowd. I was pressed almost out of breath. Then the terrible pang shot through my head, and I ceased to struggle and let everybody pass before me. I dropped down on one of the benches. I had taken a morphia pellet before I left the hotel. I had the medicine in my pocket. I took another then—"

"Very wrong, my dear. Very wrong, my dear, to meddle with that drug, without the advice of a physician."

"Yes; I know it now, but I did not know it then. The second pellet stopped my headache, and I went to the ladies' dressing room to recover myself a little, so as to be able to write a telegram saying that I would follow you by the next train, but there a stupor came over me, and I knew no more until I awoke late last night and found myself here."

"How perilous, my child! In that stupor you might have been robbed or kidnapped by persons who might have pretended to be your relations and carried you off and murdered you for your clothing," said old Aaron Rockharrt, unconscious in his native rudeness that he was frightening and torturing a very nervous invalid.

"But," urged Rose—who had grown paler at the picture conjured up—"providentially I was found by the kind lady who sent or rather brought me here, and even caused me to be put in this room instead of in a ward. Sister Susannah explained this to me as soon as I was able to make inquiries."

"Now, my dear, do you feel able to go back with us to the Blank House, where we are now again staying and waiting for Sylvanus to join us?"

"Oh, yes; I shall be glad to go, though all here are most tender and affectionate to me. But I would like to see and thank the doctor for all his goodness. How like the ideal of the beloved apostle he seems to me—so mild, so tender, so reverend."

"I think you cannot wait for that to-day, my dear. The reverend doctor is engaged with the Dean of Olivet, who is going through the hospital."

Rose Stillwater's face blanched.

"Will they—will they—will they—come into this room?"

"Of course not! And if they should, you are up and in your chair. And if you were not, they are a party of ministers of the gospel and medical doctors, and you would not mind if they should see you in bed. You are a nervous child to be so easily alarmed. It is the effect of the reaction from your stupor," said Mr. Rockharrt.

"I will go with you, however, if I may," said Rose Stillwater, touching the hand bell, that soon brought an attendant into the room.

"Will you ask Sister Susannah, please, to come to me?" said Mrs. Stillwater.

The attendant went out and was soon succeeded by the sister.

"My friends wish to take me away, and I feel quite able to go with them—in a carriage. Will you please find the doctor and ask him?" inquired Mrs. Stillwater.

The sister smiled assent and went out.

Soon the venerable man entered the room.

"I hope I find you better, my child," he said, coming to the easy chair in which sat and reclined the patient.

"Very much better, thank you, sir; so much that I feel quite able to go out with my friends, if I may."

"Certainly, my child, if you like."

"I hope I have not detained you from your friends," said Rose.

"No. I left the dean in conversation with an English patient from his old parish. It was an accidental meeting, but a most interesting one."

"Does—the dean—contemplate a long stay in the city?" Rose forced herself to ask.

"Oh, no; he leaves to-night by one of the Sound steamers for Boston and Newport. His English temperament feels the heat of the city even more than we do."

Rose felt it in her heart to wish that the climate might "burn as an oven," if it should drive the British dean away.

"But I must not leave my visitors longer. So if you will excuse me, sir," he said, turning to Mr. Rockharrt, "I will take leave of my patient and her friends here."

He shook hands all around, receiving the warm thanks of the whole party.

When the venerable doctor left the room, Mr. Rockharrt withdrew to the corridor to give the nurse an opportunity to dress the convalescent for her journey.

He walked up and down the corridor for a few minutes, at the end of which Rose Stillwater came out dressed for her drive, and leaning on the arm of Cora Rothsay.

Mr. Rockharrt hastened to meet her, and took her off Cora's hands, and drew her arm within his own.

So they went down stairs and entered the carriage that was waiting for them.

A drive of fifteen minutes brought them to the Blank House.

"Grandfather," said Cora, as they alighted and went into the house, Rose leaning on Mr. Rockharrt's arm—"Grandfather, I think, now that the rush of travelers have passed northward, you may be able to get me another room. In Mrs. Stillwater's nervous condition it cannot be agreeable to her to have the disturbance of a room-mate."

"What do you say, my child?" inquired Mr. Rockharrt of his guest.

"Sweet Cora never could disturb me under any circumstances, but it cannot be good for her to room with such a nervous creature as I am just at present," replied Rose.

"Umph! It appears to me that you two women wish to have separate rooms each only for the welfare of the other. Well, you shall have them. Take Mrs. Stillwater up stairs, Cora, while I step into the office," said Mr. Rockharrt.

Cora drew the convalescent's arm within her own, and helped her to climb the easy flight of stairs, and took her into the parlor, where they were presently joined by the Iron King.

"I have also engaged a private sitting room, so that we need not go down to the public table, and dinner will be laid for us there in a few minutes. You need not lay off your wraps until you go there; and if there is any special dish that you would particularly like, my dear, I hope you will order it at once. Come." And he offered his arm to Mrs. Stillwater, to whom, indeed, he had addressed all his remarks.

He led her from the public parlor, followed by his granddaughter. The little sitting room which Mr. Rockharrt had been able to engage was just across the hall.

On entering they found the table laid for a party of three.

Neither Mr. Rockharrt nor Cora had broken fast since their early breakfast at West Point. The old gentleman was very hungry.

Dinner was soon served, and two of the party did full justice to the good things set before them; but Rose Stillwater could touch nothing. She had not recovered her appetite since her overdose of morphia. In vain her host recommended this or that dish, for the more appetizing the flavor, the more she detested them.

At last when dinner was over, Mr. Rockharrt recommended her to retire to rest. She readily took his advice and bade him good night.

Cora volunteered to see their guest to her chamber.

"You will look at both rooms, Mrs. Stillwater, and take your choice between them," she said, as she led the guest into the new chamber engaged for one of the ladies.

"Oh, my dear Cora, I do not care where I drop myself down, so that I get rest and sleep. Oh, Cora! I have been so frightened! Suppose I had died in that opium sleep!" exclaimed Mrs. Stillwater, speaking frankly for at least once in her life.

"You should not have tampered with such a dangerous drug," said Mrs. Rothsay.

"Oh, I took it to stop the maddening pain that seemed to be killing me," exclaimed Rose Stillwater, as she let herself drop into an easy chair; not speaking frankly this time, for she had taken the morphia to quiet her nerves, and enable her to decide upon some course by which she might avoid meeting with the Dean of Olivet again, and some excuse for withdrawing herself so suddenly from her traveling party.

"So you will remain here?" inquired Cora.

"Oh, yes. I would remain anywhere sooner than move another step."

"Then I will help to get you to bed. Where is your bag?"

"Bag? Bag? I—I don't know! I have not seen it since I fell into that stupor! It must be at the depot or at the hospital."

"Then I will get you a night dress," said Cora.

And then she ran off to her own room, and soon returned with a white cambric gown, richly trimmed with lace.

When she had prepared her guest for bed, and put her into it, she lowered the gas and left her to repose. Then she went to her own room, satisfied to be alone with her memories once more. Soon after she heard the slow and heavy steps of her grandfather as he passed into his room.

CHAPTER XVII
"A MAD MARRIAGE, MY MASTERS"

When the party met at a late breakfast the next morning, Mrs. Stillwater seemed to have quite recovered her health, and what was still better, in her opinion, her complexion. She was once again a delicately blooming rose. They were still at breakfast when Sylvanus Haught burst in upon them, bowed to his grandfather, bowed to Rose Stillwater, and seized Cora Rothsay around the neck and covered her with kisses, all in a minute and before he spoke a word. Old Aaron Rockharrt glared at him. Rose Stillwater smiled on him. But Cora Rothsay put her arms around his neck and kissed him with tears of pleased affection.

"Well, sir! You have got through," said the Iron King with dignified gravity.

"Yes, sir, got through, 'by the skin of my teeth,' as I might say! And got leave of absence, waiting my commission. Hurrah, Cora! Hurrah, the Rose that all admire! I shall be your cavalier for the next three months at least, and until they send me out to Fort Devil's Icy Peak, to be killed and scalped by the redskins!" exclaimed the new fledged soldier, throwing up his cap.

"Will you have the goodness to remember where you are, sir, and endeavor to conduct yourself with some manner approximating toward propriety?" demanded Mr. Rockharrt, with solemn dignity.

"I beg your pardon, grandfather! I beg your pardon, ladies," said Sylvanus, assuming so sudden and profound a gravity as to inspire a suspicion of irony in the minds of the two women.

But old Aaron Rockharrt understood only an humble and suitable apology.

"Have you breakfasted?" he inquired in a modified tone.

"No, sir; and I am as hungry as a wolf—I mean I took the first train down this morning without waiting for breakfast."

The Iron King, whose glare had cut short the first half of the young man's reply, now rang, and when the waiter appeared, gave the necessary orders.

And soon Sylvanus was seated at the table, sharing the morning meal of his family.

"Now that my brother has joined us shall we leave for North End to-day, grandfather?" inquired Cora, as they all arose from breakfast.

"No; nor need you make any suggestions of the sort. When I am ready to go home, I will tell you. I have business to transact before I leave New York," gruffly replied the family bear.

Rose Stillwater took up one of the morning papers and ran her eyes down column after column, over page after page. Presently she came to the item she was so anxiously looking for:

"The Very Reverend the Dean of Olivet left the city last evening by the steamer Nighthawk for Boston."

With a sigh of relief she laid the paper down.

Mr. Rockharrt came and sat down beside her on the sofa, and began to speak to her in a low voice.

Sylvan, sitting by Cora at the other end of the apartment, began to tell all about the exercises at West Point which she had missed. His voice, though not loud, was clear and lively, and quite drowned the sound of Mr. Rockharrt and Mrs. Stillwater's words, which Cora could see were earnest and important. At last Rose got up in some agitation and hurried out of the room. Then old Aaron Rockharrt came up to the young people and stood before them. There was something so ominous in his attitude and expression that his two grandchildren looked dismayed even before he spoke.

"Sir and madam," he said, addressing the young creatures as if they were dignitaries of the church or state, "I have to inform you that I am about to marry Mrs. Stillwater. The ceremony will be performed at the church to-morrow noon. I shall expect you both to attend us there as witnesses."

Saying which the Iron King arose and strode out of the room.

The sister and brother lifted their eyes, and might have stared each other out of countenance in their silent, unutterable consternation.

Sylvan was the first to find his voice.

"Cora! It is an outrage! It is worse! It is an infamy!" he exclaimed, as the blood rushed to his face and crimsoned it.

Cora said never a word, but burst into tears and sobbed aloud.

"Cora! don't cry! You have me now! Oh! the old man is certainly mad, and ought to be looked after. Cora, darling, don't take it so to heart! At his age, too; seventy-seven! He'll make himself the laughing stock of the world!

Oh, Cora, don't grieve so! It does not matter after all! Such a disgrace to the family! Oh, come now, you know, Cora! this is not the way to welcome a fellow home! For any old man to make such a—Oh, I say, Cora! come out of that now! If you don't, I swear I will take my hat and go out to get a drink!"

"Oh, don't! don't!" gasped his sister; "don't you lend a hand to breaking my heart."

"Well, I won't, darling, if you'll only come out of that! It is not worth so much grief."

"I will—stop—as soon as—I can!" sobbed the young woman, "but when I think—of his reverent gray hairs—brought to such dishonor—by a mere adventuress—and we—so powerless—to prevent it, I feel as if—I should die."

"Oh, nonsense; you look at it too gravely. Besides, old men have married beautiful young women before now!" said Sylvan, troubled by his sister's grief, and tacking around in his opinions as deftly as ever did any other politician.

"Yes, and got themselves laughed at and ridiculed for their folly!" sighed Cora, who had ceased to sob.

"Behind their backs, and that did not hurt them one bit."

"Oh, if Uncle Fabian were only here!"

"Why, what could he do to prevent the marriage?"

"I do not know. But I know this, that if any man could prevent this degradation, he would be Uncle Fabian! It would be no use, I fear, to telegraph to Clarence!"

"Clarence!" said Sylvanus with a laugh, "Why he has no more influence with the Iron King than I have. His father calls him an idiot—and he certainly is weakly amiable. He would back his father in anything the old man had set his heart upon. But, Cora, listen here, my dear! You and I are free at present. We need not countenance this marriage by our presence. I, your brother, can take you to another hotel, or take you off to Saratoga, where we can stay until I get my orders, and then you can go out with me wherever I go. There! the Devil's Icy Peak itself will be a holier home than Rockhold, for you."

Cora had become quite calm by this time, and she answered quietly:

"No; you misapprehend me, Sylvan. It was not from indignation or resentment that I cried, and not at all for myself. I grieved for him, the spellbound old man! No, Sylvanus; since we feel assured that no power of ours, no power on earth, can turn him from his purpose, we must do our duty by him. We must refrain from giving him pain or making him angry; for his own poor old sake, we must do this! Sylvan, I must attend his bride to the altar; and you must attend him—as he desired us to do."

"'Desired!' by Jove, I think he commanded! I do not remember ever to have heard his Majesty the King of the Cumberland Mines request anybody to do anything in the whole course of his life. He always ordered him to do it! Well, Cora, dear, I will be 'best' man to the bridegroom, since you say so! I have always obeyed you, Cora. Ah! you have trained me for the model of an obedient husband for some girl, Cora! Now, I am going down stairs to smoke a cigar. You don't object to that, I hope, Mrs. Rothsay?" lightly inquired the youth as he sauntered out of the room.

He had just closed the door when Mrs. Stillwater entered.

She came in very softly, crossed the room, sat down on the sofa beside Cora, and slipped her arm around the lady's waist, purring and cooing:

"I have been waiting to find you alone, dearest. I just heard your brother go down stairs. Mr. Rockharrt has told you, dear?"

"Yes; he has told me. Take your arms away from me, if you please, Mrs. Stillwater, and pray do not touch me again," quietly replied the young lady, gently withdrawing herself from the siren's close embrace.

"You are displeased with me. Can you not forgive me, then?" pleaded Rose, withdrawing her arms, but fixing her soft blue eyes pleadingly upon the lady's face.

"You have given me no personal offense, Mrs. Stillwater."

"Cora, dear—" began Rose.

"Mrs. Rothsay, if you please," said Cora, in a quiet tone.

"Mrs. Rothsay, then," amended Rose, in a calm voice, as if determined not to take offense—"Mrs. Rothsay, allow me to explain how all this came to pass. I have always, from the time I first lived in his house, felt a profound respect and affection for your grandfather—"

"Mr. Rockharrt, if you please," said Cora.

"For Mr. Rockharrt, then, as well as for his sainted wife, the late Mrs. Rockharrt. I—"

"Madam!" interrupted Cora. "Is there nothing too holy to be profaned by your lips? You should at least have the good taste to leave that lady's sacred memory alone."

"Certainly, if you wish; but she was a good friend to me, and I served her with a daughter's love and devotion. In my last visit to Rockhold I also served Mr. Rockharrt more zealously than ever, because, indeed, he needed such affectionate service more than before. He has grown so much accustomed to my services that they now seem vitally necessary to him. But, of course, I cannot take care of him day and night, in parlor and chamber, unless I become his wife—'the Abisheg of his age.' And so, Cora, dear—I beg pardon—Mrs. Rothsay, I have yielded to his pleadings and consented to marry him."

"Mr. Rockharrt has already told me so," coldly replied Cora.

"And, dear, I wish to add this—that the marriage need make no difference in our domestic relations at Rockhold."

"I do not understand you."

"I mean in the family circle."

"Oh! thank you!" said Cora, with the nearest approach to a sneer that ever she made. "I have heard all you have to say, Mrs. Stillwater, and now I have to reply—First, that I give you no credit for any respect or affection that you may profess for Mr. Rockharrt, or for disinterested motives in marrying the aged millionaire."

"Oh, Cora—Mrs. Rothsay!"

"I will say no more on that point. Mr. Rockharrt is old and worn with many business cares. I would not willingly pain or anger him. Therefore, because he wills it, for his sake, not for yours, I will attend you to the altar. Also, if he should desire me to do so, I shall remain at Rockhold until the return of Mr. Fabian Rockharrt."

At the sound of this name Rose Stillwater winced and shivered.

"Then, knowing that his favorite son will be near him, I shall leave him with the freer heart and go away with my brother, withersoever he may be sent. Mr. Fabian is expected to return within a few weeks, and will probably be here long before my brother receives his orders. Now, Mrs. Stillwater, I think all has been said between us, and you will please excuse my leaving you," said Cora, as she arose and withdrew from the room.

Then Rose Stillwater lost her self-command. Her blue eyes blazed, she set her teeth, she doubled her fist, and shaking it after the vanished form of the lady, she hissed:

"Very well, proud madam! I'll pay you for all this! You shall never touch one cent of old Aaron Rockharrt's millions!"

Having launched this threat, she got up and went to her room. Ten minutes later she drove out in a carriage alone. She did not return to luncheon.

Neither did Mr. Rockharrt, who had gone down to Wall Street. Sylvan and Cora lunched alone, and spent the afternoon together in the parlor, for they had much to say to each other after their long separation, and much also to say of the impending marriage. During that afternoon many packages and bandboxes came by vans, directed to Mrs. Rose Stillwater. These were sent to her apartment. At dusk Mrs. Stillwater returned and went directly to her room. She probably did not care to face the brother and sister together, unsupported by their grandfather. A few minutes later Mr. Rockharrt came in, looking moody and defiant, as if quite conscious of the absurdity of his position, or ready to crush any one who betrayed the slightest, sense of humor. Then dinner was served, and Rose Stillwater came out of her room and entered the parlor—a vision of loveliness—her widow's weeds all gone, her dress a violet brocaded satin, with fine lace berthe and sleeve trimmings, white throat and white arms encircled with pearl necklace and bracelets; golden red hair dressed high and adorned with a pearl comb. She came in smiling and took her place at the table.

Old Aaron Rockharrt looked up at her in surprise and not altogether with pleasure. Rose Stillwater, seeing his expression of countenance, got a new insight into the mind of the old man whom she had thought she knew so well. During dinner, to cover the embarrassment which covered each member of the small party, Sylvan began to talk of the cadets' ball at West Point on the preceding evening; the distinguished men who were present, the pretty girls with whom he had danced, the best waltzers, and so forth, and then the mischievous scamp added:

"But there wasn't a brunette present as handsome as my sister Cora, nor a blonde as beautiful as my own grandmamma-elect."

When they all left the table, Mrs. Stillwater went to her room, and Mr. Rockharrt took occasion to say:

"I wish you both to understand the programme for to-morrow. There is to be no fuss, no wedding breakfast, no nonsense whatever."

Sylvan thought to himself that the marriage alone was nonsense enough to stand by itself, like a velvet dress, which is spoiled by additions; but he said nothing. Mr. Rockharrt, standing on the rug with his back to the mantlepiece and his hands clasped behind him, continued:

"Sylvan, you will wear a morning suit; Cora, you will wear a visiting costume, just what you would wear to an ordinary church service. Rose will be married in her traveling dress. Immediately after the ceremony we, myself and wife, shall enter a carriage and drive to the railway depot and take the train for Niagara. You two can return here or go to Rockhold or wherever you will. We shall make a short tour of the Falls, lakes, St.

Lawrence River, and so on, and probably return to Rockhold by the first of July. I cannot remain long from the works while Fabian is away. Now, am I clearly understood?"

"Very clearly, sir," replied Sylvan, speaking for himself and sister.

"Then, good night; I am going to bed," said the Iron King, and without waiting for a response, he strode out of the room.

"Who ever heard of a man dictating to a woman what she shall wear?" exclaimed Cora.

Sylvan laughed.

"Why, the King of the Cumberland mines would dictate when you should rise from your seat and walk across the room; when you should sit down again; when you should look out of the window, and every movement of your life, if it were not too much trouble. Good night, Cora."

The brother and sister shook hands and parted for the night, each going to his or her respective apartment. Early the next morning the little party met at breakfast. The Iron King looked sullen and defiant, as if he were challenging the whole world to find any objection to his remarkable marriage at their peril. Mrs. Stillwater, in a pretty morning robe of pale blue sarcenet, made very plainly, looked shy, humble, and deprecating, as if begging from all present a charitable construction of her motives and actions. Cora Rothsay looked calm and cold in her usual widow's dress and cap.

Sylvan seemed the only cheerful member of the party, and tried to make conversation out of such trifles as the bill of fare furnished. All were relieved when the party separated and went to their rooms to dress for church. At eleven o'clock they reassembled in the parlor. Mr. Rockharrt wore a new morning suit. He might have been going down to Wall Street instead of to his own wedding. Rose Stillwater wore a navy blue, lusterless silk traveling dress, with hat, veil and gloves to match, all very plain, but extremely becoming to her fresh complexion and ruddy hair. Cora wore her widow's dress of lusterless black silk with mantle, bonnet, veil and gloves to match. Sylvan, like his grandfather, wore a plain morning suit.

"Well, are you all ready?" demanded old Aaron, looking critically upon the party.

"All ready, sir," chirped Sylvan for the others.

"Come, then."

And the aged bridegroom drew the arm of his bride-elect within his own and led the way down stairs and out to the handsome carriage that stood waiting.

He handed her in, put her on the back seat and placed himself beside her.

Sylvan helped his sister into the carriage and followed her. They seated themselves on the front seat opposite the bridal pair.

And the carriage drove off.

"Oh!" suddenly exclaimed old Aaron Rockharrt, rummaging in the breast pocket of his coat and drawing thence a white envelope and handing it to Sylvan; "here, take this and give it to the minister as soon as we come before him."

The young man received the packet and looked inquiringly at the elder. It was really the marriage fee for the officiating clergyman, and a very ostentatious one also; but the Iron King did not condescend to explain anything. He had given it to his grandson with his orders, which he expected to be implicitly obeyed without question. They reached the church, the same church in which they had heard the dean preach on the previous Sunday. They alighted from the carriage and entered the building, old Aaron Rockharrt leading the way with his bride-elect on his arm, Sylvan and Cora following. The church was vacant of all except the minister, who stood in his surplice behind the chancel railing, and the sexton who had opened the door for the party, and was now walking before them up the aisle.

The church was empty, because this, though the wedding of a millionaire, was one of which it might be said that there was "No feast, no cake, no cards, no nothing."

The party reached the altar railing, bowed silently to the minister, who nodded gravely in return, and then formed before the altar—the venerable bridegroom and beautiful bride in the center, Sylvan on the right of the groom, Cora on the left of the bride. The young man performed the mission with which he had been intrusted, and then the ceremony was commenced. It went on smoothly enough until the minister in its proper place asked the question:

"Who giveth this woman to be married to this man?"

There was an awful pause.

No one had thought of the necessity of having a "church father" to give away the bride.

The officiating clergyman saw the dilemma at a glance, and quietly beckoned the gray-haired sexton to come up and act as a substitute. But Sylvan Haught, with a twinkle of fun in his eyes, turned his head and whispered to the new comer:

"'After me is manners of you.'"

Then he took the bride's hand and said mightily:—

"I do."

The marriage ceremony went on to its end and was over. Congratulations were offered. The register was signed and witnessed.

And old Aaron Rockharrt led his newly married wife out of the church and put her into the carriage. Then turning around to his grandchildren he said:

"You can walk back to the hotel. See that the porters send off our luggage by express to the Cataract House, Niagara Falls. They have their orders from me, but do you see that these orders are promptly obeyed. Now, good-by."

He shook hands with Sylvan and Cora, and entered the carriage, which immediately rolled off in the direction of the railway station.

The brother and sister walked back to the hotel together.

"It will be a curious study, Cora, to see who will rule in this new firm. I believe it is universally conceded that when an old man marries a pretty young wife, he becomes her slave. But our honored grandfather has been absolute monarch so long that I doubt if he can be reduced to servitude."

"I have no doubts on the subject," replied his sister.

"I have been watching them. He is not subjugated by Rose. He is not foolishly in love with her, at his age. He likes her as he likes other agreeable accessories for his own sake. I have neither respect nor affection for Rose, yet I feel some compassion for her now. Whatever the drudgery of her life as governess may have been since she left us, long ago, it has been nothing, nothing to the penal servitude of the life upon which she has now entered. The hardest-worked governess, seamstress, or servant has some hours in the twenty-four, and some nook in the house that she can call her own where she can rest and be quiet. But Rose Rockharrt will have no such relief! Do I not remember my dear grandmother's life? And my grandfather really did love her, if he ever loved any one on earth. This misguided young woman fondly hopes to be the ideal old man's darling. She deceives herself. She will be his slave, by day and night seldom out of his sight, never out of his service and surveillance. Possibly—for she is not a woman of principle—she may end by running away from her master, and that before long."

Cora's last words brought them to the "Ladies' Entrance" of their hotel.

"Go up stairs, Cora, and I will step into the office and see if there are any letters," said Sylvan.

Mrs. Rothsay went up into their private sitting room, dropped into a chair, took off her bonnet and began to fan herself, for her midday walk had been a very warm one.

Presently Sylvan came up with a letter in his hand.

"For you, Cora, from Uncle Fabian! There is a foreign mail just in."

"Give it to me."

Sylvan handed her the letter, Cora opened it, glanced over it, and exclaimed:

"Uncle Fabian says that he will be home the last of this month."

CHAPTER XVIII
A CRISIS AT ROCKHOLD

Brother and sister went to Newport and spent a month. The Dean of Olivet was in the town, but they never met him because they never went into society. Toward the last of June, Corona proposed that they should go at once to Rockhold.

The next morning brother and sister took the early train for New York. On the morning of the second day they took the express train for Baltimore, where they stopped for another night. And on the morning of the third day they took the early train for North End, where they arrived at sunset. They went to the hotel to get dinner and to engage the one hack of the establishment to take them to Rockhold.

Almost the first man they met on the hotel porch was Mr. Clarence, who rushed to meet them.

"Hurrah, Sylvan! Hurrah, old boy! Back again! Why didn't you write or telegraph? How do you do, Cora! Ah! when will you get your roses back, my dear? And how is his Majesty? Why is he not with you? Where did you leave him?" demanded Mr. Clarence in a gale of high spirits at greeting his nephew and niece again.

"He is among the Thousand Islands somewhere with his bride," answered Cora.

"His—what?" inquired Mr. Clarence, with a puzzled air.

"His wife," said Cora.

"His wife? What on earth are you talking about, Cora? You could not have understood my question. I asked you where my father was!" said the bewildered Mr. Clarence.

"And I told you that he is on his wedding trip with his bride, among the Thousand Islands," replied Cora.

Mr. Clarence turned in a helpless manner.

"Sylvan," he said, "tell me what she means, will you?"

"Why, just what she says. Our grandfather and grandmother are on the St. Lawrence, but will be home on the first of July," Sylvan explained.

But Mr. Clarence looked from the brother to the sister and back again in the utmost perplexity.

"What sort of a stupid joke are you two trying to get off?" he inquired.

They had by this time reached the public parlor of the hotel and found seats.

"Is it possible, Uncle Clarence, that you do not know Mr. Rockharrt was married on the thirty-first of last month, in New York, to Mrs. Stillwater?" inquired Cora.

"What! My father!"

"Why should you be amazed or incredulous, Uncle Clarence? The incomprehensible feature, to my mind, is that you should not have heard of the affair directly from grandfather himself. Has he really not written and told you of his marriage?"

"He has never told me a word of his marriage, though he has written a dozen or more letters to me within the last few weeks."

"That is very extraordinary. And did you not hear any rumor of it? Did no one chance to see the notice of it in the papers?"

"No one that I know of. No; I heard no hint of my father's marriage from any quarter, nor had I, nor any one else at Rockhold or at North End, the slightest suspicion of such a thing."

"That is very strange. It must have been in the papers," said Sylvan.

"If it was I did not see it, but, then, I never think of looking at the marriage list."

"I am inclined to think that it never got into the papers. The marriage was private, though not secret. And you, Sylvan, should have seen that the marriage was inserted in all the daily papers. It was your special duty as groomsman. But you must have forgotten it, and I never remembered to remind you of it," said Cora.

"Not I. I never forgot it, because I never once thought of it. Didn't know it was my duty to attend to it. Besides, I had so many duties. Such awful duties! Think of my having to be my own grandmother's church papa and give her away at the altar! That duty reduced me to a state of imbecility from which I have not yet recovered."

"But," said Mr. Clarence, with a look of pain on his fine, genial countenance, "it is so strange that my father never mentioned his marriage in any of his letters to me."

"Perhaps he did not like to mix up sentiment with business," kindly suggested Sylvan.

"I don't think it was a question of sentiment," sighed Mr. Clarence.

"What? Not his marriage?"

"No," sighed Mr. Clarence.

"Well, don't worry about the matter. Let us order dinner and engage the carriage to take us all to Rockhold. How astonished the darkies will be to see us, and how much more astonished to hear the news we have to tell! I wonder if they will take kindly to the rule of the new mistress?" said Sylvan.

"Why did not one of you have the kindness, and thoughtfulness, to write and tell me of my father's marriage?" sorrowfully inquired Mr. Clarence, utterly ignoring the just spoken words of his nephew.

"Dear Uncle Clarence, I should certainly have written and told you all about it at once, if I had not taken for granted that grandfather had informed you of his intention, as was certainly his place to do. And even if I had written to you on any other occasion, I should assuredly have alluded to the marriage. But, you see, I never wrote to any one while away," Cora explained.

"Now, Uncle Clarence, just take Cora's explanation and apology for both of us, will you, for it fits me as well as it does her? And now you two may keep the ball rolling, while I go out and order dinner and engage the hack," said Sylvan, starting for the office.

When he was gone Clarence asked Cora to give him all the details of the extraordinary marriage, and she complied with his request.

"It will make a country talk," said the young man, with a sigh, which Cora echoed.

"And you say they will be home on the first of July?" he inquired.

"Yes," said Cora.

"I wish I had known in time. I would have had old Rockhold Hall prepared as it should be for the reception of my father's bride, though I do so strongly disapprove the marriage. Do you know, Cora, that old house has never had its furniture renewed within my memory? Some of the rooms are positively mouldy and musty. And whoever heard of a wealthy man like my father bringing his wife home to a neglected old country house like Rockhold, without first having it renovated and refurnished?"

"I do not believe he ever once thought of the propriety or necessity of repairing and refitting. His mind is quite absorbed in his new and vast speculations. He spent every day down in Wall Street while we stayed in New York city."

"Well, Corona, this is the twenty-eighth of June, and we have four days before us; for I do not suppose the newly married pair will arrive before the evening of the first of July; so we must do the best we can, my dear, to make the house pleasant in this short time."

"And Uncle Fabian and his wife will be at Rockhold about the same time," added Cora.

"I knew Fabian would be at North End on the first of July, but I did not know that he would go on to Rockhold. I thought he would go on to their new house. So we shall have two brides to welcome, instead of one."

"Yes. And now, Uncle Clarence, will you please ring for a chambermaid? I must go to a bed room and get some of this railroad dust out of my eyes," said Cora.

At nine o'clock in the very warm evening, the three were sitting near the open windows, when they started at the sound of a hearty, genial voice in the adjoining room, inquiring for accommodations for the night.

"It is Fabian!" cried Mr. Clarence, springing up in joy and rushing out of the room to welcome his only and much beloved brother.

The glad voices of the two brothers in greeting reached their ears, and a moment after the door was thrown open again, and Mr. Clarence entered, conducting Mr. and Mrs. Fabian Rockharrt.

As soon as they found themselves alone, the two brothers took convenient seats to have a talk.

"How goes on the works, Clarence?" inquired Mr. Fabian.

"Very prosperously. You will go through them to-morrow and see for yourself."

"And how goes on the great scheme?"

"Even better than the works. Last reports shares selling at one hundred and thirty."

"Same over yonder. When I left Amsterdam shares selling like hot cakes at a hundred and thirty-one seventenths. How is the governor?" inquired Mr. Fabian.

"As flourishing as a successful financier and septuagenarian bridegroom can be."

"Why!—what do you mean?"

"Haven't you heard the news?"

"What is it? You—you don't mean—"

"Has our father written nothing to you of a very important and utterly unexpected act of his life?"

"No."

"I advised him to marry—"

"You! You! Fabian! You advised our father to do such an absurd thing at his age?"

"I confess I don't see the absurdity of it," quietly replied the elder brother.

"Oh, why did you counsel him to such an act?" inquired Mr. Clarence, more in sorrow than in anger.

"Out of pure good nature. I was getting married myself and wanted everybody to be as happy as I was myself, particularly my old father. Now I wonder he did not write to me of his happiness; but perhaps he has done so and the letter passed me on the sea. When did this marriage take place?"

"On the last day of May."

"Whe-ew! Then there was ample time in which to have written the news to me. And I have had at least half a dozen business letters since the date of his marriage, in any of which he might have mentioned the occurrence had he so chosen. The lady is no longer young. She must be forty-eight, and she is handsome, cultured, dignified and of very high rank. A queenly woman!"

"Do you know whom you are talking about, Fabian?"

"Mrs. Bloomingfield, the lady I recommended, whom father married."

"Oh, indeed; I thought you didn't know what you were talking about or whom you were talking of," said Mr. Clarence.

"What do you mean by that?"

"Our father never accepted your recommendation; never proposed to the handsome, high spirited Mrs. Bloomingfield."

"What!" exclaimed Mr. Fabian. "Whom, then?" "Whom? Whom should he have selected but

"'The Rose that all ad-mi-r-r-?'

"Clarence, what, in the fiend's name, do you mean? Whom has my father married?" demanded Mr. Fabian, starting up and staring at his younger brother.

"Mrs. Rose Flowers Stillwater," replied Mr. Clarence, staring back.

Mr. Fabian dropped back in his chair, while every vestige of color left his face.

"Why, Fabian! Fabian! Why should you care so much as all this? Speak, Fabian; what is the matter?" inquired the younger brother, rising and bending over the elder.

"What is the matter?" cried Mr. Fabian, excitedly. "Ruin is the matter! Ruin, disgrace, dishonor, degradation, an abyss of infamy; that is the matter."

"Oh, come now! see here! that is all wild talk. The young woman was only a nursery governess, to be sure, in our house, and then widow of some skipper or other; but she was respectable, though of humble position."

"Clarence, hush! You know nothing about it!" exclaimed Mr. Fabian, wiping his forehead with his handkerchief, and then getting up and walking the floor with rapid strides.

"I don't understand all this, Fabian. We were all of us a good deal cut up by the event, but nothing like this!" said Mr. Clarence, uneasily.

"No; you don't understand. But listen to me: I was on my way to Rockhold to join in the family reunion, and to show the old homestead to my wife; but I cannot take her there now. I cannot introduce her to the new Mrs. Rockharrt—the new Mrs. Rockharrt!" he repeated, in a tone and with a gesture of disgust and abhorrence. "I shall turn back, and take my wife to our new home; and when I go to Rockhold, I shall go alone."

"Fabian, you make me dreadfully uneasy. What do you know of Rose Stillwater that is to her discredit?" demanded Clarence Rockharrt.

His elder brother paused in his excited walk, dropped his head upon his chest and reflected for a few moments. Then he seemed to recover some degree of self-control and self-recollection. He returned to his chair, sat down, and said:

"Of my own personal knowledge I know nothing against the woman but just this—that she is but half educated, deceitful, and unreliable. And that knowledge I gained by experience after she had first left Rockhold, to which I had first introduced her for a governess to our niece. I had nothing to do with her return to the old hall, and would have never countenanced such a proceeding if I had been in the country."

"That is all very deplorable, but yet it hardly warrants your very strong language, Fabian. I am sorry that you have discovered her to be 'ignorant, deceitful, and unreliable,' but let us hope that now, when she is placed above temptation, she will reform. Don't take exaggerated views of affairs, Fabian."

The elder man was growing calmer and more thoughtful. Presently he said:

"You are right, Clarence. My indignation, on learning that that woman had succeeded in trapping our Iron King, led me into extravagant language on the subject. Forget it, Clarence. And whatever you do, my brother, drop no hint to any one of what I have said to you to-night, lest our father should hear of it; for if he should—"

Mr. Fabian paused.

"I shall never drop a hint that might possibly give our father one moment of uneasiness. Be sure of that, Fabian."

"That is good, my brother! And we will agree to ignore all faults in our young stepmother, and for our father's sake treat her with all proper respect."

"Of course. I could not do otherwise. And, Fabian, I hope you will reconsider the matter, and bring Violet to Rockhold to join our family reunion."

"No, Clarence," said the elder brother; "there is just where I must draw the line. I cannot introduce my wife to the new Mrs. Rockharrt."

"But it seems to me that you are very fastidious, Fabian. Do you expect always to be able to keep Violet from meeting with 'ignorant, insincere and unreliable' people, in a world like this?" inquired Mr. Clarence, significantly.

"No, not entirely, perhaps; yet, so far as in me lies, I will try to keep my simple wood violet 'unspotted from the world,'" replied Mr. Fabian, who, untruthful and dishonest as he was in heart and life, yet reverenced while he wondered at the purity and simplicity of his young wife's nature.

"I am afraid the pater will feel the absence of Violet as a slight to his bride," said Mr. Clarence.

"No; I shall take care that he does not. Violet is in very delicate health, and that must be her excuse for staying at home."

The brothers talked on for a little while longer; and then, when they had exhausted the subject for the time being, Mr. Clarence said he would go and look up Sylvan, and he went out for the purpose. Fabian Rockharrt, left alone, resumed his disturbed walk up and down the room, muttering to himself:

"The traitress! the unprincipled traitress! How dared she do such a deed? Didn't she know that I could expose her, and have her cast forth in ignominy from my father's house? Or did she venture all in the hope that consideration of my father's age and position in the world would shut my mouth and stay my hand? She is mistaken, the jade! Unless she falls into my plans, and works for my interest, she shall be exposed and degraded from her present position."

Mr. Fabian was interrupted by the re-entrance of Mrs. Rothsay. He turned to meet her and inquired:

"Where did you leave Violet, my dear?"

"She is in her own room, which is next to mine. I went in with her and saw her to bed, and waited until she went to sleep," replied Cora.

"Poor little one! She is very fragile, and has been very much fatigued. I do not think, my dear, that I can take her on to Rockhold to-morrow. I think I must let her rest here for a day or two."

"It would be best, not only on account of Violet's delicacy and weariness, but also on account of the condition of the house at Rockhold, which has not been opened or aired for months."

"That is true; though I had not thought of it before," said Mr. Fabian, who was well pleased that Cora so readily fell in with his plans.

"What do you think of the pater's marriage, Cora?' he next inquired.

"I would rather not give an opinion, Uncle Fabian," she answered.

"Then I am equally well answered, for that is giving a very strong opinion!" he exclaimed.

"The deed is done and cannot be undone!"

"Can it not? Perhaps it can!"

"What do you mean, Uncle Fabian?"

"Nothing that you need trouble yourself about, my dear. But tell me this—what do you mean to do, Cora? Do you mean to stay on at Rockhold?"

"I suppose I must do so."

"Not at all, if you do not like! You are an independent widow and may go where you please."

"I know that and wish to go; but I do not wish to make a scene or cause a scandal by leaving my grandfather's protection so suddenly after his marriage, which is open enough to criticism, as it is. So I must stay on at Rockhold so long as Sylvan's leave shall last, and until he shall receive his commission and orders. Then I will go with him wherever his duty may call him."

"Good girl! You have decided well and wisely. Though the post of duty to which the callow lieutenantling will be ordered must, of course, be Fort Jumping Off Point, at the extreme end of the habitable globe. Well, my dear, I must bid you good night, for, see, it is on the stroke of eleven o'clock, and I am rather tired from my journey, for, you must know, we rushed it through from New York to North End without lying over," said Mr. Fabian, as he shook hands with his niece.

He retired, and his example was soon followed by all his party.

CHAPTER XIX
A FAMILY REUNION

The next morning, after an early breakfast, the travelers assembled in the hall of the hotel to take leave of each other. Clarence, Sylvan, and Cora entered the capacious carriage of the establishment to drive to Rockhold, leaving Mr. and Mrs. Fabian Rockharrt on the porch of the hotel, at which they had decided to rest for a few days.

"We shall go to Rockhold to welcome the king and queen when they return, Cora," said Mr. Fabian, waving his hand to the departed trio, though he had not the least intention of keeping his word. He then led his pretty Violet into the house. The lumbering carriage rolled along the village street, passed the huge buildings of the locomotive works, and out into the road that lay between the fool of the range of mountains and the banks of the river.

The ferryboat was at the wharf, and the broad shouldered negro dwarf was standing on it, pole in hand.

His look of surprise and delight on seeing Sylvan and Cora was good to behold.

"Why, Lors bress my po' ole soul, young marse an' miss, is yer come sure 'nough? 'Deed I's moughty proud to see yer. How's de ole marse? When he coming back agin?" he queried, as the carriage rolled slowly across the gangplank from the wharf to the deck of the ferryboat.

"Your ole marse is quite well, Uncle Moses, and will be home on the first of the month with his new wife," said Sylvan, who could not miss the fun of telling this rare bit of news to the aged ferryman.

The old negro dropped his pole into the water, opened his mouth and eyes to their widest extent and gasped and stared.

"Wid—w'ich?" he said, at last.

"With his new wife and your new mistress," answered Sylvan.

The old negro dropped his chin on his chest, raised his knobby black fingers to his head and scratched his gray hair with a look of quaint perplexity, as he muttered,

"Now I wunner ef I tuk too heavy a pull on to dat dar rum jug, fo' I lef de house dis mornin' —I wunner if I did."

His mate stopped and pulled the pole up out of the water and began himself to push off the boat until it was afloat.

They soon reached the opposite shore, drove off the boat and up the avenue between the flowering locust trees that formed a long, green, fragrant arch above their heads, and so on to the gray old house. In a very few moments the door was opened and all the household servants appeared to welcome the returning party. Most of them looked more frightened than pleased; but when anxious glances toward the group leaving the carriage assured them that the family "Boodlejock" was not present, they seemed relieved and delighted to see the others.

With the easy, respectful familiarity of long and faithful service, the negro men and women crowded around the entering party with loving greetings.

The news of the Iron King's marriage was told by Sylvan. Had a bombshell fallen and exploded among the servants, they could not have been more shocked. There was a simultaneous exclamation of surprise and dismay, and then total silence.

At the end of the third day all was ready for the reception of Mr. and Mrs. Rockharrt.

The next day was the first of July. As soon as Mr. Clarence reached his private office at the works he found a telegram waiting him. He opened it, and read the following:

Capon Springs, July 1, 18—

Shall reach North End by the 6 p.m. train. Send the carriage to meet that train. Shall go directly to Rockhold. Order dinner there for 8 p.m.

Aaron Rockharrt.

Mr. Clarence put a boy on horseback and sent him on to Cora, with this message inclosed in a note from himself. And then he gave his attention to the duties of his office. He was still busy at his desk when Mr. Fabian strolled in.

"Well, old man, good morning. I return to duty to-day, because it is the first of the month, you know."

"And also the first of the financial year. There has been so much to do within the last few days, I am glad you have returned to your post. I would like the pater to find all right when he comes to inspect. By the way, I have just got a telegram from him. I have just sent it off to Cora, so that she may know when to send the carriage, and for what hour to order dinner. You know it would never do to have anything 'gang aglee' in which the pater is interested."

"No. Well, you and I must go to meet him. We must not fail in any attention to the old gentleman."

"Of course not. Oh! what will the people say when they hear the news? I do not think that the slightest rumor of the mad marriage has got out I know that I have not breathed it."

"Nor I. But of course it will be generally known within twenty-four hours; and then I hope the pater will do the handsome thing and give his workmen a general holiday and jollification."

"I doubt it, since he has not even refurnished the shabby old drawing room at Rockhold in honor of the occasion," said Mr. Clarence.

Then the brothers separated for the day.

Whenever the family traveling carriage happened to be sent from Rockhold to the North End railway depot, it always stopped at the North End Hotel to rest and water the horses. So when the afternoon waned, as Messrs. Fabian and Clarence Rockharrt had to remain busy in their respective offices up to the last possible minute, Sylvan was stationed on the front porch of the hotel, with the day's newspapers and a case of cigars to solace him while watching for the carriage.

It came at a quarter to five o'clock, and while the horses were resting and feeding, Sylvan sent a messenger to summon his two uncles. By the time the two horses were ready to start again, the two men came up and entered the carriage. Sylvan followed them in.

"See here, my boy," said Mr. Fabian, "you can't go, you know. There will be no room for you coming back. Clarence and myself fill two seats, and your grandfather and—"

"Grandmother fill up the other," added Sylvan. "But never mind; in coming back I can ride on the box with the coachman; but go I will to meet my venerable grandparents! Bless my wig! didn't I give away my grandmother at the altar, and shall I not pay them the attention of going to meet them on their return from their wedding tour?"

The horses started at a good pace, passed through the village street, entered the main road running miles between the great works, and rolled on into the silent forest road that led to the railway depot in the valley.

Here the carriage drew up before the solitary station house.

Soon the train ran in and stopped. Old Aaron Rockharrt got out and handed down his wife, before turning to face his sons. A man and maid servant, loaded down with handbags, umbrellas, waterproofs, and shawls, got out of another car.

"Fabian, put Mrs. Rockharrt into the carriage. I shall step into the waiting room to speak to the ticket agent," said old Aaron Rockharrt, as he strode off to the building.

Fabian Rockharrt gave his arm to the lady, who during all this time had remained closely veiled. He led her off, leaving Clarence and Sylvan on the platform to wait for the return of Mr. Rockharrt. As soon as Fabian and his companion were out of hearing of the rest of their party, he turned to her, and bending his head close to her ear, said:

"Well, Ann White, what have you to say for yourself, eh, Ann White?"

He felt her tremble as she answered defiantly:

"Mrs. Rockharrt, if you please."

"No; by my life I will never give to such as you my honored mother's name!"

"And yet I have it with all the rights and privileges it bestows, and I defy you, Fabian Rockharrt!"

"You know very little of the laws relating to marriage if you think that you have legal right to the name and position you have seized, or that I have not power to thrust you out of my father's house and into a cell."

"You are insolent! I shall report your words to Mr. Rockharrt, and then we shall see who will be thrust out of his house!"

"I think that you had better not. Listen, and I will tell you something that you do not know, perhaps."

She turned quickly, inquiringly, toward him. He stooped and whispered a few words. He felt her thrill from head to foot, felt her rock and sway for a moment, and then—he had just time to catch her before she fell a dead weight in his arms.

CHAPTER XX
THE WHISPERED WORDS

"Well! what's all this?" abruptly demanded old Aaron Rockharrt, as he came up, followed by Clarence and Sylvan, just as Fabian was lifting the unconscious woman into the carriage.

"Mrs. Rockharrt has been over-fatigued, I think, sir, for she has fainted. But don't be alarmed; she is recovering," said Mr. Fabian, as he settled the lady in an easy position in a corner of the carriage, and found a smelling salts bottle and put it to her nose.

"'Alarmed?' Why should I be?"

"No reason why, sir," answered Mr. Fabian, who then stooped to the woman and whispered: "Nor need you be so. You are safe for the present."

"Will you get out of my way and let me come to my place?" demanded the Iron King.

"Pardon me, sir," said Fabian, stepping backward from the carriage.

"Fainting?" said the old man, in a tone of annoyance, as he took his seat beside his new wife—"fainting? The first Mrs. Rockharrt never fainted in her life; nor ever gave any sort of trouble. What's the matter with you, Rose? Don't be a consummate fool and turn nervous. I won't stand any nonsense," he said roughly, as he peered into the pale face of his new slave.

"Oh, it is nothing," she faltered—"nothing. I was overcome by heat. It is a very hot day."

"Why, it is a very cool afternoon. What do you mean?" he demanded.

"It has been a very hot day, and the heat and fatigue—"

"Rubbish!" he interrupted. "If I were to give any attention to your faints, you would be fainting every day just to have a fuss made over you. Now this fainting business has got to be stopped. Do you hear? If you are out of order, I will send for my family physician and have you examined. If you are really ill, you shall be put under medical treatment; if you are not, I will have no fine lady airs and affectations. The first Mrs. Rockharrt was perfectly free from them."

"I would not have given way to the weakness if I could have helped it—indeed I would not!" said the poor woman, very sincerely.

"We'll see to that!" retorted the Iron King.

Ah, poor Rose! She was not the old man's darling and sovereign, as she had hoped and planned to be. She was the tyrant's slave and victim.

A man of Aaron Rockharrt's temperament seldom, at the age of seventy-seven, becomes a lover; and never, at any age, a woman's slave.

Mr. Fabian now got into the carriage, and sat down on the front cushion opposite his father and step-mother. Mr. Clarence was following him in, when Mr. Rockharrt roughly interfered.

"What are you about here, Clarence? What are you going to do?"

"Take my seat in the carriage, of course, sir," answered the young man, with a surprised look.

"You are going to do nothing of the sort! I don't choose to have the horses overtasked in this manner. I myself, with Fabian and my coachman, to say nothing of Mrs. Rockharrt, are weight enough for one pair of horses, and you can't come in here. Where's Sylvan?"

"On the box seat beside the driver."

"Really?" demanded the Iron King, in a sarcastic tone, "How many more of you desire to be drawn by one pair of horses? Tell Sylvan to come down off that."

"But, sir, there is not a single conveyance of any description at the station," urged Clarence.

"Indeed! And pray what do you call your own two pairs of sturdy legs? Are they not strong enough to convey you from here to North End, where you can get the hotel hack? And, by the way, why did you not engage the hack to come here and take you back?"

"Because it was out, sir."

"Then you two should not have come here to over-load the horses. But as you have come, you must walk back. Has Sylvan got off his perch? Ah, yes; I see. Well, tell the coachman to drive first to the North End Hotel. And do you two long-legged calves walk after it. If the hack should be still out when we get there, you can stay at the hotel until it comes in."

"All right, sir," said Clarence, good humoredly; and he closed the door, and gave the order to the coachman, who immediately started his horses on the way to North End.

On the way home Mr. Clarence inquired of his nephew when he expected to receive his commission and where he expected to be ordered.

"How can I tell you? I must wait for a vacancy, I suppose, and then be sent to the Devil's Icy Peak or Fort Jumping Off Place, or some such other pleasant post of duty on the confines of terra incognita. But the farther off, the stranger and the savager it is, the better I shall like it for my own sake, but it will be rough on Cora," said the youth.

"But you do not dream of taking Cora out there?" exclaimed Clarence, in pained surprise.

"Oh, but I do! She insists on going where I go. She is bent on being a voluntary, unsalaried missionary and school-mistress to the Indians just because Rule died a martyred minister and teacher among them."

"She is mad!" exclaimed Mr. Clarence; "mad."

"She has had enough to make her mad, but she is sane enough on this subject, I can tell you, Uncle Clarence. She is the most level-headed young woman that I know, and the plan of life that she has laid out for herself is the best course she could possibly pursue under the present circumstances. She is very miserable here. This plan will give her the most complete change of scene and the most interesting occupation. It will cure her of her melancholy and absorption in her troubled past, and when she shall be cured she may return to her friends here, or she may meet with some fine fellow out there who may make her forget the dead and leave off her weeds. That is what I hope for, Uncle Clarence."

And for the rest of their walk they trudged on in silence or with but few words passed between them. It was sunset when they reached North End.

That evening when Sylvan and Cora found themselves together for a moment at Rockhold House, the youth said:

"Corona Rothsay, the sooner I get my orders and you and I depart for Scalping Creek or Perdition Peak, or wherever I am to be shoveled off to, the better, my dear," said the young soldier.

"What do you think of it all now, Sylvan?" she inquired.

"I think, Cora, that while we do stay here it would be Christian charity to be very good to 'the Rose that all admire.' Nobody will admire her any more, I think."

"Why?" inquired Cora, in surprise.

"Oh, you didn't see her face. She had her mask veil, do you call it?—down, so you couldn't see. But, oh, my conscience! how she is changed in these last six weeks! She is not a blooming rose any more. She is a snubbed, trampled on, crushed, and wilted rose. Her face looks pale; her hair dull; her eyes weak; her beauty nowhere; her cheerfulness nowhere else."

Early the next morning, after a hasty breakfast, Mr. Rockharrt entered his carriage to drive to the works. Young Mrs. Rockharrt, under the plea of fatigue from her long journey, retired to her own room.

Cora said to her brother:

"Sylvan, I wish you would order the little carriage and take me to the Banks to see Violet. I should have paid her this attention sooner but for the pressure of work that has been upon me. I must defer it no longer, but go this morning."

"All right, Cora!" answered the young man, and he left the room to do his errand.

Cora went up stairs to get ready for her drive.

In about fifteen minutes the two were seated in the little open landau, that had been the gift of the late Mrs. Rockharrt to her beloved granddaughter, and that the latter always used when driving out in the country around Rockhold during the summer.

They did not have to cross the ferry, as the new house of Fabian Rockharrt was on the same side of the river as was Rockhold.

The road on this west side was, however, much rougher, though the scenery was much finer.

They drove on through the woods, which here clothed the foot of the mountain and grew quite down to the water's edge, meeting over their heads and casting the road into deep shadow.

They drove on for about three miles, when they came to a point where another road wound up the mountain side, through heavy woods, and brought them to a beautiful plateau, on which stood the handsome house of Fabian Rockharrt, in the midst of its groves, flower gardens, arbors, orchards and conservatories.

It was a double, two-storied house, of brown stone, with a fine green background of wooded mountain, and a front view of the river below and the mountains beyond. There were bay windows at each end and piazzas along the whole front.

As the carriage drew up before the door, Violet was discovered walking up and down the front porch. She looked very fragile, but very pretty with her slight, graceful figure in a morning dress of white muslin, with blue ribbons at her throat and in her pale gold hair.

She came down to meet her visitors.

"Oh, I am so glad you have come, Cora and Sylvan!" she said, throwing her arms around the young lady and kissing her heartily, and then giving her hand and offering her cheek for a greeting from the young man.

"I fear you must be lonely here, Violet," said Cora.

"Awfully lonesome after Fabian has gone away in the morning, Cora. It would be such a charity in you to come and stay with me for a little while! Come in now and we will talk about it," said the little lady, as she led the way back to the house.

"Sylvan," she continued, as they paused for a moment on the porch, "send your coachman around to the stable to put up your carriage. You and Cora will spend the day with me at the very least."

"Just as Cora pleases; ask her," said the young man with a glance toward his sister.

"Yes," she answered.

"You are a love!" exclaimed Violet as she led the way into the hall and thence into a pleasant morning room.

Cora laid off her bonnet and sank into an easy chair by the front window.

"Now, as soon as you are well rested, I wish to show you both over the house and grounds. Such a charming house, Cora! Such beautiful grounds, Sylvan!" exclaimed the proud little mistress.

Cora smiled approval, but did not explain that she herself had gone all through the establishment several times, in the course of its fitting up, to see that all things were arranged properly before the arrival of the married pair.

And when, a little later, the trio went through the rooms, she expressed as much pleasure in their appearance as if she had never seen them before.

The brother and sister spent a very pleasant day at Violet Banks, and when in the cool of the evening they would have taken leave, the young wife pleaded with them to stay all night.

In the midst of this discussion Mr. Fabian Rockharrt came home from North End.

As he entered the parlor he heard his Wood Violet at her petition. He greeted them all, kissed his wife, kissed Cora, and shook hands with Sylvan.

"Now let me settle this matter," he said, good humoredly, as he threw himself into a large arm chair.

"First tell me, Cora, what is the obstacle to your spending the night with us?"

"Only that I did not announce even this visit to the family at Rockhold."

"Do you owe any special obligation to do so?"

"It is not a question of obligation, but of courtesy. I should certainly be remiss in politeness to leave the house for a two days' visit without giving notice of my intention," she answered.

"Oh! I see. Well, I can fix all that. You will both remain to dinner. After dinner it will not be too late for Sylvan to take my sure-footed cob and ride back to Rockhold and explain to the family that Cora is to remain here overnight, and that I will myself take her home to-morrow evening if she should wish to go."

"What do you say, Cora," inquired the young man.

"I accept Uncle Fabian's offer and will remain here for the present," said the young lady.

"Like the sensible woman that you are!" exclaimed Mr. Fabian.

Half an hour later the four sat down to dinner in one of the prettiest little dining rooms that ever was seen.

Soon after the pleasant meal was over, Sylvan took leave of his friends, mounted the white cob that stood saddled at the door, and rode down the wooded hill to the river road leading to Rockhold.

The three left behind spent the remainder of the evening on the front porch, watching the deep river, the hoary mountains, the starry sky, and listening to the hum of insects, the whirl of waters and the singing of the summer breeze through the pines that clothed the precipice, and talking very little.

They retired to rest at a late hour.

Yet on the next morning they met at an early breakfast, for Mr. Fabian had to go to the works to make up for much lost time while affairs were left under the sole management of Mr. Clarence.

Cora remained with Violet, who took her into a more interior confidence, and exhibited with equal pride and delight sundry dainty little garments of fine cambric and linen richly trimmed with lace or embroidery, all the work of her own delicate fingers.

"They tell me, Cora, that I could buy all these things as cheap and as good as I can make them. But I do take such pleasure in making them with my own hands."

Cora kissed her tenderly for all reply.

Then the little lady began to ask questions about her new step-mother-in-law.

"You know, Cora, that I could not ask you yesterday while Sylvan was with us. He is in your full confidence, no doubt, and I have perfect faith in him; but for all that we cannot speak freely on all subjects before a third person, however near and dear. At least I could not ask searching questions about Mr. Rockharrt's marriage, before Sylvan. Such a strange marriage, with such a disparity in years between a man of Mr. Rockharrt's venerable age and Mrs. Stillwater's blooming youth! I saw her once by chance. She looked a perfect Hebe of radiant health and beauty."

Cora Rothsay smiled. She might have told this little lady that there was not much more difference between the ages of Rose Stillwater at thirty-seven and Aaron Rockharrt at seventy-seven than there was between Violet Wood at seventeen and Fabian Rockharrt at fifty-two. But as the young wife did not see this fact, Cora refrained from showing it to her.

Then Violet wanted to know what Cora herself thought of the marriage.

Cora said she thought it concerned only the parties in question, and only time could tell how it would turn out.

In such confidential talk passed the long summer day.

In the cool of the evening Mr. Fabian came home to dinner.

He joined his wife in trying to persuade Cora to remain with them yet another day; but Cora explained that there were many reasons for her return to Rockhold.

Finding her obdurate, Mr. Fabian ordered Mrs. Rothsay's landau to be at the door at a certain hour.

And as soon as dinner was over and Cora had put on her bonnet and taken leave of Violet, with a promise to return within a few days, Mr. Fabian placed her in the Carriage, took his seat beside her, and drove down the wooded hill to the river road below.

"It is not altogether for pleasure that I pressed you to stay till to-night, Cora, although your presence gave great pleasure to my wife and self. I wished to have a private talk with you. Cora, you ought not to stay at

Rockhold. You should come to us," said Mr. Fabian, as they bowled along the wooded road between the foot of the hills and the banks of the river.

"Why?" inquired the lady.

He did not answer at once, but drove slowly on as if to gain time for thought. At length, however, he said:

"I think that a home with Violet and myself at the Banks would be much more congenial to you than one with your grandfather and his new wife at Rockhold."

"But, my dear Uncle Fabian, under present circumstances my grandfather is my natural protector and Rockhold my proper home until my brother has one to offer me."

"Cora, you are not frank with me. I know how you feel about staying at Rockhold, and also why you feel as you do; though I do not see by what agency or intuition you could have gained the knowledge you seem to possess."

"Uncle Fabian, I have no positive knowledge of any cause why I should shrink from continuing in my natural home. I have only suspicions, which perhaps you could clear up or confirm, if you would be frank with me."

He drove on slowly in silence without answering her. She continued:

"I wrote to you while you were in Europe, informing you that Mrs. Stillwater had been invited by my grandfather to come to Rockhold to remain as long as should be convenient to herself. You never replied to my letter."

"I never got such a letter, Cora. It must have been lost with others that miscarried among the Continental mails, when they were following me from one office to another. But even if I had received such a letter, it could have made no difference. I could not have prevented Mrs. Stillwater's visit, nor the event that resulted from the visit. I could not have written or returned in time."

"Should you have prevented the visit or the marriage that followed if you could have done so?"

"Most certainly I should."

"Why?"

"For the same reason that you, or Clarence, or Sylvan would have done so. For the reason of its total unfitness. But, Cora, my dear, I repeat that you have not been frank with me. You are hiding something from me."

"And I repeat, Uncle Fabian, that I have no positive knowledge of any—"

"Yes; so you said before," he exclaimed, interrupting her. "You have no positive knowledge, but you have very strong suspicions founded upon very solid grounds! Now, what are these grounds, my dear? I am your uncle. You should give me your confidence."

If Mr. Fabian had not put the matter in this way, and if they had not been driving along the dark and over-shadowed road where the meeting branches of the trees above almost hid the light of the stars, so that only one or two occasionally gleamed through the foliage, Cora would never have been able to reply to her uncle as she did.

"Uncle Fabian, do you remember a certain warm night in September some five years ago, when we stopped at the Wirt House in Baltimore?"

"On our way home from Canada—yes, I do."

"My room was close that night and I could not sleep. A little after midnight I got up and put oil my dressing-gown and went into the adjoining room, which was our private parlor, and I sat down in a cool corner in the shadow of the curtain and in the draught of the window. I fell asleep, but was soon awakened by the sound of a door opening and some one whispering. I was about to call out when I recognized your voice. The room was pitch dark. I could not see you; but then I was about to speak, when I recognized another voice—Mrs. Stillwater's. You had let yourself in by your own key, through the door leading from the hall. She had come in through the door leading from her room, which was on the opposite side of the parlor from mine."

Cora paused to wait for the effect of her words.

Mr. Fabian drove on slowly in silence.

"I sat there quite still, too much surprised to speak or move."

"And so you overheard that interview," said Mr. Fabian, with a dash of anger in his usually pleasant voice.

"I could not escape. I was amazed, spellbound, too confused to know what to do."

"Well?"

"I gathered from your words that you and she were either secretly married or secretly engaged to be married."

"That was your opinion."

"What other opinion could I form? You were providing her with a house and an income. She was speaking of herself as a daughter-in-law sure to be acceptable to your father and mother. Of course, I judged from that that you were either wedded or betrothed, which was an incomprehensible thing to me, who had been led to believe that the lady was the wife of Captain Stillwater, remaining in Baltimore to meet her husband, whose ship was then daily expected to arrive."

"You were wrong, Cora," said Mr. Fabian, now speaking in his natural tone without a shade of anger—quite wrong, my dear; there was nothing of the sort. I was never engaged to Mrs. Stillwater."

"Then she subsequently refused you. I am telling you what I thought then, not what I think now. I have heard from her own lips that after her husband's death you proposed to her and she refused you."

Mr. Fabian shook with silent laughter. When he recovered he asked:

"And you believed her?"

"I do not know. I was in a maze. There were so many contradictory and inconsistent circumstances surrounding the woman that seemed to live and move in a web of deception woven by herself," said Cora, wearily, as if tired of the subject.

"And, after all, she is a very shallow creature, incapable of any deep scheming; there is no great harm. She knows that she is beautiful—still beautiful—and her only art is subtle flattery. She flattered your grandfather 'to the bent of his humor,' with no deeper design than to marry him and gain a luxurious home and an ample dower, as well as an adoring husband. You see she has succeeded in marrying him, poor little devil! but she has gained nothing but a prison and a jailer and penal servitude. I repeat, there is no great harm in her; and yet, Cora, my dear, I do not permit my wife to visit her, and I do not wish you to remain in the same house with her."

"Why, Uncle Fabian! you were the very first to introduce her to us! It was you who were charged with the duty of finding a nursery governess for me, and you selected Rose Flowers from a host of applicants."

"I know I did, my dear. She seemed to me a lovely, amiable, attractive girl of seventeen, not very well educated, yet quite old enough and learned enough to be nursery governess to a little lady of seven summers. And she did her duty and made herself beloved by you all, did she not?"

"Yes, indeed."

"And so she always has done and always will do. And yet, my dear, you must not live in the same house with her now, even if you did live years together when she was your governess."

"Are you not even more prejudiced against Mrs. Rockharrt than I am?"

"Bah! no, my dear; I have no ill will against the woman, though I will not let my niece live with her or my wife visit her.

"I wish, Uncle Fabian, that you would be more explicit and tell me all you know of Rose Flowers—or Mrs. Stillwater—before she became Mrs. Rockharrt."

"Have you told me all you know of her, Cora, my dear?"

"I have said several times that I know nothing, and yet—stop—"

"What?"

"In addition to that strange interview that I overheard, yet did not understand, there was something else that I saw, but equally did not understand."

"What was that?"

"Something that happened while we were in New York city in May last."

"Will you tell me what it was?"

"Yes, certainly. We were staying at the Star Hotel. We stayed over Sunday, and we went to the Episcopal church near our hotel, to hear an English divine preach."

"Well?"

"He was the celebrated pulpit orator, the Dean of Olivet—"

"Good Heav—" exclaimed Mr. Fabian, involuntarily, but stopping himself suddenly.

"What is the matter?" demanded Cora, suspiciously.

"I was too near the edge of the precipice. We might have been in the river in another moment," said Mr. Fabian.

Cora did not believe him, but she refrained from saying so.

"The danger is past. Go on, my dear."

"We were shown into the strangers' pew. The voluntary was playing. We all bowed our heads for the short private prayer. The voluntary stopped. Then we heard the voice of the dean and we lifted our heads. I turned to offer Mrs. Stillwater a prayer book. Then I saw her face. It was ghastly, and her eyes were fixed in a wild stare upon the face of the dean, whose eyes were upon the open book from which he was reading. Quick as lightning she covered her face with her veil and so remained until we all knelt down for the opening prayer. When we arose from our knees, Rose was gone."

Cora paused for a few moments.

"Go on, go on," said Mr. Fabian.

"We did not leave the church. Grandfather evidently took for granted that Rose had left on account of some trifling indisposition, and he is not easily moved by women's ailments, you know. So we stayed out the services and the sermon. When we returned to the hotel we found that Rose had retired to her room suffering from a severe attack of neuralgic headache, as she said."

"What did you think?"

"I thought she might have been suddenly attacked by maddening pain, which had given the wild look to her eyes; but the next day I had good reason to change my opinion as to the cause of her strange demeanor."

"What was that?"

"We all left the hotel at an early hour to take the train for West Point. Mrs. Stillwater seemed to have quite recovered from her illness. We had arrived at the depot and received our tickets, and were waiting at the rear of a great crowd at the railway gate, till it should be opened to let us pass to our train. I was standing on the right of my grandfather, and Rose on my right. Suddenly a man looked around. He was a great Wall Street broker who had dealings with your firm. Seeing grandfather, he spoke to him heartily, and then begged to introduce the gentleman who was with him. And then and there he presented the Dean of Olivet to Mr. Rockharrt, who, after a few words of polite greeting, presented the dean to me, and turned to find Rose Stillwater."

"Well! Well!"

"She was gone. She had vanished from the crowd at the railway gate as swiftly, as suddenly, and as incomprehensibly as she had vanished from the church. After looking about him a little, my grandfather said that she had got pressed away from us by the crowd, but that she knew her way and would take care of herself and follow us to the train all right. But when the gates were opened we did not see her, nor did we find her on the train, though Mr. Rockharrt walked up and down through the twenty cars looking for her, and feeling sure that we should find her. The train had started, so we had to go on without her. My grandfather concluded that she had accidentally missed it and would follow by the next one."

"And what did you think, Cora?"

"I thought that, for some antecedent and mysterious reason, she had fled from before the face of the Dean of Olivet at the railway station, even as she had done at the church."

"When and where did you find her?"

"Not until our return to New York city. My grandfather was in a fine state; kept the telegraph wires at work between West Point and New York, until he got some clew to her, and then, without waiting for the closing exercises at the military academy, he hurried me back to the city. We found the missing woman at St. L——'s hospital, where she had been conveyed after having been found in an unconscious condition in the ladies' room of the railway depot. She was better, and we brought her away to the hotel. The Dean of Olivet went to Newport, and Mrs. Stillwater recovered her spirits. A few days later she married Mr. Rockharrt at the church where the dean had preached. You know everything else about the matter. And now, Uncle Fabian, tell me that woman's story, or at least all that is proper for me to know of it."

"Cora, you read Rose Stillwater aright. She did on both these occasions fly from before the face of the Dean of Olivet. I will tell you all about her, for it is now right that you should know; but you must promise never to reveal it."

"I promise."

CHAPTER XXI
WHO WAS ROSE FLOWERS?

"Well, my dear Corona, I must ask you to cast your thoughts back to that year when you first came to Rockhold to live, and engrossed so much of your grandmother's time and attention that your grandfather grew jealous and impatient, and commissioned me to 'hire' a nursery governess to look after you and teach you the rudiments of education. You remember that time, Cora?" inquired Mr. Fabian, as he held the reins with a slackened grasp, so that the horse jogged slowly along the wooded road between the foot of the mountain and the banks of the river, under the star-lit sky.

"I remember perfectly," answered the girl.

"Well, business took me to New York about that time, and I thought it a good opportunity to hunt up a governess for you. So I advertised in the New York papers, giving my address at an uptown office, while my own business kept me down town.

"The first letter I opened interested me so much that I gave my whole attention to that first, and so it happened that I had no occasion to touch the others. It was from one Ann White, who described herself as a motherless and fatherless girl of sixteen, a stranger in this country, who was trying to get employment as assistant teacher, governess, or copyist, and who was well fitted to take sole charge of a little girl seven years old.

"Perhaps this might not have impressed me, but she went on to write that she had not a friend in the whole country, that she was utterly destitute and desolate, and begged me for Heaven's mercy not to throw her letter aside, but to see her and give her a trial. She inclosed her photograph, not, as she wrote, from any vanity, but that I might see her face and take pity on her.

"Cora, there was an air of childish frankness and simplicity about her letter that was well illustrated by her photograph. It was that of a sweet-smiling baby face; a sunny, innocent beautiful face. I answered the letter immediately, asking for her address, that I might call and see her. The next day I received her answer, thanking me with enthusiastic earnestness for my prompt attention to her note, and giving me the number and street of her residence in Harlem. I got on a Second Avenue car and rode out to Harlem; got off at the terminus, walked up a cross street and walked some distance to a bijou of a brown cottage, standing in shaded grounds, with sunny gleams and flower beds, and half covered by creeping roses, clematis, wisteria, and all that.

"I went in, and was received by the beautiful being that you have known as Rose Flowers. She was dressed in some misty, cloud-like pale blue fabric that set off her blonde beauty to perfection. After we were seated and had talked some time, I telling her what light duties would be required of her—only the care of one good little girl of seven years old, and of a very mild old lady who was the only lady in the house, and of the old gentleman who was the head of the family, strict but just in all his dealings; and of our country house in the mountains and our town house in the State capital—and she expressing the greatest and frankest anxiety to become a member of such a happy, amiable, prosperous family, and declaring with childish boasting that she was quite competent to perform all the duties expected of her and would perform them conscientiously, I suddenly asked her for her references.

"'I—I have not a friend in this world,' she said; and then in a timid voice, she asked: 'Are references indispensable?'

"'Of course,' I answered

"'Then the Lord help me! Nothing is left but the river. The river won't require references;' and with that she buried her little golden-haired head in the cushions of the sofa and burst into a perfect storm of sobs and tears. Now, Cora, what in the deuce was a man to do? I had never seen anything like that in all my life before. I had never seen a woman in such a fit before. All this was strange and horrible to me.

"I am a middling strong old fellow, but that beautiful girl's despair upset me, and I never could hear any one hint suicide, and she talked of the river. The river would receive her without references. The river was kinder than her own fellow creatures! The river would give her a home and rest and peace! She only wanted to do honest work for her living, but human beings would not even let her work for them without references! And I declare to you, Cora, she was not acting, as you might suspect. She was in deadly earnest. Her sobs shook her whole frame.

"At last I myself behaved like an ass. I went and knelt down beside her so as to get quite close to her, and I began to comfort her. I told her not to mind about the references; that she might have me for a reference all the days of her life; that she should have the situation at Rockhold, where I would convey her and introduce her on my own responsibility.

"While I spoke to her I laid my hand on the little golden-haired head and smoothed it all the time. Out of pity, Cora, I assure you on my honor, out of pity. After a while her sobs seemed to subside slowly. I told her that her face was to me a sufficient recommendation in her favor, and all-sufficient testimonial of character; but that I must have her confidence in exchange for my own.

"You see, Cora, I was very sorry for the poor, pretty creature, and was really anxious to befriend her; but also my curiosity was keenly piqued. I wished to know her private history, and so I assured her that she should have the position she wanted on the condition of telling me her antecedents.

"At last she yielded, and told me the story of her short, willful life. This, then, was her poor, little, pathetic story.

"Her name was Ann White. She was the daughter of Amos White, an English curate, living in a remote village in Northumberland, and of his first wife, who had died during the infancy of her youngest child, Ann, a year after which her father had married again. Ann's step-mother was one of the most beautiful women in England, and—one of the most discontented, as the wife of a widowed clergyman who was old enough to be her father, who had three sons and two daughters by a former marriage, and who was trying to support his family on a hundred pounds a year. Yet, so long as her father lived, Ann's childhood was happy. But her father, who had been a consumptive, also died when Ann was about seven years old. Then the family was broken up. The three step-sons went to seek their fortunes in New Zealand. The eldest step-daughter had been married and had gone to London a few months before her father's death; the younger step-daughter went to live with that married sister. Ann and her step-mother were permitted to remain at the parsonage until the successor of Amos White could be appointed. At last the new curate came—a handsome and accomplished man—Rev. Raphael Rosslynn. He was a bachelor, without near relatives. He called on the Widow White and at once set her heart at ease by begging her not to trouble herself to leave the parsonage, but to remain there for the present at least, and take him as a boarder. He was perfectly frank with the lovely widow, and told her that he was engaged to his own cousin, and that as soon as he should get a living promised him on the death of the present incumbent, and which was worth twelve hundred pounds a year, he should marry, but that he could not allow himself to anticipate happiness that must rise on a grave. But in the course of the year that which might have been expected happened, the young widow, who had never cared for her elderly first husband, fell desperately in love with her lodger, who was not very slow to respond, for her grace, beauty and allurements attracted, bewildered, and bedeviled him, so that he forgot or deplored his plighted vows to his good little cousin. To shorten the story, the cousin released him. In a few days the curate and the widow were married. Ann was utterly neglected, ignored, and forgotten. Her lessons, which, before the advent of the handsome curate, had been the widow's care, were now suspended. Time went on, and these ardent lovers cooled off. Not that their youth or health or beauty waned; not at all; but that their illusions were fading. Yet, as often happens, as love cooled, jealousy warmed to life—each one conscious of indifference toward the other, yet resented a corresponding indifference in the other. As years went on, six children were born to this unhappy pair, whom not the Lord but the devil had joined together, and with their increasing family came increasing poverty. It was hard to support a growing household on one hundred pounds a year.

"In the seventh year of their marriage, in desperation, the Reverend Raphael advertised his ability and readiness to 'prepare young men for college.' He obtained but one pupil one Alfred Whyte, the son of a retired brewer. You perceive that he had the same surname with the young Ann, but it was spelled differently—with a *y*, instead of an *i*, as her name was. He seems to have been a fine, hearty, good natured young fellow, about twenty years of age, with a short, stout form, a round, red face, and dark eyes and hair. He hated study, but loved children, animals, and out-door sports. It was in the course of nature that he should fall in love with the fair fifteen-year-old beauty Ann White.

"She returned his affection because since her father's death he was the only human being who had ever been kind to her. The first year that he spent at the parsonage was the happiest year Ann had ever known. Before it drew to an end, however, their happiness was clouded. The young man had over and over again assured the girl of his love for her, and at last he asked her to marry him. She consented. Then he wrote and asked permission of his father to wed the curate's step-daughter.

"The answer might have been anticipated. The purse-proud retired brewer, who had dreams of his only son and heir going into Parliament and marrying some impoverished nobleman's daughter, wrote two furious letters, one to his son, commanding his immediate return home, and another to the Rev. Raphael Rosslynn, reproaching him with having entrapped his pupil into an engagement with his pauper step-daughter.

"We can judge the effect of these letters upon the peace of the parsonage.

"The Reverend Raphael commanded his pupil into his presence, and after severely censuring him for his conduct in 'betraying the confidence of the family who had received him into its bosom,' he requested that Master Whyte should leave the house with all convenient speed.

"The youth urged that he had meant no harm and had done no harm, that he was honestly in love with the young lady, and had honestly asked leave to marry her, and that he certainly would marry her—

"'Though mammy and daddy and all gang mad.'

"Mr. Rosslynn referred him to his father's letter and ordered him to depart. And then the reverend gentleman went to his wife's room and bitterly reproached her that her forward girl had been the cause of his losing his pupil and eighty pounds a year.

"She told him that the fault was his own; that he should never have received a young man as a resident pupil in the house where there was a young girl.

"A fierce quarrel ensued, which was ended at last by the reverend gentleman going out and banging the door behind him with a force that shook the house, and in a state of mind that rendered him singularly unfit to read the prayers for the sick beside the bed of a dying parishioner to whom he was urgently summoned.

"Mrs. Rosslynn immediately hastened to wreak her vengeance on her step-daughter. She set her teeth as she seized the unlucky girl, whom she found at work in the kitchen, pushed her roughly on into the narrow passage up the steep stairs and into the little back loft that the child called her own bedroom.

"Here she took a firmer grip upon the girl, and with a dog whip that she had hastily snatched from the hat rack in passing, she lashed the hapless creature over back and shoulder.

"Ann never struggled or cried out, but held her tongue in fierce wrath and stubborn endurance. Could that woman, the victim of all ungovernable passions, have but known what she did, or foreseen its results!

"At last she ceased, pushed the bruised and wounded child away from her, sank panting to a chair, and as soon as she recovered her breath, began to insult and abuse the orphan child of her deceased husband, charging her with disgracing the house by improper conduct, of which the girl had never even dreamed; accusing her of causing the loss of their pupil and the income derived from him, and reproaching her for making discord between herself (Mrs. Rosslynn) and her husband.

"Ann replied by not one word.

"At length the maddened woman, having talked herself out of breath, got up, left the room, and locked the door, not on her victim alone, but on all the evil spirits she had raised from Tartarus and left with the girl.

"Ann sank upon the bed, weeping, moaning, and grinding her teeth, her body prostrated by pain, her soul filled with bitter wrath and scorn toward one whom she should rather have been led to love and honor. In the fiery torture of her flesh and the humiliation of her spirit she uttered but these piteous words:

"'Oh, my own mother!—oh, my lost father! do you see your child?'

"For more than an hour she lay there before the fierce smarting and burning of her scourged flesh began to subside. The short November afternoon darkened into night. No one came near her. The hour for supper passed. No one called her to the meal. She heard the family passing to their rooms. She heard her mother putting the other children to bed—a duty that she herself had hitherto performed. At last all sounds died away in the house, and she knew that all the inmates had retired, and the lights were out. She was meditating to run away; she did not know in what direction, or to what end, farther than to escape from the home that was hateful to her.

"Evil spirits were with her, suggesting many desperate thoughts; at length they infused a deadly, horrible temptation to a deed of self-destruction so ghastly that its discovery should appal the family, the parish, and the whole world; that should cover her tormentors with shame, reproach and infamy.

"She sprang up from her bed and went to search in the drawer of a little old wooden stand, until she found a half page of note paper and a bit of lead pencil.

"She took them out and wrote to her persecutors, saying that she was going to throw herself—not into the sea, nor from a precipice, because both earth and sea give up their dead—but into the quicksands, which never give up anything; they, her tormentors, should never even see again the body they had bruised and torn and degraded; and she prayed that the Lord would ever deal by them as they had dealt with her.

"It must have been near midnight when she heard a tap at her window, so light that at first she thought it was made by a large raindrop; but presently her name was softly called by a voice that she recognized. Then she understood it all, and her thoughts of the quicksands vanished.

"Her room was a small one in the rear of the house, immediately over the back kitchen, and her back window opened upon the roof of the wood shed behind the kitchen. She went and hoisted the window, and there on the roof of the wood shed stood Alfred Whyte.

"He told her that he had taken leave of the ogre and the ogress hours before, and they thought he was off to London by the four o'clock mail; but that he had gone no farther than the railway station, where he had bought a ticket, and had gone on the platform, as if to wait for his train; but when it came up, instead of taking his place on it, he had slipped away in the confusion of its arrival and had hidden himself in the woods on the other side of the road, where he had waited until it was dark, when he had come back to watch the parsonage until every one should have gone to bed, so that he could get speech with Ann.

"And then he asked her if she were 'game for a bolt?'"

"She did not understand him; but when he next spoke plainly, and inquired if she would run away with him and be married, she answered promptly that she would.

"He told her to get ready quickly, and to dress warmly, for the night was damp and cold, and to tie up a little bundle of things that she might need on the journey; but not to take much, because he had plenty of money, and could buy her all she needed.

"'Much;' Poor little thing, she had not much to take! She put on her best dress—a well-worn blue serge—a coarse, black cloth walking jacket, and a little straw hat with a faded blue ribbon. She had no gloves. She tied up a hair brush, worn nearly to the wood, a tooth brush not much better, the half of a broken dressing comb, and one clean linen collar, in a small pocket handkerchief, and she was all ready for her wedding trip.

"He told her to bolt her door before she came out, because that would take the ogres some little while to force it open, and would give the fugitives a better start.

"Ann did everything her boy lover directed, and finally stepped out of the window on to the roof below, and joined him. He let down the window, and closed the shutters with a spring that securely fastened them.

"That, he told her, would certainly give them a longer start, for it would take an hour at least to force the room open and discover her flight.

"Then they left the parsonage together.

"She had forgotten all about the parting note of malediction which she had left behind her on the stand, as she stepped along the lane leading to the highway.

"He asked her to take his arm, and when they reached the public road, he inquired if she were game for a ten mile walk.

"She told him that she could walk to the end of the world with him, because she was so happy to be beside the only one on earth who had ever been kind to her—since her father's death.

"Then he explained the steps that he had taken, and must still take, to elude pursuit; how that he had gone to the railway station and bought a first class ticket for the four o'clock express to London, and afterward, when the train came up, he had mingled with the crowd getting off and getting on, and so eluded observation, and had slipped away and hidden himself in the thicket until dark, so as to make every one concerned believe that he had gone off by the mail train alone to London.

"Now he told her that they must trudge straight on ten miles north, to take the train to Glasgow; so that while people were hunting for them in the south, they would be safe in the north.

"As they walked on he told her that he wanted to get away from England and see the world—the new world across the ocean. He had seen Europe summer after summer, traveling with his father and mother on the Continent. Now he wanted to see America; and asked her if she did not also.

"She told him that she wanted to see every place that he wanted to see, and to go everywhere he wanted to go, for that he was the only friend she had in all the wide world.

"So they walked on for about three hours, and then, about two o'clock in the morning, they reached the little railway station of Skelton. They had to wait two hours for the parliamentary train, which came heavily puffing in about five o'clock on that November morning.

"Young Whyte took second class tickets, and led his closely veiled companion to her seat on the train. And they moved off.

"They reached Glasgow about ten o'clock the next day, and found that there was a steamer bound for New York, to sail at noon. No time was to be lost, so they both went to the agency together, represented themselves as a newly married pair, and engaged the only stateroom to be procured—which happened to be in the second cabin. Their tickets were filled in with the names of Mr. and Mrs. Alfred Whyte—which indeed constituted a legal marriage in Scotland, where a marriageable pair of lovers have only to declare themselves man and wife, in the presence of competent witnesses, to be as lawfully married as if the ceremony had been performed by the Archbishop of Canterbury in his own cathedral.

"They took possession of their stateroom on the Caledonian, which sailed at noon of the same day, and in due time arrived at New York.

"They spent two days at an uptown hotel, and then took the pretty cottage at Harlem, in which they lived for several months. Ann's boy-husband often told her that she grew prettier every day, and he seemed to grow fonder of her every day. He supplied her with a nicer outfit of clothing and more pocket money than she had ever had in her poverty-stricken life, and made her much happier every way than she had ever been before, as long as his money lasted.

"He had left England with nearly one hundred pounds in his pocket—the amount of his half-yearly allowance.

"On his arrival in New York, he had written to his father and confessed his marriage with his tutor's step-daughter and begged forgiveness and—remittances.

"Ann declined to write to her step-mother or the curate, declaring that she preferred that they should believe that she had been driven by their cruelty to bury herself in the quicksands, and that they should suffer all the remorse of conscience and reprobation of society that their conduct toward her deserved.

"But weeks passed, on and no letter filled with blessings and bank notes came from the offended and obdurate father, though the boy constantly assured his girl-wife that the expected epistle would surely come in time, for he was the 'old man's' only son, whom he would not be likely to discard.

"Meanwhile their money was running low. The youth was anxious to travel and see the new world, and to take his bride with him, but he could not do so without funds. At the end of six weeks after he had written the first letter to his father he wrote a second, but received no answer; later still he wrote a third, with no better success.

"They had gone a little into debt, in order to eke out their little ready money until the longed-for letters of credit should come from England; but at the end of six months credit and cash were nearly exhausted.

"One morning in May the boy-husband took leave of the girl-wife, saying, as he kissed her good-by, that he was going down into the city to see if he could get some work to do.

"Without the least misgiving, she received his farewell kiss, and saw him depart—watched him all the way down the street, until he got to Second Avenue and boarded a down-town car.

"Then she re-entered the little gate, and began to tend the jonquils and hyacinths that were just coming into bloom in her little flower garden. She did not expect to see him until night, nor—did she see him even then. When the little gate opened at eight o'clock and a man came up the walk leading to the front door at which she stood, he was not her husband, but the letter carrier, who put a letter in her hand and went away.

"She ran into the house, and lighted the gas to read her letter. Though it gave her a shock, it did not shake her faith in her boy.

"The letter told her, in effect, that Alfred Whyte, when he left her that morning, had started to go to England in the only way by which he could get there—that is, by working his passage as a deck hand on board an outward bound ship; that he had decided on this course so as to get a personal interview with his father, to whom he would go as a penitent prodigal son; for he was sure of obtaining by this means forgiveness, and assistance that would enable him to return and bring his little wife back to England, where they would thenceforth live in comfort and luxury; that the reason he had not confided to her his intention of making the voyage was because he dreaded opposition from her that might have led him to abandon the one plan by which he hoped to better their condition.

"He concluded by entreating her not to think for one instant that he intended to desert her, who was dearer to him than his own life, but to trust in him as he trusted in her. In a postscript he told her where to find the small balance of money they had left, as he had only taken enough for his car fare to the city. In a second postscript he promised to write by every opportunity. In a third and last postscript he begged her to keep up her heart.

"It seemed a frank letter, yet it was reticent upon one point—the name of the ship on which he had sailed. This omission might have been accidental. It certainly did not raise any doubt of the boy's good faith in the mind of the girl.

"She cried a great deal over the separation from her lad, and she made a confidant of the elderly Irishwoman who was her sole servant.

"After two weeks, Ann began to watch daily for the letter carrier, in hope of getting a letter from Alfred; but day after day, week after week, passed and none came. But there came news of the wreck of the Porpoise, which had sailed from New York for London on the very day that Alfred Whyte had left the country—and which had gone down in a storm in mid-ocean with all on board.

"But as numerous ships had left New York on that day bound for various British ports, it was impossible to discover whether the boy was on board, or if he shipped under his own name or an assumed one.

"Ann cried more than ever for a few days, but then seemed to give up her lad for lost, and to resign herself to the 'inevitable.'

"She wrote to Mr. Alfred Whyte, Senior, but got no reply to her letter; again and again she wrote with no better success. The little balance of money left by her boy-husband was all gone. She began to sell off the trifles of jewelry that he had given her.

"One morning the letter carrier left a letter with a London postmark containing a bill of exchange for a hundred pounds, and not one word besides.

"Had it come from her boy-husband, or from his father? She could not tell.

"Well, to be brief, she never saw nor heard of him again. She lived comfortably with her motherly old servant, enjoyed life thoroughly and grew more beautiful every day, and this fool's paradise lasted as long as her money did. Before her last dollar was gone, she saw the advertisement in the *Pursuivant* for a nursery governess, and answered it, as has been told.

"This, my dear Cora, is the substance of the story told me by Ann White on the day that I called on her in answer to her letter. What do you think of it?" inquired Mr. Fabian when he had finished his narrative.

"I think the cruel neglect of her step-parents and the sufferings of her childhood accountable for all her faults, and I feel very sorry for her, notwithstanding that she seems to be a very heartless animal," replied Corona.

"That is the secret of the wonderful preservation of her youth and beauty even up to this present time. Nothing wears a woman out as fast as her own heart."

"You engaged her as you promised to do, but why did you introduce her at Rockhold as a single girl, and why under an alias?" gravely inquired Corona.

"I introduced her as a single girl at her own request because of her extreme youth and her timidity. She naturally shrank from being known as a discarded wife or a doubtful widow. Besides, I never did say she was a single girl. I merely presented her as Rose Flowers, and left it to be inferred from her baby face that she was so."

"But why Rose Flowers when her name was Ann White?"

"What a cross-questioner you are, Corona! but I will answer you. Again it was by her own desire that I presented her as Rose Flowers, which was not an alias, as she explained to me, but a part of her true name. She had been baptized as Rose Anna Flowers, which was the maiden name of her grandmother, her father's mother."

Cora might have asked another question, not so easily answered, if she had known the circumstances to which it related, namely: why Mr. Fabian had fabricated that false story of the young governess which he palmed upon his parents; but, in fact, Cora, at that time a child seven years old, had never heard of it. But she made another inquiry.

"What became of Rose Flowers after she left us? Did she really go to another place? Who was—Captain Stillwater?"

"Mr. Fabian drove slowly and thoughtfully on without answering her question until she had repeated it. Then he said:

"Cora, my dear, that is a story I cannot tell you. Let it be enough for me to say, the Stillwater episode in the life of this lady is the ground upon which I forbid my wife to visit her and object to my niece associating with her."

"Does Violet know the Stillwater story?"

"No; not so much of it even as you have heard. Now, look here, Cora, you think it inconsistent perhaps that I should have brought this woman to Rockhold years ago to become your governess, and now, when she is my father's wife, object to your intimacy with her. In the first instance she has been far, very far, 'more sinned against than sinning;' she had been very imprudent, that was all. She was really the wife, by Scotch law, of the boy she ran away with and then lost. I saw nothing in her case that ought to prevent her entrance into a respectable family, and Heaven knows I pitied her and tried to save her by bringing her to Rockhold. I saved her only for a few years. After she left us—but there, I cannot tell you that story! You must not be intimate with her."

"Yet she is my grandfather's wife!"

"An irreparable misfortune. I can't expose her life to him; such a blow to his pride might be his death, at his age. No! events must take their course; but I hope he will not take her to any place where she is likely to be recognized. Nor do I think he will. He is aging fast, and will be likely to live quietly at Rockhold."

"And I think she also would avoid such risks. She was terribly frightened when she recognized the Dean of Olivet. Was he really her stepfather, the once poor curate?"

"Yes. You see while they were lionizing him in the Eastern cities, his portrait, with a short biographical notice, was published in one of the illustrated weeklies, where I read of him, and identified him by comparing notes with what I had heard."

"How came he to rise so high?"

"Oh, he was a learned divine and eloquent orator. He was well connected, too. It would seem that a very few months after his step-daughter's flight he was inducted into that rich living for which he had been waiting so many years. From that position his rise was slow indeed, covering a period of twenty years, until a few months ago, when he was made Dean of Olivet."

"To think that a man capable of quarreling with his wife and ill-using their step-child should fill so sacred a position in the church!" exclaimed Cora.

"Yes; but you see, my dear, the church is his profession, not his vocation. He is a brilliant pulpit orator, with influential friends; but every brilliant pulpit orator is not necessarily a saint. And as for his quarreling with his wife and ill-using their step-daughter, we have heard but one side of that story."

When they entered the Rockhold drawing room they found Mrs. Rockharrt alone. She arose and came forward and received them with a smile.

"Your grandfather, my dear," she explained to Cora, "came home later than usual from North End, and very much more than usually fatigued. Immediately after dinner he lay down and I left him asleep."

"Where is Uncle Clarence?" inquired Corona.

"He remains at the works for the night. Will you have this chair, love?" said Rose, pulling forward a luxurious "sleepy hollow."

"No, thank you. I must go to my room and change my dress. Will you excuse me for half an hour, Uncle Fabian?" inquired Cora.

"Most willingly, my dear," replied Mr. Fabian, with a very pleased look. Cora left the room.

"I will go with you," exclaimed Rose, turning pale and starting up to follow the young lady.

"No. You will not," said Mr. Fabian, in a tone of authority, as he laid his hand heavily on the woman's shoulder. "Sit down. I have something to say to you."

CHAPTER XXII
FABIAN AND ROSE

"What do you mean?"

"I should rather ask what do you mean, or rather what did you mean, by daring to marry any honest man, and of all men—Aaron Rockharrt? It was the most audacious challenging of destruction that the most reckless desperado could venture upon." Fabian Rockharrt continued, mercilessly:

"Do you not know what, if Mr. Rockharrt were to discover the deception you put upon him, he might do and think himself justified in doing to you?"

Rose shuddered in silence.

"The very least that he would do would be to turn you out of his house, without a dollar, and shut his doors on you forever. Then what would become of you? Who would take you in?"

"Oh, Fabian!" she screamed at last. "Do not talk to me so. You will frighten me into hysterics."

"Now don't make a noise. For if you do, you will precipitate the catastrophe that you fear. Be quiet, I beg you," said Mr. Fabian, composedly, putting his thumbs in his vest pockets and leaning back.

"Why do you say such cruel things to me, then? Such inconsistent things, too. If I was good enough to marry you, I was good enough to marry your father."

"But you were never good enough to marry either of us, my dear. If you will take a little time to reflect on your antecedents, you will acknowledge that you were not quite good enough to marry any honest man," said Mr. Fabian, coolly.

"Yet you asked me to marry you," she said, sobbing softly, with her handkerchief to her eyes.

"Beg pardon, my dear. I think the asking was rather on the other side. You were very urgent that we should be married, and that our betrothal should be formally announced."

"Yes; because you led me to believe that you were going to marry me."

"Excuse me. I never led you to believe so, simply allowed you to believe so. What could a gentleman do under the circumstances? He couldn't contradict a lady."

"Oh, what a prevarication, Fabian Rockharrt, when every word, every deed, every look you bestowed on me went to assure me that you loved me and wished to marry me!"

"Softly, my dear. Softly. I was sorry for you and generous to you. I gave you the use of a pretty little house and a sufficient income during good behavior. But you were ungrateful to me, Rose. You were unkind to me."

"I was not. I would have married you. I could not have done more than that."

"But, my dear, your good sense must have told you that I could not marry you. I have done the best I could by you always. Twice I rescued you from ruin. Once when you were but little more than a child, and your boy-lover, or husband, had left you alone, a young stranger in a strange land—a girl friendless, penniless, beautiful, and so in deadly peril of perdition, I took you on your own representation, and introduced you into my own family as the governess of my niece. I became responsible for you."

"And did I not try my best to please everybody?" sobbed the woman.

"That you did," heartily responded Mr. Fabian. "And everybody loved you. So that, at the end of five years' service, when my niece was to enter a finishing school, and you were to go to another situation, you took with you the best testimonials from my father and mother and from the minister of our parish. But you did not keep your second situation long."

"How could I? I was but half taught. The Warrens would have had me teach their children French and German, and music on the harp and the piano. I knew no language but my own, and no music except that of the piano, which the dear, gentle lady, your mother, taught me out of the kindness of her heart. I was told that I must leave at the end of the term. And my term was nearly out when Captain Stillwater became a daily visitor to the house, and I saw him every evening. He was a tall, handsome man, with a dark complexion and black hair and beard. And I always did admire that sort of a man. Indeed, that was the reason why I always admired you."

"Don't attempt to flatter me."

"I am not flattering anybody. I am telling you why I liked Captain Stillwater. And he was always so good to me! I told him all my troubles. And he sympathized with me! And when I told him that I should be obliged to leave my situation at the end of the quarter, he bade me never mind. And he asked me to be his wife. I did consent to be his wife. I was glad of the chance to get a husband, and a home. So all was arranged. He advised me not to tell the Warrens that we were to be married, however. So at the end of my quarter I went away to a hotel, where Captain Stillwater came for me and took me away to the church where we were married."

"You had no knowledge that Alfred Whyte was dead, and that you were free to wed!"

"He had been lost seven years and was as good as dead to me! Besides, when a man is missing and has; not been heard of for seven years, his wife is free to marry again, is she not?"

"No. She has good grounds for a divorce that is all! To risk a second marriage without these legal formalities, would be dangerous! Might be disastrous! The first husband might turn up and make trouble!"

"I did not know that! But, after all, as it turned out, it did not matter!" sighed Rose.

"Not in the least!" assented Mr. Fabian, amiably.

"After all, it was not my fault! I married him in good faith; I did, indeed!"

"Did you tell him of your previous marriage? That is what you have not told me yet!"

"N-n-no; I was afraid if I did he might break off with me."

"Ah!"

"And I was in such extremity for the want of a home!"

"Had not my father and mother told you that if ever you should find yourself out of a situation, you should come to them? Why did you not take them at their word? They had always been very kind to you, and they would have given you a warm welcome and a happy home. Now, why need you have rushed into a reckless marriage for a home?"

"Oh, Fabian!" she exclaimed, impatiently, "don't pretend to talk like an idiot, for you are not one! Don't talk to me as if I were a wax doll or a wooden woman, for you know I am not one!"

"I am sure I do not know what you mean!"

"Well, then, I loved the man! There, it is out! I loved him more than I ever loved any one else in the whole world! And I was afraid of losing him!"

"And so it was because you loved him so well that you deceived him so much!"

"Didn't he deceive me much more?"

"There were a pair of you—well matched! So well, it seems a pity that you were parted!"

"Oh, how very unkind you are to me!"

"Not yet unkind! Only waiting to see how you are going to behave!"

"I have never behaved badly! I was not wicked; I was unhappy! Unhappy from my birth, almost! I had no evil designs against anybody. I only wanted to be happy and to see people happy. I honestly believed I was lawfully married to Captain Stillwater. He took me to the Wirt House and registered our names as Mr. and Mrs. Stillwater. And we were very happy until his ship sailed. He gave me plenty of money before he went away; but I was heartbroken to part with him, and could take no pleasure in anything until I got a little used to his absence."

"I think you told me that you met him once more before your final separation. When was that meeting? Eh?"

"Fabian Rockharrt, are you trying to catch me in a falsehood? You know very well that I never told you anything of the sort I told you that I never saw him again after he sailed away that autumn day! I waited all the autumn and heard nothing from him, I wrote to him often, but none of my letters were answered. At length I longed so much to see him that I grew wild and reckless and resolved to follow him. I took passage in the second cabin of the Africa and sailed for Liverpool, where I arrived about the middle of December. I went to the agency of the Blue Star Line, to which his ship belonged, and inquired where he was to be found. They told me he had sailed for Calcutta and had taken his wife with him! It turned me to stone—to stone, Fabian—almost! I remember I sat down on a bench and felt numb and cold. And then I asked how long he had been married—hoping, if it was true, that my own was the first and the lawful union. They told me, for ten years, but as they had no family, his wife usually accompanied him on all his voyages. So she had now gone with him to Calcutta."

"I suspect the people in that office were pretty well acquainted with the handsome skipper's 'ways and manners,' and that they understood your case at once."

"I do really believe they did," said Rose; "for they looked at me so strangely, and one man, who seemed to be a porter or a messenger, or something of that sort, said something about a sailor having a wife at every port."

"So after that you came back to New York, and did, at last, what you should have done at first—you wrote to me."

"There was no one on earth to whom, under the peculiar circumstances, I could have written but to you. Oh, Fabian! to whom else could I appeal?"

"And did I not respond promptly to your call?"

"Indeed you did, like a true knight, as you were. And I did not deceive you by any false story, Fabian. I told you all—even thing—how basely I had been deceived—and you soothed and consoled me, and told me that, as I had not sinned intentionally, I had not sinned at all; and you brought me with you to the State capital, and established me comfortably there."

"But you were very ungrateful, my dear. You took everything; gave nothing."

"I would have given you myself in marriage, but you would not have me. You did not think me good enough for you."

"But, bless my wig, child! for your age you had been too much married already—a great deal too much married! You got into the habit of getting married."

"Oh! how merciless you are to me!" Rose said, beginning to weep.

"No; I am not. I have never been unkind to you—as yet. I don't know what I may be! My course toward you will depend very much upon yourself. Have I not always hitherto been your best friend? Ungrateful, unresponsive though you were at that time, did I not procure for you an invitation from my mother to accompany her party on that long, delightful summer trip?"

"I had an impression at the time that I owed the invitation to your father, who suggested to your mother to write and ask me to accompany them."

Mr. Fabian looked surprised, and said—for he never hesitated to tell a fib:

"Oh! that was quite a mistake. It was I myself who suggested the invitation. I thought it would be agreeable to you. Was it not I myself who sent you forward in advance to the Wirt House, Baltimore, there to await the arrival of our party, and join us in our summer travel? And didn't you have a long, delightful tour with us through the most sublime scenery in the most salubrious climates on earth? Didn't you return a perfect Hebe in health and bloom?"

"I acknowledge all that. I acknowledge all my obligations to your family; but at the same time I declare that I also did my part. I was as a white slave to your parents. I was lady's maid to your mother, foot boy to your father. I don't know, indeed, what the old people would have done without me, for no hired servant could have served them as faithfully as I did."

"Oh, yes; you were grateful and devoted to all the family except to me, your best friend—to me, who gave you the use of a lovely home, and a liberal income, and a faithful friendship; and then trusted in your sense of justice for my reward."

"I would have given you all I possessed in the world—my own poor self in marriage—and you led me on to believe that you wished to marry me, but, finally, you would not have me. You went off and married another woman."

"Bah! we are talking around in a circle, and getting back to where we began. Let us come to the point."

"Very well; come to the point," said Rose, sulkily.

"Listen, then: It is not for your reckless elopement with your step-father's pupil, when you were driven from home by cruelty; it is not for your false marriage with Stillwater, when you yourself were deceived; but because with all these antecedents against you—antecedents which constituted you, however unjustly, a pariah, who should have lived quietly and obscurely, but who, instead of doing so, took advantage of kindness shown her, and betrayed the family who sheltered her by luring into a disgraceful marriage its revered father, and bringing to deep dishonor the gray head of Aaron Rockharrt, a man of stern integrity and unblemished reputation—you should be denounced and punished."

"Oh, Fabian, have mercy! have mercy! You would not now, after years of friendship, you would not now ruin me?"

"Listen to me! You checkmated me in that matter of the cottage and the income. Yes, simple as you seem, and sharp as I may appear, you certainly managed to take all and give nothing. And when you found but that you could not take my hand and my name, you waylaid me at the railway station, when I was on my wedding tour, and you swore to be revenged. I laughed at you. I advised you to be anything rather than dramatic. I never imagined the possibility of your threatened revenge taking the form of your marriage. Well, my dear, you have your revenge, I admit; but in your blindness, you could not see that revenge itself might be met by retribution! One man kills another for revenge, and does not, in his blind fury, see the gallows looming in the distance."

"What do you mean? You cannot hang me for marrying your father," exclaimed Rose.

"No; don't raise your voice, or you may be heard. No, Rose, I cannot hang you for treachery; but, my dear, there are worse fates than neat and tidy hanging, which is over in a few minutes. I could expose your past life to my father. You know him, and you know that he would show no ruth, no mercy to deception and treachery such as yours. You know that he would turn you out of the house without money or character, destitute and degraded. What then would be your fate at your age—a fading rose past thirty-seven years old? Sooner or later, and very little later, the poor-house or the hospital. Better a sweet, tidy little hanging and be done with it, if possible."

"You are a fiend to talk to me so! a fiend! Fabian Rockharrt," exclaimed Rose, bursting into hysterical sobs and tears.

"Now, be quiet, my child; you'll raise the house, and then there will be an explosion."

"I don't care if there will be. You are cruel, savage, barbarous! I never meant to do any harm by marrying Mr. Rockharrt. I never meant to be revenged on you or anybody. I only said so because I was so excited by your desertion of me. I married the old gentleman for a refuge from the world. I meant to do my duty by him, though he is as cross as a bear with a bruised head. But do your worst; I don't care. I would just as lief die as live. I am tired of trying to be good; tired of trying to please people; tired, oh, very tired of living!"

"Come, come," said soft-hearted Mr. Fabian; "none of that nonsense. Place yourself in my hands, to be guided by me and to work for my interests, and none of these evils shall happen to you. You shall live and die in wealth and luxury, my father's honored wife, the mistress of Rockhold."

He spoke slowly, tenderly, caressingly, and as she listened to him her sobs and tears subsided and she grew calmer.

"What is it you want me to do for you? What can I do for you, indeed, powerless as I am?" she inquired at last.

"You must use all your influence with my father in my interests, and use it discreetly and perseveringly," he whispered.

"But I have no influence. Never was the young wife of an old man—and I am young in comparison to him—treated so harshly. I am not his pet; I am his slave!" she complained.

"But you must obtain influence over him. You can do that. You are with him night and day when he is not at his business. You are his shadow—beg pardon, I ought to have said his sunshine."

"I am his slave, I tell you."

"Then be his humble, submissive, obedient slave; betray no disappointment, discontent, or impatience at your lot. The harsher he is, the humbler must you be; the more despotic he becomes, the more subservient you must seem. Make yourself so perfectly complying in all his moods that he shall believe you to be the very 'perfect rose of womanhood,' more excellent even than he thought when he married you, and so as he grows older and weaker in mind as well as body you will gain not only influence but ascendency over him, and these you must use in my interest."

"But how? I don't understand."

"Pay attention, then, and you will understand Mr. Rockharrt is aged. In the course of nature he must soon pass away. Fie has made no will. Should he die intestate, the whole property, by the laws of this commonwealth, would fall to pieces; that is to say, it would be divided into three parts—one-third would go to you—"

Rose started, caught her breath, and stared at the speaker; the greed of gain dilating her great blue eyes. The third of the Rockharrt's fabulous wealth to be hers at her husband's death! Amazing! How many millions or tens of millions would that be? Incredible! And all for her, and she with, perhaps, half a century of life to live and enjoy it! What a vista!

"Why do you stare at me so?" demanded Mr. Fabian.

"Because I was so surprised. That is not the law in England. In England there are usually what are called marriage settlements, which make a suitable provision for the wife, but leave the bulk of the property to go to the children—generally to the oldest son."

"And such should be the law here, but it isn't; and so if my father should die without having made a will, the great estate would break, as I said, into three parts—one part would be yours, the other two parts would be divided into three shares, to me, to my brother, and to the heirs of my sister. The business at North End would probably be carried on by Aaron Rockharrt's sons."

"But would not that be equitable?" inquired Rose, who had no mind to have her third interfered with.

"It would not be expedient, nor is such a disposition of his property the intention of Aaron Rockharrt. I know, from what he has occasionally hinted, that he means to bequeath the Great North End Works to me and my brother Clarence, share and share alike; but he puts off making this will, which indeed must never be made. The North End Works should not be a monster with two heads, but a colossus with one head with my head. So that I wish my father to make a will leaving the North End Works to me exclusively—to me alone as the one head."

"I think if I dared to suggest such a thing to him, he would take off my head!" said Rose, with grim humor.

"I think he would if you should do so suddenly or clumsily. But you must insinuate the idea very slowly and subtlely. Clarence is not for the works; Clarence is too good for this world—at least for the business of this world. I think him half an imbecile! My father does not hesitate to call him a perfect idiot. Do you begin to see your way now? Clarence can be moderately provided for, but should have no share in the North End Works."

"The North End Works to be left to you solely; Clarence to be moderately provided for; and what of the two children of the late Mrs. Haught?"

"Oh! my father never intends to leave them more than a modest legacy. They have each inherited money from their father. No; understand me once for all, Rose. I must be the sole heir of all my father's wealth, with the exceptions I have named, and the sole successor to his business, without any exception whatever. You must live, serve him and bear with him only to obtain such an ascendency over him as to induce him to make such a will as I have dictated to you. You can do this. You can insinuate it so subtlely that he will never suspect the suggestion came from you. I say you can do this, and you must do it. The woman who could deceive and entrap old Aaron Rockhartt, the Iron King, into matrimony, can do anything else in the world that she pleases to do with him if only she will be as subtle, as patient, and as complacent to him after marriage as she had been before marriage."

"If Clarence is to be so provided for, Cora and Sylvan to have modest legacies, and you to have the huge bulk of the estate—where is my third to come from?"

"Why, my dear, I could never let you have so vast a slice out of the mammoth fortune! Your third of the estate must follow Clarence's share of the business—into nothingness. You must play magnanimity, sacrifice your third, and content yourself with a suitable provision," said Fabian, equably.

"I will never do that! I would not do it to save your life, Fabian Rockharrt!"

"Oh, yes, you will, my darling. Not to save my life, but to save yourself from being denounced to Mr. Rockharrt, and turned out of this house, destitute and degraded."

"I don't care if I should be! Do you think me quite a baby in your hands? I have been reflecting since you have been talking to me. I have been remembering that you told me that the law gives the widow one third of her late husband's property when he dies intestate, and entitles her to it, no matter what sort of a will he makes."

"Unless there has been a settlement, my angel," said Mr. Fabian, composedly.

"Well, there has been no settlement in my case. So whether Aaron Rockharrt should die intestate, or whether he should make a will, I am sure of my lawful third. So I defy you, Mr. Fabian Rockharrt. You may denounce me to your father He may turn me out of doors without a penny, and 'without a character,' as the servants say, but he cannot divorce me, because I have been faithful to him ever since our marriage. I could compel him by law to support me, even though he might not let me share his home. He would be obliged by law to give me alimony in proportion to his income, and, oh! what a magnificent revenue that would be for me—with freedom from his tyranny into the bargain! And at his death, which could not be long coming at his age, and after such a shock as his dutiful son proposes to give him, I should come in for my third. And, oh, where so rich a widow as I should be! With forty or fifty years of life before me in which to enjoy my fortune! Ah, you see, my clever Mr. Fabian Rockharrt, though you frightened me out of self-possession at first, when I come to think over the situation, I find that you can do me no great harm. If you should put your threats in execution and bring about a violent separation between myself and my husband, you would do me a signal favor, for I should gain my personal freedom, with a handsome alimony during his life, and at his death a third of his vast estate," she concluded, snapping her fingers in his face.

"I think not."

"Yes; I would."

"No; you would not."

"Indeed! Why would I not, pray?" she inquired, with mocking incredulity.

"Oh, because of a mere trifle in your code of morals—an insignificant impediment."

"Tchut!" she exclaimed, contemptuously. "Do you think me quite an idiot?"

"I think you would be much worse than an idiot if, in case of my father's discarding you, you should move an inch toward obtaining alimony or in the case of the coveted 'third.'"

"Pshaw! Why, pray?"

"Because you have not, and never can have, the shadow of a right to either."

"Bah! why not?"

"Because—Alfred Whyte is living!"

She caught her breath and gazed at the speaker with great dilating blue eyes.

"What—do—you—mean?" she faltered.

"Alfred Whyte, your husband of twenty years ago, is still living and likely to live—a very handsome man of forty years old, residing at his magnificent country seat, Whyte Hall, Dulwich, near London."

"Married again?" she whispered, hoarsely.

"Certainly not; an English gentleman does not commit bigamy."

"How did you—become acquainted—with these facts?"

"I was sufficiently interested in you to seek him out, when I was in England. I discovered where he lived; also that he was looking out for the best investment of his idle capital. I called on him personally in the interests of our great enterprise. He is now a member of the London syndicate."

"Did you speak—of me?"

"Never mentioned your name. How could I, knowing as I did of the Stillwater episode in your story?"

"And he lives! Alfred Whyte lives! Oh, misery, misery, misery! Evil fate has followed me all the days of my life," moaned Rose, wringing her hands.

"Now, why should you take on so, because Whyte is living? Would you have had that fine, vigorous man, in the prime of his life, die for your benefit?"

"But I thought he was dead long ago."

"You were too ready to believe that, and to console yourself. He was more faithful to your memory."

"How do you know? You said my name was never mentioned between you."

"Not from him, but from a mutual acquaintance, of whom I asked how it was that Mr. Whyte had never married, I heard that he had grieved for her out of all reason and had ever remained faithful to the memory of his first and only love. My own inference was, and is, that the report of your death was got up by his friends to break off the connection."

"And you never told this 'mutual friend' that I still lived?"

"How could I, my dear, with my knowledge of your Stillwater affair? No, no; I was not going to disturb the peace of a good man by telling him that his child-wife of twenty years ago was still living, but lost to him by a fall far worse than death. No—I let you remain dead to him."

"Oh, misery! misery! misery! I would to Heaven I were dead to everybody! dead, dead indeed!" she cried, wringing her hands in anguish.

"Come, come, don't be a fool! You see that you are utterly in my power and must do my will. Do it, and you will come to no harm; but live and die in a luxurious home."

CHAPTER XXIII
SYLVAN'S ORDERS

While the amiable Mr. Fabian was engaged in soothing the woman whom he was resolved to make his instrument in gaining the whole of his father's great business bequeathed to him by will, carriage wheels were heard grating on the gravel of the drive leading up to the front door of the house, and a few minutes afterward the master's knock was answered by the hall waiter, and old Aaron Rockharrt strode into the drawing room.

"I did not know that you had gone out again. I left you on the library sofa asleep," said Rose, deferentially, as she sprang up to meet him.

"I was called out on business that don't concern you. Ah, Fabian! How is it that I find you here to-night?" inquired the Iron King, as he threw himself into a chair.

"I brought Cora home from the Banks," replied the eldest son.

"Ah! how is Mrs. Fabian?"

"Still delicate. I can scarcely hope that she will be stronger for some weeks yet."

"When are you going to bring her to call on my wife?" demanded the Iron King, bending his gray brows somewhat angrily and looking suspiciously on his son; for he was not pleased that his daughter-in-law's visit of ceremony had been so long delayed.

"As soon as she is able to leave the house. Our physician has forbidden her to take any long walk or ride for some time yet."

"And how long is this seclusion to last?"

"Until after a certain event to take place at the end of three months."

"Ah! and then another month for convalescence! So it will be late in the autumn before we can hope to see Mrs. Fabian Rockharrt at Rockhold!"

"I fear so, indeed, sir!"

"I do not approve of this petting, coddling, and indulging women. It makes the weak creatures weaker. If you choose to seclude your wife or allow her to seclude herself on account of a purely physiological condition, I will not allow Mrs. Rockharrt to go near her until she goes to return her call."

When Cora reached her chamber that evening, she sat down to reflect on all that her Uncle Fabian had told her of the past history of her grandfather's young wife, and to anticipate the possible movements of her brother. Her own life, since the loss of her husband—now loved so deeply, though loved too late—she felt was over. The future had nothing for herself. What, therefore, could she do with the dull years in which she might long vegetate through life but to give them in useful service to those who needed help? She would go with her brother to the frontier, and find some field of labor among the Indians. She would found a school with her fortune, and devote her life to the education of Indian children. And she would call the school by her lost husband's name, and so make of it a monument to his memory.

Revolving these plans in her mind, Cora Rothsay retired to rest. The next morning she arose at her usual hour, dressed, and went down stairs.

Old Aaron Rockharrt and his young wife were already in the parlor, waiting for the breakfast bell to ring.

She had but just greeted them when the call came, and all moved toward the breakfast room.

Just as the three had seated themselves at the table, and while Rose was pouring out the coffee, the sound of carriage wheels was heard approaching the house, and a few minutes later Mr. Clarence and Sylvan entered the breakfast room with joyous bustle.

"What—what—what does this unseemly excitement mean?" sternly demanded the Iron King, while Cora arose to shake hands with her uncle and brother; and while Rose, fearful of doing wrong, did nothing at all.

"What is the matter? What has happened? Why have you left the works at this hour of the morning, Clarence?" he requested of his son.

"I came with Sylvan, sir, for the last time before he leaves us for distant and dangerous service, and for an unlimited period."

"Ah! you have your orders, then?" said Mr. Rockharrt, in a somewhat mollified tone.

"Yes, sir," said the young lieutenant. "I received my commission by the earliest mail this morning, with orders to report for duty to Colonel Glennin, of the Third Regiment of Infantry, now at Governor's Island, New York harbor, and under orders to start for Fort Farthermost, on the Mexican frontier. I must leave to-night in order to report in time."

Cora looked at him with the deepest interest.

Rose thought now she might venture on a little civility without giving offense to her despotic lord.

"Have you had breakfast, you two?" she inquired.

"No, indeed. We started immediately after receiving the orders," said Sylvan. "And we are as hungry as two bears."

"Bring chairs to the table, Mark, for the gentlemen," said young Mrs. Rockharrt, who then rang for two more covers and hot coffee.

"Cora," whispered Sylvan, as soon as he got a chance to speak to his sister, "you can never get ready to go with me on so short a notice. Women have so much to do."

"Sylvan," she replied, "I have been ready for a month."

CHAPTER XXIV
SOMETHING UNEXPECTED

The day succeeding that on which Sylvanus Haught had received his commission as second lieutenant in the 3d Regiment of Infantry, then on Governor's Island, New York harbor, and under orders for Fort Farthermost, on the southwestern frontier, was a very busy one for Cora Rothsay; for, however well she had been prepared for a sudden journey, there were many little final details to be attended to which would require all the time she had left at her disposal.

A farewell visit must be paid to Violet Rockharrt, and—worse than all—an explanatory interview must be held with her grandfather in relation to her departure with Sylvanus Haught, and that interview must be held before the Iron King should leave Rockhold that morning for his daily visit to the works.

Cora had often, during the last year, and oftener since her grandfather's second marriage, taken occasion to allude to her intention of accompanying her brother to his post of duty, however distant and dangerous that post might be. She had done this with the fixed purpose of preparing this autocratic old gentleman's mind for the event.

Now, the day of her intended departure had arrived; she was to leave Rockhold with her brother that afternoon to take the evening express to New York. And as she could not go without taking leave of her grandfather, it was necessary that she should announce her intention to him before he should start on his daily visit to North End.

Therefore Cora had risen very early that morning and had gone down into the little office or library of the Iron King, that was situated at the rear of the middle hall, there to wait for him, as it was his custom to rise early and go into his study, to look over the papers before breakfast. These papers were brought by a special messenger from North End, who started from the depot as soon as the earliest train arrived with the morning's mail and reached Rockhold by seven o'clock.

She had not sat there many minutes before Mr. Rockharrt entered the study.

"I am going away with my brother," Cora said, without any preface whatever, "to Fort Farthermost, on the southwestern Indian frontier."

"I think you must be crazy."

"Dear grandpa, this is no impulsive purpose of mine. I have thought of it ever since—ever since—the death of my dear husband," said Cora, in a broken voice.

"Oh! the death of your dear husband!" he exclaimed, rudely interrupting her. "Much you cared for the death of your dear husband! If you had, you would never have driven him forth to his death!—for that is what you did! You cannot deceive me now. As long as the fate of Rule Rothsay was a mystery, I was myself at somewhat of a loss to account for his disappearance—though I suspected you even then—but when the news came that he had been killed by the Comanches near the boundaries of Mexico, and I had time to reflect on it all, I knew that he had been driven away by you—you! And all for the sake of a titled English dandy! You need not deny it, Cora Rothsay!"

"It would be quite useless to deny anything that you choose to assert, sir," replied the young lady, coldly but respectfully. "Yet I must say this, that I loved and honored my husband more than I ever did or ever can love and honor any other human being. His departure broke my spirit, and his death has nearly broken my heart—certainly it has blasted my future. My life is worth nothing, nothing to me, except as I make it useful to those who need my help."

"Rubbish!" exclaimed old Aaron Rockharrt, turning over the leaves of his paper and looking for the financial column.

"Grandfather, please hear me patiently for a few minutes, for after to-day I do not know that we may ever meet again," pleaded Cora.

The old man laid his open paper on his knees, set his spectacles up on his head, and looked at her.

"What the devil do you mean?" he slowly inquired.

"Sir, I am to leave Rockhold with my brother this afternoon, to go with him, first to Governor's Island, and within a few days start with him for the distant frontier fort which may be his post of duty for many years to come. We may not be able to return within your lifetime, grandfather," said Cora, gravely and tenderly.

"And what in Satan's name, unless you are stark mad, should take you out to the Indian frontier?" he demanded.

"I might answer, to be with my only brother, I being his only sister."

"Bosh! Men's wives very seldom accompany them to these savage posts, much less their sisters! What does a young officer want his sister tagging after him for?"

"It is not that Sylvan especially wants me, nor for his sake alone that I go."

"Well, then, what in the name of lunacy do you go for?"

"That I may devote my time and fortune to a good cause—to the education of Indian girls and boys. I mean to build—"

"That, or something like that, was what Rothsay tried to do when you drove him away, as if he had been a leper, to the desert. Well, go on! What next? Let us hear the whole of the mad scheme!"

"I mean to build a capacious school house, in which I will receive, board, lodge, and teach as many Indian children as may be intrusted to me, until the house shall be full."

"Moonstruck mania! That is what your mad husband driven mad by you—attempted on a smaller scale, and failed."

"That is why I wish to do this. I wish to follow in his footsteps It is the best thing I can do to honor his memory."

"But he was murdered for his pains."

Cora shuddered and covered her face with her hands for a space; then she answered, slowly:

"There may be many failures; but there will never be any success unless the failures are made stepping stones to final victory."

"Fudge! See here, mistress! No doubt you suffer a good many stings of conscience for having driven the best man that ever lived—except, hem! well—to his death! But you need not on that account expatriate yourself from civilization, to go out to try to teach those red devils who murdered your husband and burned his hut, and who will probably murder you and burn your school house! You have been a false woman and a miserable sinner, Cora Rothsay! And you have deserved to suffer and you have suffered, there is no doubt about that! But you have repented, and may be pardoned. You need not immolate yourself at your age. You are a mere girl. You will get over your morbid grief. You may marry again."

Cora slowly, sadly, silently shook her head.

"Oh, yes; you will."

"No, no; no, dear grandpa. I will bear my dear, lost husband's name to the end of my life, and it shall be inscribed on my tomb. Ah! would to Heaven that at the last, I might lay my ashes beside his," she moaned.

"Now don't be a confounded fool, Cora Rothsay! To be sure, all women are fools! But, then, a girl with a drop of my blood in her veins should not be such a consummate idiot as you are showing yourself to be. You shall not go out with Sylvan to that savage frontier. It is no place for a woman, particularly for an unmarried woman. You would come to a bad end. I shall speak to Sylvan. I shall forbid him to take you there," said the old autocrat.

Cora smiled, but answered nothing. She had firmly made up her mind to go with her brother, whether her grandfather should approve the action or not; but she thought it unnecessary to dispute the matter with him just now.

"So, mistress, you will stay here, under my guardianship, until you accept a husband, like a respectable woman," continued old Aaron Rockharrt.

Still Cora remained silent, standing by his chair, with her hand resting on the table, and her eyes cast down.

The egotist seemed not to object to having all the talk to himself.

"Come!" he exclaimed, with sudden animation, sitting bolt upright in his chair, "When I found you in this room just now, you said you had something to tell me. And you told it. Naturally, it was not worth hearing. Now, then, I have something to tell you, which is so well worth hearing that when you have heard it your missionary madness may be cured, and your Quixotic expedition given up: in fact, all your plans in life changed—a splendid prospect opened before you."

Cora looked up, her languor all gone, her interest aroused. Something was rising in her mind; not a sun of hope ah! no—but nebula, obscure, unformed, indistinct, yet with possible suns of hope, worlds of happiness, within it. What did her grandfather mean? Had he heard something about— Was Rule yet—

Swift as lightning flashed these thoughts through her mind while her grandfather drew his breath between his utterances.

"Listen! This is what I had to tell you: I had a letter a few days ago from an old suitor of yours," he said, looking keenly at his granddaughter.

Cora's eyes fell, her spirits drooped. The nebula of unknown hopes and joys had faded away, leaving her prospect dark again. She looked depressed and disappointed. She could feel no shadow of interest in her old suitors.

"I received this letter several days since, and being at leisure just then. I answered it. But in the pressure of some important matters I forgot to tell you of it, though it concerned yourself mostly, I might say entirely. Shouldn't have remembered it now, I suppose, if it had not been for your foolish talk about going out for a missionary to the savages. Ah! another destiny awaits your acceptance."

Cora sighed in silence.

"Now, then. Of course you must know who this correspondent is."

"Without offense to you, grandfather, I neither know nor care," languidly replied the lady.

"But it is not without offense to me. You are the most eccentric and inconsistent woman I ever met in all the course of my life. You are not constant even to your inconstancy."

Having uttered this paradox, the old man threw himself back in his chair and gazed at his granddaughter.

"I am not yet clear as to your meaning, sir," she said, coldly but respectfully.

"What! Have you quite forgotten the titled dandy for whom you were near breaking your heart three years ago? For whom you were ready to throw over one of the best and truest men that ever lived! For whom you really did drive Regulas Rothsay, on the proudest and happiest day of his life, into exile and death!"

"Oh, don't! don't! grandfather! Don't!" wailed Cora, sinking on an office stool, and dropping her hands and head on the table.

"Now, none of that, mistress. No hysterics, if you please. I won't permit any woman about me to indulge in such tantrums. Listen to me, ma'am. My correspondent was young Cumbervale, the noodle!"

"Then I never wish to see or hear or think of him again!" exclaimed Cora.

"Indeed! But that is a woman all through. She will do or suffer anything to get her own way. She will defy all her friends and relations, all principles of truth and honor; she will move Heaven and earth, go through fire and water, to get her own way; and when she does get it she don't want it, and she won't have it."

"Grandfather!" pleaded Cora.

"Silence! Three years ago you would have walked over all our dead bodies, if necessary, to marry that noble booby. And you would have married him if it had not been for me! I would not permit you to wed him then, because you were in honor bound to Regulas Rothsay. I shall insist on your accepting him now, because poor Rothsay is in his grave, and this will be the best thing to do for you to help you out of harm's way from redskins and rattlesnakes and other reptiles. I don't think much of the fellow; but he seems to be a harmless idiot, and is good enough for you."

Cora answered never a word, but she felt quite sure that not even the iron will of the Iron King could ever coerce her into marriage with any man, least of all with the man whose memory was identified with her heart's tragedy. The old man continued his monologue.

"The best thing about the fellow is his constancy. He was after your imaginary fortune once. I am sure of that. And he was so dazzled by the illumination of that *ignis fatuus* that he didn't see you, perhaps, and didn't recognize how much he really cared for you. At all events, in his letter to me—and, by the way, it is very strange that he should write to me after the snubbing I gave him in London," said the Iron King, reflectively.

Cora did not think that was strange. She, at least, felt sure that it was as impossible for the young duke to take offense at the rudeness of the old iron man as at the raging of a dog or the tearing of a bull. But she did not drop a hint of this to the egotist, who never imagined passive insolence to be at the bottom of the duke's forbearance.

"In his letter to me," resumed old Aaron Rockharrt, "the young fool tells me that, immediately after his great disappointment in being rejected by you, he left England—and, indeed, Europe—and traveled through every accessible portion of Asia and Africa, in the hope of overcoming his misplaced affection, but in vain, for that he returned home at the end of two years with his heart unchanged. There he learned through the newspapers that you had been recently widowed, through the murder of your husband in an Indian mutiny. That's how he put it. He farther wrote that, in the face of such a tragedy as that, he felt bound to forbear the faintest approach toward resuming his acquaintance with you until some considerable time should have elapsed, although, he was careful to add, he always believed that you had given him your heart, and would have given him your hand had you been permitted to do so. He ended his letter by asking me to give him your address, that he might write to you. He evidently supposed you to be keeping house for yourself, as English widows of condition usually do. Well, my girl, what do you think I did?"

"You told me, sir, that, being at leisure just then, you answered his letter immediately," coldly replied Cora.

"Yes; and I told him that you were living with me. I gave him the full address. And I told him that I was pleased with his frankness and fidelity, qualities which I highly approved; and I added that if he wished to renew his suit to you, he need not waste time in writing, but that he might come over and court you in person here at Rockhold, where he should receive a hearty, old-fashioned welcome."

Cora gazed at the old man aghast.

"Oh, grandfather, you never wrote that!" she exclaimed.

"I never wrote that? What do you mean, mistress? Am I in the habit of saying what is not true?"

"Oh, no; but I am so grieved that you should have written such a letter."

"Why, pray?"

"Because I cannot bear that any one should think for a moment that I could ever marry again."

"Rubbish!"

"Well, it does not matter after all. If the duke should come on this fool's errand, I shall be far enough out of his reach," thought Cora; but she said no more.

The breakfast bell rang out with much clamor, and the old man arose growling.

"And now you have cheated me out of my hour with the newspapers by your foolish talk. Come, come to breakfast and let us hear no more nonsense about going on that wild goose chase to the Indian frontier."

At the end of the morning meal he arose from the table, called his young wife to fetch him his hat, his gloves, his duster, and other belongings, and he got ready for his daily morning drive to the works.

"I shall remain at North End to bid you good-by, Sylvan. Call at my office there on your way to the depot," he said, as he left the house to step into his carriage waiting at the door.

As the sound of the wheels rolled off and died in the distance, Rose turned to Cora and inquired:

"My dear, does he know that you are going out West with Sylvan?"

"He should know it. I have spoken freely of my plans before you both for months past," said Cora.

"But, my dear, he never took the slightest notice of anything you said on that subject. Why, he did not even seem to hear you."

"He heard me perfectly. Nothing passes in my grandfather's presence that he does not see and hear and understand."

"Well, then, I reckon he thinks you have changed your mind; for he spoke of meeting Sylvan at North End to bid him good-by, but said not a word about you."

"He will believe that I am going when he sees me with Sylvan," said Cora.

And then she touched the bell and ordered her carriage to be brought to the door.

"We must go and take leave of Mrs. Fabian Rockharrt," she said to Rose.

Twenty minutes later Cora and Sylvan entered the pony carriage. Sylvan took the reins and started for Violet Banks.

They soon reached the lovely villa, where they found Violet seated in a Quaker rocking-chair on the front porch, with a basket workstand beside her, busily and happily engaged in her beloved work—embroidering an infant's white cashmere cloak. She jumped up, dropped her work, and ran to meet her visitors as they alighted from the carriage. She kissed Cora rapturously, and Sylvan kissed her.

"How lovely of you both to come! Wait a minute till I call a boy to take your chaise around to the stable. And, oh, sit down. You are going to stay all day with me, too, and late into the night—there is a fine moon to-night. Or maybe you will stay a week or a month. Why not? Oh, do stay," she rattled on, a little incoherently on account of her happy excitement.

"No, dear," said Cora, "we can only stay a very few minutes. The rising moon will see us far away on our route to New York."

"W-h-y! You astonish me! How sudden this is! Where are you going?" asked Violet, pausing in her hurry to call a groom.

"Let me explain," said Cora, taking one of the Quaker chairs and seating herself. "Sylvan has just received his commission as second lieutenant in the 3d Regiment of Infantry, now on Governor's Island, New York harbor, but under orders for Fort Farthermost, on the extreme frontier of the Indian Reserve. He leaves by the afternoon express, and I go with him."

"Cora!" exclaimed Violet, as she dropped into her chair. "I know you have talked about this, but I never thought you would do such a wild deed! Please don't think of going out among bears and Indians!"

"I must, dear, for many reasons. Sylvan and myself are all and all to each other at present, and we should not be parted. More than that, I wish to do something in the world. I can not do anything here. I am not wanted, you see. I must, therefore, go where I may be wanted and may do some good."

"But what can you do—out there?"

Cora then explained her plan of establishing a missionary home and school for Indian children.

"What a good, great, but, oh, what a Quixotic plan! Sylvan, why will you let her do it?" pleaded Violet.

"My dear, I would not presume to oppose Cora. If she thinks she is right in this matter, then she is right. If her resolution is fixed, then I will uphold and defend her in that resolution," said the young lieutenant, loyally. But all the same his secret thought was that some fine fellow in his own regiment might be able to persuade Cora to devote her time and fortune to him, instead of to the redskins.

After a little more talk Cora got up and kissed Violet good-by. Sylvan followed her example with a little more ardor than was absolutely necessary, perhaps.

At Rockhold luncheon was on the table, and young Mrs. Rockhart waiting for them. Mr. Clarence was also at home, having determined to risk his father's displeasure and to neglect his business on this one day—this last day, for the sake of the niece and the nephew who were so dear to his heart.

After luncheon Sylvan went out to oversee the loading of the farm van, which was drawn by two sturdy mules, with the many heavy trunks and boxes that contained Cora's wardrobe and books—among the latter a large number of elementary school books. Mr. Clarence stood by his side to help him in case of need. Cora went up to her room, where nothing was now left to be done but to pack her little traveling bag with the necessaries for her journey, and then put on her traveling suit. She had a quantity of valuable jewelry, but this she put carefully into her hand bag, intending to convert it all into money as soon as she should reach New York, and to consecrate the fund, with the bulk of her fortune, to her projected home school for the Indian children.

As she sat there, she was by some occult agency led to think of her grandfather's young wife—to think of her tenderly, charitably, compassionately. Poor Rose! In infancy, from the day of her father's death, an unloved, neglected, persecuted child; in childhood, driven to desperation and elopement by the miseries of her home; in girlhood, deceived and abandoned by her lover; now, in womanhood, as friendless and unhappy as if she had not married a wealthy man, and was not living in a luxurious home. Poor Rose! She had lost her sense of honor, or she never would have married Mr. Rockharrt, even for a refuge. But, through all her sins and sorrows, she had not lost her tender heart, her sweet temper, or her amiable desire to serve and to please. She had now a hard time with her aged, despotic husband. He had not gratified her ambition by taking her into the upper circles of society, for he seemed now to have given up society; he had not pleased her harmless vanity with presents of fine dress and jewelry; no, nor even regarded her services with any sort of affectionate recognition.

Cora sat there feeling sorry that she had ever shown herself cold and haughty to the helpless creature who had always done all that she could to win her (Cora's) love, and whom she was about to leave to the tender mercies of a hard and selfish old man, who, though he highly approved of his young wife's meekness, humility and subserviency, and held her up as an example to her whole sex, yet did not care for her, did not consult her wishes in anything, did not consider her happiness.

Cora sat wondering what she could do to give this poor little soul some little pleasure before leaving her. Suddenly she thought of her jewels. She resolved to select a set and give it to Rose with some kind parting word.

She took her hand bag and withdrew from it case after case, examining each in turn. There was a set of diamonds worth many thousand dollars; a set of rubies and pearls, worth almost as much; a set of emeralds, very costly; but none of them as lovely as a set of sapphires, pearls, and diamonds, artistically arranged together, the sapphires encircled by a row of pearls, with an outer circle of small diamonds; the whole suggesting the blue color, the foam, and the sparkle of the sea.

This Cora selected as a parting present to her grandfather's young wife.

She took them in her hand and hurried to Rose's room, knocked at the door and entered. Rose was seated in a white dimity-covered arm chair, engaged in reading a novel. She looked surprised, and almost frightened, at the sight of Cora, who had never before condescended to enter this private room.

"Have I disturbed you?" inquired Cora.

"Oh, no; no, indeed. Pray come in. Please sit down. Will you have this arm chair?" eagerly inquired the young woman, rising from her seat.

"No, thank you, Rose; I have scarcely time to sit. I have brought you a keepsake which I hope you will sometimes wear in memory of your old pupil," said Cora, opening the casket and displaying the gems.

Rose's face was a study—all that was good and evil in her was aroused at the sight of the rich and costly jewels—vanity, cupidity, gratitude, tenderness.

"Oh, how superb they are! I never saw such splendid gems! A parure for a princess, and you give them to me? What a munificent present! How kind you are, Cora! What can I do? How shall I ever be able to return your kindness?" said Rose, as tears of delight and wonder filled her eyes.

"Wear them and enjoy them. They suit your fair complexion very well. And now let me bid you good-by, here."

"No, no; not yet. I will go down and see you off—see the very last of you, Cora, until the carriage takes you out of sight. Oh, dear, it may indeed be the very last that I shall ever see of you, sure enough."

"I hope not. Why do you speak so sadly?"

"Because I am not strong. My father died of consumption; so did my elder brothers and sisters, the children of his first marriage, and often I think I shall follow them."

Mrs. Rothsay looked at the speaker. The transparent delicacy of complexion, the tenderness of the limpid blue eyes, the infantile softness of face, throat, and hands, certainly did not seem to promise much strength or long life; but Cora spoke cheerfully:

"Such hereditary weakness may be overcome in these days of science, Rose. You must banish fear and take care of yourself. Now, I really must go and put on my bonnet."

"Very well, then, if you must. I will meet you in the hall. Oh, my dear, I am so very grateful to you for these precious jewels, and more than all for the friendship and kindness that prompted the gift," said Rose; and perhaps she really did believe that she prized the giver more than the gift; for such self-deception would have been in keeping with her superficial character.

Cora left the room and hurried to her chamber, where she put on her bonnet and her linen duster. She had scarcely fastened the last button when her brother knocked at the door, calling out:

"Come, Cora, come, or we shall miss the train."

Cora caught up her traveling bag, cast

"A long, last, lingering look"

around the dear, familiar room which she had occupied when at Rockhold from her childhood's days, and then went out and joined her brother.

In the hall below they were met by Rose

"Be good to her, poor thing," whispered Cora to Sylvan.

"All right," replied the young lieutenant.

Rose's eyes were filled with tears. It seemed to the friendless creature very hard to lose Cora, just as Cora was beginning to be friendly.

"Good-by," said Mrs. Rothsay, taking the woman's hand. But Rose burst into tears, threw her arms around the young lady's neck, hugged her close, and kissed her many times.

"Good-by, my pretty step-grandmother-in-law," said Sylvan, gayly, taking her hand and giving her a kiss. "You are still

'The rose that all admire,'

but the best of friends must part."

And leaving Rose in tears, he opened the door for his sister to pass out before him. But she, at least, passed no farther than the front porch, where she stood looking down the lawn in surprise and anxiety, while Sylvan hurried off to see what was the meaning of that which had so suddenly startled them. What was it? What had happened?

A crowd of men, silent, but with faces full of suppressed excitement and surrounding something that was borne in their midst, was slowly marching up the avenue.

Cora watched Sylvan as he went to meet them; saw him speak to them, though she could not hear what he said; saw them stop and put the something, which they bore along and escorted, down on the gravel; saw a parley between her brother and the crowd, and finally saw her brother turn and hurry back toward the house, wearing a pale and troubled countenance.

"You may take the carriage back to the stables, John," said the lieutenant to the wondering negro groom, as he passed it in returning to the porch.

"What is the matter, Sylvan? What has happened? Why have you sent the carriage away?" Cora anxiously inquired.

"Because, my dear, we must not leave Rockhold at present," he gravely replied. "There has been an accident, Cora."

"An accident! On the railroad?"

"No, my dear; to our old grandfather."

"To grandfather! Oh, Sylvan! no! no!" she cried, turning white, and dropping upon a bench, all her latent affection for the aged patriarch—the unsuspected affection—waking in her heart.

"Yes, dear," said Sylvan, softly.

"Seriously? Dangerously? Fatally? Perhaps he is dead and you are trying to break it to me! You can't do it! You can't! Oh, Sylvan, is grandfather dead?" she wildly demanded.

"No, dear! No, no, no! Compose yourself. They are bringing him here, and he is perfectly conscious. He must not see you so much agitated. It would annoy him. We do not yet know how seriously he is hurt. He was thrown from his carriage when near North End. The horses took fright at the passing of a train. They ran away and went over that steep bank just at the entrance of the village. The carriage was shattered all to pieces; the coachman killed outright—poor old Joseph—and the horses so injured that they had to be shot."

"Poor old Joseph! I am so sorry! so very sorry! But grandfather! grandfather!"

"He was picked up insensible; carried to the hotel on a mattress laid on planks, borne by half a dozen workmen, and the doctor was summoned immediately. He was laid in bed, and all means were tried to restore consciousness. But as soon as he came to his senses he demanded to be brought home. The doctor thought it dangerous to do so. But you know the grandfather's obstinacy. So a stretcher was prepared, a spring mattress laid on it, and he has been borne all the way from North End to Rockhold Ferry by relays of six men at a time, relieving each other at short intervals, and escorted by the doctor and our two uncles. That, Cora, is all I can tell you."

He then entered the house, followed by Cora.

They found Rose still in the front hall, where they had left her a few minutes before. She was seated in one of the oak chairs wiping her eyes. She had not seen the approaching procession with the burden they carried. And of course she had not heard their silent movements.

She looked up in surprise at the re-entrance of Cora and Sylvan.

"Oh!" she exclaimed "Have you forgotten anything? So glad to see you back, even for half a minute. For, after all, I couldn't see you drive away. I just shut the door and flung myself into this chair to have a good cry. Can't you put off your journey now, just for to-night and start to-morrow? You will have to do it anyhow. You can't catch the 6:30 express now," she added, coming toward them.

"We shall not attempt it, Rose," said Sylvan, in a kinder tone than he usually used in speaking to her.

"I am so glad," she said, but her further words were arrested by the grave looks of the young man.

"What is the matter with you?" she suddenly inquired.

"There has been an accident, Rose. Not fatal, my dear, so don't be frightened. My grandfather has been thrown from his carriage and stunned. But he has recovered consciousness, and they are bringing him home a deal shaken, but not in serious danger."

While Sylvan spoke, Rose gazed at him in perfect silence, with her blue eyes widening. When he finished, she asked:

"How did it happen?"

Sylvan told her.

Rose dropped into a chair and covered her face with her hands. She was more shocked than grieved by all that she had heard. If her tyrant had been brought home dead, I think she would only have sighed

"With the sigh of a great deliverance!"

"Let us go now, Rose, and prepare his bed. Sylvan will stay hereto receive him," said Cora.

The two women went up to the old man's room and turned down the bedclothes, and laid out a change of linen, and many towels in case they should be needed, and then went to the head of the stairs and waited and listened.

Presently, through the open hall door, they heard the muffled tread and subdued tones of the men, who presently entered, bearing the stretcher on which was laid the huge form of the Iron King, covered, all except his face, with a white bed-spread. Slowly, carefully, and with some difficulty they bore him up the broad staircase head first—preceded by the family physician, Dr. Cummins, and followed by Messrs. Fabian and Clarence.

Rose and Cora stood each side the open chamber door, and when the men bore the stretcher in and set it down on the floor, the two women approached and looked down on the injured man.

His countenance was scarcely affected by his accident. He was no paler than usual. He was frowning—it might be from pain or it might be from anger—and he was glaring around. Rose was afraid to speak to him, prone on the stretcher as he was, lest she should get her head bitten off. Cora bent over him and said tenderly:

"Dear grandfather, I am very sorry for this. I hope you are not hurt much."

And she had her head immediately snapped off.

"Don't be a confounded idiot!" he growled, hoarsely. "Go and send old black Martha here. She is worth a hundred of you two."

Rose hurried off to obey this order, glad enough of an excuse to escape. And now the room was cleared of all the men except the family physician, the two sons, and the grandson.

These approached the stretcher and carefully and tenderly undressed the patient and laid him on his bed.

Then the physician made a more careful examination.

There were no bones broken. The injuries seemed to be all internal; but of their seriousness or dangerousness the physician could not yet judge. The nervous shock had certainly been severe, and that in itself was a grave misfortune to a man of Aaron Rockharrt's age, and might have been instantaneously fatal to any one of less remarkable strength.

Dr. Cummins told Mr. Fabian that he should remain in attendance on his patient all night. Then, at the desire of Mr. Rockharrt, he cleared the sick room of every one except the old negro woman.

When the door was shut upon them all, and the chamber was quiet, he administered a sedative to his patient and advised him to close his eyes and try to compose himself.

Then the doctor sat down on the right side of the bed, with old Martha on his left.

There was utter silence for a few minutes, and then old Aaron Rockharrt spoke.

"What's the hour, doctor?"

"Seven," replied the physician after consulting his gold repeater. "But I advise you to keep quiet and try to sleep," he added, returning his timepiece to his fob.

As if the Iron King ever followed advice! As if he did not, on general principles, always run counter to it!

"Didn't I see my fool of a grandson among the other lunatics who ran after me here?" he next inquired.

"Yes."

"Where is he now?"

"With the ladies, I think."

"Send—him—up—to—me!"

The doctor shrugged his shoulders and went to obey the order. The obstinacy of this self-willed egotist was surely growing into a monomania, and perhaps it would have been more dangerous to oppose him than to comply with his whim. In a few moments Dr. Cummins re-entered the room, followed by Sylvan Haught.

"I hope you are feeling easier," said the lieutenant, as he bent over his grandfather.

"I have not complained of feeling uneasy yet, have I?" growled the Iron King.

"You sent for me, sir. Can I do anything for you?"

"For me? No; not likely! But you can do your duty to your country! How is it that you are not on your way to join your regiment?"

"I had actually bidden good-by and left the house to start on my journey, when I met men bringing you home."

"What the demon had that to do with it?"

"I could not go on, sir, and leave you under such circumstances."

"Look here, young sir!" said the Iron King, speaking hoarsely, faintly, yet with strong determination. "Do you call yourself a soldier or a shirk? Let me tell you that it is the first duty of a soldier to obey orders, at all times, under all circumstances, and at all costs! If you had been a married man, and your wife had been dying—if you had been a father, and your child had been dying, it would have been your duty to leave them!"

"But, sir, there was no real need that I should go by this night's express. If I should start to-morrow morning, I shall be in good time to report for duty. It was only my zeal to be better than prompt which induced me to start earlier than necessary. To-morrow will be quite time enough to leave for New York."

"Very well; then go to-morrow by the first train," said the Iron King in a more subdued manner, for the sedative was beginning to take effect.

At a hint from the doctor the young lieutenant bade his grandfather good-night and softly stepped out of the room.

CHAPTER XXV
THE SICK LION

Early the next morning Dr. Cummins came down stairs and joined the family at the breakfast table.

In answer to anxious inquiries, he reported that Mr. Rockharrt had slept well during the night, and had just taken refreshment prepared by old Martha under the physician's own orders, and had composed himself to sleep again.

"He would not admit any of us last night. Will he see me this morning?" inquired Rose Rockharrt.

"Of course, after a little while. It was best that I and the old nurse should have watched him alone together last night, but the woman now needs rest, and I must presently take leave, to look after my other patients. You two ladies must take the watch to-day, with one of these gentlemen within call. I will give you full directions for my patient's treatment, and will see him again in the afternoon."

"Does my father's present condition admit of my leaving him to go and look after the works this morning?" inquired Mr. Fabian, who had spent the night at Rockhold.

"Yes," replied the doctor, after some little hesitation. "Yes; I think so. If your presence here should be absolutely needed, you can be promptly summoned, you know; but one of you should remain on guard."

"Clarence will stay home, then," replied Mr. Fabian.

"Doctor, you heard my grandfather order me to leave Rockhold this morning to join my regiment. Now, what do you think? May I see him before I go?" inquired the young lieutenant.

"I will let you know when he wakes," said Dr. Cummins.

"Must you leave us to-day, Sylvan? Could you not be excused under the circumstances?" inquired Mrs. Rockharrt.

"No; I could not be excused. I must join my regiment, Rose."

"But, Cora! Oh, Cora! You will not leave us now? You are not under orders, and—and—I wish you would stay," pleaded Rose.

"I shall stay, Rose. It is as much my bounden duty to stay as it is that of Sylvan to go," answered Cora.

"Oh, that is such a relief to my feelings!" exclaimed the other lady.

Dr. Cummins looked up in surprise, glancing from one woman to the other.

Sylvan undertook to explain.

"My sister was going out with me, sir. I am her nearest relative, as she is mine, and we do not like to be separated."

"Ah!" said the doctor. "And now, very properly, she decides to stay here."

"For a while, Dr. Cummins—until the case of my grandfather shall be decided. Later I shall certainly follow my brother," Cora explained.

Before another word could be uttered the door opened, and Violet Rockharrt, in a silver gray carriage dress, entered the room. Mr. Fabian sprang up to meet her.

"My dear child, why have you come out here against all orders?"

Mrs. Fabian Rockharrt saluted all the company at the breakfast, who had risen to receive her, and then replied to her husband's question.

"I have come to see how our father is. It was twelve o'clock last night when your messenger arrived at the Banks and told me that you would not be able to return that night, because an accident had happened to Mr. Rockharrt. Not a dangerous one, but yet one that would keep you with him for some hours. I know very well how accidents are smoothed over in being reported to women; so I was not reassured by that clause, and I would have set out for Rockhold immediately if it had not been a starless midnight, making the road dangerous to others as well as myself. But I was up at daybreak to start this morning, and here I am."

"Sit down, my child; sit down. You look pale and tired. Ah! did not our good doctor here forbid you taking long walks or rides?"

"I know, Fabian; but sometimes a woman must be a law to herself. It was my duty to come in person and inquire after our father; so I came, even against orders," said Violet, composedly.

"Now look at that little creature, doctor. She seems as soft as a dove, as gentle as a lamb; but she is perfectly lawless. She defies me, abuses me, and upon occasion thrashes me. Would you believe it of her?" demanded Mr. Fabian, gazing with pride and delight on his good little wife.

"Oh, yes; I can quite believe it. She looks a perfect shrew, vixen, virago! Oh, how I pity you, Mr. Fabian!" said the doctor.

Cora filled out a cup of coffee and brought it to the visitor, whispering:

"I am glad you came, Violet. I do not believe it will hurt you one bit in any way."

"Can I see father? I want to see for myself, and to kiss him, and tell him how sorry I am; and I want to help to nurse him. Say, can I see him?"

"Not just now, dear. None of us have seen him since he was put to bed last evening except the doctor and the nurse; but in the course of the day you may. You will spend the day with us?" Cora inquired.

"I will spend the day and the night, and to-morrow and to-morrow night, and this week and next week, and just as long as I can be helpful and useful to father, if you and mamma there will permit me. And, by the way, I have not kissed mamma yet. Only shaken hands with her." And so saying, Violet put down her untasted cup of coffee, went around the table, put her arms round Rose's neck, and kissed her fondly, saying:

"You are very sweet and lovely, mamma, and I know I shall love you. I wanted to come and see you before this, but the doctor there wouldn't allow it. But now I have come to stay as long as I may be wanted."

"I should want you forever, sweet wood violet," cooed Rose, returning her caresses.

Mr. Fabian turned away, half in wrath, half in mirth. He was much too good humored to be seriously offended as he said to the doctor:

"Ah! these dove-eyed darlings! How mistaken we are in them! You are an old bachelor, Cummins; but if you should ever take it into your head to repent of celibacy, don't marry a dove-eyed darling, if you don't want to be defied all the days of your life."

"I won't," said the doctor; "but now I must go and see how Mr. Rockharrt is getting on, and take leave to look after my other patients."

And he left the breakfast room, followed by Mr. Fabian.

"You and Sylvan will not leave Rockhold for some time," said Violet, with a little air of triumph.

"Sylvan must leave this morning. I shall remain until grandfather gets well," said Cora—"or dies," she added, mentally.

In a few minutes Dr. Cummins returned and said that Mr. Rockharrt would see Lieutenant Haught first, and afterward the other members of his family.

Then the physician bade the family good morning, and left the house.

Sylvan went up stairs to their grandfather's room.

There they found Mr. Fabian seated by the bedside.

Old Martha had gone to her garret to lie down and rest. The windows were all open, and the summer sun and air lighted and cooled the room.

"Come here, Sylvan," said the Iron King, and his voice, though hoarse and feeble, was peremptory.

"The young lieutenant went up to the bedside and said:

"I hope you are feeling better this morning, sir."

"I hope so, too; but don't let us waste words in compliments. Cummins tells me that you wished to bid me good-by."

"Yes, sir."

"Well, bid good-by, then."

"Grandfather, have you anything to say to me before I go?" respectfully inquired the young man.

"If I had, don't you suppose that I could say it? Well, if you wish advice, I will give it you very briefly: You are an 'officer and a gentleman'—that is the phrase, I believe?"

"I hope so, sir."

"Then behave as one under all circumstances. Never lie—even to women; never cheat—even the government. That is all. I cannot bless you if that is what you want. No man can bless another—not even the Pope of Rome or the Archbishop of Canterbury. No one under heaven can bless you. You can only bless yourself by doing your whole duty under all circumstances. You will have men in authority over you. Obey them. You will have authority over other men. Make them obey you. There, good-by!" said old Aaron Rockharrt, holding out his hand to his grandson.

Sylvan noticed how that hand shook as its aged owner held it up. He took it, lifted it to his lips, and pressed it to his heart.

"There, there; don't be foolish, Sylvan! Good-by! Good-by! And you, Fabian! What are you loitering here for, when you should be looking after the works?" impatiently demanded the Iron King.

"The carriage stands at the door, sir, waiting to take Sylvan to his train. I shall go with him as far as North End and try to do your work there in addition to my own."

"Quite right. Where is Clarence?"

"At North End, sir, where he went directly after he saw you safe in bed under the doctor's care," said Mr. Fabian, lying as fast as a horse could trot.

"Very well. Send the two women here."

"There happen to be three women below at present, sir. Violet has come to see you."

In the morning sitting room below stairs Sylvan and Fabian found the three ladies with Clarence, all in a state of anxiety to hear from the injured man.

Sylvan was more agitated in leaving his sister than any young soldier should have been. At the last, the very last instant of parting, when Mr. Fabian had left the parlor and was on his way to the carriage, Sylvan turned back and for the third time clasped Cora in his arms.

"Never mind, Sylvan, as soon as I possibly can, without violating my duty to the only one on earth to whom I owe any duty, I shall go out to you. I can see now, now in this hour of parting, how very right I was in deciding to go with you. My journey is not abandoned, it is only postponed. God bless you, my dear."

After standing at the front door until they had watched the carriage out of sight, the three went up stairs and softly entered the room of the injured man, so softly that he did not hear their entrance. They stood in a silent group, believing him to be asleep, and afraid to sit down, lest a chair should creak and wake him up.

In a few seconds, however, they heard him clear his throat, knew that he was awake, and went up to his bedside.

Rose spoke, gently, for all.

"You sent for us, Mr. Rockharrt. We are all here, and we hope that you are much better," she said.

"Oh, you do! Stand there—all three of you at the foot of the bed, so that I can see you without turning."

The three women obeyed, placing themselves in line as he had directed, and perceived that he lay upon the flat of his back, looking straight before him, because he could not turn on either side without great pain.

He scanned them and then said:

"Ah, Violet, you are there! You have a proper sense of duty, my girl. So you have come to see how it is with me yourself, eh?"

"Yes, father; and also to stay and help to nurse you, it I may be permitted to do so."

"Rubbish! My wife can nurse me. It is her place. I don't want a lot of other women around me! I won't have more than one in the room with me at a time! Violet, get into your carriage and return to your home."

"Oh, papa, how have I offended you?"

"Not in any way as yet; but you will offend me if you disobey me. You must go home at once. You are not in a condition to be of any service here. You would only injure your own health, and distract the attention of these women from me. Wherever there is a lot of women, there is sure to be more talk than duty. So you must go. When I get well, and you get strong again, you may come and stay as long as you like. So, now, bid me good-by and be off with yourself."

Violet, feeling much chagrined, went around to the side of the bed, took the hand of her father-in-law, bent over and kissed him good-by.

"Now, Cora, take her out and see her off."

Violet took leave of her young mother-in-law, and followed Cora from the sick room.

"Now, Rose, close all the shutters; darken the room and sit beside the head of my bed. Don't speak until you are spoken to; don't move; don't even read; but sit still, silent, attentive, while I try to rest."

Rose obeyed all his orders, and then sat like a dead woman, back in the resting chair beside him. She had noted how weak and husky his voice had been in giving his instructions to his "womankind," with what pain and effort he had spoken, while his strong will bore him through the interview, which, short as it was, had left him prostrate and exhausted.

Rose wished to offer him the cordial the doctor had left, but he had ordered her not to move or speak until she was spoken to, and Rose dared not disobey. She did not know what might be the result of her passive obedience to him, nor, to tell the truth, did she very much care. Rose was weary of life!

Meanwhile, Cora and Violet went down stairs together.

At six o'clock the doctor came, and made anxious inquiries into the state of the injured man; but Cora could only report that he seemed to have passed a quiet day, watched by his wife, but unapproached by any other member of his family, all of whom he had forbidden to come near him unless called.

"A very wise provision, my dear Mrs. Rothsay. I will go up now and see him," said Dr. Cummins.

A few minutes later Rose came down and entered the parlor, looking very faint and white except for two small, deep crimson spots on the cheeks.

"Here, Rose, take this chair," said Violet, vacating the most comfortable seat in the room, on which she had sat all the afternoon.

The woman dropped into it, too weak and weary to stand upon ceremony.

"How did you leave grandfather?"

"I hardly know; but doing well, I should think, for he has been dozing all day, only waking up to ask for iced beef tea, or milk punch, and then, when he had drank one or the other, going to sleep again. I have been fanning him all the time except when I have been feeding him."

While Rose was sipping some tea which had been promptly brought to her, the doctor came in and reported Mr. Rockharrt as doing extremely well.

"You will stay to dinner with us, Dr. Cummins," said Rose.

"Thank you, my dear lady, but I cannot. I shall just wait to see Mr. Fabian Rockharrt and give my report to him in all its details, as I promised, and then hurry home and go to bed. I have had no sleep for the last twenty-four—no, bless my soul! not for the last thirty-six hours!" replied the physician. He had scarcely ceased to speak when Mr. Fabian entered the room.

"Oh! home so soon!" exclaimed Violet, starting up to meet him.

"Yes; how is the father?"

"There is the doctor; ask him."

"Ah, Dr. Cummins! Good afternoon? How is your patient?"

"Come with me into the library, Mr. Fabian, and I will give you a full report."

"Where is Clarence?" inquired Fabian.

"Up stairs somewhere. He did not come to luncheon," replied Cora.

"Poor Clarence! He is awfully cut up!" said Mr. Fabian, as he left the parlor with Dr. Cummins. As they passed through the hall they were joined by Mr. Clarence, who had just heard of the doctor's arrival.

"I left him very comfortable, carefully watched by old Martha, who has waked up refreshed after a ten hours' sleep and has taken her place by his bedside. There is no immediate cause for anxiety, my dear Clarence," said the physician, in reply to the questions put to him.

"The worst of it is, doctor, that while it was absolutely necessary for me to stay here during Fabian's absence, I dare not go into my father's room. He thinks that I am at North End. And he would become very angry if he knew that I was here against his will and his commands. Besides which, I hate deception and concealment," complained Mr. Clarence.

"It is rather a difficult case to manage, my boy, but it is absolutely necessary that either yourself or your brother should be on hand here day and night; it is equally necessary that your father should be kept quiet. So I see nothing better to do than for you to stay here and keep still until you are wanted," replied the doctor.

And then the three went into the little library or office at the rear of the hall, and what further was said among them was whispered with closed doors. At the end of fifteen minutes they came out. The doctor took leave of all the family and went away.

Mr. Fabian went up to his father's door and rapped softly.

Old Martha came to admit him.

"How is your master? Is he awake? Can I see him?" he inquired.

"Surely, Marse Fabe! Ole marse wide awake, berry easy, and 'quiring arter you. Come in, sar!"

Mr. Fabian entered the room, which was in some darkness from the closed window shutters, and went up to his father's bed.

"I hope you are better, sir," he said.

"I don't know," said the injured man, in a faint voice.

"How are the works getting on?"

"Famously, sir! Splendidly! Pray do not feel the least anxiety on that score."

"Where is Clarence?"

"At North End, sir. Of course, he would not think of leaving the works while both you and myself are absent."

"I don't know," sighed the weary invalid, for the third time. "But you had better not, either of you, attempt to deceive me while I am lying here on my back."

"Not for the world, my dear father! Pray do not be doubtful or anxious. We are your dutiful sons, sir, and our first—"

"Rubbish!" exclaimed the broken Iron King. "That will do! Go send Rose to me. Why the deuce did she leave? I—I—I—" His voice dropped into an inarticulate murmur.

Mr. Fabian bent over him, and saw that he had dozed off to sleep.

"Dat's de way he's been a-goin' on ebber since de doctor lef'. It's de truck wot de doctor give him," said old Martha.

Fabian stole on tiptoe out of the room. Dinner was waiting for him down stairs. He would not deliver his father's selfish message to Rose, because he wished the poor creature to dine in peace. He told Clarence to give her his arm to the dining room.

While they were all at dinner Violet explained to her husband why Mr. Rockharrt had directed her to return home. Poor Violet was very loth to stir up any ill feeling between the father and son; but she need not have feared. Mr. Fabian understood the autocrat too well to take offense at the dismissal of his wife.

The next morning when the family physician arrived, and visited the injured man, he found him suffering from restlessness and a rising fever.

He reported this condition to Mr. Clarence Rockharrt, left very particular directions for the treatment of the patient, and then took leave, with the promise to return in the evening and remain all night.

Later in the afternoon the doctor, having finished all other professional calls for the day, arrived at Rockhold. He found his patient delirious. He took up his post by the sick bed for the night, and then peremptorily sent off the worn-out watcher, Rose, to the rest she so much needed.

The condition of Aaron Rockharrt was very critical. Irritative fever had set in with great violence, and this was the beginning of the hard struggle for life that lasted many days, during which delirium, stupor, and brief lucid intervals followed each other with the rise and fall of the fever. A professional nurse was engaged to attend him; but the real burden of the nursing fell on Rose.

CHAPTER XXVI
A VOLUNTARY EXPIATION

Rose never lost patience. She stayed by the bedside always until the doctor turned her out of the room. She came back the moment she was called, night or day.

Weeks passed and Mr. Rockharrt grew better and stronger, but Rose grew worse and weaker. The fine autumn weather that braced up the convalescent old man chilled and depressed the consumptive young woman.

It was certain that Mr. Rockharrt would entirely regain his health and strength, and even take out a new lease of life.

"I never saw any one like your grandfather in all my long practice," said the doctor to Cora one morning, after he had left his patient; "he is a wonder to me. Nothing but a catastrophe could ever have laid him on an invalid bed; and no other man that I know could have recovered from such injuries as he has sustained. Why in a month from this time he will be as well as ever. He has a constitution of tremendous strength."

"But the poor wife," said Cora.

"Ah, poor soul!" sighed the doctor.

"And yet a little while ago she seemed such a perfect picture of health."

"My dear, wherever you see that abnormally clear, fresh, semi-transparent complexion, be sure it is a bad sign—a sign of unsoundness within."

"Can nothing be done for Rose?"

"Yes; and I am doing it as much as she will let me. I advise a warmer climate for the coming winter. Mr. Rockharrt will be able to travel by the first of November, and he should then take her to Florida. But, you see, he pooh-poohs the whole suggestion. Well—'A willful man must have his way,'" said the doctor, as he took up his hat and bade the lady good-by.

A week after this conversation, on the day on which Aaron Rockharrt first sat up in his easy chair, Rose had her first hemorrhage from the lungs. It laid her on the bed from which she was never to rise.

Cora became her constant and tender nurse. Rose was subdued and patient. A few days after this she said to the lady:

"It seems to me that my own dear father, who has been absent from my thoughts for so many years, has drawn very near his poor child in these last few months, and nearer still in the last few days. I do not see him, nor hear him, nor feel him by any natural sense, but I do perceive him. I do perceive that he is trying to do me good, and that he is glad I am coming to him so soon. I am sorry for all the wrong I have done, and I hope the Lord will forgive me. But how can I expect Him to do it, when I can scarcely forgive—even now on my dying bed I can scarcely forgive—my step-mother and her husband for the neglect and cruelty that wrecked my life? Oh, but I forget. You know nothing of all this."

Cora did know. Fabian had told her; but he had also exacted a promise of secrecy from her; so she said nothing in reply to this.

Rose continued, speaking in a low, meditative tone:

"Yes; I am sorry, sorry for the evil I have done. It was not worth while to do it. Life is too short—too short even at its longest. But, oh! I had such a passionate ambition for recognition by the great world! for the admiration of society! Every one whom I met in our quiet lives told me, either by words or looks, that I was beautiful—very beautiful—and I believed them; and I longed for wealth and rank, for dress and jewels, to set off this beauty, and for ease and luxury to enjoy life. Oh, what vanity! Oh, what selfishness! And here I am, with the grave yawning to swallow me up," she murmured, drearily.

"No, dear; no," said Cora, gently laying her hand on the blue-white forehead of the fading woman. "No, Rose. No grave opens for any human being; but only for the body that the freed human being has left behind. It is not the grave that opens for you, Rose, but your father's arms. Would you like to see a minister, dear?"

"If Mr. Rockharrt does not object."

"Then you shall see one."

Rose's sick room was on the opposite side of the hall from Mr. Rockharrt's convalescent apartment.

If the Iron King felt any sorrow at his young wife's mortal illness, he did not show it. If he felt any compunction for having taxed her strength to its extremity, he did not express it. He maintained his usual stolid manner, and merely issued general orders that no trouble or expense must be spared in her treatment and in her interest. He came into her room every day, leaning on the arm of his servant, to ask her how she felt, and to sit a few minutes by her bed.

Violet could no longer come to Rockhold, because a little Violet bud, only a few days old, kept her a close prisoner at the Banks. But Mr. Fabian came twice a week. The minister from the mission church at North End came very frequently, and as he was an earnest, fervent Christian, his ministrations were most beneficial to Rose.

On the day that Mr. Rockharrt first rode out, the end came, rather suddenly at the last.

There was no one in the house but Cora and the servants, Mr. Clarence having gone back to North End. Cora had left Rose in the care of old Martha, and had come down stairs to write a letter to her brother. She had scarcely written a page when the door was opened by Martha, who said, in a frightened tone:

"Come, Miss Cora—come quick! there's a bad change. I'm 'feard to leave her a minute, even to call you. Please come quick!"

Both went to the bedside of the dying woman, over whose face the dark shadows of death were creeping. Rose could no longer raise her hand to beckon or raise her voice to call, but she fixed her eyes imploringly on Cora, who bent low to catch any words she might wish to say. She was gasping for breath as in broken tones she whispered:

"Cora—the Lord—has given me—grace—to forgive them. Write to— my step-mother. Fabian—will tell you—where—"

"Yes; I will, I will, dear Rose," said Cora, gazing down through blinding tears, as she stooped and pressed her warm lips on the death-cold lips beneath them.

Rose lifted her failing eyes to Cora's sympathetic face and never moved them more; there they became fixed.

The sound of approaching wheels was heard.

"It is my grandfather. Go and tell him," whispered Cora to old Martha without turning her head.

The woman left the room, and in a few moments Mr. Rockharrt entered it, leaning on the arm of his valet.

When he approached the bed, he saw how it was and asked no questions. He went to the side opposite to that occupied by Cora, and bent over the dying woman.

"Rose," he said in a low voice—"Rose, my child."

She was past answering, past hearing. He took her thin, chill hand in his, but it was without life.

He bent still lower over her, and whispered:

"Rose."

But she never moved or murmured.

Her eyes were fixed in death on those of Cora.

Then suddenly a smile came to the dying face, light dawned in the dying eyes, as she lifted them and gazed away beyond Cora's form, and murmuring contented;

"Father, father—" and

"With a sigh of a great deliverance,"

she fell asleep.

They stood in silence over the dead for a few moments, and then Mr. Rockharrt drew the white coverlet up over the ashen face, and then leaning on the arm of his servant went out of the room.

Three days later the mortal remains of Rose Rockharrt were laid in the cemetery at North End.

It was on the first of November, a week after the funeral, that Mr. Rockharrt, for the first time in three months, went to the works.

On that day, while Cora sat alone in the parlor, a card was brought to her—

"The Duke of Cumbervale."

The Duke of Cumbervale entered the parlor.

Cora rose to receive him; the blood rushing to her head and suffusing her face with blushes, merely from the vivid memory of the painful past called up by the sudden sight of the man who had been the unconscious cause of all her unhappiness. Most likely the old lover mistook the meaning of the lady's agitation in his presence, and ascribed it to a self-flattering origin.

However that might have been, he advanced with easy grace, and bowing slightly, said:

"My dear Mrs. Rothsay, I am very happy to see you again! I hope I find you quite well?"

"Quite well, thank you," she replied, recovering her self-control.

In the ensuing conversation, Cora made known her grandfather's accident and the death of Rose.

"I am truly grieved to have intruded at so inopportune a time," asserted the visitor, and arose to take leave.

Then Cora's conscience smote her for her inhospitable rudeness. Here was a man who had crossed the sea at her grandfather's invitation, who had reached the country in ignorance of the family trouble; who had come directly from the seaport to North End, and ridden from North End to Rockhold—a distance of six or seven miles; and she had scarcely given him a civil reception. And now should she let him go all the way back to North End without even offering him some refreshment?

Such a course, under such circumstances, even toward an utter stranger, would have been unprecedented in her neighborhood, which had always been noted for its hospitality.

Yet still she was afraid to offer him any polite attention, lest she should in so doing give him encouragement to urge his suit, that she dreaded to hear, and was determined to reject.

It was not until the visitor had taken his hat in his left hand, and held out the right to bid her good morning, that she forced herself to do her hostess' duty, and say:

"This is a very dull house, duke, but if you can endure its dullness, I beg you will stay to lunch with me."

A smile suddenly lighted up the visitor's cold blue eyes.

"'Dull,' madam? No house can be dull—even though darkened by a recent bereavement—which is blessed by your presence. I thank you. I shall stay with much pleasure."

And now I have done it! thought Cora, with vexation.

At length the clock struck two, the luncheon bell rang, and Cora arose with a smile of invitation. The duke gave her his arm, they went into the dining room. The gray-haired butler was in waiting. They took their places at the table. Old John had just set a plate of lobster salad before the guest when the sound of carriage wheels was heard approaching the house. In a few minutes more there came heavy steps along the hall, the door opened, and old Aaron Rockharrt entered the room. Cora and her visitor both arose.

"Ah, duke! how do you do? I got your telegram on reaching North End; went to the hotel to meet you, and found that you had started for Rockhold. Had your dispatch arrived an hour earlier I should have gone in my carriage to meet you," said the Iron King with pompous politeness.

Now it seemed in order for the visitor to offer some condolence to this bereaved husband. But how could he, where the widower himself so decidedly ignored the subject of his own sorrow? To have said one word about his recent loss would have been, in the world's opinion and vocabulary, "bad form."

"You are very kind, Mr. Rockharrt; and I thank you. I came on quite comfortably in the hotel hack, which waits to take me back," was all that he said.

"No, sir! that hack does not wait to take you back. I have sent it away. Moreover, I settled your bill at the hotel, gave up your rooms, saw your valet, and ordered your luggage to be brought here. It will arrive in an hour," said the Iron King, as he threw himself into the great leathern chair that the old butler pushed to the table for his master's accommodation.

The duke looked at the old man in a state of stupefaction. How on earth should he deal with this purse-proud egotist, who took the liberty of paying his hotel bill, giving up his apartments and ordering his servants? and doing all this without the faintest idea that he was committing an unpardonable impertinence.

"You are to know, duke, that from the time you entered upon my domain at North End, you became my guest—mine, sir! John, that Johannisberg. Fill the duke's glass. My own importation, sir; twelve years in my cellar. You will scarcely find its equal anywhere. Your health, sir."

The duke bowed and sipped his wine.

His future bearing to this old barbarian required mature reflection. Only for the duke's infatuation with Cora, it would have not have needed a minute's thought to make up his mind to flee from Rockhold forthwith.

When luncheon was over Mr. Rockharrt invited the duke into his study to smoke. Before they had finished their first cigar the Iron King, withdrawing his "lotus," and sending a curling cloud of vapor into the air, said:

"You have something on your mind that you wish to get off it, sir. Out with it! Nothing like frankness and promptness."

"You are right, Mr. Rockharrt. I do wish to speak to you on a point on which my life's happiness hangs. Your beautiful granddaughter—"

"Yes, yes! Of course I knew it concerned her."

"Then I hope you do not disapprove my suit."

"I don't now, or I never should have invited you to come over to this country and speak for yourself. The circumstances are different. When I refused my granddaughter's hand to you in London, it was because I had already promised it to another man—a fine fellow, worthy to become one of my family, if ever a man was—and I never break a promise. So I refused your offer, and brought the young woman home, and married her to Rothsay, who disappeared in a strange and mysterious manner, as you may have heard, and was never heard of again until the massacre of Terrepeur by the Comanche Indians—among whom, it seems, he was a missionary—when the news came that he had been murdered by the savages and his body burned in the fire of his own hut. But the horror is two years old now, and I am at liberty to bestow the hand of my widowed granddaughter on whomsoever I please. You'll do as well as another man, and Heaven knows that I shall be glad to have any honest white man take her off my hands, for she is giving me a deal of trouble."

"Trouble, sir? I thought your lovely granddaughter was the comfort and staff of your age, and, therefore, almost feared to ask her hand in marriage. But what is the nature of the trouble, if I may ask?"

"Didn't I tell you? Well, she has got a missionary maggot in her head. It's feeding on all the little brains she ever had. She wants to go out as a teacher and preacher to the red heathen, and spend her life and her fortune among them. She wants to do as Rule did, and, I suppose, die as Rule died. Oh, of course—

"'Twas so for me young Edwin did,
And so for him will I!'

"And all that rot. I cannot break her will without breaking her neck. If you can do anything with her, take her, in the Lord's name. And joy go with her."

The young suitor felt very uncomfortable. He was not at all used to such an old ruffian as this. He did not know how to talk with him—what to reply to his rude consent to the proposal of marriage. At length his compassion, no less than his love for Cora, inspired him to say:

"Thank you, Mr. Rockharrt. I will take the lady, if she will do me the honor to trust her happiness to my keeping."

"More fool you! But that is your look-out," grunted the old man.

The next morning when they met at breakfast Mr. Rockharrt invited his guest to accompany him to North End to inspect the iron mines and foundries, the locomotive works and all the rest of it.

The duke had no choice but to accept the invitation.

The two gentlemen left directly after breakfast, and Cora rejoiced in the respite of one whole day from the society of the unwelcome guest.

She saw the house set in order, gave directions for the dinner, and then retired to her own private sitting room to resume her labor of love, the life of her lost husband.

Earlier than usual that afternoon the Iron King returned home accompanied by their guest and by Mr. Clarence, who had come with them in honor of the duke. The evening was spent in a rubber of whist, in which Mr. Rockharrt and the duke, who were partners, were the winners over Cora and Mr. Clarence, their antagonists. The evening was finished at the usual hour with champagne and sago biscuits.

The next morning, when Mr. Rockharrt and Mr. Clarence were about to leave the house for the carriage to take them to North End, the Iron King turned abruptly and said to his granddaughter:

"By the way, Cora, Fabian and Violet are coming to dinner this evening to meet the duke. It will be a mere family affair upon a family occasion, eh, duke! A very quiet little dinner among ourselves. No other guests! Good morning."

And so saying the old man left the house, accompanied by his son.

Cora returned to the drawing room, where she had left the duke. He arose immediately and placed a chair for her; but she waved her hand in refusal of it, and standing, said very politely:

"You will find the magazines of the month and the newspapers of the day on the table of the library on the opposite side of the hall, if you feel disposed to look over them."

"The papers of to-day! How is it possible you are so fortunate as to get the papers of to-day at so early an hour, at so remote a point?" inquired the duke, probably only to hold her in conversation.

"Mr. Clarence Rockharrt's servant takes them from the earliest mail and starts with them for Rockhold. Mr. Rockharrt usually reads the morning papers here before his breakfast."

"A wonderful conquest over time and space are our modern locomotives," observed the duke.

Cora assented, and then said:

"Pray use the full freedom of the house and grounds; of the servants also, and the horses and carriages. Mr. Rockharrt places them all at your disposal. But please excuse me, for I have an engagement which will occupy me nearly all day."

The duke looked disappointed, but bowed gravely and answered:

"Of course; pray do not let me be a hindrance to your more important occupations, Mrs. Rothsay."

"Thank you!" she answered, a little vaguely, and with a smile she left the room,

"Rejoicing to be free!"

The duke anathematized his fate in finding so much difficulty in the way of his wooing, his ladylove evading him with a grace, a coolness, and a courtesy which he was constrained to respect.

He strolled into the library, and then loitered along on the path leading down to the ferry.

Here he found the boat at the little wharf and old Lebanon on duty.

"Sarvint, marster," said the old negro, touching his rimless old felt hat. "Going over?"

"Yes, my man," said the duke, stepping on board the boat.

"W'ich dey calls me Uncle Lebnum as mentions ob me in dese parts, marster," the old ferryman explained, touching his hat.

"Oh, they do? Very well. I will remember," said the passenger, as the boat was pushed off from the shore.

"How many trips do you make in a day?" inquired the fare.

"Pen's 'pon how many people is a-comin' an' goin'. Some days I don't make no trip at all. Oder days, w'en dere's a weddin' or a fun'al, I makes many as fifty."

The passage was soon made, and the duke stepped out on the west bank.

"Is there any path leading to the top of this ridge, Uncle—Lemuel?" inquired the duke.

"Lebnum, young marster, if you please! Lebnum!—w'ich dere is no paff an' no way o' gettin' to de top o' dis wes' range, jes' 'cause 'tis too orful steep; but ef you go 'bout fo' mile up de road, you'd come to a paff leadin' zigzag, wall o' Troy like, up to Siffier's Roos'."

"Zephyr's—what?"

"Roos', marster. Yes, sar. W'ich so 'tis call 'cause she usen to roos' up dar, jes' like ole turkey buzzard. W'en you get up dar, you can see ober free States. Yes, sar, 'cause dat p'ints w'ere de p'ints o' boundy lines ob free States meets—yes, sah!"

"I think I will take a walk to that point. I suppose I can find the path?"

"You can't miss it, sah, if you keeps a sharp look-out. About fo' miles up, sah"

"Very well. Shall you be here when I come back?"

"No, sah. Dis ain't my stoppin' place; t'other side is. But I'll be on de watch dere, and ef you holler for me, I'll come. I'll come anyways, 'cause I'll be sure to see you."

"Quite so," said the duke, as he sauntered up that very road between the foot of the mountain and the bank of the river down which the festive crowd had come on Corona Haught's fatal wedding day.

An hour's leisurely walk brought him to the first cleft in the rock.

From the back of this the path ascended, with many a double, to the wooded shelf on which old Scythia's hut had once stood—hidden. When he reached the spot he found nothing but charred logs, blasted trees, and ashes, as if the spot had been wasted by fire.

A ray of dazzling light darted from the ashes at his feet. In some surprise he stooped to ascertain the cause, and picked up a ring; examined it curiously; found it to be set with a diamond of rare beauty and great value. Then in sudden amazement he turned to the reverse side of the golden cup that clasped the gem and saw a monogram.

"I thought so," he muttered to himself; "I thought that there was not another such a peculiar setting to any gem in the world but that; and now the monogram proves it beyond the shadow of a doubt to be the same. But how in the name of wonder should the lost talisman be found here—in the ashes of some charcoal burner's hut?"

With these words he took out and opened his pocket-book and carefully placed the ring in its safest fold, closed and returned the book to his pocket, and arose and left the spot. The duke turned to descend the mountain.

At length, however, he reached the foot, and then, under the shadow of the ridge that threw the whole narrow valley into premature twilight, he hurried to the ferry.

The boat was not there. Indeed, he had not expected to find it after what old Lebanon had told him. It was too obscure in the valley to permit him to see across the river, so he shouted:

"Boat!"

"All wight, young marster, but needn't split your t'roat nor my brain pan, nider! I can hear you! I's coming!" came the voice from mid-stream, for the old ferryman was already half across the river with a chance passenger.

In a few minutes more the boat grated upon the shore and the passenger jumped out, tipped his hat to the duke, and hurried up the river road toward North End.

"Dat pusson were Mr. Thomas Rylan', fust foreman ober all de founderies. Dere's a many foremen, but he be de fust. Come down long ob de ole mars dis arternoon arter some 'counts, I reckon, an' now gone back wid a big bundle ob papers an' doc'ments. Yes, sah. Get in. I's ready to start," said the ferryman, as he cleared a seat in the stern of the boat for the accommodation of the passenger.

"Who used to live in that hut on the mountain before it was burned down?" inquired the duke as he took his seat.

"Ole Injun 'oman named Siffier."

"Where did she come from?"

"Dunno dat nudder. Nobody dunno."

"Can't you tell me something about such a strange person who lived right here in your neighborhood?"

"Look yere, marster, leas' said soones' mended where she's 'cerned. I can't tell you on'y but jes' dis: She 'peared yere 'bout twenty year ago, or mo'. She built dat dere hut wid her own han's, an' she use to make baskets an' brackets an' sich, an' fetch 'em roun' to de people to sell. She made 'em out'n twigs an' ornimented 'em wid red rose berries an' hollies an' sich, an' mighty purty dey was, an' de young gals liked 'em, dey did. An' she made her libbin outen de money she got for her wares. She use to tell fortins too; an' folks did say as she tole true, an' some did say as she had a tell-us-man ring w'ich, when she wore it, she could see inter de futur; but Lor', young marse, dey was on'y supercilly young idiwuts as b'leibed dat trash! But she nebber would take no money for tellin' fortins—nebber!—w'ich was curous. De berry day as de gubner-leck was missin' ob, she wanished too. When de cons'able went to 'rest her, he foun' her gone an' de hut burnt up. Now, yere we is, young marse, at de lan'in', an' you can get right out yere 'dout wettin' your feet," said the old ferryman, as he pushed the boat up to the dry end of the wharf.

The passenger astonished the old ferryman by putting a quarter of an eagle in his hand, and then sprang from the boat and ran up the avenue leading toward the house. There was no light visible from the windows of the mansion. The dinner party was a strictly private family affair, and nothing but the solitary lamp at the head of the avenue appeared to guide the pedestrian's steps through the darkness of the newly fallen night.

He reached the house, and was admitted by the old servant.

When his toilet was complete, the duke went down to the drawing room to join the family circle.

The dinner, quiet as it was, was a success. To be sure, the diners were all in deep mourning and the conversation was rather subdued; but, then, it was perhaps on that account the more interesting.

The many courses, altogether, occupied more than an hour.

When the cloth was drawn and the dessert placed upon the table, at a signal from the Iron King the butler went around the table and filled every glass with champagne, then returned and stood at his master's back. Mr. Rockharrt arose and made a speech, and proposed a toast that greatly astonished his company and compromised two of them. With his glass in his hand, he said:

"My sons, daughters, and friend: You all doubtless understand the object of this family gathering, and also why this celebration of an interesting family event must necessarily be confined to the members of the family. In a word, it is my duty and pleasure to announce to you all the betrothal in marriage of his grace the Duke of Cumbervale and my granddaughter, Mrs. Corona Rothsay. I propose the health of the betrothed pair."

Cora put down her glass and turned livid with dismay and indignation. All the other diners, the duke among them, arose to the occasion and honored the toast, and then sat down, all except the duke, who remained standing, and though somewhat embarrassed by this unexpected proceeding on the part of the Iron King, yet vaguely supposed it might be a local custom, and at all events was certainly very much pleased with it. Being in love and being taken by surprise, he could not be expected to speak sensibly, or even coherently. He said:

"Ladies and gentlemen: This is the happiest day of my life as yet. I look forward to a happier one in the near future, when I shall call the lovely lady at my side by the dearest name that man can utter, and I shall call you not only my dear friends, but my near relatives. I propose the health of the greatest benefactor of the human race now living. The man who, by his mighty life's work, has opened up the resources of nature, compelled the everlasting mountains to give up their priceless treasures of coal and iron ore; given employment to thousands of men and women; made this savage wilderness of rock, and wood, and water 'bloom and blossom as the rose,' and hum with the stir of industry like a myriad hives of bees. I propose the health of Mr. Aaron Rockharrt."

All, except Cora, arose and honored this toast.

Mr. Fabian Rockharrt replied on the part of his father.

Then the health of each member of the party was proposed in turn. When this was over the two ladies withdrew from the table and went into the drawing room, leaving the gentlemen to their wine.

"Oh, my dear, dear Cora! I am so glad! I wish you joy with my whole, whole heart!" exclaimed Violet, effusively, but most sincerely and earnestly, as she clasped Corona to her heart. The next instant she let her go and gazed at Cora in surprise and dismay.

"Why, what is the matter, Cora? You are as white and as cold as death. What is the matter?" demanded Violet as she led and half supported Corona to an easy chair, in which the latter dropped.

"Tell me, Cora. What is it, dear? What can I do for you? Can I get you anything? Is all this emotion caused by the announcement of your betrothal to the duke?" demanded Violet, hurrying question upon question, and trembling even more than Cora.

"Sit down, Violet. Never mind me. I shall be all right presently. Don't be frightened, darling," said Cora, as well as she could speak.

"But let me do something for you!"

"You can do nothing."

"But what caused this?"

"My feelings have been outraged!—outraged! That is all!"

"How? How? Surely not by Mr. Rockharrt's announcement of your betrothal to the duke? It was rather embarrassing to the betrothed pair, I admit; but surely it was the proper thing to do."

"'The proper thing to do!' Violet, it was false! false! I am not betrothed to the duke. I never was. I never shall be. I would not marry an emperor to share a throne. My life is consecrated to good works in the very field in which my dear husband died. I have said this to my grandfather and to you all, over and over again. If it had not been for Mr. Rockharrt's accident that endangered his life, I should have gone out to the Indian Territory with my brother, and should have been at work there at this present time. I shall go at the first opportunity."

Cora spoke very excitedly, being almost beside herself with wrath and shame at the affront which had been put upon her.

"I thought the duke was an old admirer of yours, and had come over on purpose to marry you," said Violet.

"That is too true. He came against my will. I have never given him the slightest encouragement. How could I when my life is consecrated to the memory of my husband and to the work he left unfinished? I fear Mr. Rockharrt assured the duke of my hand; and when he heard the false announcement of our betrothal, he took it for granted that it was all right. He must have done so; though he himself was much taken by surprise."

"How very strange of Mr. Rockharrt to do such a thing. If I had been you, Cora, I should have got up and disclaimed it."

"No you would not. You would not have made a scene at the dinner table. I was in no way responsible for the announcement made by my grandfather, and in no way bound by it. The silence that seemed to indorse it was rendered absolutely necessary under the circumstances."

"But what shall you do about it?"

"As soon as I can speak of it without making a scene, I shall tell Mr. Rockharrt and the Duke of Cumbervale that a most reprehensible liberty has been taken with my name. I will say that I never have been, and never will be, engaged to the Duke of Cumbervale, or to any other man. That is what I shall do about it."

"It would mortify the duke very much."

"I do not care if it does."

"And, indeed, it would put Mr. Rockharrt into a terrible rage."

"I cannot help it. Here come the gentlemen."

At that moment the four gentlemen entered the drawing room. The duke came directly up to Cora, and bending over her, said in a low voice inaudible to the rest of the party:

"Corona, you have blessed me beyond the power of words to express! Only the dedication of a life to your happiness—"

There the ardent lover was suddenly stopped by the cold look of surprise in Cora's eyes. His face took on a disturbed expression.

"I think there is some serious mistake here, sir, which we may set right at some more fitting opportunity. Will you have the kindness not to refer to the comedy enacted at our dinner table to-night?"

"I will obey you, although I do not understand you," said the duke.

"Oblige me, duke! I want to show you a map of the projected Oregon and Alaska railroad," said the Iron King, coming toward his guest with a roll of parchment in his hands.

The duke immediately arose and went off with his host to a distant table, where the map was spread out, and the two gentlemen sat down to examine it. Mr. Fabian and Mr. Clarence came over to join Cora and Violet.

"This is a pretty march you have stolen on us, Cora! I had no more idea of this than the man in the moon! But I congratulate you, my dear! I congratulate you! Your present from me shall be a set of the most splendid diamonds that can be got together by the diamond merchants of Europe. No mere set that can be picked up ready set, eh? Diamonds that shall grace a duchess, my dear!" said Mr. Fabian ostentatiously.

"Cora, my dear, I was as much surprised as Fabian. But, oh! I was happy for your sake. The duke is a good fellow, I am sure, and awfully in love with you. Ah! didn't he offer a just and heartfelt tribute to the father! I declare, Cora, I never fully appreciated my father, or realized what a great benefactor he was to the human race, until the duke made that little speech in proposing his health. How appreciative the duke is! Really, Cora, dear, you are a very happy woman, and I congratulate you with all my heart and soul; indeed, I do," said Mr. Clarence, wringing the young lady's hand, and turning away to hide the tears that filled his eyes.

"Thank you, Uncle Clarence. Thank you, Uncle Fabian. I am grateful for your congratulations, on account of your good intentions; but— congratulations are quite uncalled for on this occasion."

"Why—what on earth do you mean, Cora?" inquired Mr. Fabian, while Mr. Clarence looked full of uneasiness.

"I mean that I have never been engaged to the Duke of Cumbervale, and never mean to marry him. Mr. Rockharrt's announcement was unauthorized and unfounded. It was just an act of his despotic will, to oblige me to contract a marriage which he favors."

The two men looked on the speaker in mute amazement.

"We will not talk more of this to-night. But the matter must be set right to-morrow," said Cora.

A little later Mr. and Mrs. Fabian Rockharrt took leave and departed for their home.

CHAPTER XXVII
UNREQUITED LOVE

The Duke of Cumbervale, weary of a sleepless pillow, arose early and rang his bell, startling his gentlemanly valet from his morning slumbers; dressed himself with monsieur's assistance, and went down stairs with the intention of taking a walk before the family should be up.

But his intention was forestalled by the appearance of Mr. Rockharrt coming out of his chamber on the opposite side of the hall.

The Iron King looked up in some surprise at the apparition of his guest at so early an hour; but quickly composed himself as he gave him the matutinal salutation:

"Ah, good morning, duke. An early riser, like myself, eh? Come down into the library with me, and let us look over the morning papers."

A cheerful coal fire was burning in the grate, a very acceptable comfort on this chill November morning.

This was one of the happy days when there is "nothing in the papers" — that is to say, nothing interesting, absorbing, soul harrowing, in the form of financial ruin, highway robbery, murder, arson, fire, or flood. Everything in the world at the present brief hour seemed going on well, consequently the papers were very dull, flat, stale and unprofitable, and were soon laid aside by the host and his guest, and they fell into conversation.

"You took a long walk yesterday, I hear—went across in the ferry boat, and strolled up to the foot of Scythia's Roost."

"I did. Can you tell me anything about that curious spot?"

"No; nothing but that it was the dwelling of an Indian woman, who pretended to second sight, and who should have been sent to the State's prison as a felon, or, at the very least, to the madhouse as a lunatic. She was burned out, or perhaps burned herself out, and vanished on the same night that Governor Rothsay disappeared. She was in some way cognizant of a plot against him that would prevent him from ever entering upon the duties of his office. I, in my capacity as magistrate, issued a warrant for her arrest, but it was too late. She was gone. It is said by some people that she is a Mexican Indian, who had been very beautiful in her youth, and who had become infatuated with an English tourist who admired her to such a degree that he married her—according to the rites of her nation. He was a false hearted caitiff, if he was an English lord. Having committed the folly of marrying the Indian woman, he should have been true to her—made the best of the bad bargain. Instead of which he grew tired of her, and finally abandoned her."

"Did he return to his native country, do you know?"

"He did not. She never gave him time. She went mad after he left her, followed him to New Orleans and tomahawked him on the steamboat. She was tried for murder, acquitted on the ground of insanity, and sent to a lunatic asylum. After a time she was discharged, or she escaped. It is not known which; most probably she escaped, as she certainly was not cured. She was as mad as a March hare all the time she lived here; but as she was harmless—comparatively harmless—it seemed nobody's business to have her shut up! And as I said, when at last I thought it was time to have her arrested on a charge of vagrancy, it was too late. She had fled."

"Why do you suspect that she had some knowledge of a plot to make away with the governor-elect?"

"I suspect that she was in the plot. Developments have led me to the conclusion. By these I learned that Rothsay was not murdered, as his friends feared, nor abducted, as some persons believed, but that he went away, and lived for many months among the Indians in the wilderness, without giving a sign of his identity to the people among whom he lived, or sending a hint of his whereabouts, or even of his existence, to his anxious friends. But that the massacre of Terrepeur—in which he was murdered and his hut was burned—occurred when it did, we might never have learned his fate."

"Yet, still, I cannot see the ground upon which you suspect this Indian woman of complicity in the man's disappearance," said Cumbervale.

"But I am coming to that. Scythia was a Mexican Indian. It is well known to travelers that the Mexican Indians possess the secret of a drug which, when administered to a man, will not kill him, or do him any physical harm, but will reduce him to a state of abject imbecility, so that his free will is destroyed, and he may be led by any one who may wish to lead him. This drug administered to Rothsay, by the woman, must have so deprived him of his reason as to induce him to follow any one influencing him."

"What interest could she have had in reducing the man to this state of dementia?"

"She had been like a mother to the young man, and had sheltered him in her hut for years, when he had no other home. She was very much attached to this adopted son of hers; she was longing to go back to her tribe and die among her own people. It may be that she wished to take him with her, and so gave him the drug that destroyed his will. Or, she may have been the tool of others. All this is the merest conjecture. But the facts remain that she foretold his fate, and that she vanished on the same day on which he disappeared, and that he remained in exile, voluntarily, until he was murdered by the Indians. Still—there might have been another cause for this self-expatriation."

"May I inquire its nature?"

"No, duke; it is only in my secret thought. I have no just right to speak of it to you. But if the question be not indiscreet, will you tell me why you take so deep an interest in the unreliable story of this Indian woman's life?"

"Certainly; because the wild young blade who married and left her, and paid down his life for that desertion, was my own uncle, my father's elder brother, Earl Netherby, the heir to the dukedom, by whose death my father, and subsequently myself, succeeded to the title."

"You astonish me! Are you sure of this?"

"Reasonably sure. I was but five years old when my uncle came to bid us good-by, before setting out for America. But I remember his having on his finger a wonderful ring, a large solitaire diamond with certain flaws in it; but these flaws were very curious; they were faint traces left by the hand of nature shaping out a human eye. When ordinary mortals like myself looked at the diamond, they saw the delicate outline of an eye traced by the flaws in the stone; but it was said that whenever a clairvoyant looked into it they could see, not the human eye, but, as through a telescope, they could view the panorama of future events."

"What nonsense!" said Mr. Rockharrt.

"Nonsense, of course," assented the duke. "I did not speak of the ring on account of its supposed magic power, but because it was so peculiar a jewel that it would be impossible to mistake it for any other ring, or any other ring for itself; and to lead up to the statement that its discovery enabled me to identify the Mexican Indian woman with the maniac who murdered my uncle, as you will see very soon. When my uncle took leave of us, my father, noticing the family talisman—which, by the way, was picked up by our ancestor, Raoul-de-Netherbie, the great Crusader, on the battle field of Acre, and was said to have belonged to an Eastern magician, and has remained an heirloom with the head of our family ever since—inquired of his brother whether he was going to wear that outre jewel in open view upon his finger. My uncle answered that he was; and half laughing, and wholly incredulous, he added:

"'You know, Hugh, that this stone is a talisman against shipwreck, fires, floods, robbery, murder, illness, and all the perils by land or by sea, and all the ills that flesh is heir to. While I wear this ring I expect to be safe from the evils of the world, the flesh, and the devil. So it shall never leave my living hand while I am away; but it shall bring me home safe to live to a patriarchal age and then die peacefully in my bed, with my children and children's children of many generations weeping and wailing around me.'

"These or words to this effect he was speaking, while I, standing by the chair in which he sat, toyed with his hand, and gazed curiously upon the talismanic jewel, and got into my mind an impression of it that never was lost. My uncle soon after left the house, and we never saw him alive again."

"He was the victim of this mad woman?"

"I know it. News was slow in those days. We seldom heard from my uncle. His letters were but the mark of the cities he stopped at. We had one letter from Boston; a month later one from New York; a fortnight later, perhaps—for I only remember these matters by hearing them talked over by my parents—from Philadelphia; later still, and later, Baltimore, Washington, Nashville, New Orleans, and so on as he journeyed southward. Then came a long interval, during which we heard nothing from him, while all his family suffered the deepest anxiety, fearing that he had fallen a victim to the terrible fever that was then desolating the Crescent City. Then at length came a letter from his valet—a deep black-bordered letter—which announced the terrible news of the murder of his master by a Mexican Indian woman, supposed to be mad. There were no details, but only the explanation that he, the valet— who had seen the murder, which was the work of an instant—was detained in New Orleans as a witness for the prosecution, and should not be able to return home until after the trial. It was two months after the latter that the valet came back to England in charge of his late master's effects, which had all been sealed by the New Orleans authorities, and reached us intact. Only the family talisman was missing, and could nowhere be found. And as the family's prosperity, and even continuity, was supposed to depend upon the possession of that ring, its loss was considered only a less misfortune than my uncle's death. Later, my uncle's remains were brought home from New Orleans and deposited in the family vault at Cumbervale Castle.

"The ring was never again heard of. On the death of my grandfather, the seventh duke, my father, who was the second son, succeeded to the title. But fortune seemed to have deserted us. By a series of unlucky land speculations my father lost nearly all his riches, which calamities preyed upon his mind so that his health broke down and he sank into premature old age and died. I came into the title with but little to support it. So that when I honestly loved a lady believed to be wealthy, my motives were supposed to be mercenary."

The Iron King might have felt this thrust, but he gave no sign. The duke continued:

"My after life does not concern the story of the ring. On learning, since my return from long travel in the East, that your fair granddaughter was widowed nearly two years before, you know I wrote to you asking her address, with a view of renewing my old suit. You replied by telling me that Mrs. Rothsay made her home with you, and inviting me to visit you. I refer to this only to keep the sequence of events in order. I came. Yesterday morning I went to Scythia's Roost, climbed from that shelf to the top of the mountain and viewed the scene from it. After I came down again to Scythia's Roost I sat down to rest. The sun was sinking behind the ridge, but through a crevice in the rocks a ray—'a line of golden light'—pierced and seemed to strike fire and bring out an answering ray from some living light left in the ashes. I went to see what it was, and picked up the magic ring, the family talisman. There it was, the wonderful stone for which no other could possibly be mistaken, the gem of intolerable light and fire that had to be shaded before it could be steadily looked at and before the delicate lines of its flaws delineating the human eye could be discerned. Here is the ring, Mr. Rockharrt. Examine it for yourself."

Mr. Rockharrt took the ring, examined it curiously, turned it toward the clouded window, then toward the blazing sea coal fire; in both positions it burned and sparkled just like any other diamond. Then he shaded it and looked at it through his eye-glasses; finally he shook his head and returned it to its owner, saying:

"It is a fine gem, barring a flaw, and I congratulate you on its recovery, but I see no human eye in it. I see some indistinct lines, fine as the thread of a spider's web, that is all. There is the breakfast bell, duke. We will go into the drawing room and find Cora. She must be down by this time."

Cora was standing at one of the front windows, looking out upon the driving rain. She turned as the two gentlemen entered the room, and responded to their greeting.

"Well, now we will go in to breakfast. Did the fresh venison come in time, Cora?"

"I think so, sir."

"We cook it on the breakfast table, duke, each one for himself. Put a slice on a china plate over a chafing dish. The only way to eat a venison cutlet," said old Aaron Rockharrt, as he led the way into the breakfast room, where his eyes were immediately rejoiced by the sight of three chafing dishes filled with ignited charcoal ready for use, and a covered china dish, which he knew must contain the delicate venison cutlets.

When breakfast was over and they had all left the table, the Iron King, addressing his guest, said:

"Well, sir, I must be off to North End. I hope you will find some way of entertaining yourself within doors, for certainly this is not a day to tempt a man to seek recreation abroad. Nothing but business of importance could take me out in such weather."

"I regret that any cause should take you out, sir," replied the guest.

As soon as the noise of the wheels had died away, the duke, who had lingered in the hall to see his host depart, turned and entered the drawing room, where he found Cora as before, standing at a window looking out upon the dull November day.

"Will you permit me now to speak on the subject nearest my heart?" he pleaded, taking the hand which had dropped down by her side.

"I had rather that the subject had never been started, but under the circumstances, after what was said last night at dinner, I feel that the sooner we come to a perfect understanding the better it will be," said Cora, leading the way to a group of chairs and by a gesture inviting him to be seated. Then, to prevent him further committing himself and incurring a humiliating refusal, she herself took the initiative and said:

"If any other person than Mr. Rockharrt had made the public announcement that he did yesterday, I should have denounced the act as an unpardonable outrage; but of him I must say that he must have labored under some strange hallucination to have made such reckless assertions without one shadow of foundation. You yourself must have known that there was not one syllable of truth in his announcement."

"My dearest Mrs. Rothsay, I supposed that Mr. Rockharrt thought, even as I hoped, that our betrothal was but the question of a few days, or even of a few hours, and that he took the occasion of the family gathering to announce the fact. He had already given his consent to my suit for the blessing of your hand, and if he committed an indiscretion in that premature announcement, I did not know it. I thought such announcement might be a local custom, and I blessed him in my heart for observing it. Cora!" he said, taking her hand and dropping his voice to a pleading tone, "dear Cora, it was only premature."

"Duke of Cumbervale," she answered, coldly and gravely, withdrawing her hand, "it is not premature. It was utterly false and groundless; it was the declaration of an engagement that not only had never taken place, but could never take place—an engagement forever impossible!"

"Oh, do not say that! I have kept my faith. After your grandfather's rejection of me in your name I could rest nowhere in England. I went to the Continent, and thence to the East; but still could rest nowhere, because I was pursued by your image. When I came back to England, I learned that you had been widowed from your wedding day and almost as long as I had been absent. I determined to renew my suit, for I remembered that it was not you, but your grandfather in your name, who rejected my proposal. I remembered that you had once given me hope."

"You refer to a time of sad self-deception on my part, which led me even to unconsciously deceiving you. My imaginary preference for you was a brief hallucination. Let it be forgotten. The memory to me is humiliating. You must think of me only as the wife of Regulas Rothsay."

"As the widow, you would say. Surely that widowhood can be no bar to my suit."

"I do not call myself the widow of Rule Rothsay, but his wife," said Cora, solemnly.

"But, my dear lady, surely death has—"

"Death has not," said Cora, fervently interrupting him—"death cannot sever two souls as united as ours. I mean to spend the years I have to live on earth, temporarily and partially separated from my husband, in good works of which he would approve; with which he would sympathize and which would draw his spirit into closer communion with mine; and I hope at that ascension to the higher life which we miscall death to meet him face to face, to be able to tell him, 'I have finished my work, I have kept the faith,' and to be with him forever in one of the many mansions of the Father's kingdom."

"I see," said the suitor, with a deep sigh, "that my suit would be utterly useless at present. But I will not give up the hope that is my life—the hope that you may yet look with favor on my love. I will merit that you should do so. Cora Rothsay, I will no longer vex you with my presence in this house. I will take leave of you even now, and only ask of your courtesy the use of a dog cart to take me to the North End Hotel."

"You are good, you are very good to me, and I pray with all my heart that you may meet some woman much more worthy of your grace than am I, and that you may be very happy. God bless you, Duke of Cumbervale," said Cora, earnestly.

He lifted her hand to his lips, kissed it, bowed over it and silently left the room.

Cora stepped after him and shut the door; then she hastened across the floor, threw herself down on the sofa, buried her face in the cushions and gave way to the flood of tears that flowed in sympathy with the pain she had given. Meantime the duke went up to his room and rang for his valet.

That grave and accomplished gentleman came at once.

"Dubois, go down and order the dogcart to be at the door in half an hour; then return here to assist me."

The Frenchman bowed profoundly and withdrew.

"I have come a long way for a disappointment," murmured the rejected lover, as he threw himself languidly upon the outside of the bed and clasped his hands above his head. "A fanatic she certainly is. A lunatic also most probably. Yet I cannot get her out of my head. I would go to Canada—to Quebec—if it was not so abominably cold. Vane is there with the 110th. But the climate is too severe. I must move southward, not northward— southward, through California, and thence to the Sandwich Islands, New Zealand, and Australia. That will be a pleasant winter voyage. Talbot is at Sydney, and the climate, and the scenery, and the fruits and vegetables said to be the finest in the world. It will be a new experience, and if I can't forget her among soldiers and convicts, miners and bushmen—well, then, I will come back and make a third attempt. Well, Dubois, what is it?" This question to his valet, who just then re-entered the room.

"The carriage will be at the door on time, your grace."

"Right. Now attend to my directions. I am going immediately to North End, and shall leave thereby the six o'clock express, en route for San Francisco. After I shall have left Rockhold you are to pack up my effects. I shall send a hack from the hotel to fetch them. Be very sure to be ready."

The duke went out and entered the dog cart, received his valise from his valet, gave the order to the groom and was driven off, without having again seen Cora.

But from behind the screen of her lace-curtained window she watched his departure.

"I hope he will soon forget me," she murmured, as she turned away and went down stairs to the library to look over the morning' papers, which she had not yet seen. But before she touched a paper her eyes were attracted by a letter stuck in the letter rack, directed to herself in her brother's well known handwriting.

"To think that my grandfather should have neglected to give me my letter," she complained, as she seized and opened it.

It was dated Fort Farthermost, and announced the fact of the regiment's arrival at the new quarters near the boundary line of Texas, "in the midst of a wilderness infested with hostile Indians, half-breeds, wild beasts, rattlesnakes and tarantulas. Only two companies are to remain here; my company—B—for one. Two first lieutenants are married men, but they have not brought their wives. One of the captains is a widower, and the other an old bachelor. In point of fact, there are only two ladies with us—the colonel's wife and the major's. And when they heard from me that my sister was coming to join me, they were delighted with the idea of having another lady for company. All the same, Cora, I do not advise you to come here. Will write more in a few days; must stop now to secure the mail that goes by this train—wagon and mule train to Arkansaw City, my dear."

This was the substance of the young lieutenant's letter to his sister.

"But 'all the same,' I shall go," said Corona. And she sat down to answer her brother's letter.

CHAPTER XXVIII
A DOMESTIC STORM

It is a truth almost too trite for reference, that in the experience of every one of us there are some days in in which everything seems to go wrong. Such a day was this 13th of November to the Iron King.

When he reached North End that morning, the first thing that met him in his private office was the news that certain stocks had fallen. The news came by telegraph, and put him in a terrible temper.

This was about ten o'clock. Two hours later it was discovered that one of the minor bookkeepers, a new employe who had come well recommended about a month before, had just absconded with all he could lay his hands on—only a few thousand dollars—the merest trifle of a loss to Rockhartt & Sons, but extremely exasperating under the circumstances. So taking one provocation with another, at noon on that 13th of November old Aaron Rockharrt was about the maddest man on the face of the earth.

It was his custom to lunch with his sons in the private parlor of Mr. Clarence's suit of rooms at the North End Hotel, every day at two o'clock.

To-day, however, he showed no disposition to eat or drink. And although the two younger men were famishing for food they dared not go to lunch without him, or even urge him to make an effort to go with them. It was then three o'clock, an hour later than their usual hour, that Mr. Rockharrt made a movement in the desired way by rising, stretching his limbs, and saying:

"We will go over to the hotel and get something to eat."

The three men crossed the street and went directly to Mr. Clarence's room, where the table for luncheon was set out. But there was nothing on it but cut bread, casters, and condiments, for these men always preferred hot luncheon in cold weather, and it was yet to be dished up.

The Iron King was not in a humor to wait. He hurried the servants. And at length when the dishes, which had been punctually prepared for two o'clock, were placed on the table at twenty minutes past three, everything was overdone, dried up, and indigestible.

It was the Iron King's own fault for not coming to the table when the meal was first prepared to order. But he would not admit that into consideration. He ordered the waiter to take everything away and throw it out of doors, declared that he would have a restaurant started on the opposite side of the street where a man could get a decent meal, and rose from the table in a rage.

It was while the Iron King was in this amiable and promising state of mind that a waiter brought in a card and laid it before him. He took it up and read aloud:

"The Duke of Cumbervale."

"Show him in," said Mr. Rockharrt.

A few minutes later the visitor entered the parlor, bowed to his host, and then shook hands with the two younger men, whom he had not seen since the evening before.

"So you braved the storm after all, duke? You found the old house too dreary for a long, rainy day. Take a seat," said Mr. Rockharrt, waving his hands majestically around the chairs.

"No; it was not the weather that made Rockhold insupportable to me. But, sir, I have come a long way for a great disappointment," said the rejected lover.

"What! what! what! Explain yourself, if you please, sir!" exclaimed the Iron King, bending his heavy gray brows over flashing eyes.

"Mrs. Rothsay has rejected me."

"What! what! Rejected you! Why, your engagement was declared in the family conclave only last night."

"Mrs. Rothsay states that the declaration was erroneous, and that no such engagement ever has been or ever could be made between us."

"How dare she say that? How dare she try to break off with you in this scandalous manner? But she shall not! She shall keep faith with you or she is no granddaughter of mine! I will have nothing to do with false women! How did this breach occur? Tell me all about it! Fabian—Clarence! Go about your business. I want to have some private conversation with the duke."

The two younger men, thus summarily dismissed, nodded to the visitor and left the room, glad enough to go down below to the saloon and get something to eat and drink.

"Now, then, sir, what's the row with my granddaughter?" demanded the Iron King, wheeling his chair around to face his visitor.

"There is no 'row,'" said the young man, with the faintest possible hint of disgust in his tone and manner. "Mrs. Rothsay rejects me, positively, absolutely. She repudiates the announcement of our betrothal as unauthorized and erroneous."

"But you know, as we all know, that she was engaged to you! Yes; and she shall keep her engagement. I'll see to that!"

"Pardon me, Mr. Rockharrt, I am grieved to say that you have made a mistake. The lady was right. There was no engagement, between Mrs. Rothsay and myself at the time you made that announcement, nor has there been one since, nor, I fear, can there ever be."

"Sir!" exclaimed the Iron King, rising in his wrath. "Did you not come to this country for the express purpose of asking my granddaughter's hand in marriage? Did I not promise her hand to you in marriage?"

"You did, provi—"

"Then if that did not constitute an engagement, I do not know what does—that is all. But some people have very loose ideas about honor. You ask the hand of my granddaughter; I bestow it on you, and announce the fact to my family."

"Pardon me, Mr. Rockharrt, you promised me the hand of your granddaughter, provided she should be willing to give it to me."

"'Provided' nothing of the sort, sir. I gave her hand unconditionally, absolutely, and announced the betrothal to the family."

"But, my dear Mr. Rockharrt, the lady's consent is a most necessary factor in such a case as this," urged the young man, who began to think that the despotic egotism of the Iron King had in these later years grown into a monomania, deceiving him into the delusion that his power over family and dependants was that of an absolute monarch over his subjects. This opinion was confirmed by the next words of the autocrat.

"Of course her consent would follow my act. That was taken for granted."

"But, sir, her consent did not follow your act. Quite the contrary; for my rejection followed it. It is of no use to multiply words. The affair is at an end. I have bidden good-by to Mrs. Rothsay. I am here to say good-by to you."

"You cannot mean it!"

"I have left Rockhold finally. I shall leave North End by this six p.m. train, en route for the South," continued the rejected lover.

"Then, by — —! if she has driven you out of my house, she shall go herself! I have done the best I could for the woman, and she has repaid me by ingratitude and rebellion. And she shall leave my house at once!" exclaimed the despot in a tone of savage resolution.

"Mr. Rockharrt, I must beg that you will not visit my disappointment on the head of your unoffending granddaughter."

"Duke of Cumbervale, you must not venture to interfere with me in the discipline of my own family. I don't very much like dukes. I think I said that once before. I rejected you for my granddaughter two years ago when she was bound to Rule Rothsay. Now that she is a widow and is free, I accepted your suit and bestowed her on you, not that I like dukes any better now than I did then, but I like you better as a man."

The young duke bowed with solemn gravity at this compliment, repressing the smile that fluttered about his lips. At this moment a waiter entered the room, and said that "the gentleman's" servant had arrived with his master's luggage, and requested to know where it was to be put.

"Tell him to get his dinner, and then take the luggage in the same carriage to the station," said the duke, and the messenger withdrew.

"Have you lunched, duke?" inquired Mr. Rockharrt, mindful, even in his rage, of his duties as a host.

"I have not thought of doing so," replied the young man.

"Umph! I suppose not!" grunted the Iron King, as he rang the bell.

A waiter appeared.

"Any game in the house?"

"Yes, sir; fine venison."

"Don't want venison—had it for breakfast. Anything else?"

"A very fine wild turkey, sir."

"Bother! Takes three hours to dress, and I want a hot lunch got up in twenty-five minutes, at longest. Any small game?"

"Uncommon fine partridges, sir."

"Then have a dozen dressed and sent up, with proper accompaniments; and lose no time about it! Also put a bottle of Johannisberg on ice."

"Yes, sir."

The waiter vanished.

"I must bid you good-by now, Mr. Rockharrt," said the duke, rising.

"No; you must not. Sit down. Sit down. You must lunch with me, and drink a parting glass of wine. Then you will have plenty of time to secure your train, and I to drive to Rockhold at my usual hour. Say no more, duke. Keep your seat."

Cumbervale looked at the iron-gray man before him, thought certainly this must be their last meeting and parting on earth, and that therefore he would not cross the patriarch in his humor.

"You are very kind. Thank you. I will break a parting bottle of wine with you willingly."

In double-quick time the broiled partridges were served, the wine placed, and all was ready for the two men.

"Go and tell Mr. Fabian and Mr. Clarence that I wish them to come here. You will find them somewhere in the house," said Mr. Rockharrt.

"Beg pardon, sir; both gentlemen have gone over to the works," replied the waiter.

This was true. Both "boys" had gorged themselves with cold ham, bread and cheese, washed down with quarts of brown stout, and were in no appetite to enjoy partridge and Johannisberg, even if they had been found in the hotel.

"Glad they have found out that they must be attentive to business. You and I, duke, will discuss the good things on the table before us. Come."

The two lingered over the luncheon until it was time for the duke to start for the depot.

"I will send over for my two sons, that you may bid them good-by," said Mr. Rockharrt, and he turned to the waiter, and told him to go and dispatch a messenger to that effect.

Messrs. Fabian and Clarence soon put in an appearance, and expressed their surprise and regret at the sudden departure of their father's guest, and their hope and trust to see him again in the near future. Neither of them seemed to know that the betrothal declared at the dinner table on the night before had no foundation in fact. The duke thanked them for their good wishes, invited them to visit him if they should find themselves in England, and then he took a final leave of the Rockharrts, entered the carriage, and drove off, through a pouring rain, to the railway station—and out of their lives forever.

"A fine thing Mistress Rothsay has done!" exclaimed the Iron King, when his guest had gone, and he explained Cora's action.

Corona had spent the day at Rockhold drearily enough. She felt reasonably sure that her rejection of the duke's hand would deeply offend her grandfather and precipitate a crisis in her own life. When she had finished her letter to her brother, in which she told him of the death of Mr. Rockharrt's wife and added her own resolution soon to set out to join him in his distant fort, she began to make preparations for her journey in the event of having to leave Rockhold suddenly. She knew her grandfather's temper and disposition, and felt that she must hold herself in readiness to meet any emergencies brought about by their manifestations. So she set about her preparations.

She had not much to do. The trunks that she had packed and dispatched to the North End railway station three months before at the hour when her own journey was arrested by the accident to her grandfather, had remained in storage there ever since.

The contents of her large valise, which was to have been her own traveling companion in her long journey to and through the "Great American Desert," and which was well packed with several changes of clothes and with small dressing, sewing and writing cases, supplied all her wants during the three months of her further sojourn at Rockhold.

She had only now to collect these together, cause all the soiled articles to be laundered, and then repack the valise. This occupied her all the afternoon of the short November day.

At six o'clock she came down into the parlor to see that the lamps were trimmed and lighted, and the coal fire stirred up and replenished, so that her grandfather should find the room warm and comfortable on his return home. Then she brought out his dressing gown and slippers, hung the first over his arm chair and put the last on the warm hearthstones.

At length the carriage wheels were heard faintly over the soft, wet avenue and under the pouring rain.

Old John, waiting in the hall to be ready to open the door in an instant, did so before the Iron King should leave the carriage, and hoisting a very large umbrella, he went out to the carriage door and held it over his master while they walked back to the house and entered the hall.

"Here! take off my rubber cloak! Take off my overcoat! Now my rubber boots! What a night!" exclaimed the old man, as he came out of his shell, or various shells.

Corona had the pitcher of punch on the table now with a cut-glass goblet beside it.

"I hope you have not taken cold, grandfather," she said, drawing his easy chair nearer the fire.

"Hold your tongue! Don't dare to speak to me! Leave the room this instant! John! come in here. Pour me out a glass of that punch, and while I sip it draw off my boots and put on my slippers," said the Iron King, throwing himself into his big easy chair and leaning back.

Corona was more pained than surprised. She had expected something like this from the Iron King. She replied never a word, but passed into the adjoining dining room and sat down there. Through the open door she could see the old gentleman reclining at his ease, and sipping his fragrant hot punch while old John drew off his boots, rubbed his feet, and put on his warm slippers. Presently the waiter brought in the soup, put it on the table, and rang the dinner bell. Mr. Rockharrt put down his empty glass, and arose and came to the table. Cora took her place at the head of the board, hardly knowing whether she would be allowed to remain there. But her grandfather took not the slightest notice of her. She filled his plate with soup, and put it on the waiter held by the young footman, who carried it to his master. In this manner passed the whole dinner in every course. Corona carved or served the dishes, filled the plate for her grandfather, which was taken to him by the footman. At the end of the heavy meal the Iron King arose from the table and said:

"I am going to my own room. Mistress Rothsay, I shall have something to say to you in the morning;" and he went out.

CHAPTER XXIX
CORONA'S OPPORTUNITY

Corona Rothsay stood behind her chair at the head of the breakfast table, waiting for Mr. Rockharrt. He entered presently, and returned no answer to her respectful salutation, but moodily took his seat, raised the cover from the hot dish before him, and helped himself to a broiled partridge. After the gloomy meal was finished the Iron King arose from the table and pushed back his chair so suddenly and forcibly as to nearly upset his servant.

"Come into the library! I wish to have a decisive talk with you!" he said, in a harsh voice, to his granddaughter, as he strode from the dining room.

Corona, who had finished her own slight breakfast some minutes before, immediately arose and followed him. On reaching the bookery, old Aaron Rockharrt sank heavily into his big leathern armchair, and pointed, sternly, to an opposite one, on which Corona obediently seated herself.

"Look at me, mistress!" he said, placing his hands upon the arms of his chair, bending forward and gazing on her with fixed, keen eyes, that burned like fire beneath the pent roof of his shaggy iron-gray brows.

Corona looked up at him.

"Do you know, madam, that in rejecting the hand of the Duke of Cumbervale you have offered me an unpardonable affront?"

"No, grandfather, I did not know it; and certainly I never meant—never could possibly have meant—to affront you," said Corona, deprecatingly. "If I have been so unhappy as to disappoint your wishes, I am very sorry, my dear grandfather, but—"

He harshly interrupted her.

"Do not you dare to call me grandfather, either now or ever again! I disclaim forever that relationship, and all relationship with the false, flirting, coquettish, unprincipled creature that you are! Your late suitor may forgive your treachery to him, beguiling him by your once pretended preference to pass by all eligible matches and cross the ocean for your sake! Yes; he may forgive you, because he is a fool (being a duke)! But as for me—I will never pardon the outrageous affront you have put upon me, in rejecting the man of my choice! Never, as long as I live, so help me—"

"Oh!—oh, grandfather!" cried Corona, arresting his half-sworn oath, "don't say that! I am sorry to have crossed your will in this matter, or in any way; but, oh, my dear grandfather—"

"Stop there!" vociferated the Iron King, with a stamp. "I am no grandfather of yours! How dare you insult me with the name when I have forbidden you to do so?"

"I beg your pardon, sir. It was a mere slip of the tongue. I spoke impulsively. I had forgotten your prohibition. I shall not certainly offend in that way again," said Corona, quietly.

"You had better not!"

"I was about to say, when you interrupted me," resumed Cora, earnestly, "that I am grieved to have been compelled to disappoint you by rejecting the Duke of Cumbervale; but, sir, I could not do otherwise. I could not accept a man whom I could not love. To have done so would have been a great sin. Surely, sir, you must know it would have been a sin," pleaded Corona.

"Stuff and nonsense!" roared the Iron King. "Don't dare to talk such sentimental rubbish to me! You can't love him, can't you? Tell that to an idiot, not to me! When we were in London, two or three years ago, you loved him so well that you were ready to break your engagement with your betrothed husband, Regulas Rothsay, in order to marry this duke. Yes; and you would certainly have done so if I had not put a stop to the affair by having an explanation with the suitor, telling him of your prior engagement, and also of your want of fortune, and bringing you back home to your forgotten duties."

"Oh, sir, I deserve all your reproaches for that forgetfulness. I was very wrong then," said Cora, with a sigh.

"Bosh! You are always wrong!" sneered old Aaron Rockharrt. "And you always will be wrong! You were wrong when you wished to break your engagement with Regulas Rothsay to marry the Duke of Cumbervale, and you are wrong, now that you are free, to reject the man. Why, look at it: Now that you have been a widow for more than two years, and Cumbervale has proved his constancy by remaining a bachelor two years for your sake, and crossing the ocean and coming down here to propose for you again, and even after I—I myself—have positively promised him your hand, and have given a family dinner in honor of the occasion, and have announced the engagement, and after speeches have been made and toasts have been drank to the happiness and prosperity of your married life, and all due formalities of betrothal had been observed, then, mistress, what do you do?" severely demanded old Aaron Rockharrt.

"Only my duty under the circumstances. I was not in the least bound or compromised by or responsible for anything that was said or done at that dinner table," replied Corona.

"This is what you do: You dare to set me at defiance! You dare to set your will against mine! You dare to reject the man whom I chose for your husband, whom I announced as your betrothed husband! You dare to drive him away from my house, grieved, disappointed, humiliated, to become a wanderer over the face of the earth for your sake, even as you drove Regulas Rothsay from the goal of his ambition into exile, and—"

A sharp cry from Corona suddenly stopped him in full career.

"Do not, oh! do not speak of that! I—I would have given my life to have prevented Rule's loss, if I could! As for this man—this duke—he is nothing whatever to me, and never can be!"

"And yet you were ready to fall down and worship him three years ago!"

"It was a brief insanity—a self-delusion. That is past. Cumbervale never was and never can be anything to me. No man can ever be anything to me! I could not live Rule's wife, but I will die Rule's widow; and I do not care how soon—the sooner the better, if it were the Lord's will!" moaned Corona.

"Drivel!" angrily exclaimed old Aaron Rockharrt. "I am tired of your idiotic, imbecile hypocrisies! Here are two men driven away by your unprincipled vacillation—to call your conduct by the lightest name. One driven to his death; one driven, it may be, to his ruin. It is quite time you were sent to follow your victims. Look you! I am just about to start for North End. I shall return home at my usual time this evening. Do not let me find you here when I arrive, for I never wish to see your false face again!" said the Iron King, rising from his arm chair and striding from the room.

Corona started up and ran after him, pleading, imploring—

"Grandfather! Dear grandfather! Oh, I beg pardon! I forgot! Sir! sir! Oh, do not part from me in this way!"

He turned sharply, stared at her mockingly, and then demanded:

"Come! Shall I call Cumbervale back? Tell him that you have changed your whirligig mind, and are ready to marry him, if he will only take time by the forelock and return before you shift around again? I can easily do that. I can send a telegram that will over-take him and turn him back so promptly that he may be here in twenty-four hours! Come! Shall I do that?"

Corona, who had been gazing at the mocking speaker scarcely knowing whether he spoke in earnest or in irony, now answered despairingly:

"Oh, no, no! not for the world! I have not changed my mind. I could not do so for any cause."

"Then don't stop me. I'm in haste. I am going to North End. Don't let me find you here when I come back. Don't let me ever see or hear from you again, without your consent to marry the man I have chosen for you. John!"

"Oh, sir, consider—" began Corona, pleadingly.

"John!" vociferated the Iron King, pushing rudely past her.

The old servant came hurrying up, helped his master on with his overcoat and with his rubber coat, then gave him his hat and gloves, and finally hoisted a large umbrella to hold over his master's head as he passed from the house to the carriage in front.

Corona stood watching until the carriage rolled away and old John came back into the hall and closed the door. Then she returned to the library and sank sobbing into the big leathern chair. She now realized for the first time what the parting with her grandfather would be—the parting with the gray old man who had been the ogre of her childhood, the terror of her youth, and the autocrat of her maturity, and yet whom, by all the laws of nature, she tenderly loved, and whom by the commandment of God she was bound to honor.

She glanced mechanically toward the card rack, and saw there another letter in the handwriting of her brother—a letter that had come in the morning's mail and had been stuck up there, and in the excitement of the hour had been neglected or forgotten.

She seized it eagerly and tore it open, wondering what could have urged Sylvan to write so soon after his last letter.

It was dated three weeks later than the one she had received only the day previous, the first one having, no doubt, been delayed somewhere along the uncertain route.

In this letter Sylvan complained that he had not received a word from his dear sister since leaving Governor's Island, and mentioned that he himself had written all along the line of march and three times since the arrival of his regiment at Fort Farthermost.

But he admitted, also, that the mails beyond the regular United States mail roads were very uncertain and irregular. Then he came to the object of this particular epistle.

"It is, my dear Cora, to tell you," he wrote, "that if you should still be resolved to come out and join me here, an opportunity for your safe conduct will be offered you this autumn which may never occur again. Our senior captain—Captain Neville, Company A—has been absent on leave for several months. So he did not come out here with the regiment. His leave expires on the 30th of November. He will be obliged to start in the latter part of October in order to have time enough to accomplish the tedious journey by wagon from Leavenworth to Fort Farthermost, which is, as I believe I told you, in the southern part of the Indian Reserve, bordering on Texas. He is to bring his wife with him.

"But our colonel thinks it is I who want you, and, moreover, I who need you; for he says that, next to a wife, a sister is the best safeguard a young officer can have out in these frontier forts, and he gave me the address of Captain Neville and advised me to write to him and ask him and his wife to take charge of my sister on the route.

"And then, dear, he went further than that. He took my letter after I had written it, and inclosed it in one from himself. So now, my dear, all you have to do is to go to Washington, call on Mrs. Neville, at Brown's Hotel, Pennsylvania Avenue, and send up your card. She will expect you. Then you must hold yourself in readiness to start when the captain and his wife do."

Cora had no time to indulge in reverie. She must be up and doing.

Her luggage had long been stored in the freight house of the North End railway station, and her traveling bags had been packed the day before. The servants knew she was going out to join her brother, though they did not know that her grandfather had discarded her. She had very little to do for herself on that day, but she resolved to do all that she could for the comfort of her grandfather before she should leave the house forever.

So she went and ordered the dinner—just such a dinner as she knew he would like. Then she called old John to her presence and directed him to have the parlor prepared for his master just as carefully as if she herself were on the spot to see it done; to have the fire bright; the hearth clean; the lamps trimmed and lighted; the shutters closed and the curtains drawn; the easy chair, with dressing gown and slippers, before the fire, and, lastly, a jug of hot punch on the hearth.

Old John promised faithfully to perform all these duties. Then Cora went and wrote two letters.

One to her brother Sylvan, in which she acknowledged the receipt of his letter, expressed her thanks to the colonel for his kindness, and assured him that she should gladly avail herself of the escort of the Nevilles and go out under their protection to Fort Farthermost.

This letter she put in the mail bag in the hall ready for the messenger to take to the North End post office.

The second letter was a farewell to her grandfather, in which she expressed her sorrow at leaving him even at his own command; her grief at having offended him, however unintentionally; her prayers for his forgiveness, and her hope to meet him again in health, happiness and prosperity.

This letter Corona stuck on the card rack, where he would be sure to find it.

Then she ordered her own little pony carriage, and went and put on her bonnet and her warm fur-lined cloak and called Mark to bring her shawls and traveling bags down to the hall.

When all this had been done, Corona called all the servants together, made them each a little present, and then bade them good-by.

Then she stepped into the little carriage and bade the groom to drive on to Violet Banks.

"I think I shall go no further than that to-night, my friends, and leave for Washington to-morrow morning," she said, in a broken voice, as the pony started.

"Then all ob us wot kin get off will come to bid yer annurrer good-by to-morrow mornin'!" came hoarsely from one of the crowd, and was repeated by all in a chorus.

The carriage rolled down the avenue to the ferry—not that Corona intended to cross the river, for Violet Banks, it will be remembered, was on the same side and a few miles north of Rockhold—but that she would not leave the place without taking leave of old Moses, the ferryman. Fortunately the boat lay idle at its wharf, and the old man sat in the ferry house, hugging the stove and smoking his pipe.

He came out at the sound of wheels. Corona called him to the carriage, told him that she did not want to cross the river, but that she was going away for a while and wished to take leave of him.

Now old Moses had seen too many arrivals and departures to and from Rockhold to feel much emotion at this news; besides he had no idea of the gravity of this departure. So he only touched his old felt hat and said:

"Eh, young mist'ess, hopes how yer'll hab a monsous lubly time! Country is dull for de young folks in de winter. Gwine to de city, s'pose, young mist'ess?"

"Yes, Uncle Moses, I am going to Washington first," replied Corona.

"Lors! I hear tell how so many folkses do go to Washintub! Wunner wot dey go for? in de winter, too! Lors! Well, honey, I wish yer a mighty fine time and a handsome husban' afore yer comes home. Lor' bress yer, young mist'ess!"

"Thank you, Uncle Moses. Here is a trifle for you," said Cora, putting a half eagle in his hand.

"Lor' bress yer, young mist'ess, how I do tank yer wid all my heart! I nebber had so much money at one time in all my life!" exclaimed the overjoyed old ferryman.

CHAPTER XXX
FAREWELL TO VIOLET BANKS

Along the north road, between the thickly wooded east ridge and the swiftly running river, Corona drove on her last journey through that valley. Three miles up, the road turned from the river, and, with several windings and doublings, ascended the mountain side to the elevated plateau on which were situated the beautiful house and grounds called Violet Banks.

As the carriage reached the magnificent plateau, Corona stopped the horse for a moment to take in the glory of the view. In the midst of her admiration of this scenery, two distinct thoughts were strongly borne in on the mind of Corona. One was that Violet Rockharrt would never be willing to leave this enchanting spot to make her home at Rockhold. She might consent to do so to please others, but she would suffer through it.

The other thought was that old Aaron Rockharrt would never consent to live in a place which, however beautiful it might be, was too difficult of access and egress for a man of his age.

What, then, could be done to cheer the old man's solitude at his home? The only hope lay in the chance of Mr. Clarence finding a wife who might be acceptable to his father, and bringing her home to Rockhold.

The carriage drew up before the long, low villa, with its vine-clad porch, where, though the roses had faded and fallen, the still vivid green foliage and brilliant rose berries made a gay appearance.

Violet was not sitting on the porch, beside her little wicker workstand basket, as she always had been found by Cora in the earlier months of her residence there, but, nevertheless, she saw her visitor's approach from the front windows of her sitting room, and ran out to meet her.

"Oh, so glad to see you! And such a delightful surprise!" were the words with which she caught Cora in her arms, as the latter alighted from the carriage.

"How well you look, dear. A real wood violet now, in your pretty purple robe," said Corona, with assumed gayety, as she returned the little creature's embrace, and went with her into the house.

"I am going to send the carriage to the stable. You shall spend the afternoon and evening with me, whether you will or not, and whether the handsome lover breaks his heart or not!" exclaimed Violet, as they entered the parlor.

"Don't trouble yourself, dear. See, the man is driving around to the stable now, and I have come, not only to spend the afternoon, but the night with you," said Cora, sitting down and beginning to unfasten her fur cloak. "Will my uncle be late in returning this evening?"

"Fabian? Oh, no! this is his early day. He will be home very soon now. But where did you leave his grace? Why did he not escort you here?" inquired the little lady.

"Have you not heard that he has left Rockhold?" asked Corona, in her turn.

"Why, no. I have heard nothing about him since the night of the dinner given in honor of your betrothal. Are you tired, Cora, dear? You look tired. Shall I show you to your room, where you may bathe your face?" inquired Violet, noticing for the first time the pale and weary aspect of her visitor.

"No; but you may bring the baby here to see me."

"My baby? Oh, the little angel has just been put to sleep—its afternoon sleep. Come into the nursery, and I will show it to you," exclaimed the proud and happy mother, starting up and leading the way to the upper floor and to a front room over the library, fitted up beautifully as a nursery. Corona, on entering, was conscious of a blending of many soft bright colors, and of a subdued rainbow light, like the changes of the opal.

Violet led her directly to the cradle, an elegant structure of fine light wood, satin and lace, in which was enshrined the jewel, the treasure, the idol of the household—a tiny, round-headed, pink-faced little atom of humanity, swathed in flannel, cambric and lace, and covered with fine linen sheets trimmed with lace, little lamb's-wool blankets embroidered with silk, and a coverlet of satin in alternate tablets of rose, azure and pearl tablets.

The delighted mother and the admiring visitor stood gazing at the babe, and talking in low tones for ten or fifteen minutes perhaps, and were then admonished by the nurse—an experienced woman—that it was not good for such young babies to be looked over and talked over so long when they were asleep.

Violet and her visitor softly withdrew from the cradle, and Corona had leisure to look around the lovely room, the carpet of tender green, like the first spring grass, and dotted over with buttercups and daisies; the wall paper of pearl white, with a vine of red and white roses running over it; the furniture of curled maple, upholstered in fine chintz, in colors to match the wall paper. But the window curtains were the marvels of the apartment. There were two high front windows, draped in rainbow silk—that is, each breadth of the hangings was in perfect rainbow stripes, and the effect of the light streaming through them was soft, bright, and very beautiful.

"It is a creation! Whose?" inquired Corona, as she stood before one of the windows.

"Well, it was my idea, though I am not at all noted for ideas, as everybody knows," said Violet, with a smile. "But I wanted my baby's first impressions of life to be serenely delightful through every sense. I wanted her to see, when she should open her eyes in the morning, a sphere of soft light and bright, delicate shades of color. So I prepared this room."

"But where did you find the rainbow draperies?"

"Oh, them! I designed them for my baby, and Fabian sent the pattern to Paris, and we received the goods in due time. I will tell you another thing. I have an Æolian harp for her. It is under the front window of the upper hall, but its aerial music can reach her here when it is in place. When she is a little stronger I am going to have a music box for her. Oh, I want my little baby to live in a sphere of 'sweet sights, sweet sounds, soft touches.'"

A brisk, firm footstep, a cheery, ringing voice in the hall below, arrested the conversation of the two women.

"It is Fabian! Come!" exclaimed Violet, joyfully, leading the way down stairs.

Mr. Fabian stood at the foot. He embraced his young wife boisterously, and then seeing Cora coming down stairs behind Violet, went and shook hands with his niece, saying:

"Glad to see you! Glad to see you! Has Violet been showing you our little goddess? I tell you what, Cora: everything has changed since that usurper came. This place is no longer 'Violet Banks' It is the Holy Hill. This house is the temple; that nursery is the sanctuary; that cradle is the altar; and that babe is the idol of the community. Now go along with Violet. Oh! she is high priestess to the idol. Go along. I'm going to wash my face and hands, and then I'll join you."

Mr. Fabian went up stairs, and Cora followed Violet into the parlor.

"Here are the English magazines, my dear, come this morning. Will you look over them, while I go and see to the dinner table? I will not be gone more than ten minutes," said Violet, lifting a pile of pamphlets from a side table and placing them on a little stand near the easy chair into which Corona had thrown herself.

"Certainly, Violet, love. Don't mind me. Go."

Violet kissed her forehead and left the room.

Cora never touched the magazines, but sat with her elbow on the stand and her forehead resting on her hand.

She sat motionless, buried in painful thought until her Uncle Fabian entered the room.

Then she looked up.

He came and sat down near her; looked at her inquiringly for a few moments; and then, as she did not break the silence, he said:

"Well, Cora?"

"Well, Uncle Fabian?"

"What is up, my dear?"

"I would rather defer all explanations until after dinner, if you please."

"Very well, my dear Cora."

And indeed there was no time for further talk just then, for Violet came hurrying into the room laughing and exclaiming:

"I am the pink of punctuality, Cora, dear. Here I am back again in just ten minutes."

The next moment the dinner bell rang, and they all went into the dining room.

Violet—trained by Mrs. Chief Justice Pendletime, who was a great domestic manager—excelled in every housekeeping department, especially, perhaps, in the culinary art; so the little dinner was an exquisite one, and thoroughly enjoyed by the master and mistress of the house, and might have been equally appreciated by their visitor if her sad thoughts had not destroyed her appetite.

After dinner, when they adjourned to the parlor, Violet said:

"Again I must beg you to excuse me, Cora, dear, while I go up and put baby to sleep. It is a little weakness of mine, but I always like to put her to sleep myself, though I have the most faithful of all nurses. You will excuse me?"

"Why, of course, darling!" Corona heartily replied; and the happy little mother ran off.

"Now then, Cora, what is it? You said you would explain after dinner. Do so now, my dear; for if it is anything very painful I would rather not have my Wood Violet grieved by hearing it," said Mr. Fabian, drawing his chair nearer to that of Corona.

"It is very painful, Uncle Fabian, and I also would like to shield Violet as much as possible from the grief of knowing it. But—is it possible that you do not know what has happened at Rockhold?" gravely inquired Corona.

"I know this much: That the announcement of an engagement between yourself and the Englishman was premature and unauthorized; that you have finally rejected the suitor—who has since left Rockhold—and by so doing you have greatly enraged our Iron King. I know no more than that, Cora."

"What! Has not my grandfather told you anything to day?"

"Not one word."

"Then I must tell you. He has cast me off forever."

"Cora! Cora!"

"It is true, indeed. This morning he ordered me to quit his house; not to let him find me still there on his return; never to let him see or hear from me again unless it was with my consent to recall and marry my English suitor."

"But, Cora, my dear, why can you not come into his conditions? Why can you not marry Cumbervale? He is a splendid fellow every way, and he loves you as hard as a horse can kick. He is awfully in love with you, my dear. Now, why not marry him and make everybody happy and all serene?"

"Because, Uncle Fabian, I don't happen to be in love with him," replied Corona, with just a shade of disdain in her manner.

"Well, my dear, I will not undertake to persuade you to change your mind. If you have inherited nothing else from the Iron King, you have his strength of will. What are you going to do, Cora?"

"I am going to carry out my purpose of going to the Indian Reserve as missionary to the Indian tribes, to devote all my time and all my fortune to their welfare."

"A mad scheme, my dear Cora. How are you, a young woman, going to manage to do this? Under the auspices of what church do you act?"

"Under that of the broad church of Christian charity—no other."

"But how are you going to reach the field of your labors? How are you going to cross those vast tracts, destitute of all inhabitants except tribes of savages, destitute of all roads except the government 'trails'?"

"You know, if you have not forgotten, that it was my purpose to join my brother at his post, and to establish my school near his fort and under its protection."

"Well, yes; I remember hearing something of the sort; but really, Cora, I thought it was all talk since Sylvan went away."

"But it is more than that. Some time late in this month I shall go out to Fort Farthermost under the protection of Captain and Mrs. Neville. They are now in Washington, where I am going immediately to join them. When you read this letter, which I received after my grandfather had left me in anger this morning, you will understand all about it," said Corona, drawing her brother's last letter from her pocket and handing it to her uncle.

Mr. Fabian took it and read it carefully through; then returned it to her, saying:

"Well, my dear, it does seem as if there were a fate in all this. But what a journey is before you! At this season of the year, too! But, Cora, do not let Violet know that the grandfather has discarded you. It would grieve her tender heart too much. Just tell her that you are going out to your brother. Do not even tell her so much as that to-night. It would keep her from sleep."

"I will not hint the subject this evening, Uncle Fabian. I love Violet too much to distress her."

"You will have to explain that your engagement with the Englishman is at an end."

"Or, rather, that it has never had a beginning," said Corona.

"Very well," assented Mr. Fabian. "And now I must go and dispatch a messenger to North End to fetch Clarence here to spend the night. A hasty leave-taking at the railway depot would hardly satisfy Clarence, Cora."

"I know! And I thank you very much, Uncle Fabian," replied Corona.

"Ah, Violet! here you are, just in time to take my place. I am going out to send for Clarence to spend the evening with us," said Mr. Fabian, as he passed his young wife, who entered the room as he left it.

Instead of sending a messenger, Fabian put his fastest horse into his lightest wagon, and set off at his best speed himself. He reached North End Hotel in twenty minutes, and burst in upon Clarence, finding that gentleman seated in an arm chair before a coal fire.

"Anything the matter, Fabian?" he inquired, looking up in surprise.

"Yes! The devil's to pay! The monarch has driven his granddaughter from court!" exclaimed the elder brother, throwing his hat upon the floor, and dropping into a chair.

"You don't mean to say—"

"Yes, I do! Father has turned Cora out of doors because she refused to marry the Englishman."

"Good Heaven!"

"Come! There is no time to talk! Cora is at my house. She leaves for Washington to join Captain and Mrs. Neville, and go out with them to Fort Farthermost."

"But, look here, Fabian. Why do you let her do that?"

"Don't be a fool! Who is to stop her if she is bound to go? Come, hurry up; put on your overcoat and get into my trap, and I will take you back with me, see Cora, and stay all night with us."

Mr. Clarence started up, rang for a waiter to see to his rooms, then put on his overcoat, and in five minutes more he was seated beside his brother in the light wagon, behind the fastest horse in Mr. Fabian's stables, bowling out of the village at a rate of speed that I would not dare to state. It was not nine o'clock when they reached Violet Banks.

Mr. Fabian drove around to the stables, gave his team up to the groom, and walked back to the house with Clarence.

"You must not drop a word to Violet about Cora's intended journey. She thinks that Cora has only come to spend the night with her. If she knew otherwise she would be too distressed to sleep. Not until after breakfast to-morrow is she to be told that Cora is going away; and never is she to know that our niece has been driven away."

"I understand, Fabian. Who is going to Washington with Cora?"

"No one that I know of; but she is quite able to take care of herself, so far."

"I will not have it so, Fabian. I will go with our niece!" said Mr. Clarence.

"Are you mad? The monarch would never forgive such misprision of treason. He would discard you, Clarence!" exclaimed Mr. Fabian, in consternation.

"I do not think so. Our father is too just for that. And in any case I shall take the risk."

"The Iron King is just in all his business relations; he would not be otherwise to save himself from bankruptcy. But has he been just to Cora?"

"From his point of view. He has not been kind; that is all. I must be kind to our niece at all costs."

This brought them to the door of the house, which Mr. Fabian opened with his latch key, and the two men entered the parlor together.

"Why, how soon you have come! I am so glad!" exclaimed Violet, rising to welcome the new visitor.

"That is because, instead of sending, I went for him," explained Mr. Fabian.

"So I suspected when I found that you did not return immediately to the parlor," said Violet.

Mr. Clarence meanwhile went to his niece, took her hand and kissed her in silence. He could not trust his voice to speak. She understood him, and returned the pressure of his hand. If it had not been for Violet, the evening would have passed very gloomily; but she, who knew nothing of the domestic tempest that had driven Cora from home, nor even of the impending separation in the morning, and who heartily enjoyed the presence of her two favorite relatives in the house, kept the party enlivened by her own good spirits and gay talk.

Once during the evening Clarence and Cora found themselves far enough off from their friends for a short tete-a-tete, in which there was a brief but perfect explanation between them.

Then Clarence announced his intention of escorting her to Washington and seeing her safe under the protection of the Nevilles.

Cora strongly opposed this plan, on the ground that his escort was unnecessary and might be deeply offensive to Mr. Rockharrt.

But Clarence was firm.

"You may turn your back on me, Cora. You may refuse to speak to me during the whole journey. But you cannot prevent me from going on the same train with you, and so becoming your guardian on the journey," said Clarence.

Cora's answer to this was prevented by the approach of Violet, who said:

"Clarence, it is half past eleven o'clock, and Cora looks tired to death. Your room is ready whenever you would like to retire."

Acting upon this very broad hint, Mr. Clarence laughed, kissed his niece good night, shook hands with his sister-in-law, and left the room, preceded by Mr. Fabian, who offered to show him to his chamber. Violet conducted Cora to the room prepared for her, and, with a warm embrace, left her to repose for the last time in that house.

CHAPTER XXXI
"IT IS THE UNEXPECTED THAT HAPPENS"

After her exciting and fatiguing day, Corona slept long and heavily, and when she reached the family sitting room she found her two uncles there in conversation.

"I am sorry I kept you waiting, Uncle Fabian," she said, hurriedly.

"You have not done so, my dear. The bell has not yet rung."

"Then I'm glad. Good morning, Clarence," she said, turning to her younger uncle.

"Good morning, Cora. How did you sleep?"

"Perfectly, Clarence dear. I hope you will set out for North End immediately after breakfast. I shall not start for Washington until to-night. I shall spend the day here, so that after telling Violet of my intended journey I may have some little time to reconcile her to it."

"How good you are, Cora. I do appreciate this consideration for Violet," said Mr. Fabian earnestly.

"It is only her due, uncle. Well, Clarence, since you are determined to escort me to Washington, whether or not, you may meet me at the depot for the 6:30 express. I feel that it is every way better that I should go by the night train; better for Violet, with whom I can thus spend a few more hours, and better for Clarence, who need not by this arrangement lose this day's work."

"Quite so," assented Mr. Fabian. "And now," he added, as light footsteps were heard approaching the room, "here comes Violet. Not a word about the journey until after breakfast."

They all went into the breakfast room, where a fragrant, appetizing morning meal was spread.

How different this was from the breakfast at Rockhold on the preceding-day, darkened by the sullen wrath of the Iron King and eaten in the most gloomy silence! Here were affectionate attentions and jests and laughter. Violet was in such gay spirits that her vivacity became contagious, and

Fabian and Clarence often laughed aloud, and Corona was won to smile at her sallies.

At last Mr. Fabian arose with a sigh, half of satisfied appetite, half of reluctance to leave the scene, and said:

"Well, I suppose we must be moving. Clarence, will you drive with me to North End?"

"Certainly. That is all arranged, you know," replied the younger brother.

"Mr. Fabian walked out into the hall, saying as he left the breakfast room:

"Corona, a word with you, my dear."

Corona went to him, and he said:

"After you have had an explanation with Violet, persuade her to accompany you to North End. You had better come in your own pony carriage, my dear; it is so easy and the horse so safe. And then, after you have left us, I can drive her home in the same vehicle. And, by the way, my dear, what shall you do with that little turnout? Shall I send it to Hyde's livery stable for sale? You can get double what was given for it. And remit you the price?"

"No, Uncle Fabian; it is not to be sold. And I am glad you reminded me of it. I have intended all along to give it to our minister's wife. She has no carriage of any sort, and she really needs one, and she will enjoy this because she can drive the pony herself. So, after I have gone, will you please send it to Mrs. Melville, with my love?"

"Certainly, my dear; with the greatest pleasure. Cora, that is well thought of. Now I must go up to the nursery and bid good-by to baby, or her mother would never forgive me."

And high and heavy Mr. Fabian tripped up the stairs like a lamplighter.

Corona lingered in the hall, talking with Mr. Clarence, who had now come there to put on his overcoat. Presently Mr. Fabian came hurrying down stairs alone. He had left Violet in the sanctuary.

"Come, come, Clarence, hurry up! We are late! What if the monarch should reach the works before us? I shouldn't like to meet him in his roused wrath! Should you?

"Old age ne'er cooled the Douglass blood!"

said Mr. Fabian, hurriedly pulling on his overcoat, seizing hat and gloves, and with a hasty—

"Good-by, Cora, until to-night," hurried out of the front door.

He need not have been in such haste—the Iron King was not destined to reach North End in advance of his sons that morning.

Mr. Clarence kissed Corona good-by, and hurried after his elder brother, and then stopped short at what he saw.

Mr. Fabian was standing before the carriage door with one foot on the step.

Beside him was a horseman who had just ridden up—the horse in a lather of foam, the man breathless and dazed—telling some news in broken sentences; Mr. Fabian listening pallid and aghast.

"Great Heaven! how sudden! how shocking!" he exclaimed at last, turning back toward the house, and hurrying up the steps.

"What is it? What is the matter? What has happened, Fabian?" anxiously demanded Clarence.

"The father has had a stroke! No time for particulars now! Take the fastest horse in the stable and go yourself to North End to fetch the doctor. You can bring him sooner than any servant. I must go directly on to Rockhold. Cora must delay her journey again. Be off, Clarence!" said Mr. Fabian.

And while the elder brother returned to the house, the younger went to get his horse.

"Cora!" called Mr. Fabian.

Corona came out of the parlor.

"You cannot go away to-day."

"Why?" inquired the young lady.

"Don't talk! Listen! Your grandfather is ill—very ill. Old John has just come from Rockhold to tell me."

"Oh! I am very sorry."

"No time for words! Go put on your bonnet, and come along with me; the carriage that was to have taken me to North End must take us both to Rockhold. Hurry, Cora."

"But Violet?"

"I will go and tell Violet that the grandfather is not feeling very well, and has sent for you. I can do this while you are getting ready to go. Then come into the nursery and bid Violet good-by."

Corona hurried up to her room, and quickly put on her bonnet and fur-lined cloak, and then ran into the nursery, where she found Violet nursing her baby, looking serious but composed, and evidently unconscious of old Aaron Rockharrt's danger. Mr. Fabian was standing at the back of her chair, so that she might not read the truth in his face.

"So you are going home so suddenly, Cora, dear? I am so sorry the father is not feeling well that I cannot even ask you to stay here a moment longer. Give my love to the father, and tell him if he does not get better in a day or two I shall be sure to come and nurse him."

She could not rise without disturbing her precious baby, but she raised her head and put up her lips, that Cora might kiss her good-by. Then Cora followed her uncle down stairs, and in five minutes more they were seated in the carriage, slowly winding their way down the dangerous mountain pass to the river road that led to Rockhold.

"Uncle Fabian," said Corona, gravely, "I have been trying to think what is right for me to do. This sorrowful news took me so completely by surprise, and your directions were so prompt and peremptory, that I had not a moment for reflection; so that I followed your lead automatically. But now, Uncle Fabian, I have considered, and I ask you as I have asked myself—am I right in going back to Rockhold, after my grandfather has sent me away, and forbidden me ever to return? Tell me, Uncle Fabian."

"My dear, what do you yourself wish to do?" he inquired.

"To return to Rockhold and nurse my grandfather, if he will allow me to do so."

"Then by all means do so."

"But, Uncle Fabian—against my grandfather's express command?"

"Good Heaven, girl!" Those 'commands' were issued by a well and angry man. You are returning to minister to an ill and perhaps a dying one."

"Still, Uncle Fabian, would it not seem to be taking advantage of my grandfather's helpless state to return now, after he had forbidden me to enter his house? I think it would. And the more I reflect upon the subject, the surer I feel that I ought not to enter Rockhold unbidden. And—I will not."

"You will not! What! Can you show resentment to your stricken—it may be dying—grandfather?"

"Heaven forbid! But I must not disobey his injunction, now that he is too helpless to prevent me. No, Uncle Fabian, I must not enter the house. But neither will I be far from it. I will remain within call."

"Where?"

"At the ferryman's cottage. Will you, Uncle Fabian, as soon as you have an opportunity, say that I am deeply grieved for all that has estranged us. Will you ask him to forgive me and let me come to him?"

"Yes; I will do so, my dear, if there is an opportunity. But, Cora, I think you are morbidly scrupulous. I think that you should come to the house. He may wish to see you if he should have a lucid interval, and there may not be time to send for you."

"I must risk that rather than disobey him in his extremity."

"As you will," replied Mr. Fabian. And no more was said on the subject.

When they reached the foot of the mountain and the level of the river road, the horses were put upon their speed, and they soon arrived at Rockhold.

"I will wait in the carriage until you go in and inquire how he is," said Corona, as the vehicle drew up before the front door.

Mr. Fabian got out and hurried up the steps. The door stood open, cold as the day was, and all things wore the neglected aspect of a dwelling wherein the master lay stricken unto death. The housekeeper, Martha, was coming down the stairs and crying.

"How is your master?" breathlessly inquired Mr. Fabian.

"Oh, Marse Fabe, sir, jes' livin', an' dat's all!" sobbed the woman. "Dunno nuffin. Layin' dere jes' like a dead corpe, 'cept for breavin' hard," wept the woman.

"Who is with him?"

"Me mos' times an' young Mark. I jes' come down to speak 'long o' you, Marse Fabe, w'en I see de carriage dribe up."

"Well, go back to your master. I will speak to my niece, and then come in," said Mr. Fabian, as he hurried out to the carriage. All his interview with the housekeeper had not occupied two minutes, but Cora was pale with suspense and anxiety.

"How is he?" she panted.

"Unconscious, my poor girl. Oh, Cora! come in!"

"No, no; I must not. Not until he permits me. I will stop at the ferryman's cottage. Oh, if he should recover consciousness—oh, Uncle Fabian, ask him to let me come to him, and send me word."

"Yes, yes; I will do it. I must go to him now. Charles," he said, turning to the coachman, "drive Mrs. Rothsay down to the ferry house, and then take the carriage to the stables."

And then, with a grave nod to Corona, Mr. Fabian re-entered the house. The coachman drove the carriage down to the ferryman's cottage and drew up. The door was open and the cottage was empty.

"Boat on t'other side, ma'am," said Charles.

"For the doctor, I suppose—and hope," said Corona, looking across the river, and seeing a gig with two men coming on to the ferryboat.

She watched from the door of the ferryman's cottage while Charles drove off the empty carriage toward the stables and the two ferrymen poled their boat across the river. She retreated within the house before the boat touched the land, for she knew that the doctor, if he should see her there, would wonder why she was not at her grandfather's bedside, and perhaps— as he was an old friend—he might ask questions which she would find it embarrassing to answer. The boat touched the shore; the gig, containing the doctor and Mr. Clarence, rolled off the boat on along the drive leading to the house.

Meanwhile Mr. Fabian had re-entered the hall and hurried up to his father's room. He found the Iron King in bed, lying on his right side and breathing heavily. His eyes were half closed.

"Father," said the son, in a low voice, taking his hand and bending over him.

There was no response.

"It ain't no use, Marster Fabe. Yer can't rouse him, do wot yer will. Better wait till de doctor come, young marse. I done been tried all I knowed how, but it wa'n't no use," said Martha, who stood on the other side of the bed watching her insensible master.

"Tell me when this happened. Come away to the upper end of the room and tell me about it."

"Might's well tell yer right here, marse. 'Twon't sturve him. Lor! thunder wouldn't sturve him, the way he is in."

"Then tell me, how was it? When was he stricken?"

"We don't know, marse. He was found jes' dis way by John dis mornin'—not jes zackly dis way, howaseber, case he was a-layin' on his lef side, w'ich was berry bad; so me an' John turn him ober jes so like he is a-layin' now. Den we sent right off for you, marse, to ketch yer at home 'fore yer went to de works."

"Did he seem well when he came home last night?'

"Jes 'bout as ujual, marse. He came in, an' John he waited on him. An he ax, ole marse did, 'was Mrs. Rossay gone?' W'ich John tole him she were. Den he ordered dinner to be fotch up. An' John he had a pitcher ob hot punch ready. An' ole marse drank some. Den he went in to dinner all by hisself. An' young Mark he waited on de table, w'ich he tell me, w'en I ax him dis mornin', how de ole marse eat much as ujual, wid a good relish. Den arter dinner he went to de liberairy and sot dere a long time. Ole John say it were midnight 'fo' de ole marse walk up stairs an' call him to wait on him."

"Was John the last one who saw my father before he was found unconscious this morning?"

"Hi! yes, young marse, to be sure he were. De las' to see de ole marse in healt' las' night, an' de firs' to fine him dis way dis mornin'.'"

"How came he to find his master in this condition?"

"It was dis way. Yer know, young marse, as dere is two keys to ole marser's do', w'ich ole marse keeps one in his room to lock hisse'f in, an' John keeps one to let hisse'f in wen de ole marse rings for him in de mornin'.'"

"Yes; I know."

"Well, dis mornin' de ole marse didn't ring at his ujual hour. An' de time passed, an' de breakfast were ready an' spilin'. So I tole John how he better go up an' see if ole marse was well, how maybe he didn' feel like gettin' up an' might want to take his breakfas' in bed. But Lor! I nebber participated sich a sarious 'tack as dis. Well, den, John he went an' rapped soft like. But he didn't get no answer. Den he rap little louder. But still no answer. Den John he got scared, awful scared. Las' John he plucks up courage, an' unlocks de do', slow an' saf', an' goes in on tiptoe to de bedside, an'—an'—an'—dis yer is wot he seen. He t'ought his ole marse were dead sure, an' he come howlin' an' tumblin' down to me, an' tole me so, an' I called young Mark to follow me, case ole John wa'n't no good, an' I run up yere, an'—an'—an' dis yer is wot I foun'! O'ly he were a layin' on his lef side, an' I see he were breavin' an' I turn' him ober on his right, an' did all I could for him, an' sent John arter you."

"I wish the doctor would come," said Mr. Fabian, anxiously, as he took his father's hand again and tried to feel the pulse.

The door opened very quietly, and Clarence came into the room. Fabian beckoned him to approach the bed.

"How is he?" inquired the younger man.

"As you see! He was found in this condition by his servant this morning. He has shown no sign of consciousness since," replied the elder.

"The doctor is below. Shall he come up now?"

"Certainly."

Clarence left the room and soon returned with the physician. After a very brief examination of pulse, temperature, the pupils of the eyes of the patient, prompt measures were taken to relieve the evident pressure on the brain. The doctor bled the sufferer, who presently opened his eyes, and looked slowly around his bed. His two sons bent over him.

He tried to speak.

They bent lower still to listen.

After several futile efforts he uttered one word:

"Cora."

"Yes, father—she is here. Go, Clarence, and fetch her at once. She is at the ferryman's cottage."

The last sentence was added in a low whisper. Clarence immediately left the room to do his errand. A few minutes later the door opened softly, and Clarence re-entered the room with Cora.

Mr. Fabian went to meet her, saying softly:

"He has called for you, my dear! The only word he has spoken since he recovered consciousness was your name."

"So Uncle Clarence told me," she said, in a broken voice.

"Come to him now," said Fabian, leading her to the bedside.

She sank on her knees and took the hand of the dying man and kissed it, pleading:

"Grandfather, dear grandfather, I love you. I am grieved at having offended you. Will you forgive me—now?"

He made several painful efforts to answer her, before he uttered the few disconnected words:

"Yes—forgive—you—Cora."

She bathed his hand with her tears. All on her part also was forgotten now—all the harshness and despotism of years was forgotten now, and nothing was remembered but the gray-haired man, always gray-haired in her knowledge of him, who had protected her orphanage and given her a home and an education. She knelt there, holding his hand, and was presently touched and comforted because the lingers of that hand closed on hers with a loving pressure that they had never given her in all her life before. That was the last sign of consciousness he gave for many hours.

Mr. Fabian took the doctor aside.

"Ought I to send for my wife?" he inquired.

"Yes; I think so," replied the physician.

And the son knew that answer was his father's sentence of death. Not one of the family could be spared from this death bed to go and fetch Violet. So Mr. Fabian went down stairs to the library and wrote a hasty note:

Dear Violet: You offered to come and help to nurse the father, who is sicker than we thought, but with no contagious fever. Come now, dear, and bring baby and nurse, for you may have to stay several days.

Fabian.

He inclosed this letter in an envelope, sealed and directed it, and took it down to the stable, where he found his own groom Charles in the coachman's room.

"Put the horses to the carriage again, and return to Violet Banks to bring your mistress here. Give her this note. It will explain all," said Mr. Fabian, handing the note to the servant.

He found the same group around the death bed. Clarence and the doctor standing on the left side, Cora kneeling by the right side, still holding the hand of the dying man, whose fingers were closed upon hers and whose face was turned toward hers, but with "no speculation" in it. Two hours passed away without any change. The sound of wheels without could be heard through the profound stillness of the death chamber. Mr. Fabian again left the room to receive his wife.

He met Violet in the hall, just as old John had admitted her. She was closely followed by the nurse and the child.

"How is father?" she inquired.

"He is very ill, my dear, but resting quietly just at present. Here is Martha; she will take you to your room and make you and the baby comfortable. Then, as soon as you can, come to the father's chamber; you know where to find it," said Mr. Fabian, who feared to shock his sensitive wife by telling her that he was sinking fast, and thought that it would be safer to let her come into the room and join the group around the bed, and gradually learn the sad truth by her own observation.

"Yes; I can find my way very well," answered Violet, as she handed her bag, shawl, and umbrella to Martha, and followed the housekeeper up stairs, with the nurse and baby.

Mr. Fabian returned to the chamber of the dying man, around whose bed the group remained as he had left it, and where in a very few minutes he was joined by Violet. She entered the room very softly, so that her approach was not heard until she reached the bedside. Then she took and silently pressed the hands that were silently held out by Cora, and finally she knelt down beside her.

More hours passed; no one left the sick room, for no one knew how soon the end might come. Old John thoughtfully brought in a waiter of refreshments and set it down on a side table for any one who might require it.

Day declined. Through the front windows of the death room the western sky could be seen, dark, lowering, and stormy. A long range of heavy clouds lay massed above the horizon, obscuring the light of the sinking sun, but leaving a narrow line of clear sky just along the top of the western ridge.

Presently a singularly beautiful effect was produced. The sun, sinking below the dark cloud into the clear gold line of sky, sent forth a blaze of light from the mountain heights, across the river, and into the chamber of death! Was it this sudden illumination that kindled the fire of life in the dying man into a last expiring flame, or was it indeed the presence of a spiritual visitant, visible only to the vanishing spirit? Who can tell?

Suddenly old Aaron Rockharrt opened his eyes—those great, strong black eyes that had ever been a terror to the evil doer—and the well doer also—and stared before him, held up his hands and exclaimed:

"Deborah! Deborah!"

And then he dropped his arms by his side, and with a long, deep-drawn sigh fell asleep. The name of his old wife was the last word upon his dying lips.

No one but the doctor knew what had happened. He bent over the lifeless shell, gazed on the face, felt the pulse, felt the heart, and then stood up and said:

"All is over, my dear friends. His passage has been quite painless. I never saw an easier death."

And he drew up the sheet over the face of the dead.

Although all day they had hourly expected this end, yet now they could not quite believe that it had indeed come.

The huge, strong man, the rugged Iron King—dead? He who, if not as indestructible as he seemed, was at least constituted of that stern stuff of which centenarians are made, and whom all expected should live far up into the eighties or nineties—dead? The father who had lived over them like some mighty governing and protecting power all their lives, necessary, inevitable, inseparable from their lives—dead?

"Come, my dear," said Mr. Clarence, gently raising Corona and leading her away. "You have this to console you: he died reconciled to you, holding your hand in his to the last."

"Ah, dear Uncle Clarence, you have much more to console you, for you never failed even once in your duty to him, and never gave him one moment of uneasiness in all your life," replied Corona, as she left him in front of her old room.

She entered and shut the door and gave way to the natural grief that overwhelmed her for a time.

When she was sufficiently composed she sat down and wrote to her brother, informing him of what had occurred, and telling him that she still held her purpose of going out to him with the Nevilles.

CHAPTER XXXII
"SIC TRANSIT GLORIA MUNDI"

If old Aaron Rockharrt, the Iron King, had never been generally loved, he was certainly very highly respected by the whole community. The news of his sudden death fell like a shock upon the public. Preparations for the obsequies were on the grandest scale.

They occupied two days. On the first day there were funeral services at Rockhold, performed by the Rev. Luke Melville, pastor of the North End Mission Church, and attended by all the neighboring families, as well as by all the operatives of the works. After these were over, the whole assembly, many in carriages and many more on foot, followed the hearse that carried the remains to the North End railway depot, where the coffin was placed in a special car prepared for its reception, and, attended by the whole family, it was conveyed to the State capital and deposited in the long drawing room of the Rockharrt mansion, where it remained until the next day. On the second day funeral services were held at the town house by the bishop of the diocese, assisted by the rector of the church of the Lord's Peace, and attended by a host of the city friends of the family.

After these services the long funeral procession moved from the house to the cemetery of the Lord's Peace, where the body was laid in the Rockharrt vault beside that of his old wife.

On the return of the family to the house they assembled in the library to hear the reading of the will of Aaron Rockharrt, which had been brought in by his solicitor, Mr. Benjamin Norris.

There were present, seated around the table, Fabian, Violet, and Clarence Rockharrt, Cora Rothsay, the doctor and the lawyer. Standing behind these were gathered the servants of the family.

Mr. Norris blew his nose, cleared his throat, put on his spectacles, opened the will and proceeded to read it.

The testament may be briefly summed up as follows:

First there were handsome legacies left to each of the old servants. One full half of the testator's vast estate was left to his elder son, Fabian; one quarter to his younger son, Clarence; and one quarter to be divided equally between his grandson, Sylvan Haught, and his granddaughter, Corona Rothsay.

Fabian was appointed sole executor.

The lawyer folded up the document and handed it to Fabian Rockharrt.

"Clarence, old boy, I hardly think this is altogether fair to you," said Fabian, good naturedly, and ready to deceive him into the delusion that he had not schemed for this unequal division of the enormous wealth.

"It is all right, Fabian. Altogether right. You are the eldest son, and now the head of the firm, and you have ten times over the business brains that I have. I am perfectly satisfied, and even if I were not, I would not dream of criticising my father's will," replied Clarence, with perfect good humor and sincerity.

The legacies were promptly paid by Fabian Rockharrt. Mr. Clarence decided to remain as his brother's junior partner in the firm that was henceforth to be known as "Aaron Rockharrt's Sons," and to leave all his share of the money invested in the works.

When Corona was asked when and how she would receive her own, she also declared that she would leave it for the present where it was invested in the works, and the firm might pay her legal interest for its use, or make her a small silent partner in the business. Sylvan had yet to be consulted in regard to the disposal of his capital.

The month of October was in its third week. It was high time for Corona to go to Washington and make the acquaintance of the Nevilles, if she wished to go to travel west under their protection. She had several times spoken of this purpose in the presence of Violet, so as to accustom that emotional young woman to the idea of their separation. But Violet, absorbed in her grief for the dead, paid but little attention to Corona's casual remarks.

At the end of a few days Fabian Rockharrt began to talk about going back to Violet Banks, and invited Corona to accompany his wife and himself to their, pleasant country home.

It was then that Corona spoke decisively. She thanked him for his invitation and reminded him of her unalterable resolution to go out to Fort Farthermost to join her brother.

When Fabian Rockharrt tried to combat her determination, she informed him that she had during the funeral week received a joint letter from Captain and Mrs. Neville, inviting her to join their party to the frontier. This letter had been written at the suggestion of the colonel of Captain Neville's regiment, and had not been mentioned or even answered until after the funeral. She said that she had accepted this kind invitation, and had forwarded all her baggage, which had been so long stored at North End, to Washington to wait her arrival in that city.

"Very well, then," said Fabian. "If you are set upon this expedition, I cannot hinder you, and shall not try to do so. But I tell you what I will do. I will take Violet to Washington with you, and get rooms at some pleasant house before the rush of winter visitors. We shall not be able to go into general society, but there is a great plenty of sightseeing in the national capital with which to divert the mind of my poor little girl. Her old guardians, the Pendletimes, are there also, and it will comfort her to see them. With them she will be able to let you depart without breaking her poor little heart."

"Oh, Uncle Fabian, I am so glad you have thought of this! It will be so good for Violet. She has had a sad time since her home-coming. She needs a change," said Corona, eagerly.

"I think she will be very much pleased with the plan. Now, Cora, when do you wish to go?"

"As soon as possible; but since you are so kind as to accompany me, my wish must wait on yours, Uncle Fabian."

"Let us go and consult Violet," said Fabian Rockharrt, rising and leading the way to the nursery, which had been hastily fitted up for the accommodation of the Rockharrt baby and her nurse, and where he felt sure of finding the young mother, too.

Violet, when told of the scheme to go immediately to Washington and see her old friends, was more than "pleased;" she was delighted. To show her baby to her more than mother, as she often called Mrs. Pendletime, would fill her soul with pride and joy.

Very early the next morning Mr. Fabian and his party left the city by the express train en route for the national capital, leaving Mr. Clarence to go to North End and take charge of the works. They reached Baltimore at 11 p.m., and remained over night. The next day they went on to Washington, where they arrived about noon, and went directly to the hotel where Captain and Mrs. Neville were staying.

Violet, very much fatigued, lay down to rest and to get her baby to sleep at her bosom. Mr. Fabian, as we must continue from habit to call him, though his rightful style was now Mr. Rockharrt, went down to the reading room to send his own and his wife's cards to Chief Justice and Mrs. Pendletime, and to collect Washington gossip.

Corona changed her traveling dress, went down into the ladies' parlor, and sent her card to the rooms of the Nevilles. And presently there entered to her a very handsome middle-aged pair.

The captain was a fine, tall, broad-shouldered, soldierly-looking man, with a bald head and a gray mustache. He was clothed in a citizen's morning suit. The captain's wife was also rather tall, slender, dark complexioned, with a thin face, black eyes, and black hair very slightly touched with gray, which she wore in ringlets over her ears, and in a braid behind her neck. Her dress was a plain, dark cashmere, with white cuffs and collar.

"It is very kind of you to take charge of me," said Corona to Mrs. Neville, as the three seated themselves on a group of chairs near together.

"My dear, I am very glad to have your company, as well on the long and dreary journey over the plains as at that distant frontier fort. You will find life at the fort with your brother a severe test to your affection for him," said Mrs. Neville, with her rather doubtful smile.

"You have some experience of life at Fort Farthermost?" remarked Corona pleasantly.

"No; not at that particular fort. We have never been quite so far as that yet. It is a new fort—an outpost really on the extreme southwestern frontier, as I understand. We shall have to cross what used to be called the Great American Desert to reach it. We go first to Leavenworth, and, of course, the journey to Leavenworth is easy enough. But from Leavenworth the long, tedious traveling by army wagons over the plains and through the wilderness to the southwestern forts will try your endurance, my dear."

"Come, come!" said the captain, heartily; "it is not all unmitigated dreadfulness. To be sure we have no railroads through the wilderness, no fine city hotels to stay at; but, then, there are some few forts along the line of travel, where we can stop a day or two to rest, and have good sport. And when we have no fort at the end of a day's journey, it is not very awful to bivouac under the shelter of some friendly rock or in the thicket of some forest. The wagons by day make good couches by night; and as for the bill of fare, a haunch of venison from a deer shot by some soldier on the road, and cooked on a fire in the open air, has a very particularly fine flavor. All civilized condiments we carry with us. As for amusements, though we have no theaters or concerts, yet there is always sure to be some fellow along who can sing a good song, and some other fellow who can tell a good story. I rather think you will enjoy the trip as a novelty, Mrs. Rothsay. I observe that most young people do."

"I really think I shall enjoy it," assented Corona.

"I hope that you will be able to endure it, my dear," added Mrs. Neville.

"You see the journey is no novelty to my wife, Mrs. Rothsay. She has spent all her married life on the frontier. Thirty years ago, my dear lady, I received my first commission as second lieutenant in the Third Infantry, and was ordered to Okononak, Oregon. I married my sweetheart here, and took her with me, and she has been with me ever since; for we both agreed that anything was better than separation. We have raised children, and they have married and left us, and we have never been parted for a week. We have lived on the frontier, and know every fort from the confines of Canada to those of Mexico. We have lived among soldiers, savages, pioneers, scouts, border ruffians, wild beasts, and venomous reptiles all the days of our married life. What do you think of us?"

"I think it is unjust that some military officers have to vegetate all their days in those wilds of the West, while others live for all that life is worth in the Eastern centers of civilization."

"Bless you, my dear, we don't vegetate. If nothing else should rouse our souls the Indians would, and make it lively for us, too! It is not an unpleasant life, upon the whole, Mrs. Rothsay; but you see we are growing old, and my wife is tired of it, that is all."

"How soon shall we leave for the West?" inquired Corona.

"How soon can you be ready, my dear young lady?"

"I am quite ready now."

"Then on Monday, I think. What do you say, Mrs. Neville?" inquired the captain.

"Monday will do," replied the wife.

"Now here are some people coming in to interrupt us," said the captain in a vexed tone.

Corona looked up and said:

"They are Chief Justice and Mrs. Pendletime, come to call on their late ward, Mrs. Fabian Rockharrt. You know them?"

"Not a bit of it. So if you please, my dear, we will retire at once and leave you to receive them, especially as we are both engaged to dine at the arsenal this afternoon," said the captain; and he arose, and with his wife withdrew from the parlor.

Cora went forward to receive the new visitors. They both greeted her very warmly, and then expressed the deepest sympathy with her in her sorrow at the loss of her grandfather, and made many inquiries for the particulars of his illness.

When Corona had answered all their questions, and they had again expressed their sympathy, she inquired:

"Have you sent for Violet? Does she know you are here? If not, I will go and call her."

"Oh, yes; the servant took up our card. And here she comes! And the baby in her arms, by all that is beautiful!" said Mrs. Pendletime, as she arose to meet her favorite, and took the infant from the fond mother and covered both with caresses.

"To think of my child coming to a hotel instead of directly to my house!" said the elder lady, reproachfully.

"But I wished to stay a day or two with Corona before she leaves for the West. And after I meant to go to you and stay as long as you would let me," Violet replied.

"Mrs. Rothsay going West!" exclaimed the old lady.

"Yes; she is," said Violet, emphatically and impatiently. And then there ensued more explanations, and exclamations, and remonstrances.

And finally Mrs. Pendletime inquired:

"And when do you leave on this fearful expedition, my dear?"

"On Monday next I go, with Captain and Mrs. Neville," replied Corona.

"Well, I am truly sorry for it; but, of course, I cannot help it. On Monday, therefore, after your friend has taken leave of you, you will remove to my house, Violet?"

"Oh, yes; the thought of going to you is the only comfort I have in parting from Corona," replied Mrs. Fabian Rockharrt.

CHAPTER XXXIII
CORONA'S DEPARTURE

On the Sunday following her arrival in Washington, the last day of her sojourn in the capital, the day before her departure for the frontier, Corona Rothsay rose early in the morning, and soon as she was dressed went down to the ladies' parlor. Neither her uncle nor his young wife had yet left their rooms. In fact, so early was it that none of the ladies staying in the house had yet come down to the parlor. The place was vacant.

Corona went up the long room and sat down by one of the front windows, to look down on the passing life of the avenue below.

While she sat looking out of the window she heard a movement at the lower end of the room. Some one entered and sat down to wait. And some one else went out again. Corona never turned round to see who was there. She continued to look through the window. She was not interested in the comers and goers into and out of the hotel.

Presently some one came in again and said:

"Mrs. Rothsay is not in her room, sir."

"Then I will wait here until she can be found," replied the new comer in a familiar voice.

But then Corona started up and rushed down the length of the room, crying eagerly:

"Uncle Clarence! Oh, Uncle Clarence! Is this you? Is this indeed you? I am so glad to see you once more before I go! I had thought never to see you again! Or, at least, not for many years! And here you are!"

He caught the hands she held out as she reached him, drew her to his bosom and kissed her as he answered:

"Yes, my dear, it is I, your old bachelor uncle, who was not satisfied with the leave taking on last Thursday, but longed to see you again before your departure."

"You dear Uncle Clarence!"

"So yesterday afternoon I telegraphed to Fabian to ask him when you were to start for the West. He telegraphed back that you expected to leave Washington on Monday morning. I got this answer about five o'clock in the afternoon. And, as it was Saturday night and I had a clear day, the blessed Sabbath, before me, I only waited to close the works at six o'clock, as usual, and then I hurried away, packed a carpet bag and caught, by half a minute, the six-thirty express for Baltimore and Washington, and came straight through! It was a twelve hours' journey, my dear, without stopping except to change cars, which connected promptly, and so you see I have lost no time! I have just arrived, and did not have to wait five minutes even to see you, for you were here to receive me! And now that I am here, my dear, I shall stay to see you off with the Nevilles. You go to-morrow, as I understand? There has been no change in the programme?"

"We go to-morrow, Uncle Clarence," replied Corona, in a grave, sorrowful tone, for she was sympathizing with him.

"By what train, my child?"

"The eight-thirty express, Baltimore and Ohio Railroad."

"Then I need not part with you here in Washington. Our routes are the same for some hundred miles. I shall travel with you as far as the North End Junction, and take leave of you there. That will be seeing the very last of you, up to the very last minute."

Just at this moment Mr. Fabian entered the parlor, and recognizing his younger brother and junior partner, approached him with a shout:

"Clarence! by all that's magical! Pray, did you rise from the earth, or fall from the skies, that I find you here?"

"How do you do, Fabian? I came in the most commonplace way you can imagine—by the night express train—and have only just now arrived," replied Mr. Clarence.

"And how goes on the works?" inquired Fabian Rockharrt.

"Admirably."

"Glad to hear it. And what brought you here, if it is a civil question?"

"It isn't a civil question, but I'll answer it all the same. I came to see Cora once more, to spend the last Sabbath with her and to accompany her as far on the journey to-morrow as our way runs together, which will be as far as the North End Junction."

"And you will not reach North End before Monday night! A whole day lost at the works, Clarence! Ah! it is well you have me to deal with instead of the father—Heaven rest his soul!"

"See here, Fabian," said Mr. Clarence, "for a very little more I will go with Cora all the way to Fort Farthermost, as her natural protector and helper in her missionary work. What, indeed, have I to keep me here in the East since the father left us? Nothing whatever. You have your wife and child; I have no one. Cora is nearer to me than any other being."

"Come! Come down to breakfast. You have been traveling all night without food, I feel sure; and fasting and vigils never were means of grace to a Rockharrt. Come!" said Mr. Fabian, with a laugh.

"I must get a room and go to it first. Look at me!" said Clarence.

"You do look like the ash man or blacksmith, certainly. Well, come along; we'll go to the office and get a room, and then you can get some of that dust off you. It won't take ten minutes. After that we will go to breakfast."

The brothers left the parlor together.

The next moment Violet entered it, and bade good morning to Corona, who in turn told her of the new arrival.

"Clarence! Oh, I am so glad! What an addition he will be to our party, Cora, especially after you have left us, my dear, when we shall miss you so sadly," said Violet.

Cora made no reply. She disliked to tell Violet that she, Violet, would lose the society of Clarence at the same time that she would lose that of herself, as her uncle was to leave Washington by the same train.

While they were still talking the two brothers re-entered the parlor.

When Fabian demanded whether they were ready to go down to breakfast, and received a satisfactory answer, he drew the arm of his wife within his own, and led the way down stairs. Clarence and Corona followed. When they entered the breakfast saloon, the polite waiter came forward and ushered them to a table at which Captain and Mrs. Neville were already seated. Morning greetings were exchanged, and Mr. Clarence was introduced and welcomed.

After breakfast all the party went to church.

Then Clarence and Corona spent the afternoon together at one end of the long parlor, which was so long and had so many recesses that half a dozen separate groups might have isolated themselves there, each without fear of their conversation being overheard by the others.

All the members of our party sat up late that evening to eke out the time they might spend together before parting. It was after midnight when they retired.

The travelers met at an early breakfast the next morning. Their baggage had been sent on and checked in advance. They had nothing to do but make the most of the few remaining minutes.

When the meal was over they all hastily left the table and went to their rooms to put on their traveling wraps.

Fabian and Violet were to accompany the travelers to the railway depot to see them off, so that there was to be no leave taking at the hotel except of the baby.

Corona went into the nurse's room, took the mite in her arms, held it to her bosom, caressed and kissed it tenderly, but dropped no tear on its sweet, fair face or soft white robe.

The baby received all this love with delight, leaping and dancing in Corona's arms, then gazing at her with intense eyes, and crowing and prattling in inarticulate and unintelligible language, of some happy, incommunicable news, some joyful message it would deliver if it could.

"Come, Cora. We are waiting for you, my dear," sounded the voice of Mr. Fabian in the hall outside.

Corona kissed the baby for the last time, blessed it for the vague sweet hope it had infused into her heart, and then laid it in its nurse's arms and left the room.

"We shall barely catch the train, if we catch it at all. And the captain is as nearly in a 'stew' as an officer and a gentleman permits himself to get. We have been looking for you everywhere," said Mr. Fabian.

"I was in the nurse's room, bidding good-by to the baby," replied Cora.

"Oh!"

No more was said. Baby was excuse for any amount of delay, even though it had caused the missing of their train and the driving of the captain into a war dance.

They hurried down stairs and entered the carriages that were waiting to take them to the depot—Fabian, Violet, Clarence and Corona in one; Captain and Mrs. Neville, and Mrs. Neville's maid, in the other. And so they drove to the depot, and arrived just in time to take their tickets and rush to their seats on the train, with no further leave taking than a kiss all around, and a general, heartfelt "God bless you!"

The train was speeding away, leaving Washington City behind, when our party first began to realize that they were really "off" and to take in their surroundings.

Captain and Mrs. Neville sat together about midway in the car. Clarence and Corona sat immediately behind them. On the opposite side sat Mrs. Neville's colored maid, Manda, and in the rear corner, on the same side, the captain's orderly—a new recruit. About half the remaining seats in the car were occupied by other travelers.

At Harper's Ferry, amid the most beautiful and sublime mountain scenery of Virginia, the train stopped twenty minutes for dinner, which, in those ante-bellum days, was well served from the hotel at the depot. After dinner, the train started off again at express speed, stopping but at few stations, until near night, when it reached North End Junction, where Mr. Clarence was to get off.

"Cora, my darling, we must part here," said Mr. Clarence, gathering up his effects, as the train slackened speed.

"Oh, Uncle Clarence! Dear Uncle Clarence! God bless you! God bless you!" sobbed Corona.

"Keep up your heart, dear one. You may see me sooner than you dream of. The missionary mania is sometimes contagious. You have it in its most pronounced form. And I have been sitting by you for eight hours," replied Mr. Clarence, forgetting his prudent resolution to say nothing to Corona of an incipient plan in his mind.

"What do you mean, dear Uncle Clarence?" she anxiously inquired.

"I hardly know myself, Corona. But ponder my words in your heart, dear one. They may mean something. Here we are! Good-by! Good-by! God bless you!" exclaimed Mr. Clarence.

"Good-by! God bless you!" cried Corona, and they parted—Clarence jumping off the train just as it started again, at the imminent risk of his life, yet with lucky immunity from harm.

Corona, looking through the side window, saw him standing safely on the platform waiting a North End train to come up—saw him only for an instant as her train flashed onward, and "pondered his words in her heart," and wondered what they meant.

CHAPTER XXXIV
ON THE FRONTIER

Traveling in the ante-bellum days, even by steamboats and railway trains, was not the rapid transit of the present time. It took one day for our travelers to reach Wheeling. There they embarked on a river steamer for St. Louis. On Monday morning they took a steamboat for Leavenworth, where they arrived early in the evening.

This was the first and best part of their long journey. The second part must of necessity be very different. Here their railway and steamboat travel ceased, and the remainder of their course to the far southwestern frontier must be by military wagons through an almost untrodden wilderness.

I know that since the days of which I write this section of the country has been wonderfully developed, and the wilderness has been made to "bloom and blossom as the rose," but in those days it was still laid down on the maps as "The Great American Desert." And Fort Leavenworth appeared to us as an extreme outpost of civilization in the West, and a stopping place and a point of new departure for troops en route for the southwestern frontier forts.

Captain Neville and his party landed at Leavenworth on the afternoon of a fine November day. The captain led the way to the colonel's quarters. A sentinel was walking up and down the front. He saluted the captain, who passed into the quarters, where an orderly received the party, showed them into a parlor, gave them seats, and then took the captain's card to the colonel.

In a few moments Col. —— entered the parlor, looked around, recognized Captain Neville, and greeted him with:

"Ah, Neville! delighted to see you! Mrs. Neville, of course! I remember you well, madam! And this young lady your daughter, I presume?" he added, turning from the elders to shake hands with Corona.

"No; not our daughter, I wish she were; but our young friend, Mrs. Rothsay, who is going with us to Farthermost," Captain Neville explained.

"To join her husband! One of the new set of officers turned out by the Academy! Happy man!" exclaimed the colonel, warmly shaking Corona's hand.

"No, sir; Mrs. Rothsay is a widow. She goes out to join her only brother, Lieutenant Haught!" the captain again explained, in a low and faintly reproachful tone.

"Oh! ah! I beg pardon, I am sure. The mistake was absurd," said the colonel, with a penitent air.

"When did you leave Washington?"

"A week ago to-day; but the boats were slow."

"Pleasant journey, I hope?"

"Oh, yes, so far."

At this moment the colonel's wife came into the room. She was a tall, gray-haired woman with a fair complexion and blue eyes, and dressed in black silk and a lace cap. She shook hands with Captain and Mrs. Neville, who were old friends, and who then presented Mrs. Rothsay, whom the hostess received with much cordiality.

Meanwhile the colonel and the captain strolled out upon the piazza, to smoke each a cigar. The former inquired more particularly into the history of the beautiful, pale woman who had come out under the protection of the captain and his wife.

Captain Neville told him all he knew of Mrs. Rothsay's story—namely, that she was the granddaughter of the famous Iron King, Aaron Rockharrt, lately deceased, and that she was the widow of the late Regulas Rothsay, who so mysteriously disappeared on the evening of his wedding before the day of his expected inauguration as governor of his native State, and who was afterward discovered to have been murdered by the Comanche Indians.

In the evening, when a number of officers dropped into the drawing room of the colonel's quarters, our party were quite able to receive them.

One unexpected thing happened. Among the callers was a certain Major ----, a childless widower of middle age, short, thick-set, black-bearded and red-faced, with a bluff presence and a bluff voice, who fell—yes, tumbled—heels over head in love with Corona at first sight.

This catastrophe was so patent to all beholders as to excite equal wonder and mirthfulness.

Only Corona of all the company remained ignorant of the conquest she had made; ignorant, that is, until the visitors had all left the quarters, when her hostess said to her in a bantering tone:

"You have subdued our major, my dear, utterly subdued him. This is the first case of love at first sight that ever came under my notice, but it is an unmistakable one. And, oh, I should say a malignant, if not a fatal, type of the disorder."

So closed the day of our travelers' arrival at Fort Leavenworth.

It was Saturday afternoon, on the sixth day of the visitors' stay at the fort, and the ladies were on the parade ground watching the drill, when the word came that the steamer was coming up the river with troops on board.

"Our raw recruits at last," said Captain Neville, who was standing with the ladies.

"And that means, I suppose, that we are to start for Farthermost at once," said Mrs. Neville.

"Not on the instant," laughed the captain.

"This is Saturday afternoon. To-morrow is Sunday. We shall leave on Monday morning."

"Rain or shine?"

"Fair or foul, of course," said the captain.

It was really the steamer with the new recruits on board. Half an hour later they landed and marched into the fort, under the command of the recruiting sergeant, and they were received with cheers.

That evening Captain Neville announced his intention to set out for Farthermost on Monday morning. Of course this was expected. And equally, of course, not one word was said to induce him to defer his departure for one day. Military duty must take precedence of mere politeness.

The next day being the Sabbath, the ladies attended the morning service in the chapel of the fort. The irrepressible Major — — was present, and after the benediction, attached himself to Captain Neville's party, and walked home with them to the colonel's quarters, but not next to Cora, who walked with Mrs. Neville.

As the major paused at the door, Mrs. —— had no choice but to invite him to come in and stay to dinner, adding that this was the last day of the Nevilles' and Mrs. Rothsay's sojourn at the fort.

The major thanked the lady, and followed her into the drawing room, where he sat talking to the colonel, while the ladies went to their rooms to lay off their bonnets and cloaks. They came down only when called by the bell to the early Sunday dinner.

As this was the last day of the guests' stay at Fort Leavenworth, many of the officers dropped in to say good by; so that the party sat up rather later than usual, and it was near midnight when they retired to rest.

Corona did not go to bed at once. She sat from twelve to one writing a letter to her Uncle Clarence, not knowing how the next was to be mailed to him.

The next morning was so clear, bright, and beautiful that every one said that it must be the perfection of Indian summer.

On the road outside the walls five strong army wagons, to which stout mules were harnessed, stood in a line. These were to serve the men as carriages by day and couches by night. Besides these, there were two carriages of better make and more comfortable fittings for the captain and the ladies of his party.

The farewell breakfast at the colonel's quarters partook of the nature of an official banquet. It was unnecessarily prolonged.

At length the company left the table.

Mrs. Neville and Mrs. Rothsay went to their rooms to put on hats and cloaks. As soon as they were ready they came down to bid good by to Mrs. ---- and some other ladies who had come to the colonel's quarters to see them off.

When these adieus were all said, the colonel gave Mrs. Rothsay his arm to lead her to the carriage, which stood in line with the army wagons on the road outside the walls.

Captain and Mrs. Neville had gone on before.

"There, the steamer has landed, and here are some people coming up from it," said the colonel, pausing at the gate with Corona on his arm, as a heavy carriage, drawn by a pair of powerful draught horses, came up from the steamboat landing and drew up at the gate.

A tall man, in a long overcoat and a fur cap, jumped down and approached Corona.

"Uncle Clarence! Oh, heaven of heavens! Uncle Clarence!" she exclaimed, pale and faint with excess of surprise and joy.

"Yes, my dear; I am going with you. See, I have my own carriage and horses, brought all the way by steamer from St. Louis. Our own servants, brought all the way from North End. Now introduce me to your friend here, and later I will tell you all about it," said the new comer, with a smile, as he kissed his niece.

"Oh, Colonel — —, this is my dear Uncle Clarence—Mr. Clarence Rockharrt, I mean," said Corona, in a rapture of confusion.

"How do you do, sir? I am very glad to see you. Really going over the plains with this train?" inquired the colonel, as the two gentlemen shook hands.

CHAPTER XXXV
THE NEW COMERS

"Yes, colonel," briskly replied Clarence, "I am really going out to the frontier! I have not enlisted in the army, nor have I received any appointment as post trader or Indian agent from the government, nor missionary or schoolmaster from any Christian association. But, all the same, I am en route for the wilderness on my own responsibility, by my own conveyance, at my own expense, and with this outgoing trail—if there be no objection," added Clarence, with a sudden obscure doubt arising in his mind that there might exist some military regulation against the attachment of any outsider to the trail of army wagons going over the plains from fort to fort.

"'Objections!' What objections could there possibly be, my dear sir? I fancy there could be nothing worse than a warm welcome for you," replied the colonel.

At that moment Captain Neville, who had put his wife in their carryall, came up to see what had delayed his guest.

"My dear Mrs. Rothsay, we are ready to start," he said. Then seeing Mr. Clarence, whom he had met in Washington and liked very much, he seized his hand and exclaimed:

"Why, Rockharrt, my dear fellow! You here! This is a surprise, indeed! I am very glad to see you! How are you? When did you arrive?" and he shook the hand of the new comer as if he would have shaken it off.

"I am very well, thank you, captain, and have just landed from the boat. I hope you and your wife are quite well."

"Robust, sir! Robust! So glad to see you! But so sorry you did not arrive a few days sooner, so that we might have seen more of you. You have come, I suppose, all this distance to bid a last, supplementary farewell to your dear favorite niece?"

"I have come to go with her to the frontier, if I may have the privilege of traveling with your trail of wagons."

"Why, assuredly. We are always glad of good company on the way," heartily responded the captain.

"Oh, beg pardon, and thank you very much; but I did not intend to 'beat' my way. Look there!" exclaimed Clarence, with a brighter smile, as he pointed to the commodious carriage, drawn by a pair of fine draught horses, that stood waiting for him, and to the covered wagon, drawn by a pair of stout mules, that was coming up behind.

"Oh! Ah! Yes, I see! You are traveling with your retinue. But is not this a very sudden move on your part?" demanded the captain.

"So sudden in its impulse that it might be mistaken for the flight of a criminal, had it not been so deliberate in its execution. The fact is, sir, I am very much attached to my widowed niece, and not being able to dissuade her from her purpose of going out into the Indian country, and being her natural protector and an unincumbered bachelor, I decided to follow her. And now I feel very happy to have overtaken her in the nick of time."

"I see! I see!" said the captain with a laugh.

While this talk was still going on, Corona turned to take a better look at the great, strong carriage in which her uncle had driven up from the steamboat landing. There, to her surprise and delight, she saw young Mark, from Rockhold, seated on the box. He was staring at her, trying to catch her eye, and when he did so he grinned and bobbed, and bobbed and grinned, half a dozen times, in as many half seconds.

"Why, Mark! I am so surprised!" said Corona, as she went toward him. "I am so glad to see you!"

"Yes'm. Thanky'm. So is I. Yes'm, an'dar's mammy an' daddy an' Sister Phebe 'hind dar in de wagon," jerking his head toward the rear.

Corona looked, and her heart leaped with joy to see the dear, familiar faces of the colored servants who had been about her from her childhood. For there on the front seat of the wagon sat old John, from Rockhold, with the reins in his hands, drawing up the team of mules, while on one side of him sat his middle-aged wife, Martha, the housekeeper, and on the other his young daughter, Phebe, once lady's maid to Corona Rothsay.

Corona uttered a little cry of joy as she hastened toward the wagon. The three colored people saw her at once, and, with the unconventionally of their old servitude, shouted out in chorus:

"How do, Miss C'rona?"

"Sarvint, Miss C'rona!"

"Didn't 'spect to see we dem come trapesin' arter yer 'way out yere, did yer now?"

And they also grinned and bobbed, and bobbed and grinned, between every word, as they tumbled off their seats and ran to meet her.

Mr. Clarence hoisted the two women to their seats, one on each side of the driver, and then turned to Corona.

"Come, my dear. Let me put you into our carriage," he said, as he drew her arm within his own and led her on.

"Oh! I have not taken leave of Colonel — — yet.

"Where is he?" she inquired, looking around.

"Here I am, my dear Mrs. Rothsay. Waiting at the carriage door to put you in your seat and to wish you a pleasant journey. And certainly, if this initial day is any index, you will have a pleasant one, for I never saw finer weather at this season of the year," said the colonel, cheerily, as he received Corona from her uncle's hand, and, with the stately courtesy of the olden time, placed her in her seat.

"I thank you, colonel, for all the kindness I have received at your hands and at those of Mrs. — —. I shall never forget it. Good by," said Corona, giving him her hand.

He lifted the tips of her fingers to his lips, bowed, and stepped back.

Mr. Clarence entered the carriage and gave the order to the young coachman. Carriage and covered wagon then fell into the procession, which began to move on. A farewell gun was fired from the fort.

"Uncle Clarence," said Corona, after the party had been on the road some hours—"Uncle Clarence, how came you first to think of such a strange move as to leave the works and come out here? And when did you first make up your mind to do it?"

"I think, Cora, my dear, that the idea came vaguely into my mind, as a mere possibility, after my father's death. It occurred to me that there was no absolute necessity for my remaining longer at the works. You see, Cora, however much I might have wished for a change in my life, I never could have vexed my father by even expressing such a wish, while he lived. After his death I thought of it vaguely."

"Oh! why didn't you tell me?"

"My mind was not made up; therefore I spoke of the matter to no one. I only hinted something to you, when on bidding you good by at North End Junction I told you that you might possibly see me before you would expect to do so."

"Yes; I remember that well. I thought you only said that to comfort me. And you really meant that you might possibly follow me?"

"Yes, my dear; that is just what I meant. I could not speak more plainly because I was not sure of my own course. I had to think of Fabian."

"Yes. How, at last, came you to the conclusion of following your poor niece?"

"Fabian and myself could not agree upon a certain policy in conducting our business. There was no longer the father's controlling influence, you see, and Fabian is the head of the firm; and I could not do business on his principles," said Mr. Clarence, flushing up to his brow.

"No; I suppose you could not," said Cora, meditatively; and then she was sorry that she had said anything that might imply a reproach to the good-humored uncle she had left behind.

"Still, I said nothing about a dissolution of partnership until Fabian complained that I, or my policy, was a dead weight around his neck, dragging him down from the most magnificent flights to mere sordid drudgery. Then I proposed that we should dissolve partnership. And he said he was sorry. And I believe he was; but also glad, inconsistent as that seems. For he was sorry I could not come into his policy, and stay in the firm; but since I could not so agree with him, he was relieved when I proposed to withdraw from it. We disagreed, my dear Cora, but we did not fall out; we parted good friends and brothers with tears in our eyes. Poor little Violet cried a good deal. But you know she has such a tender heart, poor child!—Look at that herd of deer, Cora, standing on the top of that swell of the land to the right, and actually gazing at the trail without a motion or a panic. I hope nobody will shoot at them!" exclaimed Mr. Clarence, suddenly breaking off in his discourse to point to the denizens of the thicket and the prairie, until upon some sudden impulse the whole herd turned and bounded away.

So they fared on through that glorious autumn day—over the vast, rolling, solitary prairie—now rising to a smooth, gradual elevation that revealed the circle of the whole horizon where it met the sky; now descending into a wide, shallow hollow, where the rising ground around inclosed them as in an amphitheater; but everywhere along the trail, the prairie grass, dried and burnished by the autumn's suns and winds, burned like gold on the hills and bronze in the hollows, giving a singularly beautiful effect in light and shade of mingling metallic hues.

At noon the captain ordered a halt, and all the teams were drawn up in a line; and all the men got out to feed and water the horses and mules, and to prepare their own dinner.

They were now beside a clear, deep, narrow stream, a tributary of the Kansas River, running through a picturesque valley, carpeted with long grass, and bordered with low, well-wooded hills on either side. The burnished gold and bronze of the long dried grass on the river's brim, dotted here and there with a late scarlet prairie flower, the brilliant crimson and purple of the autumn foliage that clothed the trees, the bright blue of the sky and the soft white of the few downy clouds floating overhead, and all reflected and duplicated in the river below, made a beauty and glory of color that must have delighted the soul of an artist, and pleased the eye of even the most careless observer.

Mike O'Reilly, the captain's orderly, was busy spreading a table cloth on the grass, at the foot of a hill on the right, and old John, Mr. Clarence's man, was emulating Mike by spreading a four-yard square of white damask at a short distance behind him.

Our friends had nearly finished their lunch, when something—she never could tell what—caused Corona to look behind her. Then she shrieked! All looked to see the cause of her sudden fright.

There stood a group of Indians, with blankets around their forms, and gleaming tomahawks about their shoulders.

"Pawnees—friendly. Don't be afraid. Give them something to eat," said the captain, in a low tone, addressing the first part of his conversation to Corona and the last part to Mrs. Neville.

But Corona had never seen an Indian in her life, and could not at once get over her panic caused by the sight of those bare, keen-edged axes gleaming in the sun.

Captain Neville spoke to them in their native tongue, and they replied. The conversation that ensued was quite unintelligible to Clarence and Corona, but not to Mrs. Neville, who beckoned to two squaws who stood humbly in the rear of the braves. They were both clothed in short, rude, blue cotton skirts, with blankets over their shoulders. The elder squaw carried a pack on her back; the younger one carried a baby snugly in a hood made of the loop of her blanket at the back of her neck.

They both approached the ladies, chattering as they came; the elder one threw down her pack on the grass and began to open it, and display a number of dressed raccoon skins stretched upon sticks, and by gibbering and gesticulations expressed her wish to sell them.

Neither of the ladies wished to buy; but Mrs. Neville give her loaves of bread and junks of dried beef from the hampers on the grass, and Corona gave her money.

She put the money in a little fur pouch she carried at her belt, and she packed the bread and beef in the bundle with the highly flavored raccoon skins. She was not fastidious.

While Mrs. Neville and Corona were occupied with the squaw, Captain Neville and Mr. Clarence had been feasting the braves, and the attendants had been washing dishes, repacking hampers, and reloading wagons for a fresh start.

When all was ready the wayfarers took leave of the Indians and re-entered their conveyances and resumed their route, leaving the savages still feasting on the fragments that remained.

It was now two o'clock in the afternoon, as the long trail of carryalls and army wagons passed up from the beautiful valley and out upon the vast prairie that still rolled on before them in hills and hollows of gold and bronze, blazing under the bright autumnal sun.

Men and women, mules and horses, had all been rested and refreshed by their mid-day halt and repast.

The people, however, seemed less inclined to observe and converse than in the forenoon.

Even Clarence saw more than one flock of birds sail over their heads, and made no sign; saw a herd of deer stand and gaze, and said not a word.

At length Clarence took out his cigar and lit it, and as he smoked he watched the descending sun until it sank below the horizon and sent up the most singular after-glow that Clarence had ever seen—a shower of sparks and needle-like flames from the edge of the prairie immediately under the horizon.

"Looks like de worl' was ketchin on fire ober dere, Marse Clarence," said young Mark, speaking for the first time since they had resumed their march.

"It is only the light reflected by the prairie, my boy," kindly replied Mr. Clarence. And then he smoked on in silence, while the after-glow died out, the twilight faded, and one by one the stars came out. Corona seemed to be slumbering in her seat. Young Mark crooned low, as if to himself, a weird, old camp meeting hymn. It was so dark that he could not have seen to guide his horses, had not the captain's carryall been immediately in front of his own, and the long trail of wagons in front of the captain's, with lantern carried by the advance guard to show the way.

"What's the matter?" suddenly called out Mr. Clarence, who was aroused from his reverie by the halt of the whole procession.

"We 'pears to got sumwhurze," replied Mark, strongly pulling in his horses, which had nearly run into the back of the captain's stationary carryall in front.

"We are at Burley's," called out Captain Neville from his seat.

While he spoke Mike O'Reilly brought up a lantern to show their way to the house.

Clarence alighted and handed down his niece, took her arm, and followed Captain and Mrs. Neville past the wagons and mules and groups of men through a door that admitted them into a long, low-ceiled room, lighted by tallow candles in tin sconces along the log walls, and warmed by a large cooking stove in the middle of the floor. Rude, unpainted wooden chairs, benches and tables were the only furniture, if we except the rough shelves on which coarse crockery and tinware were arranged and under which iron cooking utensils were piled.

Captain Neville and Mr. Clarence returned to the wagons to see for themselves that their valuable personal effects were safely bestowed for the night, and that the horses and mules were well cared for. The proprietor of this place attended them.

While Mrs. Neville and Corona still walked up and down in the room, a small dark-haired woman came in and nodded to them, and asked if they would like to go upstairs and have some water to wash their faces.

Both ladies thankfully accepted this offer, and followed the landlady up a rude flight of steps that led up from the corner of the room to an open trap door, through which they entered the garret.

This was nothing better than a loft, whose rough plank floor formed the ceiling of the room below, and whose sloping roof rose from the floor front and back, and met overhead.

Here they rested through the night.

Let us hasten on. It was the thirteenth day out. The trail had crossed nearly the whole of the Indian Territory, and were within one day's march of Fort Farthermost, on the Texan frontier.

They had passed the previous night at Fort W., and at sunrise they had crossed the Rio Negro, and before noon they had made nearly a score of miles toward their destination. They halted beside a little stream that took its rise in a spring among the rocks on the right hand of the trail. Here the party meant to rest for two hours before resuming the march to Fort Farthermost, which they hoped to reach that same night.

As usual at the noon rest, mules and horses were unharnessed and led down to the stream to be watered and fed. Fires were built and rustic cranes improvised to hang the pots and kettles gypsy style. Since the first day out old Martha had been constituted cook and old John butler to our party.

In a short time Martha had prepared such a hot dinner as was practicable under the circumstances, and John had laid the cloth.

When all was ready the party of four sat down on the dry grass to partake of the meal, to every course of which they all did ample justice.

"This is our last *al fresco* feast," said Captain Neville, after dinner, as he filled the glasses of the two ladies and of Clarence Rockharrt and proposed the toast:

"Our lasting friendship and companionship."

It was honored warmly.

Next Clarence proposed:

"Mrs. Neville," which was also honored and responded to by the captain in a neat little speech, at the end of which he proposed:

"Mrs. Rothsay."

This was duly met by Clarence with a brief acknowledgment. Mr. Clarence was no speechmaker. But he proposed the health of—

"Our gallant captain," which was drank with enthusiasm.

The captain responded, and proposed—

"Mr. Clarence Rockharrt," which was cordially honored.

Then Mr. Clarence made his last little speech of personal thanks.

After this the company arose and separated, to wander about the camping ground, to stretch their cramped limbs before returning to their seats on their carryalls.

"Come, Clarence, let us follow this little stream up to its head. It cannot be far away," said Corona.

Mr. Clarence silently drew her arm within his, and they walked on up the little valley until it narrowed into a gorge, clothed with stunted trees in brilliant autumn hues, through which the gray rocks jutted. The tinkling of the spring which supplied the stream could be heard while it was yet out of sight.

"Did you bring your drinking cup with you, Clarence? I should like a draught from the spring," said Corona.

"Oh, yes," said her uncle, producing the silver cup. They clambered up the side of the gorge until they reached the spring—a great jet of water issuing from the rock. But there both stopped short, spellbound, in amazement. On a ledge of rock above the spring, and facing them, stood a majestic man, clothed in coat of buckskin, faced and bordered with fur, leggings of buckskin and sandals of buffalo hide. On his head he wore a fur cap that half concealed his tawny hair. The face was fine, but sunburnt and half covered with a long, tawny beard. Corona looked up, and recognized— Regulas Rothsay!

With a cry of terror, she struck her hands to her eyes, as if to dispel an optical illusion, and sank half fainting, to be caught in the arms of her uncle and laid against the side of the rocks, while he sprinkled her face with water from the spring.

She recovered her breath, opened her eyes, and looked anxiously, fearfully, all around her.

There was no one in sight anywhere. The apparition had vanished. Corona and her uncle were alone.

CHAPTER XXXVI
THE MEETING ON THE MOUNT

"What is this? Am I mad? Have I seen a spirit? Oh, Clarence, what is it?" cried Corona, in a tumult of emotion in which her life seemed throbbing away as she clung to her uncle for support.

"Try to compose yourself, dear Cora," he answered, as he gently laid her down on the mossy rocks, and went and brought her water from the spring in his pocket cup.

She raised herself and drank it at his request, and then staring wildly at him, repeated her questions:

"Oh, what was it? Who was here just now? Or was it—or was it—was it—delusion?"

"For Heaven's sake, Cora, calm yourself. It was Regulas Rothsay who stood here a moment ago."

"Rule himself, and no delusion! But, oh! I knew it! I knew it all the time!" she exclaimed, still trembling violently.

"My darling Cora, try—"

"Where did he go? Where?" she cried, staggering to her feet and clinging to her uncle. "Where? Oh, take me to him!"

"Do you see that log cabin on the plateau above us, Cora, to the right?" he said, pointing in the direction of which he spoke.

Her eyes followed his index, and she saw a cottage of rough-hewn logs standing against the rocky steep at the back of the broad ledge above them.

"What do you mean? Is he up there? Is he up there?" she breathlessly demanded.

"Yes; he is in that hut. I saw him climb the rocks and enter it, and close the door. But, for Heaven's sake! compose yourself, my dear. You are shaking as with an ague, and your hands are cold as ice," said Clarence.

"In that hut, did you say? So near? So near?"

"Yes, dear Cora; but be calm."

"Take me there! Take me there! Oh, give me your arm, Uncle Clarence, and help me. My limbs fail now, when I need them more than ever before. Ah! and my heart fails, too!" she moaned, growing suddenly pale and fainter as she leaned heavily against her uncle.

"Cora, darling! Cora, rouse yourself, my girl! This weakness is not like you. Take courage; all will be well," said Mr. Clarence, caressingly, laying his hand on her head.

She sighed heavily as she asked:

"How will he receive me? Oh, how will he receive me? Will he have me now? But he must! Oh, he must! For I will never, never, never go down this mountain side again without him! I will perish on its rocks sooner! Oh, come, come! Help me to reach that hut, Clarence."

There was no resisting her wild and passionate appeal. Clarence put his arm around her waist, to sustain her more effectually, as he said:

"Now lean on me, Cora, and step carefully, for the path is almost hidden, and very rugged."

"Oh, Clarence, did he recognize me? did he, Clarence? did he?" she eagerly inquired.

"Yes, Cora, he did," gravely answered the young uncle.

"And turned and went away! And turned and went away! Went away and left me without one word!" she wailed, in doubt and distress.

"Cora, my dear, pray control yourself," said Clarence, uneasily.

"Did he speak to you?" she suddenly inquired.

"Not one word."

"Did you speak to him?"

"No; for he was gone in an instant, before I recovered from my astonishment at his appearance."

"How did he look?—how did he look when he recognized me? In anger?"

"No, Corona; but in much sorrow, pity, and tenderness," gravely replied Clarence.

"Then, why did he leave me? Oh, why did he turn away from me?"

"My dear, he had every reason to think that his sudden appearance had frightened you, and that his presence grieved and distressed you."

"Why, oh, why should he have thought so?" she demanded, with increasing agitation.

"My dear girl, you were frightened. I might say appalled. You saw him suddenly, and with a half-smothered scream threw your hands to your eyes as if to shut out the sight, and then sank to the ground. Now what could the man think but that you feared and hated the sight of him?"

"Just as he thought before! Just as he thought before!"

"And he turned sorrowfully away and walked up to his cabin on the mount, entered, and shut the door. I saw him do it."

"Just as he did before! Just as he did before! Oh, Rule! what a fatality! That appearances should always be false and disastrous between us!" she moaned.

"Not in this case, Cora. At least not from this hour. Come, we are on the ledge now!" said Clarence, as he helped his niece, who with one more high step stood on the top of the plateau, her back to one of the most glorious prairie scenes in nature, her face to a rocky, pine-dotted precipice, against which stood a double log cabin, with a door in the middle and a window on each side.

"There is the hut! Now, shall I take you there, or shall I wait here and let you go alone?" he inquired, as they stood side by side gazing on the hut.

She did not answer. Her eyes were riveted on the door of the cabin, while she leaned heavily on the arm of her uncle.

"I see how it is: you are weakening, losing courage. Let me support you to the door," said Clarence, putting his arm around her waist.

But she drew herself up suddenly.

"Oh, let me go alone, dear Uncle Clarence. My meeting with Rule should be face to face only," she replied, still trembling, but resolute.

"Are you sure you can do it?"

"Oh, yes, yes! My limbs shall no longer refuse their office!"

Clarence threw himself down at the foot of a pine tree to sit and await events.

He took out his watch and looked at the time.

"It is one o'clock," he said to himself. "At two sharp the trail will move, or ought to do so. Perhaps Neville might give us half an hour's grace, though. At any rate, I will wait here three-quarters of an hour, and if in that time I hear nothing from Rothsay or Cora, I shall go down the mountain to explain the situation to Neville."

So saying, Mr. Clarence took out his pipe, filled and lighted it, and smoked.

Corona, like a somnambulist or a blind woman, went slowly toward the log cabin, holding out her hands before her. She soon reached it, leaned for a moment against the log wall to recover her breath and her courage, and then knocked.

The door was instantly opened, and Regulas Rothsay stood on the threshold, still clothed in his hunter's suit of buckskin, but without the fur cap—the same Rule, unchanged except in habiliments and in the length of his untrimmed, tawny hair and beard.

In the instant of meeting she raised her eyes to his, and read in them the undying love of his heart.

With a cry of rapture, of infinite relief and infinite content, she sank upon his doorstep, clasped his knees, and laid her beautiful head down prone on his feet. Only for a second.

He instantly raised her in his arms, pressed her to his heart, kissed her, and kissed her again and again, bore her into the cabin, placed her in the only chair, and knelt down beside her.

She turned and threw her arms around his neck, and dropped her head upon his bosom.

And not a word was spoken between them. The emotions of both were too great for utterance, too great almost for endurance.

They were bathed in a flood of light from the noonday sun pouring its rays through the open door and windows of the cabin. It was the apotheosis of love.

Rule was the first to speak.

"You are welcome, oh, welcome, as life to the dead, my love! But I do not understand my blessedness—I do not," he said, dropping his head on her shoulders, while she still lay on his bosom, in a dream, a trance of perfect contentment.

"Oh, Rule, my husband, my lord, my king! I have come to you, unconsciously led by the Divine Providence! But I have come to you, to stay forever, if you will have me! I have come, never, never, never to leave you, unless you send me away!" she said.

"I send you away, dear? I send away my restored life from me? Ah, you know, you know how impossible that would be! But if I should try to tell you, dear, all that I feel at this moment, I should fail, and talk folly, for no human words can utter this, dear! But I am amazed—amazed to see you here with me, as the dead to the material world might be, on awaking amid the splendors of Paradise!"

"You wish to know how I came?"

"No! I do not! Amazed as I may be, I am content to know that you are here, dear—here! But," he said, looking around on the rudeness of his hut, "oh, what a place to receive you in! I left you in a palace, surrounded by all the splendors and luxuries of civilization! I receive you in a log cabin, bare of even the necessaries and comforts of life!" he added, gravely.

"But you left me a discarded, broken-hearted woman, and you receive me a restored and happy wife!" she exclaimed.

"But, oh, Cora! can you live with me here, here? Look around you, dear! Look on the home you would share!—the walls of logs, the chimney of rocks, the floor of stone, the cups and dishes of earthenware, pewter and iron, the—"

She interrupted him, passionately:

"But you are here, Rule! You! you! And the log hut is transfigured into a mansion of light! A mansion like the many in our Heavenly Father's House! Oh, Rule! you, you are all, all to me! life, joy, riches, splendor, all to me! Am I all to you, Rule?"

"All of earth and heaven, dear."

"Oh, happy I am! Oh, I thank God, I thank God for this happiness! Rule, we will never part again!—never for a single day! But be together, to-day and

'To-morrow and to-morrow and to-morrow,
To the last syllable of recorded time,'

and through the endless ages of eternity! Oh, Rule, how could we ever have mistaken our hearts? How could we ever have parted?"

"The mistake was mine only, dear. After what you told me on our marriage day, I lost all hope, all interest and ambition in life. I had toiled and striven and conquered, for the one dear prize; all my battle of life was fought for you; all my victories were won for you, and were laid at your feet. But when I found that all my love and hope had brought only grief and despair to you—then, dear, all my triumphs turned into Dead Sea fruit on my lips! Then I left all and came into the wilderness; left no trace behind me; effaced myself from your life, from the world, as effectually as I could do it; and so—believing it to be for your good and happiness—died to the world and died to you!"

"Oh, Rule! Miserable woman that I was! I wrecked your life! I wrecked your career!"

"No, dear, no; the mistake, I said, was mine! I should have trusted your heart. I should have given you the time you implored; I should not have fled in the madness of suddenly wounded affection."

"Oh, Rule? if you could have only looked back on me after you went away, only known the anguish your disappearance caused me and the inconsolable sorrow of the time that followed it."

"If I could have supposed it possible even, I would have hastened to you, from the uttermost parts of the earth!"

"And then they reported you dead, murdered by the Comanches, in the massacre of La Terrepeur, and sorrow was deepened to despair."

"Yes; I heard of that massacre. The report of my death must have arisen in this way: I had lived at La Terrepeur for many months, but had left and come to this place some days before the massacre. Some other unfortunate was murdered and burned in the deserted hut, whose bones were found in ashes. I did not return to contradict the report. I wished to be dead to the world, as I was dead to hope, dead to you, dead to myself!"

"Oh, Rule! in all that time how I longed, famished, fainted, died, for your presence! Yes, Rule; died daily."

"My own, dear Cora, how could I have mistaken you? Oh! if I had only known!"

"Ah, yes! if you had only known my heart, or I had only known your whereabouts! In either case we should have met before, and not lost four years out of our lives! But now, Rule," she said, with sudden animation— "now 'We meet to part no more,' as the hymn says. I will never, never, never, leave you for a day! I will be your very shadow!"

"My sunshine, rather, dear!"

"And are you content, Rule?"

"Infinitely."

"And happy?"

"Perfectly."

"Thank God! So am I. But why, oh, why when we met by the spring just now, why, when I was crazed with joy and fear at the sudden sight of you, why did you turn away and leave me?" she passionately demanded.

He looked at her serenely, incisively, and answered, calmly, quietly:

"Dear, because you shrank from me, threw your hands up before your eyes, as if to shut out the sight of me. Dear, your own sudden appearance before me at the spring, to which I had gone for my noonday draught of water, nearly overwhelmed me; but I readily recovered myself and understood it, connected it with the trail below, and concluded that you were on your way to Farthermost to join your brother, whom I had heard of as one of the officers of the new fort. Then, believing that my presence distressed you, I went away."

"Oh, Rule!"

After a little while Rothsay inquired:

"Was not that Mr. Clarence Rockharrt whom I saw with you by the spring?"

"Yes; Uncle Clarence. He helped me up to this ledge, and then he stayed outside while I came in here to look for you."

"Let us go and bring him in now, dear," said Rule.

And the two walked out together.

But no one was to be seen on the plateau; only, on the ground under the pine tree where Mr. Clarence had rested was a piece of white paper, kept in place by a small stone laid upon it.

Rule picked up the stone, and handed the paper to Cora.

It proved to be a leaf from Mr. Clarence's pocket tablets, and on it was written:

> "I am going down the mountain to tell Captain Neville that my party will camp here to-night, and join him at the fort to-morrow, so that he may go on with his train at once, if he should see fit. Clarence."

"He saw you receive me; he knew it was all right; then he grew tired of waiting for me. He thought I had forgotten him, and so I had, and he left this paper and went down to the trail," Corona explained with a smile.

"Shall we go down and see your friends, Cora? Tell me what you wish, dear," said Rothsay.

Corona looked at her watch, and then replied:

"Courtesy would have required me to go down and take leave of Captain and Mrs. Neville before leaving them, but it is too late now. Their caravan is on the march by this time. They were to have resumed their route at two o'clock. It is after three now."

"We can go to Farthermost later, dear. It is but half a day's ride from here. Shall we go down the mountain and join Clarence? Is it your wish, Cora?"

"No, not yet. He is very well as he is. He can wait for us. Let us sit down here together. I have so much to tell, and so much to hear," said Corona.

"Yes, dear; and I also have 'so much to tell, and so much to hear,'" assented Rothsay, as they sat down at the foot of the young pine tree, with their backs to the rising cliffs and their faces to the descending mountain, the brook at its foot, and the vast, sunlit prairie, in its autumn coat of dry grass, rolling in smooth hills and hollows of gold and bronze off to the distant horizon.

"Tell me, dear, of all that has befallen you in these dark years that have parted us. Tell me of your grandparents. Do they still live?" inquired Rothsay.

"Ah, no!" replied Corona. And then she entered upon the family history of the last four years and four months, since Rule had disappeared, and told him of the sudden death of her dear old grandmother on the very day on which the false report of Rothsay's murder reached them.

She told him of her Uncle Fabian's marriage to Violet Wood a year later.

Of her widowed grandfather's second marriage to Mrs. Stillwater, whom Rothsay had known in his childhood as Miss Rose Flowers.

Of the recent death of this second wife, followed very soon after by that of the aged widower.

And finally she told him of her own resolution to follow her brother Sylvan to his post of duty at Fort Farthermost, to open a mission home school for Indian children, and to devote her life and fortune to their service; and of the good opportunity offered her by the kindness of Colonel Z. in procuring for her the escort of Captain and Mrs. Neville, who were on their way to Farthermost with a party of recruits.

"And Clarence? How came he to be of the company?" inquired Rothsay.

"Uncle Clarence could not agree with Uncle Fabian in business policy. So they dissolved partnership very amicably and with mutual satisfaction. This was after I had left Rockhold. Clarence gathered up his wealth, brought three devoted servants with him, and set out to follow me. At St. Louis he purchased wagons, tents, horses, mules, and every convenience for crossing the plains. He overtook and surprised us at Fort Leavenworth on the very day of our intended departure for Farthermost."

"Clarence came for your sake."

"Yes; and he has enjoyed the journey. On the free prairie he has been like a boy out of school—so buoyant, so joyous—the life of the whole company."

"What will he do now?"

"I think he will go on to Farthermost for this season. After this I do not know what he will do or where he will go."

"He will remain in this quarter, which offers a grand field for a man like Clarence Rockharrt," said Rothsay.

"I should think it might—in the future," replied Corona.

"In the near future. The tide of emigration is pouring into this section so fast that very soon the ground will be disputed with the Mexican government, and true men and brave men will be much wanted here."

"Yes," said Corona, indifferently, for she cared very little at this moment for public interests. "But tell me of yourself, Rule. I long to hear you talk of yourself."

Rothsay was no egotist. He never had been addicted to speaking of himself or of his feelings.

Now, at her urgent request, he told her in brief how he had renounced all his honors in the country for the sake of the woman for whose sake, also, he had first striven to win them and had won them.

"Dear," he said, "from the time you first noticed me, when you were a sweet child of seven summers and I a boy of twelve—yes, winters—for while all your years had been summers, dear—summers of love, shelter, comfort, luxury—all my years had been winters of loss, want, orphanage, and destitution—you were my help, support, inspiration. I longed to be worthy of your friendship, your interest, your sympathy. And for all these things I toiled, endured, and struggled."

"I know! Oh, I know!" said Corona, earnestly.

"Yes, dear, you know it all. For who but you were with me in the spirit through all the struggle, helping, supporting, encouraging, until you seemed to me my muse, my soul, my inner and purer and higher self. Dear, I wronged you when I connected your love with this world's pride. I wronged you bitterly, and I have suffered for it and made you suffer—"

"Oh, no, no, no, Rule! The fault was all my own! I am not so good and wise as you!" exclaimed Corona.

"Hush, dear! Hush! Hear me out!" said Rothsay, laying his hand gently on her head.

"Well, go on, but don't blame yourself. Oh, '*chevalier sans peur et sans reproche*,'" said Corona, fervently.

He resumed very quietly:

"When I had reached a position in this world's honor to which I dared to invite you, then I laid my victory at your feet and prayed you to share it. And, Corona, when the bishop had blessed our nuptials, I dreamed that we were blessed indeed. You know, dear, what a miserable awakening I had from that dream on the evening of our wedding day."

"It was my fault! It was my fault! Oh, vain, foolish, infatuated woman that I was!" cried Corona.

"No, dear; you were not to blame. You were true, candid, natural through it all. Our betrothal, dear, was on your part the betrothal of friends. You did not know your own heart then. You went abroad with your grandparents, and, after two years of travel, you were thrown in the court circles of London, and exposed to all the splendors, temptations and fascinations of rank, culture and refinement, such as you had never met at home in your rural neighborhood. You were caught, dazzled, bewildered. You thought you loved the English duke who sought your hand—"

"But I never did, Rule. Oh, Heaven knows I never did. It was all self-delusion," broke in Corona.

"No; you never did. I saw that in the first instant that I met your eyes in the log cabin up yonder. You never did! It was a self-delusion. Yet you were under the influence of that self-delusion when I found you on our wedding evening in such a paroxysm of grief and despair that I—astonished and amazed at what I saw—shared your delusion and imagined that you loved this duke when you married me. What could I do, my own dear Cora, for whom I would have lived or died at bidding—what could I do but efface myself from your life?"

"Oh! you could have given me time—time to recover from my mental illness, since I had done no evil willingly. Since I had kept my troth as well as I could. Since I had vowed to love and serve you all the days of my life. You should have given me time, Rule, to recover my senses and keep my vow."

"Yes; I should have done so! But, you see, I did not know. How could I know? Oh, my dear Cora! It cost me little to lay down all the honors I had won, for they were worthless to me if not shared by you, for whom they were won. But it cost my life almost to resign you. Mine was 'not the flight of a felon' or a coward, but the retirement of one sick, sick unto death of the world and of all the glory of the world. Some men in my case might have sought relief in death, but I—I knew I must live until the Lord of life should himself relieve me of duty. So I left the city on the night of my wedding day, the night also before my inauguration day."

"Oh, Rule! and as if it required that supreme act of renunciation to tear the veil from my eyes and let me see you as you were, and see my own heart as it was—from that hour I knew how much, how deeply, how eternally I loved you!" said Corona.

Rothsay raised her hand to his lips and kissed it. Then he resumed:

"I wrote two letters—one to you, explaining my motives for leaving, and advising you not to repeat to any one the subject or substance of our last interview, lest it should be misunderstood or misrepresented, and should do you unmerited injury with an evil-thinking world—"

"Yes, Rule. See! See! I have that letter yet!" exclaimed Corona, hastily unbuttoning the front of her bodice and pulling up the little black silk bag which she wore next her heart, suspended from the silken cord around her neck, and taking from it the old, yellow, broken paper which contained the last lines he had written to her.

"You kept that all this time, dear?" he inquired, gently taking the paper and looking at it.

"Yes. Why not? It was the last relic I possessed of you. And it has never left me. I never showed it to a human being, because you did not wish me to do so. But you said you had written two letters. To whom was the other? We never heard of it."

Rothsay looked at her in surprise for a moment and answered:

"The other letter? Why, of course it was my letter of resignation."

"Then it was never found! Never! If it had been, it would have saved much trouble. No one knew what had become of you, Rule. Not even I, except that you had left me on account of that last conversation between us, which you adjured me never to divulge. And oh! what amazement your disappearance caused! and what conjectures as to your fate! Many thought that you had been assassinated and your body sunk in the river. Oh, Rule! Many others thought that you had been abducted by some political enemy— as if any force could have carried you off, Rule!"

Rothsay laughed for the first time during the interview. Corona continued:

"Advertisements were placed in all the papers, offering large rewards for information that should lead to the discovery of your fate or whereabouts, living or dead. And, oh! how many impostors came forward to claim the money, with information that led to nothing at all. A sailor returning from Rio de Janeiro swore that you had shipped as a man before the mast and gone out with him, and that he had left you in the capital of Brazil. A fur trader from Alaska reported you killing seals in that territory. A returned miner swore that he had left you gold digging in California. A New Bedford sailor made his affidavit that he had seen you embark on a whaling ship for Baffin's Bay. These were the most hopeful reports. But there were others. There was never the body of an unknown man found anywhere that was not reported to be yours. Oh, Rule! think of the anguish all these rumors cost your friends!"

"Cost you, my poor Corona! I doubt if they cost any other human being a single pang."

"But all these rumors proved to be false, and your fate remained a mystery until it was apparently cleared up by the report of your murder by the Comanches in the massacre of La Terrepeur."

"A report as false as any of the others, as you see, yet with a better foundation in probability than any of those, as I have explained. But how my letter of resignation should have been lost I cannot conjecture. I posted it with my own hand," said Rothsay, reflectively.

"Why, letters are occasionally lost in the mail! But, Rule, how was it that you never heard of all the amazement and confusion that followed your flight, for the want of your letter to explain it?"

"Because, dear, from the time I left the State capital to this day I have never seen a newspaper or spoken to a civilized being."

"Rule!"

"It is true, dear! Look at me. Have I not degenerated into a savage?"

"No, no, no, Regulas Rothsay! you could never do that! Ah! how much nobler you look to me in that rude forest garb than ever in the fine dress of the drawing room! But tell me about your journey from the city into the wilderness, and of your life since."

"I have been trying to do so, Cora, but every time I try to begin my narrative by reverting to the hour of my flight, I seem spellbound to that hour and cannot escape from it. But I will try again," he said, and he began his story.

He told her, in brief, that on leaving the Rockhold house and going out upon the sidewalk, he found the streets still alight with illuminated houses and alive with the orgies of revelers who had come to the inauguration.

In moving through the crowd he was unrecognized, for who could suspect the black-coated figure passing alone along the street at midnight to be the governor-elect of the State, in whose honor the assembled multitudes were getting drunk?

His first intention had been to take a hack, drive to the railway depot, and board the first train going West. But the hacks were all engaged as sleeping berths by men who could not get accommodations in any of the houses of the overcrowded city.

So he set off to walk, and almost immediately came face to face with old Scythia, the friend of his childhood.

"Old Scythia!" exclaimed Corona, interrupting the narrative.

"Yes, dear; the old seeress of Raven Roost, as they used to call her. Of course, I never, even as a boy, believed in the supernatural powers of divination ascribed to her, but I must credit her with wonderful intuitions. She had divined the very crisis that had come, and in that hour of my agony and humiliation she exercised a strange power over me," said Rothsay; and then he took up the thread of his narrative again.

He told her that on leaving the State capital he had taken neither railway carriage nor river steamboat, but had tramped, with old Scythia by his side, all the way from the Cumberland Mountains to the Southwestern frontier.

The journey had taken them all the summer, for they traveled very slowly—sometimes walking no more than ten miles a day, sometimes sleeping on pallets made of leaves under the trees of the forest, sometimes reaching a pioneer's log hut, where they could get a hot supper and a night's lodging. Sometimes stopping over Sunday in some settlement where there was no church, and where Rule, though not an ordained minister, would on Christian principles hold a service and preach a sermon.

So they journeyed over the mountains, and through the valleys and forests, until at length, in the end of October, they arrived at the poorest, loneliest, and most forlorn of all the pioneer settlements they had seen.

This was La Terrepeur, on the borders of the Indian Reserve. It was a settlement of about twenty log huts, in a small valley shut in by densely wooded hills, and watered by a narrow brook. It was too near the country of the Comanches for safety, and too far from the nearest fort for protection. There was neither church nor school house within a hundred miles.

The travelers were hospitably received by the pioneers, and here, as the autumn was far advanced, and travel difficult, they determined to halt for the winter, at least, and in the spring to go farther south in search of Scythia's tribe, the Nez Percees, who had been moved away from their former hunting grounds.

They were feasted and lodged by the hutters that night. The next morning the men turned out in a body, felled trees and cleared a spot on the slope of a wooded hill, sawed logs and built two huts, one for Rothsay, and one for old Scythia. They were finished before night. And then the settlers had a house-warming, which was a breakdown dance to the music of the one fiddle in the settlement, and a supper of such eatables and drinkables as the place could afford.

But there was no furniture in these two primitive dwellings. So once more these wayfarers had each to sleep on a bed of leaves.

On the second day the man who owned the only mule and cart, and was the only expressman and carrier to the settlement, offered to go to the nearest post trader's station—a distance of fifty miles—and purchase anything that the strangers might need, if said strangers had the money to buy.

Rothsay had money in notes, hardly thought of, and never looked at, except when, on their long journey, he had to take out his pocket book to pay for accommodations at some log cabin, or to purchase a change of under clothing at some post trader's.

Also old Scythia had a pouch of silver and gold coin, saved from the money that had been regularly sent to her by Rule from the time when he first began to earn wages to the time when they set out for the wilderness in company.

Of this money they gave the frontier expressman all that he required to purchase the plainest furniture for the log cabins—bedding, cooking utensils, crockery ware, and some groceries.

"Yer can't buy bed or mattresses at the post trader's; but yer can buy ticking, and we can sew it up for yer, and the men will stuff with straw. There's plenty of straw," said one of the kindly women, speaking for all her neighbors.

And the expressman set out with his list.

In three days he was back again with a satisfactory supply. The women made the straw beds and pillows and hemmed the sheets. The men filled the ticks and "knocked together" a pine table and a few rude, three-legged stools. And so Rothsay and old Scythia were settled for the winter.

Rothsay took upon himself the office of teacher and preacher. Among the articles brought from the post trader's were a few Bibles, hymn books, and elementary school books, slates and pencils.

He began his labors by holding a religious service in his own cabin on the first Sabbath of his sojourn at La Terrepeur, which—perhaps for its rarity—was attended by the whole of the little community. And on the next day he opened his little school in his hut, where he taught the children all day, and where he slept at night. Old Scythia's cabin was kitchen and dining room.

All that autumn, winter and spring Rule labored among the pioneers of La Terrepeur. It was not true, as had been reported, that he was a missionary and schoolmaster to the Indians; for no one of the savages who occasionally came into the settlement could be induced to approach the "school."

It was in June that old Scythia became restless and anxious to find her tribe—the wandering Nez Percees.

Rothsay gave his school a vacation and set out with Scythia to find the valley where they were reported to be in camp.

"This valley below, Cora, dear," said Rothsay, interrupting the course of the narrative. "But when we reached it, the Nez Percees had disappeared. A lonely old hunter, who had built this hut, was the only human being in the place, and he was slowly dying, and he would have died alone but for the opportune arrival of old Scythia and myself. He told us that the Nez Percees had crossed the river about two weeks before, and were far on their migration west."

"Old Scythia sat down flat on the floor, drew up her knees, folded her hands upon them, dropped her head, and died as quietly as a tired child falls to sleep."

"Oh!" exclaimed Corona, "how sad it was."

"Yes; it was sad; age, fatigue and disappointment did their work. I buried her body under that pine tree where your Uncle Clarence sat down. The old hunter's struggle with dissolution was longer. He lingered five days. I waited on him until death relieved him, and then laid his body to rest beside old Scythia's. I was then preparing to return to La Terrepeur, when a wandering scout brought me the news of the massacre of the inhabitants and the destruction of the settlement. Since that time, dear Corona, I have lived alone on this mountain. That is all. Come, shall we go down and see your uncle?"

"Yes," said Corona.

And they arose and walked down into the valley.

They soon found the wagon camp of Clarence Rockharrt and his followers.

The horses and mules, which had been unharnessed, watered and fed, were now tethered to the scattered tree trunks, and were nosing about under the dried leaves in search of the tender herbage that was still springing in that genial soil beneath the shelter of the fallen foliage. The wagons had been drawn up under cover of the thicket and prepared as sleeping berths.

On the grass was spread a large white damask table cloth, and on that was arranged a neat tea service for three.

Martha was busy at a gypsy fire boiling coffee and broiling venison steaks.

"You are just in time, Rule. How do you do?" exclaimed Mr. Clarence, emerging from among the horses, and coming forward to shake hands with Rothsay as if they had been in the daily habit of meeting for the last four years.

The two men clasped hands cordially.

"I always had a secret conviction that you were living, Rule, and always secretly hoped to meet you again, 'somehow, somewhere;' and now my prescience is justified in our meeting to-day."

"Clarence," gravely replied Rothsay, "you ask me no questions, yet now I feel that you are entitled to some explanation of my strange flight and long sequestration. And I will give it to you to-morrow."

"My dear Rothsay, I have divined much of the mystery, but you may tell me what you like, when you like. And now supper is ready," said Clarence, heartily, as the four servants came up, each with a dish to set on the cloth, quite an unnecessary pageantry where one would have been enough, but that they all wanted to see the long-lost man. And with the warmth and freedom of their race they quickly set down their dishes and gathered around the stranger to give him a warm welcome, expressing loudly their surprise and delight in seeing him.

"Dough 'deed I doane wonner at nuffin' wot turns up in dis yere new country!" old Martha declared.

Then followed a gay and happy *al fresco* supper.

By the time it was over the sun had set, and the autumn evening air, even in that southern clime, was growing very chilly.

So the three friends arose from the table.

Rothsay and Corona turned to go up the hill. Clarence escorted them, carrying Corona's bag.

They parted at the door of the log cabin.

"I shall have our tent pitched at the foot of the mountain early to-morrow morning, and breakfast prepared. You will come down and join me," said Mr. Clarence, as he bade the reunited pair good night.

The wagon camp did not break up the next day, nor the day after that.

On the third day who should arrive but Lieut. Haught, absent on leave, and come to look up his relations. His meeting with them was a jubilee. His sister wept for joy; his brother-in-law and his uncle would have embraced him if they had expressed their emotions as continental Europeans do; even the negroes almost hugged and kissed him.

On Lieut. Haught's representations and at his persuasions the little camp broke up, and with Rothsay and Cora in company, marched off to Fort Farthermost, where they were cordially received by the commandant and the officers, and where the reunited pair commenced life anew.

My story opened with the marriage and mysterious separation of the newly married pair. It should close with their reunion.

The later life of my young hero belongs to history. It would require a pen more powerful than mine to pursue his career, which was as grand, heroic and romantic as that of any knight, prince, or paladin in the days of old.

His pure name and fame became identified with the rise and progress of a great State in that Southwestern wilderness. Soldier, statesman, patriot, benefactor, all in one, his memory will be honored as long as his country shall last. And yet, perhaps, the crowning glory of his character was his power of self-renunciation—proved in every act of his public life, but shown first, perhaps, when, to leave the life of one beloved woman free, he renounced not only the hand of his adored bride, but

"The kingdoms of the world and the glory."